Debbie Johnson
works in Liverpool. She writes fantasy, crime and romance,
which is about as confusing as it sounds. Find out more
at www.debbiejohnsonauthor.com, www.facebook.com/
debbiejohnsonauthor and @debbiemjohnson

Praise for *Dark Vision*

'A sassy and often very funny fantasy romp, lifted
above the mass by the wit of protagonist Lily and her
best friend, the fabulously ballsy Carmel . . . Clever and
full of sharp wisecracks . . . a deftly told entertainment
that shows there is certainly room in the world for a
Liverpudlian Charlaine Harris'
Guardian

'Very *Mortal Instruments*, very *Secret Circle* . . . Yet,
there is a little something extra to be found in *Dark
Vision* . . . she has the insight to blend in the right
amount of otherwordly action, humour, Irish folklore
and the magnificent setting of Liverpool'
ScifiNow

'A sizzling debut about goddesses, vampires and rock
'n' roll, you'll love Debbie Johnson's sassy page-turner'
Jane Costello

'If future instalments build on the strength of
this debut, they'll be ones to look out for'
Starburst magazine

Also by Debbie Johnson:

Dark Vision

DARK TOUCH

DEBBIE JOHNSON

DEL REY

1 3 5 7 9 10 8 6 4 2

Del Rey, an imprint of Ebury Publishing
20 Vauxhall Bridge Road,
London SW1V 2SA

Del Rey is part of the Penguin Random House
group of companies whose addresses can be found at
global.penguinrandomhouse.com

First published in 2015 by Del Rey

www.eburypublishing.co.uk

A CIP catalogue record for this book is
available from the British Library

ISBN 9780091953614

Penguin Random House is committed to a sustainable future for
our business, our readers and our planet. This book is made from
Forest Stewardship Council® certified paper.

MIX
Paper from
responsible sources
FSC
www.fsc.org   FSC® C018179

Typeset in Palatino LT Std by Palimpsest Book Production Limited,
Falkirk, Stirlingshire

Printed and bound by Clays Ltd, St Ives plc

To Dom, Keir, Dan and Lou – I love you all so much.
Viva forever, Skyfall!

Prologue

The boy scurried under the bed, screwing his tiny body up into a defensive, trembling ball. Maybe, he thought, maybe if I make myself small enough he won't notice me, he'll leave me alone, just for one night. One night of peace. One night without fear and pain and loneliness.

The sound of heavy workman's boots echoed along the narrow hallway. He could practically feel the floorboards vibrating as the steps got closer. There was a pause, a familiar grunt, outside his door.

The boy felt the warm, humiliating stain of moisture at his groin, felt it spreading over his shaking body as he clenched his eyes tight against the tears. Every night now. For weeks. Every night the footsteps, the pause, the door quietly opening, the sound of the belt being tugged from its loops. The rough, beer-stained voice, telling him he was worthless. That he needed to be made a man. That he needed to be punished.

He clenched his tiny fists and, for the millionth time, he prayed. Prayed to be left alone. Prayed for his mother to believe him. Prayed for this man to die. Prayed to whatever gods he knew about, and any that he didn't. Prayed to the land of his fathers, to the king his family worshipped.

1

So far, they'd all been silent. The only sounds in his life now were sounds of fear and anger and hatred. The sounds of leather and metal hitting skin. The sounds of delicate flesh being slapped and torn. The sounds of tears and pain and lonely desperation. Nobody was listening, he knew. Nobody was coming to rescue him. Nobody cared. He *was* worthless.

He looked up at the small window in his room. Saw the stars, the moon, and everything else that ignored him. The whole universe had abandoned him.

Except . . . one star. It was vast. Much bigger than the others. It looked to be redder, as well, and the light of it made it look like it was blinking at him. At this pathetic scrap of humanity, cowering beneath a bed, soaked in his own urine and drenched in his own terror.

He blinked away the tears and stared, for one moment concentrating on that rather than the sound of a rough hand reaching out to push that door open. It reminded him of something – of one of the old legends his father, his real father, used to tell him. From the story books he used to read. About an all-powerful being who once battled in their lands. A mighty warrior, long gone.

Tomorrow . . . tomorrow he would find those books. The few things left from his father. He'd read about mighty warriors and powerful foes and vanquishing everyone who harmed him. And maybe, if he worked hard enough at it, he could find some of that power for himself. Enough power to fight back, even if he was only ten. Even if the whole universe had abandoned him.

For a few seconds the thought comforted him, gave him hope. Then the door opened, the boots marched in, and all he could do was whimper.

Chapter One

We'd travelled to New York on a magical boat.

Yeah, I know. Sounds crazy. It is crazy. The tragic part is I'm getting used to saying things like that.

It was six weeks after I took my first ride on the Goddess Train at Tara, the ancient seat of even more ancient High Kings. Six weeks after I accepted my fate, and my responsibilities, as Mabe, Mother of the Mortals. Which also sounds crazy. Six weeks after a terrifying ceremony that had seen me turn my back on my nice, safe, solitary human existence as Lily McCain, Liverpool pop writer and social retard – and walk into one that included magical boats, vampires, gods and witches. Not a long time to get my head around it all, really. And it certainly didn't feel long enough to prepare me for this – for our trip to New York, where I'd be presented to some equally freaky supernatural High Council for their approval. Just saying – a girl's allowed to be a bit messed up when her life takes that kind of turn.

We'd all met up at Liverpool's docklands, which is a mysterious place at the best of times. Depending on where you are on the waterfront, you could be swilling champagne with footballers' wives (or wives in training),

3

dazzled by the perfect displays of veneered teeth, spray-tanned legs and Russian hair extensions. Or you could be inhaling rust and corroded metal from the mountains of scrap and dry-docked ships in for salvage. Same city, same river, very different story.

On the day we were leaving for New York, I found myself huddled in a damp, drizzly group on a dock I've never even seen before – and considering that much of my angst-ridden teenaged life was spent tramping around sad and lonely places just like this, that's a minor miracle.

Gabriel had driven us from his apartment up past Seaforth, bumping and jumping as the car bounced over the potholed dock road in the moonlight, passing the parked-up cabs of sleeping lorry drivers and the massive hulks of ghostly old warehouses. Past the silos and the garages and the lock-ups under the dripping brick arches. All the way towards Crosby – where there wasn't a dock. Honest guv'nor. They're big places – it's not like you could forget one.

Carmel, my best friend and mystical Champion (is that ever going to stop sounding weird?), summed it up as she staggered out of the Audi, possibly a bit the worse for wear after consuming most of a bottle of vodka before we set out.

'Fucking hell,' she said, gazing out at the perfect working harbour, her curly black hair whipping around her face in the wind. It was the second week in December, and the weather was nigh-on apocalyptic. Gale force gusts; torrential rain, and bouts of hailstones so large they could give you a really cool piercing if they caught you at the right angle.

The perfect night, obviously, to set off on a sea voyage to a distant land. That's why Carmel had been drinking so much. Well, that and the fact that she's a journalist, of course. They all drink a lot; it comes with the shorthand notes and the swearing.

'Tell me again why we have to do this,' she said. 'And while you're at it, where the hell are we? This should be a marina. We should be looking at dinghies and canoes. Why is there a bloody great big boat there at all?'

'Ship,' I corrected automatically, which earned me a deserved scowl. Carmel is the adopted daughter of a large Scouse Irish family, and has six big brothers. She's also – and this gets a little hazy, so bear with me – Egyptian by birth, and seems to have some connection to a mysterious warrior woman called Menhit. That, combined with the vodka and her newly-gained fighting skills, makes her one scary chick. Luckily, she's on my side.

Gabriel followed us out of the car, carrying our bags from the boot. We'd become lazy with that kind of thing – why bother pulling a muscle hefting luggage around, when there was a super-strong Irish High King to do it for you? He's really good at changing light bulbs as well. All part of the package when you're a centuries-old supernatural monarch, sworn to protect, serve, and carry out minor domestic tasks.

'I'm going to check everything's ready. You – don't go anywhere,' Gabriel said, his face stern in the shadowed night. His eyes were such a deep shade of blue that I couldn't see them, and his body language was doing that 'big bad protector' thing he enjoys so much. His thick dark hair spilled to shoulder level, the waves swaying in the breeze.

He was as handsome as a slightly decadent angel, with his pale skin, high cheekbones and luscious lips, but what can I say? He really annoyed me when he tried to tell me what to do. Which was all the time. Honestly, give a boy a title, and a stupid name – Cormac macConaire, give or take a few syllables – and it goes right to his head.

I smiled sweetly and gave him a magical finger gesture.

My goddess status seems to have had absolutely zero effect on Gabriel treating me like a petulant child, or in fact on me behaving like one when I'm around him. Perhaps it would come with time. He glowered at me and sprinted off towards the gangplank, bags tucked under his arms as though they were empty instead of containing Carmel's Imelda Marcos-like shoe collection.

Car tyres crunched in the gravel behind us, and the clunking of doors told me the rest of the gang had arrived.

The gang would be Finn, a stocky mock-leprechaun wider than he is tall; Kevin, the one-eyed barman from a Liverpool nightclub, who is also a bad-guy slayer on the side; and Connor, a Daniel Craig lookalike who I suspected was bonking Carmel on the quiet. Naughty sausages.

Luca was also with them, as it was no longer safe for him and Gabriel to be in an enclosed space together for any length of time. Luca is a vampire. The kind that rustic maidens would have swooned over in Hammer movies. I'd saved his life – long story, needs alcohol – and unwittingly bound him to me as a result. Not in a 'yes, mistress' Renfield kind of way – more in an 'always around to bug me' kind of way. Although not as much as he bugged Gabriel, that's for sure. They had one thing in common: their loyalty to me. I think the only thing that stopped them killing each other was the fact that I'd be pretty peeved if they did. All of which boded well for a week-long sea crossing, I thought.

The vessel we'd be using to make that crossing loomed before us, impossibly present on a dock that didn't exist. It was all sleek white lines, glimmering in the moonlight, bearing an eerie resemblance to the luxury liners of bygone eras. Sort of a *Honey I Shrunk the Titanic* vibe. It says a lot about the turn my life had taken that I didn't feel even remotely surprised.

'Don't worry, angel,' said Luca, oozing his way behind

me and snuggling up so close I could feel the muscle of his thighs pressed into the back of mine. 'I will keep a lookout for the icebergs.'

'Ha bloody ha,' I replied, leaning back into him, enjoying the connection more than I should. I've become a lot better at touching human beings and not sinking to the ground with hideous, skull-crunching visions. For most of my human life, I'd been cursed with them. The touch of skin against skin, and I'd be risking a glimpse of that person's future – which I'd learned to my cost was often not a good thing. Since Tara, I'd worked hard with Fionnula, my witchy mentor, to learn how to control them. To protect myself against them. To find a way to touch and be touched without the paralysing fear of what that might bring with it. I was getting much, much better.

Which is a good thing, right? But there's still room for improvement, and in the back of my mind there's always that fear, always that slight hesitation before I allow myself to be touched. First, I had to concentrate to draw down my mental armour, which didn't exactly make for a carefree tactile existence. 'Fancy a snog, Lily?' 'Yeah, just give me a few minutes to blank out your possible cancer diagnosis . . .' No. Not romantic at all.

With Luca, it was different. As a vampire, he was technically dead. He had no human future that could blitzkrieg its way across my brain, and I had nothing to fear, not on that front anyway. The fact he was my devoted slave, set on getting into my knickers, and perfectly capable of draining me of blood in one chomp, however – well, that was all something to fear, in its own way. I'd accidentally inherited Luca from Donn, the Lord of the Dead, and we were both still adjusting to our new circumstances.

If I'd been a normal girl, I'd have dealt with the knickers bit a long time ago. There was one occasion – when I was under the influence of some powerful supernatural urges that make party drugs look like popcorn – when I'd come very close to doing it. With him, and with Gabriel, and possibly with every man in the room. I felt myself go red at the memory, and was glad it was dark.

'You're blushing, aren't you?' said Luca, wiggling his hips into me in a way that told me he knew exactly what I was thinking about.

'No,' I lied, striding away, 'we're not all obsessed with sex. Now, where's my dog? You haven't eaten her, have you?'

'Don't be ridiculous – what kind of a man do you think I am?' he said, laughter still tingeing his voice. Luca was born in Italy, like, hundreds of years ago. He has olive skin and chocolate-drop eyes and dark blond hair – and when he's amused, or angry, or hurt, his accent becomes obvious. It's kind of sexy, but I'd never admit that to him.

I heard one of the others clicking open the car boot and, on cue, my dog gracefully leapt out and ran towards me. I'd acquired the dog at Tara, round about the same time I'd chosen Gabriel as my mate. Yeah, that's right – my mate. The one I bickered with and swore at and kept at arm's length and certainly never, ever . . . well, mated with. What can I say? In Facebook-ese, it's complicated.

So far – apart from surviving and saving the human race, blah blah blah – the dog has been absolutely the best thing to come out of it.

She remains nameless – unless you count The Dog – which is a very bad oversight on my part. She looks like a greyhound crossed with a lurcher crossed with a growth hormone, all legs and skinny ribs and powerful haunches. When she stands on her back legs, she's taller than me, and her velvety soft black fur is underlaid with sparkles. Seriously, she is a Diamond Dog – and she's very, very pretty.

She jumped up, rested her paws on my shoulders, and licked my face while I stroked her seal-like head and went all mushy inside. Yup. I definitely loved The Dog, one hundred per cent and without reservation. Perhaps there was hope for me yet.

Carmel, I noted, had slunk off to stand next to Connor, who had a very unnecessary hand on her back. Deffo something going on there. Something . . . earthy. I pulled a face and gently pushed The Dog down. I was only jealous. My job title might be Mother of the Mortals, and I might be a fertility goddess, but 'earthy' is something I've never really pulled off. I've had glimpses, here and there, tempting little twitches in the nether regions, but never, you know, the full monty. I am Liverpool's oldest virgin, and getting a bit sick of it. My 'mate' – the afore-mentioned Cormac macConaire – was keen to change that state of affairs, because he's a bloke after all, but I wasn't ready.

I don't know what I'm waiting for. Some mystical sign from up above. To master control of my visions. To meet an even hotter guy, which would be impossible. Who knows? Perhaps I'd never be ready, and die like an old spinster lady, getting eaten by my collection of feral cats. I always found it ironic that I could see other people's futures by touching them, but my own remained a complete mystery.

I didn't even have anyone to really talk to about it. I had what you might call a dysfunctional childhood. My family is gone – my parents sacrificed themselves to save me, and they now live in the Otherworld, where time moves like a hundred times faster than here. All of which makes visiting for parental advice a bit difficult.

I seem to have several identities, and pretty much all of them are having a crisis.

Years ago, when I was small, I was Maura Delaney. One of three girls, any one of whom could have been

9

destined to be the Goddess Mabe, all living with different families. Except, for the other two – the spirit sisters I'd never known – it didn't end well. They were found, and they were slaughtered by the Faidh – a maverick bunch of bad guys who were pretty keen on the world ending.

Once I was the only one left, Gabriel kicked everything up a level in his drive to protect me. Francis and Sarah, my parents, effectively killed themselves in a car accident near our home in London, taking with them a sacrificial lamb: Lucy, a mortal woman and friend of the High King's, who had been magically transformed into the body of a little girl at the time of the crash. Everyone – including, for a while, the Faidh – assumed the little girl was me.

Straight after, I had been silently spirited away to a quiet backstreet in the shadow of Liverpool Football Club, given a new name, and a whole new life. A life that totally sucked. Raised by a fake nan called Coleen, without love or affection or touch. Plagued by visions and constantly on the edge of a nervous breakdown as a result.

Is it any wonder I was a bit on the introverted side?

Now, I was left in an equally dysfunctional present. Carmel and The Dog I loved, no doubt. Gabriel . . . I sometimes loved. Luca mainly exasperated me, but I couldn't really imagine life without him. Without any of them – which, for a naturally solitary soul like myself, was a bit of a conundrum. Like I said. Having a crisis had kind of become my default setting.

Rescuing me from my as-per-usual inane ramblings, the quiet of the night was cracked open by the ear-shattering cawing of a crow. I felt a flutter in the air around my head, and stood perfectly still as it approached.

Two spindly black feet landed on my shoulder, their grip surprisingly strong through the padding of my coat. I twisted my head around and met coal black eyes, shining up close and personal, and a beak that leaned forward to peck softly at my nose.

Around me, the usual reaction: everyone fell to their knees and grovelled, including Carmel. Especially Carmel, in fact, who looked like she might be planning to tunnel her way to New York. They'd settle down after a while, but whenever she appeared for the first time, they all tended to eat dirt for a few moments.

They were terrified of the crow, mainly because it wasn't a crow at all. It was the Morrigan, an ancient goddess of war and fertility. The Harbinger of Death, the bringer of doom – and my kind-of big sister.

If she'd landed on anyone else's shoulder like that, it would have meant death was coming for them. With me, it was just a sign of affection.

What can I say? I'm just special.

Chapter Two

'You're a lovely shade of green,' I said, smirking at Carmel's face.

She hadn't taken well to the journey, and spent the whole time bleating about how she'd far prefer to be in a Virgin Upper Class cabin sipping champagne.

Tough for her, really. Gabriel had organised the sea crossing for a number of reasons. Firstly, there was some kind of issue with Kevin's passport and possible entry into the States. It seemed he'd slaughtered half of Dakota last time he was there – all in the name of truth, justice, and the supernatural way. So, we were doing some probably highly illegal sneaking past border-control manoeuvre.

Secondly, we had three passengers who would struggle with long-haul flights – Luca (the undead), The Dog and Morrigan.

The last one was weird, given the fact that she could basically fly anyway, but the last time she'd tried it in a plane had ended with a crash landing in the Welsh Black Mountains. It's like this: the Morrigan is kind of a bird, in her other form. And she has this crazy affinity for birds, who follow her everywhere. You've seen those freaky starling things on nature shows, where they all swoop and flock into weird, bird-based shadow storms? Well that happened around her all the time. It was like she was their mummy bird and they all came swooping in for a cuddle.

Unfortunately, if that happens while she's on a plane, it results in bird soup. Not nice, and really not safe.

The other reason Gabriel had cited – and I must admit this one made me laugh, which wasn't perhaps the reaction he was looking for – was that it would be 'like a honeymoon'.

Technically, I had accepted him as my consort. In my reality, however, he was the physical embodiment of the 'love/hate relationship'. And I'd yet to hear about any kind of honeymoon where the bride shared a cabin with her female best friend while the groom patrolled the corridors wielding a huge sword – and I don't mean that in a saucy metaphorical way.

It was the night before we were due to dock in New York – presumably somewhere we could smuggle Kevin and The Dog in with no questions asked, or entirely possibly in a pier that didn't even exist. I'd given up questioning this stuff – it happened too often, and my brain would explode if I tried to understand it all.

We were all gathered in the ship's equivalent of an office boardroom, sitting around a huge blonde wood table. Carmel, after flicking me the Vs in response to my jibe, went back to staring at the water glasses, watching the liquid gently slosh around in them as the ship rolled, gripping on to the arm rests of her chair until her knuckles went white.

The Dog was curled at my feet, sitting on my toes like a huge black carpet, and Luca was paring an apple with a very small, very sharp knife. He didn't need to eat food – he'd brought charmingly squishy chilled bags of blood with him, which he kept in a fridge in his room like a twelve-pack of Peroni. Yuk to infinity, but nobody's perfect I suppose. I guess he just really liked apples, because I'd seen him peeling loads of them throughout the journey.

This time, he was doing it slowly, licking the juice off the knife in a way that could have earned him a lead role in a porno. Seriously, it was obscene – and seemed to rile Gabriel no end. Luca's very existence seemed to rile Gabriel no end, though, so no surprises there.

Gabriel himself, when he wasn't glaring at Luca, was talking urgently to Connor, Finn and Kevin, and jotting down notes on a small pad he had in front of him. I felt a smile tugging at my mouth as I realised they bore a striking resemblance to a team of high-flying businessmen preparing for some killer presentation. If he produced a mystical flipchart or a primeval Powerpoint, I was going to pee my pants.

'Cormac Mor,' said the Morrigan, lounging with her legs draped across the backs of three chairs – she's six foot tall and built like a female wrestler in her human form, not quite as petite as the crow – 'I grow tired of waiting and watching you confer with your cronies. I am sure I speak for the Goddess when I say we have better things to be doing.'

She'd used one of his traditional titles – Cormac 'Mor', which loosely translates as the Great, the Mighty, or some other superlative – but her tone implied she was less than impressed.

I nodded, keeping my face stern and serious and goddess-like. In fact, the only thing I'd been doing was watching Too Cute Kittens on Animal Planet and holding Carmel's hair out of her face while she puked – but they didn't need to know that.

Gabriel glanced over at her, and I saw his shoulders twitch under the knit of his sweater. The name Cormac Mor is also super-appropriate for a man who already has an ego the size of Jupiter. It might also be related to the fact that when he is angry, or stressed, or fired up with those protective alpha-king urges of his, he swells. Literally. Sometimes it's just a few extra inches in height and bulk; sometimes it's hide-under-the-table-the-ceiling-is-coming-in huge. And every now and then – when he's in full-on battle mode – he turns into a monster.

Yep, my mate, the incredible expanding man. Told you it was complicated. Right now, I could tell, he was struggling to control his annoyance at being interrupted – no point going all swell-o on the Morrigan's ass; she could eat him for breakfast, then sit contentedly back and belch out his remains. She's a great role model for any young woman: what do you want to be when you grow up, Lily? Well, a super-strong goddess of war and fertility would be nice.

'Yeah,' muttered Carmel, who had now laid her head flat on the table, cradled by her arms, 'get the fuck on with it or I'm gonna puke all over your high kingly shoes.'

Connor stared at her, concern and . . . yep, disappointment, in his eyes. Carmel had come late to their merry gang of slayers, and she'd never quite mastered the correct levels of etiquette and respect that they thought their king deserved. God bless her.

Gabriel rose above it – in fact he rose above everything, as he was now a good five inches over his usual six two – and nodded abruptly at the Morrigan.

'We are here to prepare for the events of the next few days,' he said, 'and the role that the Goddess must fulfil when she meets the Comhairle –'

'Excuse me, sir,' I said, raising my hand and smiling, 'but could you please call me Lily? In fact, I kind of insist on it. And also, why are we meeting a koala?'

The Morrigan laughed so hard her biker boots slapped up and down on the table, and Finn assumed his usual

15

expression of shock. The one he wore whenever I was disrespectful, which is pretty much all of the time.

'The Comhairle,' repeated Gabriel, smiling back at me just as sweetly, 'is the Council. I suspect you already know that . . . *Lily*.'

He was kind of right. When I'd visited my parents in the Otherworld – Tir na nOg, the land of the eternally young, eternally happy and eternally Stepford Wives – I had been able to understand the sounds of the ancient Irish words they used. Back here, in the land of the eternally confused, I understood some of it, some of the time. I'd figured out that when Gabriel called me 'a ghra', he was expressing his love. I'd figured out the name structure, and I'd started to get to grips with some of the tongue-twisting pronunciations. The whole language was batshit crazy, which was I suppose just about right for me.

Still, I was battling on behalf of the lowest common denominator here – which would be me and Carmel.

'Sorry, my Lord,' I replied, 'please forgive my impertinent interruption, and continue speaking a foreign language that is barely understood by the Goddess you claim to serve. I'm sure you know best. Also, if it's not too intrusive to ask, if we're meeting leaders from other cultures and other worlds, why do we still give them the silly Irish names?'

Luca sniggered, and I saw Gabriel's eyes flare purple. His physical landscape was an ever-changing one: as well as the body expansion, his eyes often changed colour too, varying between deep blue to such a dark purple they were almost black. That usually happened when he was a wee bit vexed. Like now, in fact.

Gabriel sucked in a deep breath, visible to all, which was pretty much an admission of stress on his part, and ploughed on. I almost felt sorry for him – public speaking isn't easy at the best of times, and he was getting heckled by two goddesses, a love-rival vampire and a very seasick Egyptian warrior woman. Life at the top, eh?

'I can give you the names they use, if you prefer? But you'd probably think they were equally silly.'

I ignored him. It was a fair point. He continued.

'We will be presenting the Goddess – Lily – to the Comhairle, for their approval. Each of the representatives present will have the chance to talk to her, to question her, and to signify their acceptance of her as the Mother. The leader of the Council, the Taoiseach, will guide the proceedings, guard against any wrongdoing, and complete the ritual that accepts the Goddess fully.'

Hmmm. I already knew a lot of this, and didn't totally understand it. If there were the equivalents of Gabriel from these other worlds, how did that work? Did they all hang out in different parts of the Otherworld that I'd visited, like on Earth? Or was it like those Enid Blyton books I'd read as a kid, with an enchanted tree in a faraway wood, with a different land at the top each time? Either way, it kind of sucked. Big time.

At the Feast of Samhain – Halloween to you and I, kiddos – I had been forced to make a choice that I never wanted to make. I'd stood at the Lia Fail, the ancient standing stone on the Hill of Tara, dressed up like a Pussycat Goddess, with the fate of the world resting on my shoulders.

If I chose Gabriel – a man I often wanted to poke through the eye with a chopstick, and the man who had condemned me to a miserable childhood with an apparently unloving fake-gran – then all would be well with the world. Humanity would continue to tiptoe through the tulips, reap bounty, commit genocide, and all its other popular hobbies.

If I chose Fintan – the leader of an Otherworld rebel group called the Fintna Faidh – then it would all have been gone. In the blink of a Goddess's eye. Humanity, the

17

world as I knew it, would have ceased to be, replaced by the never-ending saccharine sunshine of the Otherworld. That would have suited some people just fine, involving as it did a life of endless feasting, eating, and partying on, dudes. But for others, it would have been an eternal prison – maybe not for many, but for some. And I decided that I couldn't take that choice from them.

There was one of those big heavy scenes – Lords of the Undead urging my potential hubbie to rape me; eyes getting gouged out; people transforming into crows; knife fights; me turning into a blazing white light, that kind of thing – and then I made my choice. I chose Gabriel, and I thought, honestly and naively thought, that that was it – job done. I even had a new hair colour to show for it – my previously red locks had turned entirely white, which was apparently some kind of cosmic tell for saving the known universe. I'd freaked out to start with, but must admit it's pretty cool.

Hair make-over aside, I'd been flunking Goddess school for some time, so it shouldn't have come as a surprise that it was only the beginning. I'd half hoped that I'd be able to tick that box (yup, world saved) and move on. Grieve for my gran, who'd died in the middle of all of it, proclaiming her love on her deathbed and throwing the basis of my whole life on its head; go back to my normally abnormal life as a pop writer on the *Liverpool Gazette*; see some bands; control some visions; drink some fucking beer and eat pizza and put my feet up for a bit.

But no. In fact hell, no. It was all go in the life of a goddess – and I learned soon after that I had to make this journey and meet with a council of Gabriel's equivalents from all over the world. Once I'd picked myself off the floor at the thought of there being more out there like him, I got mightily annoyed. Essentially, I was getting paraded like a dog at a show – allowing this supernatural council of nigh-on immortal bureaucrats to poke me and prod me and make sure I was fit for the job. I'd have happily told them straight off that I wasn't, and would be happy to take up any redundancy package they were offering, but apparently that wasn't in the rules. Typical.

So, yeah, I knew what was coming. But Gabriel had mentioned one thing in that tiny speech that I'd not really picked up on before.

'What do you mean, guard against wrongdoing?' I asked, feeling a sense of dread seeping through me. 'Is Fintan going to be there? Donn?'

Donn was the Lord of the Dead, and he didn't much like me. To be fair, last time we'd met I'd stabbed him in the leg, lost him an eye, and unintentionally stolen one of his favourite vampires. He was obviously the grudge holding type.

'No, child,' replied the Morrigan, interceding before Gabriel had a chance to reply. 'But in all my centuries I have yet to meet a council that is united in thought and deed, that does not curl in on itself like exposed entrails, rotting and stinking and feasted upon by maggots in the midday sun.'

I heard Carmel grunt beside me, which at least proved she was still alive. It was a pretty gross image – the Morrigan is nothing if not eloquent.

'Lily,' said Gabriel, his eyes narrowing in on me like I was the only person in the room, sparkling purple and intense, 'you know that you will be safe. I will be there, your mate and your protector, as well my men, who are willing to –'

'Yeah, I know already,' I said, waving my hands at them, 'willing to lie on their swords for me. I'm just a little uncertain as to why I'll be needing all that protection – isn't this council, well, on your side? Isn't this just a . . . formality?'

'It will indeed be formal,' he replied, 'and yes, we have many allies on the Council. But the Morrigan speaks truly

– like any meeting of power, there are rivalries and factions, a jostling for position. All may not be as it seems on the surface.'

As I started to try and digest this – life in danger again, yay for me – Luca finally paused from making sweet love to his apple.

'It will be like casting her into a barrel of snakes,' he said. 'And you forgot to include me on that list, Cormac Mor. I am Lily's to command. My life – my soul and my body – are hers already.'

God, I wish he'd shut up about that. Especially the body part. I'd saved Luca from dying a second time round by feeding him my ever-so-sacred blood, and by doing that I'd unwittingly gained an unwanted extra guard dog. One that never sat for treats and might possibly eat the postman. I felt far more comfortable around the one keeping my toes warm under the table.

Gabriel's body started to swell and grow, and the seams of his sweater strained as the bulk pushed outwards. Something about Luca just drove him nuts.

Luca looked on, a slight smirk at the corner of his mouth. He knew exactly what he was doing, the sneaky bastard.

He picked up the remains of his apple, slowly peeled the very last scrap of skin from it, and licked the knife in a way that could only be described as lascivious.

'Yum,' he said, grinning right at Gabriel, 'I do love the juice of a freshly plucked apple, don't you, High King? Never before tasted and so sweet to the tongue . . .'

I had no idea what was going on, or why Luca's fruit-eating habits were such a big deal, but the High King in question instantly went berserk.

He threw himself over the table, growling and snarling, and dragged Luca to the floor with him. I could hear the sounds of slapping and punching and biting as they disappeared beneath it, and took the precaution of lifting my glass from the surface. Eventually, as I'd suspected, the whole thing flew up in the air, crashing to one side and almost taking Carmel's prone head with it.

Luca and Gabriel emerged upright, spitting and slashing at each other; Gabriel huge and furious, Luca smaller but just as predator-deadly.

'What's going on?' I said to the Morrigan, who was looking on with such glee I half expected her to start clapping her hands and chanting 'fight, fight, fight'.

'Oh,' she replied, tearing her eyes away from the blood-letting for a moment, 'it is the vampire and the apple. Don't you see, you silly child?'

'Uh, no,' I replied. Silly child indeed. No argument there.

'The apple is you. The apple is the symbol of the Goddess. The symbol of rebirth and fertility, from the ancient tree of life. The vampire knows this, and has pushed our pretty High King past his limits.'

Ah. Well, that explained a lot. Luca had, essentially, been winding Gabriel up for the whole trip, rather than indulging in a passion for Granny Smiths. And that last little speech had – for those in the know, which as usual didn't include me – basically referred to him doing something unspeakable to me.

I stood up, feeling The Dog move to my side, whipping my legs with her cord-like tail. I still didn't have a full grip on my powers, and what I could and couldn't do, but before we left I'd been working with Fionnula the Fair, my terribly tipsy spiritual mentor, and had continued with the Morrigan during the journey.

A few times before, I'd pulled off spectacular light shows using nothing but Goddess power, but the problem was, I never really figured out how I did it. Much of what Fionnula had taught me seemed to come down to power of will, strength of intent, and making my wishes a reality, so I took a deep breath and gave it a go.

I started by clearing my head, using my favoured

technique of a fluffy white cloud to shunt out everything else. Then I called up my power, gave myself a pep talk, and waited a beat as I felt it gathering within me. I had nothing to lose: either it would work, and I'd give myself a mental high five, or it wouldn't and I'd just look a bit of a tit, not for the first time. There was, of course, a third option – that it would work too well, I'd kill both of them with a blast of super-power, and blow a hole in the side of the ship.

Nah. That seemed unlikely. And heck, there'd be life-boats, right?

I paused until Gabriel and Luca were at an especially violent point, which seemed to involve attempting to smash each other's heads through the wall, and closed my eyes for a second. I know, I said I was trying to wean myself off that bad habit – but I needed, at least for a moment, to block out the sights and sounds around me and focus purely on the crazy stuff my brain was capable of channelling.

I had the urge to point my fingers or use a wand, but guessed that was just from watching too much *Harry Potter*. I simply exhaled my breath, and let the energy flow, visualising my targets in my mind's eye.

Previously, I'd been bathed in the light myself – it shone from me, like I was the Human Torch in chick form. A five foot nine glow stick in Doc Marten's. This time, perhaps because I was focusing so much on the two roiling dickheads in front of me, it shot straight at them, like a blast of cold fire.

As soon as it hit them, they both froze, then fell to the floor. Luca was holding his temples in his hands, and stayed on his knees, grimacing. Gabriel used the edge of the broken table to drag himself back upright, though I could see it was killing him to do it; to resist. I surged harder against him and he flew back against the wall, hitting it so hard the framed picture of the Manhattan skyline fell off. Still he stayed on his feet, with his eyes narrowed and his teeth clamped together and sweat beading on his forehead. He wouldn't go down. My vision blinkered until all I could see was him, all I could hear was his laboured breathing, all I could feel was his panic and strength and spirit.

Part of me really wanted to force him. To push this power to its limits, to really see what I was capable of; to simply humiliate him, make him submit to the Goddess, but even as I thought the words, I realised it wasn't me speaking. It wasn't Lily McCain at least, which was the 'me' I was fighting to keep. That was someone different, older, and much, much scarier. Someone I wasn't entirely in control of.

I closed my eyes, flicked off the mental switch, and let reality flood back in. The Dog was nudging my knees with her long black head. Carmel was looking on, eyes huge and distressed. Connor, Finn and Kevin were standing around like muscular toadstools, frozen between duty to their High King and allegiance to the Goddess.

Luca climbed to his feet, warily backing off from me like a whipped dog. Maybe I could have just told him to back down – he was my almost-willing slave, after all. But that stranger inside me hadn't really been in the mood for negotiation.

Gabriel stood tall, muscles trembling from the effort it had cost him to fight me, glaring at me from across the room: he knew what I'd been tempted to do, and his purple-flecked eyes told me he'd die before he let me do it.

I met his gaze and threw my own attitude back at him. Truthfully, I felt a bit embarrassed at showing off so much, and slightly concerned at the way I almost lost control. But he didn't know that – and maybe now he'd think twice before he tried to boss me around.

The Morrigan started a long, slow round of applause.

'Now that,' she said, smiling at me like her favourite pupil, 'is how a goddess deals with snivelling curs.'

Chapter Three

We'd docked somewhere called Dumbo, which left me and Carmel in fits of childish laughter. There really is no limit to how much fun can be had from flapping your fingers at the sides of your face to imitate cartoon elephant ears. Yep, the world really is in safe hands.

The ship had somehow slid into a deserted pier that was, from the signage, usually used by water taxis. It was a tricky operation and one skilfully handled by the captain. The captain I'd never seen – he was probably made of skeleton parts and wearing a peaked hat at a jaunty angle on his bony skull, whistling the theme to Popeye from between empty tooth sockets.

There were no people around at all, which I don't suppose was strange for 4 a.m. on a freezing December night, but perhaps I'd been expecting more nocturnal activity in the city that never sleeps. And there certainly wasn't anything remotely approaching a customs official hanging about – good news for Kevin, and backing up my belief that Something Magical Was Afoot. Da da da!

I'd never been to New York before – in fact, the furthest I'd ever been away from home was Ireland. What can I say? I'm a ginger (or at least I was) who doesn't like being touched. Package holidays to Ibiza were never going to be my thing, and I'd always been too – I could try and find a more flattering word, but ultimately 'scaredy-pants' is just about right – to go further afield. The thought of being trapped in the press of crowds, of being shoved around with a mass of tourists, was repellent to me back then. I still wasn't keen, but I knew I'd be able to do it – protect myself and them from the impact of my touch.

We had cars waiting for us, to sweep us away to whatever luxury pad Gabriel had on his books in New York, but first I wanted to stop and to stare and to try and soak some of it up. This was big. This was the States. This was New York. The Big Apple – though now I knew from the Morrigan that that could also be used as a metaphor for my fine self, I wasn't too keen on anyone taking a bite out of it any time soon.

The weather was shockingly cold, but free of the bluster and drizzle we'd left at home in the UK. I was wrapped head to toe in a long-length puffer that made me look like the Michelin man, with knee-high boots and very snazzy black leather gloves Carmel's mum had given me for the journey, bless her. I had a black beanie hat crammed on to my head, pulled down around my ears, and my long white hair was wrapping itself around my neck like a scarf. The only part of me that could feel the encroaching frost was my face, and I knew my naturally pale cheeks would now be perfectly pink.

I looked around at the hazily lit streets; the red brick warehouses and faded industrial grandeur; the cobble stones and the iron tracks that were testament to the days when cargo was shunted from place to place, of sugar and coffee and boxes being hauled from docks to shore to shed.

'It looks,' said Carmel, standing beside me, 'a bit like—'

'Liverpool!' I finished for her, grinning.

'Yeah, except this time it really does,' she replied,

shoving her curls into the collar of her coat and zipping it up over her chin.

It was a standing joke between us that Carmel suffered from a common Scouse affliction: she thought Liverpool was the centre of the whole world, and everywhere we went, she found comparisons – usually unfavourable ones. This time, though, she'd nailed it – something about the shared industrial heritage definitely made it reminiscent of home.

'Come on,' said Gabriel, ushering us towards our car. 'We're in Brooklyn, and we're heading into Manhattan, but I'll show you something on the way if you like. Something I suspect might be very . . . interesting.'

'Interesting as in "this could have its own Wikipedia entry", or interesting as in "the world is about to burst and spray poo all over my face"?' I asked. Because, frankly, it could go either way with me.

Gabriel smiled down at me, and I felt my heart literally do a little bump. He looked damn fine in moonlight. In any light in fact, but there was something about the shimmer of pale silver dancing in the waves of his hair, and the gleam of affection in his deep blue eyes, that just made me go a bit gooey right then. Maybe it was the soft Irish accent. Maybe it was the cable knit sweater, which I've always found strangely enticing in a sexy-Cornish-fisherman way. Or the scarf. Or the boots. Or all the bits in between.

'Hopefully the former, Lily, but life with you does have a tendency not to go to plan. In fact, since I met you, I've given up planning completely. I just live my life one day at a time, and hope for the best.'

'Yeah, right,' I murmured, looking away. I always looked away. I always fought it when I found him too attractive, when the pull was too strong. Completely bonkers, really, considering I'd been ready to do anything to save him just a few short weeks ago. I probably still would if push came to shove – but in the cold light of, well, night, it sometimes felt too much. I was only just starting to feel in control of myself – and giving in to Gabriel's undoubted charms would mean undoing it all.

Anyway, he was fibbing. Gabriel was one of the most devious and ruthless men I knew. The day he gave up planning and scheming was the day he gave up breathing. He'd planned and schemed my whole life for me, from childhood through to my recent acceptance of my role as his mate, without the slightest consideration for my feelings.

Until the end, that is. Until the end of that terrible night in Tara, when he'd finally freed me to make my own choice . . . and I was still there. Still with him, kind of. So either I'm a complete dumb ass, or I secretly believe there may be a happy ending for life, the universe and everything after all.

'Stop thinking so much,' he said, nudging my padded coat with his elbow. 'You've got that look on your face that tells me you're analysing why the colour blue is blue, and wondering if it's all a trick.'

'Yeah,' chipped in Carmel. 'You do have that look a lot, Lily. Your eyes kind of screw up and your lips go a bit pouty and your head tilts to one side like a very confused budgie. It's not flattering. I call it your "what's the story morning glory?" look.' She drawled the last few words in an almost-convincing Liam Gallagher whine.

I was about to sputter in objection, but realised my head was at exactly that angle, my eyes were in fact screwed up and, well, why *was* the colour blue blue? And anyway, hadn't I earned a bit of confusion after everything that had happened to me? Growing up with a fake name and a fake identity and a fake nan? Finding out I was a bloody goddess and not just a pop writer after all? They could both just—

'Fuck right off,' I said, walking away to stroke my dog. She never criticised me.

I looked on as Finn and Connor loaded the bags into the cars, absently scratching The Dog behind her silky ears, and held my sulk. I was tired. I was cold. I was a long way from home. Luca raised his eyebrows at me in a question, and I quickly shook my head: back off buster. He backed off. Something about me blasting him to the ground in a super-charged ray of magical light had made him a lot more acquiescent.

'Come on,' shouted Gabriel, 'get in. You can sulk later – don't let your inner teenager spoil your first sight of New York.'

Bastard. I hated him.

I got in.

Chapter Four

Within a couple of minutes, we'd pulled up again, somewhere called Brooklyn Heights. Behind us were rows of
pretty brownstone houses, several storeys high, creeping
ivy crawling darkly around railings and doors. In front
of us lay . . . everything.

The promenade was dotted with benches, and I could
see the reason why – they came with probably the best
view in the world. Across the river, lit up like an urban
fairytale, was Manhattan. The shiny points and spines of
the skyscrapers; millions of shining windows; man-made
structures reaching up to poke the inky black sky with
electric-gold fingers. To the side was the far off blink of
the Statue of Liberty and, spanning it all, the enormous
fairy lights of a giant suspension bridge, even now
flashing with the headlights of passing cars.

It was unreal. It was like a scene from a movie, a
picture from the front of a postcard. Even Carmel was
silent, staring across the shimmering water in amazement.

I am a Goddess of the Earth – but ironically I'm a city
girl at heart. That's growing up in Liverpool for you.
New York was, obviously, the ultimate city – giving a
hefty 'screw you' to nature, to the encroaching mud and
water of the rivers, creeping in to eat away at some of

the world's most expensive real estate. The whole of Manhattan, in fact, looked like it shouldn't even exist – balanced there so precariously, an island of humanity stranded in the middle of a sea of nature.

But exist it did. Majestically.

I felt overwhelmed – possibly also a bit exhausted from the journey, from firing up my goddess power the night before, and from the ongoing emotional battle-ground of my life. I imagined the millions of people over there, across that sparkling bridge, with their busy lives and their loves and their jobs and their families and their annoying bosses and all their normality.

It was beautiful, and I felt tears spring, stinging, into my eyes, the moisture starting to freeze on my eyelashes as soon as it leaked out. I am officially a wuss, I thought, blinking back the tears and swallowing down the rush of emotion.

I saw the Morrigan whoop and swoop and run, one giant step at a time, down towards a wooden bridge. The Dog ran after her, stretching her elegantly long legs in an effortless pursuit, skidding to a halt in the middle. The Morrigan started jumping up and down, yelling out her joy in a way that would freeze muggers at fifty paces. As she leapt, the bridge started to shake and wobble, and she laughed so hard I could almost feel the vibrations.

On cue, a flock of birds swooped towards her – they looked like gulls and ducks and herons to me, but I could have sworn some eagles and hawks had joined the party. They flapped and whirled around her head, and she waved her hands, directing them into obscure black shapes as The Dog jumped and snapped and gave in to her predatory nature, the diamond sparkles beneath her skin gleaming like the cats' eyes on the side of the road. All of this, bathed in the shower of light from the angular shapes of the Manhattan skyscrapers. Well. That was just plain weird.

'Lily, come here,' said Gabriel, distracting me.

I gave him a pointed look, and he added, between gritted teeth: 'Pretty please.'

'Only if you add sugar on top,' I murmured under my breath, walking towards him. Of course I'd temporarily forgotten his annoying High King super hearing, and he smiled at me, the grin white in the darkness.

'I'll give you sugar on top any time you want, *a ghra,*' he said.

'Stop that – you sound on the lechy side,' I replied, drawing up close to him. 'Now what did you want to show me? If that's not a leading question.'

'Look at this,' he said, pointing at a series of images on the pavement. They were embedded in the stone, and seemed to be some kind of engravings. A series of them, all showing the view I'd just been wowed by, in different eras. One pictured a relatively bucolic scene of sail boats and higgledy piggledy buildings on the edge of Manhattan, only a few church spires piercing the sky. One showed it a few years later, with cranes and industrialisation. The next were modern, with skyscrapers past and skyscrapers present.

'Why don't you see what you can do?' he suggested, looking at me hopefully. 'This is a place of great power, a special place. I know you see the past as well as the future. I know you've been working hard to control it all. Stand here, and test it out.'

'Are you mad?' I half said and half screeched. 'You have no idea what happens to me. It's like deliberately inviting someone to whack me round the head with a sledgehammer! That might mean nothing to you Terminator types, but I'm not keen. I'm not doing it. If I want to see what old New York looks like, I'll visit the bloody museum, OK?'

I've seen the past a few times before – the first time was unintentional, during a school trip on the Mersey

Ferries. That time, as a more-confused-than-usual teen-ager, I'd seen ancient monks waving at me from across the river. Yeah, I know – bit of a mind warp. It had happened since, including once when my teacher Fionnula the Fair had forced me to see her own personal (and pretty traumatic) history. Frankly, I didn't much like it – especially as it often involved collapsing afterwards like a heap of blancmange having an aneurysm.

Grudgingly, part of me knew that Gabriel was right. I'd learned a lot since then, and had a newfound, if very small, level of confidence in my own abilities. Fionnula and the Morrigan had both told me that I could control all of this, that it was up to me what I saw, didn't see, or felt. Hum. Easy for them to say – they had centuries of experience. I was still firmly wearing my 'L' plates.

He looked down at me patiently, like a teacher encouraging an awkward student, as though he could see the cogs whirring in my brain, which made me feel even more irate.

'You need to start learning more about your powers, Lily. Yes, you can throw your pretty light shows at me and Luca – and maybe we deserved it. But you can't go through life every day tip-toeing around what might happen. You need to know, and to control it.'

I was torn between agreeing, and wanting to throttle him with his own scarf. Yes, my control was limited – and that was because of him. Because he, arrogant fool that he is, decided when I was a child that the 'safest' option was to keep me ignorant of what I was; to let me grow up just feeling weird and scared and out of place wher-ever I went. I should have had decades to come to terms with what I was and, thanks to him, I'd had little over a month.

I was about to launch into an undoubtedly eloquent speech on that very subject when Carmel intervened, even more eloquently.

'Chicken!' she said, and went into a crowd-pleasing charade of flapping her imaginary wings and making squawking noises. I saw Connor staring at his feet in an attempt not to laugh, and Finn and Kevin staring firmly off into the distance like FBI special agents trying to ignore the madness in their midst.

I didn't want to rise to the bait. I was too old to be goaded like a child in the school playground. I was a goddess, for fuck's sake and I should have more dignity. I shouldn't care what Gabriel said, what Carmel squawked, or what anybody thought of me. I was a strong, independent woman with a mind of my own.

I pushed Gabriel out of the way and jumped on the first plaque. It was the oldest one, and as I stood there, shivering, I tried to remember all the lessons Fionnula had given me, all the pithy comments the Morrigan had made. Anything I'd picked up through trial and error, which was very little, as I'd spent most of my life avoiding this kind of thing, not seeking it out. It felt alien and disturbing and I was way out of my comfort zone. Admittedly my comfort zone is a very small place – a room on my own with my dog – but this definitely wasn't it.

When I was younger, and I'd seen the past through eyes that were rooted in the present, it usually resulted in me falling over and my classmates gathering round in a circle and laughing at me. 'Cause kids are nice like that. Not high on my list of idyllic childhood memories, especially when combined with the pain of my brain juddering against the sides of my skull.

This time, I was doing it all on purpose, for the first time ever. Scary.

I gazed out at the view of Manhattan, and lowered the ever-present control that I now held about me pretty much all of the time. It felt nice: like taking your bra off at the end of the night, a sense of relief at the removal of a subtle pressure you'd not even realised was there until it was gone. I'd grown used to it being there, guarding me against accidental visions and unwanted brain invasions, but was nowhere near experienced enough for it to feel effortless.

I closed my eyes once, cleared my mind of the here and now, and blocked out the sights and sounds of the reality around me – opening up space for a different reality altogether.

I opened my eyes and looked again. The vista had changed. Fewer lights. Darkened buildings, tiny in the distance. A black river, and boats with old-fashioned sails. Different sounds, different smells – it was coming at me in 4D, and I let it. Not for too long though – didn't want to accidentally fall into an invisible time portal and wake up facing off with the *Gangs of New York*. Hey, it could happen!

I dragged myself away, jumped on to the next plaque, shaking off Gabriel's touch as he tried to guide me. Repeated the process: saw Manhattan as it grew and changed and developed, dark smoke billowing over the harbour. My mind gobbled it up, and I felt a thrill run through me: I was doing it. On purpose. All by myself – because I wanted to, not because the great gods of head-fuck had decided to give me a celestial Glasgow kiss. I closed it down, glorying in the fact that I could and, full of a kind of mental sugar rush, went to hop onto another picture.

'That's enough now,' said Gabriel, reaching out to take hold of me. 'Don't push yourself too far in one night.'

He was using that tone again. The I-will-be-obeyed voice. I shoved him aside in a blaze of strength, fixing him with a glare as old as time. Default setting: stop bossing me around, big boy.

I was so distracted by asserting my state of independence that I didn't notice the warning signs before it was too late. Incoming: one of my totally adorable visions.

DARK TOUCH

There was a powerful buzz flooding my brain, like a swarm of very pissed-off hornets was invading. A searing white pain slashing through my mind as the vision swamped me, grabbing me by the shoulders and giving me a damn good shaking. Utter agony. Aural hallucinations. Complete collapse into unconsciousness. Ah, home sweet home. My last coherent thought was: damn him, he was right.

When I came to, I was lying in Gabriel's arms, my head cradled against his chest, beanie hat knocked over my eyes. I clutched up at his face, my gloved hands seeking out comfort and reality and solidity as I shook and shuddered and surrendered myself to the aftershock.

'What?' he murmured, pulling up the hat and scanning my face, looking for damage. 'What is it? What did you see? Are you alright?'

'No,' I replied, feeling the world's biggest headache clamp down around my skull. 'I'm not. I saw an eye . . .'

Chapter Five

My freaky eye vision had thrown everyone into a raging ball of chaos, and I was wrapped in metaphorical cotton wool for the rest of the night. I think if he'd had enough, it wouldn't even be metaphorical – Gabriel would have rolled me up in bubble wrap.

We'd all piled back into the cars and driven to Greenwich Village. I was exhausted, and still in the kind of pain that was so strong you tried your very best to hide it. I was fooling no one, I knew. I'm usually pale but after that episode, I was channelling Casper, and I found it impossible to take part in the forced banter that Carmel and Gabriel tried to keep up during the drive. I couldn't even raise a smile when Carmel got excited about seeing the building where the Friends used to live, wondering out loud if she could pick up Joey in Central Perk.

Gabriel's home was off Ash Street, a picture-perfect New York collection of brownstones and coffee shops and iron fire escapes. It was tucked away in a quiet courtyard, gated with a picturesque set of frost-bitten bars, four storeys high and fronted with a bright red door. The courtyard held a small garden, and a fountain that tinkled and sprinkled through the night, tiny sprays of water glittering in the moonlight.

The cars had crunched to a stop on the gravel, and we'd all scurried inside before the first fingers of sunshine started to poke through the clouds and turn our vampire into Rip van Winkle. As soon as our coats were shed, Luca held me close to him, kissing me gently on my still throbbing temples, for once tender and concerned instead of flirtatious.

'I must go now, Lily. But keep yourself safe while I am gone – you know I can't live without you.'

That last comment wasn't helping my headache any, nor was the way Gabriel was lurking in the background pretending he wasn't watching, two huge suitcases clutched under his arms and a scowl on his face.

When Luca said he couldn't live without me, was he being sentimental? Or would he actually pop his clogs if I wasn't around? I was really hoping for the former. I already had way too much responsibility for comfort.

I shook it away, which is my usual coping mechanism for thoughts that are bothering me. I am at championship level when it comes to mental evasion. I think if someone did an autopsy on my brain, they'd find it jammed full of tiny ribboned boxes, all crammed with thought processes I'd abandoned half-way through and hidden away to think about never.

Luca disappeared off upstairs, and Gabriel immediately corralled me into a book-lined room that I assumed was some kind of superhero study. It looked and smelled like a law library, the whiff of leather bindings and furniture polish and old paper. The huge dark wood desk was covered with charts and maps, and I had an entertaining moment where I imagined Gabriel and Finn in here, shoving miniature tanks around with pointy sticks, like a scene from an old war movie. Celtic Crazies.Top Secret HQ. Stiff upper lip, chaps, sword arms at the ready – keep calm and carry on.

'OK, master and commander,' I said, falling wearily

into a swivel chair and tapping my Docs onto the floor to give myself a swing. 'Out with it – I can tell you have a big speech brewing, and I really really want to go to sleep.'

He frowned, obviously not enjoying the fact that I'd caught him out. Maybe even wondering if I'd read his mind – I'd done that a few times, and it was always sensationally strange. I'd learned enough control now to keep him out of my own head – where he used to occasionally pop in for an unplanned visit, like a tipsy uncle – but I had no intention of ever doing it to him again. Some things are just plain wrong.

'No, I didn't read your mind,' I said, enjoying the look of doubt on his face, 'you're just very predictable. You pretty much always have a big speech brewing, and I'm usually on the receiving end of it. You're like a disapproving dad, lecturing his daughter on inappropriate behaviour. It's really not very sexy at all.'

If he hadn't been an iron man of legend with centuries of experience under his belt, his jaw might have dropped. Instead, he just grinned.

The grin was followed by a blur of movement, and a few seconds where I had no idea where he was at all, spinning round on my swingy chair to try and see where he was going.

Then he was there. Behind me. Scooping my hair up from my neck, bundling it loosely over my shoulder to leave my skin exposed. I felt the soft whisper of his breath just beneath my ear, and the silken touch of fingertips caressing me.

I breathed in, deeply, focusing my energy on blocking out visions, and inhaled a hefty dose of Gabriel with it: something woody and spicy and uniquely him. He leaned down, placed his lips on the sensitive flesh at the side of my neck, and kissed me. So soft, so slow, I could almost pretend it wasn't happening – if it wasn't for the fact that my whole body was going nuts in response to his touch. I felt my head fall to one side, inviting more, and long strong fingers moved around to stroke my throat, my shoulders, and a very silly spot where my collarbones met that just made me crazy.

Stroking, nuzzling, kissing, sighing. The sighing would be me, feeling my whole being scream for more – for those fingertips to reach down, to touch my breasts, to undo the buttons I seemed to have been trapped by for the whole of my life. To take everything away apart from the way I felt right then.

He spun me around in the chair, and lifted me up until I was crushed against him, holding me steady with one arm. He was tall and strong and hard and all mine, and my legs just weren't working any more. He smiled, tracing his fingers over my cheekbones and the flush I knew would be flaming away; running them across the outline of lips that were open and willing and pretty damn desperate to be kissed; gazing into eyes that I knew were heavy and dilated and drugged with lust.

'Is that sexy enough for you?' he murmured, the Irish lilt more pronounced than usual, his own eyes flaming violet in the dimly lit room. 'Or do you want more?'

I stretched up, kissed him, wrapping my arms around his neck and pulling his head down to mine. Right then, I wanted more. I wanted as much as he could give. Gabriel is the only man I've ever properly kissed – in a tongues and all kind of way – and he was pretty damn good at it. My headache was gone, and all I could think about was hanging on to him, touching more of him, and making sure he didn't stop kissing me. Possibly until I blacked out from oxygen deprivation.

But even as I lost myself in the moment, even as I felt hidden parts of me tighten and swell and get ever so excited, I could tell he was holding back, not quite giving in to the desire that I knew was in him. I could feel tension in the coiled muscles of his shoulders, and slight hesitancy in his kiss. His hands were firmly placed in the small of my back, holding me to him but not wandering or moving or caressing. My hips had taken on a life of their own against him; writhing and wriggling and generally acting all slutty, while he remained perfectly still.

His body was sending out messages so mixed they needed to see a therapist: definite boy response in the trouser area, which was shamefully thrilling to feel pressed up against me, but all that . . . reserve. Control. He was having to fight himself, and I didn't quite know why. I didn't know why, but I didn't like it. I don't know much about this man–woman stuff, but I knew enough to realise it had to be mutual. He had to want me as much as I wanted him. Otherwise, it was just plain undignified.

I pulled away, tried to put some distance between us, and ended up falling very gracefully back into the swivel chair, with him looming above me. OK. So I'd managed to successfully engage in a making-out session with Gabriel without visions. I'd managed to keep my control in place, and still go pretty much wild with lust. That was a big step forward for me. I should have been pleased. He should have been pleased. This could have been the start of a beautiful relationship – or at the very least a pretty hot one. Which was what he'd given every indication of wanting, and I'd been resisting. Until, you know, he touched me. Then I changed my mind pretty damn fast. I repeat: he should have been pleased.

Instead, the violet of his eyes was shading down to navy, and the hands that just seconds ago were driving me deliberately wild were shoved firmly into the pockets of his Levis, like he was trying to stop them from reaching out. He was backing off, and I felt my heart plummet to somewhere near my ankles, where it started to bawl like a baby.

'Yes,' I replied, once my breathing had settled, looking up at him sadly. 'I did want more. But you appear not to, oh mate of mine. And I'm sure, as ever, that you have your reasons. You always have your reasons, don't you?'

As I said it, a few of them flooded back to me: the reasons he'd used to justify it all. The reasons he'd left me with Coleen when I was six. The reasons he'd left me with my life-fucking visions. The reasons he'd kept me isolated from the rest of the world, emotionally crippled, staggering along on half-power until he appeared one night to change everything. Keeping me safe. Protecting the Goddess. Saving the world. All very . . . reasonable. And, you know, borderline evil.

This was the kind of thought process I'd usually shove into one of those boxes I mentioned before, but this time I welcomed them. They made me feel angry and determined – which was a hell of a lot better than rejected and embarrassed.

Gabriel stepped away, putting the width of the war-desk between us before he risked slipping his hands from his pockets. He used one to run through his hair, and I watched the thick dark waves fall between his fingers like silk. He did that when he was stressed. When he was thinking hard. Very often when he was about to lie. It was his little tell, and I don't think he knew he even had it.

'Lily, you know I want you. You know I've waited my whole life for you. That there is nothing my body wants more than to feel you beneath me, to touch what I've only before seen. To feel you shake and shiver as I explore you, and to hear my name on your lips as I do it. You are my mate, you are my love. But this . . . isn't right.'

He gestured around him, at the sparklingly clean library and the old wooden shelves and the hundreds of books. It all looked pretty fine to me. What was he waiting for? Beds scattered with rose petals and gypsy violinists?

A romantic meeting at the top of the Empire State Building, cocktails, and a tender night on a bearskin rug in front of a roaring log fire? That was all romance. That was all stage setting. I didn't need that, any of it. The Morrigan had told me once that my nature was to be fertile and of the earth – the subtext being I really liked having a shag – and I hadn't believed her.

Now, sitting here, fighting down twin demons of anger and lust, I was starting to think she was right.

Hmmph. There wasn't much I could do, other than run over there and jump on him. I'd done it before, and I could do it again. But he might say no, and I didn't think I was quite up to that, thank you very much. I'd lived my whole life without love or touch or sex, and done just fine. I could carry on like that as long as I needed to.

I told myself it was no biggie as I climbed to my unsteady feet, holding on to the side of the desk in an attempt to hide my collywobbles.

'OK,' I replied, sauntering towards the door in a way I hoped was nonchalant but knowing full well it wasn't, 'it isn't right. If you say so, High King. I'm sure, as ever, that you know best. But do me a favour in future? Don't start what you can't finish.'

I'd almost crawled up the stairs after that fairly humiliating scene, wandering along the corridors of the upper floors, randomly opening doors to try and find the room that contained my suitcase.

In one room, I'd seen Luca, sprawled naked and dead to the world on a four-poster bed. I paused to silently appreciate the work of art that he was, and moved on. I flung open the next door to see Finn sitting at the side of his bed with his back to me, wearing boxer shorts, and his hand moving rapidly in a frenzied up-and-down motion.

I jerked away, completely mortified at interrupting what seemed to be a highly personal moment, until he turned around slightly and I saw he was merely polishing his sword. As it were.

I spluttered my apologies and walked on. I stopped outside the next door and gave pause before bursting in. The noises coming from inside told me I'd made a very wise decision. Muffled yelps, laughter, little cries of pleasure. One male, one female. Carmel and Connor, indulging in a spot of recreation together. I lingered there for perhaps a few moments more than necessary, I'm ashamed to say. A tiny part of me felt a voyeuristic urge to listen in, to share vicariously in the mindlessly good time they were obviously having. To at least imagine something I felt like I'd never have.

But my blood was still up from having Gabriel lick my neck like a Cornetto, and it just felt too weird to be marginally turned on while my best friend was having sex. I moved on and wished them well.

I was sad and lonely and completely drained by the time I found the right room. I knew it was the right room because The Dog was in it, tail whipping in excitement.

I untied my boots, hopping on one leg as I tried to pull each off, and fell onto the bed fully clothed, staring at the ceiling and trying to figure out what had just happened. If there had been one thing I'd been used to taking for granted, it was that Gabriel wanted to be my mate in more than just name.

Now, when the opportunity presented itself in all its throbbing glory, he'd pulled back. Said no. What had he expected to happen when he started that . . . foreplay? Perhaps he underestimated his own prowess and didn't expect me to be so keen? Nah, that didn't feel right – Gabriel *never* underestimated his own prowess. It must have been me he underestimated, as ever – my control, my ability to tolerate his touch, the fact that I turned into a nympho at the drop of a hat. He hadn't expected it, and he clearly hadn't wanted it.

I felt a rush of the familiar isolation and solitary fear I'd felt when I was growing up – when I'd become so used to other people rejecting me that in the end, I started doing it on their behalf before anybody ever got a chance to get close. Nobody had been interested in pursuing a relationship with me – Coleen, the school friends who sensed my weirdness, work colleagues who thought I was insane in the membrane. Carmel was the only exception, and even that had its limits.

I was used to being alone. I was used to people not wanting me, and used to clamping down on any sense at all that I might want them.

Now, without even noticing it was happening, I'd started to let that go – I'd made my choice, that night at Tara. I'd chosen Gabriel and this life, and with it the companionship that had begun to edge its way into my whole existence. Being with Carmel so much; having Connor, Kevin and Finn around; expecting the Morrigan to land on my shoulder; knowing that Luca was always nearby. And him. Gabriel. There at the heart of it all. The man who loved me.The man I maybe loved, depending on what mood I was in.

It had all started to feel normal. Like a family. And as I lay there on that strange bed in yet another strange house I was expected to call home, I realised that was a mistake. I was Lily McCain. Freak show. And I was better off on my own.

Well, I thought, as I felt the dull thud of an athletic body land next to mine, and the warmth of a muzzle slipping itself under my hand, apart from The Dog.

Chapter Six

It was the day. We were in a pub. Some things never change.

It was, shockingly enough, an Irish pub – although to be fair that seemed to be the only kind I'd seen in New York. We'd spent a bit of time sightseeing that morning, accompanied of course by my faithful pack, which would have been fun – apart from the unshakeable feeling I had of being watched. Which may have been pure paranoia on my part – but you know how the old saying goes? Just because you're paranoid, it doesn't mean the giant flaming mystical eyeball isn't out to get you.

We were somewhere near Bleecker Street, and as soon as we walked through the doors, my head was almost knocked off by the eardrum-splitting decibel level of the music karate-chopping its way out of the speakers. The Dropkick Murphys, dropkicking the bejezus out of Rose Tattoo. Ah. Beer. Loud music. I felt instantly at home.

The place was empty apart from us, the barman, and one enormous cat that was curled up in the sawdust on the floor. It looked up at us with one lazy blink, and went back to sleep. Been there, done that, it seemed to say. I momentarily wished I hadn't left The Dog back at the house: it would have been fun to see her chase Mr Feline

Groovy around for a few minutes. See how blasé he was then.

The bar was long and dark and set up with draft taps for Guinness and Harp and Blue Moon and Kilkenny, all reflecting in the mirror behind them. There was a TV mounted on the wall, showing baseball to the soundtrack of Celtic punk, and neat rows of empty stools. The walls were covered in randomly placed posters for gigs in Dublin and boxing photos and pictures of the aforementioned enormous cat and Irish and US flags, all stuck up like a crazy-paving collage.

When he spoke, the barman had a fresh-off-the-boat accent, pausing in his glass-drying to give Gabriel the once over and a respectful nod first. He stared at me briefly, then quickly averted his eyes.

'You'll be busy today, I expect,' he said. 'So I'll close up for a few hours, shall I?'

Gabriel nodded back, and the barman strode over to the door, reaching out to flip the 'Closed' sign face forward. He hadn't gone as far as genuflecting or quaking in fear, but he was obviously a bit overwhelmed. He knew who we were, he knew how to behave, but he was still terrified.

I looked on as everyone trailed to a group of seats set up around scratched wooden tables, already laid with beer mats for the pints the barman was now pulling. Carmel, face still bearing the jagged scar she'd gained in a battle with the Faidh; Finn, Connor and Kevin moving with the easy grace and coiled violence of the warriors they were; the Morrigan, six foot tall, covered in weapons, red hair striped with dazzling white, and Gabriel. Cormac Mor himself. The High King. He Who Must Be Obeyed.

Yep, it was a pretty strange bunch. Can't say that I blamed the barman for being so scared. I reached out, went to touch him on the hand as he passed over the ale.

Intending to comfort him, show him the 'human' face of this carnival of weird.

He yelped as our skin brushed, and dropped the glass to the ground, shattering on the stone floor in a foaming blend of creamy froth and shards. He dragged his hand away from me, cradling it like it was burned, and looked over at me. If I'd thought he was terrified before, I'd been wrong. *This* was terrified.

'I-I'm sorry,' he stuttered, backing away so far his spine cracked into the cash till. I dropped my guard a fraction, and allowed tendrils of my mind to reach out to his. I'm not telepathic, but I've been learning to use the power I do have to pick up on senses, images, sometimes random names or words. I don't do it often – let's face it, it's rude. But this time, I just wanted to get a better sense of him. Of this blubbering wreck of a hospitality profes- sional, standing in front of me with Guinness lapping round his trainers, too scared to move. I wanted to find out what he found so frightening.

As ever when you eavesdrop, you never find anything good out, do you? It didn't take a lot of probing to discover exactly what it was he found so frightening. It was little old me – Lily McCain. The only one in our band of merry travellers who hadn't actually killed anybody.

It was *me* he found so frightening. Not the King, or the men with swords, or the huge woman who could turn into a death-eating crow. No. I was bringing on his panic attack – the 'human' face of the freak show, as I'd been arrogant enough to think of myself. Even the slightest connection to his frantic mind told me that. He was petrified of me. Scared of the legends that had built up around me. That if I touched him, I could take away his free will. Steal his soul. Change his destiny. Make him infertile. Turn him into stone. Exile him to the Otherworld.

I gasped in shock and backed away myself. I'd been

cruising through all of this seeing myself as a victim, truth be told. I'd never asked to be a frigging goddess. I'd never asked to see people's futures, or to save the world, or for my hair to turn white when I saved it, or to shack up with a King. I'd never asked for anything other than to be left alone – and now here I was. The stuff of legend. The Big Scary Goddess Girl. Scaring the poor barman, still not getting laid, and failing to impress the enormous cat, who was now looking at me with one unblinking eye as it licked its own arse.

'It's all right,' I said to the barman, not sure which of us was more shocked. 'I'm not going to do anything to hurt you. I don't do that. I don't hurt people.'

Part of me wanted to stamp my feet and shout a bit. It didn't seem fair that I'd been forced into this role – and in fact had, let's not forget, saved the fucking world after all – and now found myself the subject of fear and loathing in New York. But that didn't seem very grown up and, at the end of the day, what difference did it really make? People had always been a bit scared of me, anyway. What did I think, that one blessing-the-whole-of-humanity session would turn me into Little Miss Popular? That being able to finally touch people would make me normal? Well, maybe I had. But now, I could see, I was very much mistaken. Because some people would now be scared of *me* touching *them*, instead of the other way round. Different cause – same effect. The same delightful merry-go-round I'd always been on.

I realised the barman was never going to leave his catatonic state while I was standing so close to him, so I carried three pints over to the table.

He followed, at a cautious distance, with the rest of the drinks on a tray, his hands still shaking so much the beer was sloshing over the sides.

Once he'd retreated to the safety of his bar, where he turned the music down low enough for us to talk, he seemed to calm down and went back to drying his glasses. Poor bloke. I swigged half my glass of Guinness before anyone even touched theirs and was aware of everyone staring at me as I slammed the jar back down on the table.

'What?' I snapped at them all. 'Lightweights.'

The Morrigan laughed and downed hers in one before raising the empty glass to me in a silent salute. We were of the same blood, she and I. Descended from the same spirits, kinship there for the world to see in our ridiculous hair and our even more ridiculous drinking abilities. If we traced it all back, she was my big sister a thousand times removed, or something. That was kind of cool, at least.

'We must talk more about the vision you had last night, Lily,' said Gabriel, pretty much the first words we'd shared since the embarrassing sex scene in the study. I knew he'd been itching to discuss it more, and had seen him and the Morrigan having conflabs about it. I knew it was important and that it was partly my fault we'd become all 'distracted' the night before – but my heart was far from in it. I was still a bit freaked out by the whole barman mind-dive incident. 'Must we?' I asked, wiping my Guinness 'tash away with the back of my hand. 'What'll happen if we don't?'

'Then we will go in to potential battle tomorrow unprepared and could all be killed. Is that what you want, Goddess?'

I glared at him through slitted eyes. Yeah. Maybe it was. And I wasn't too keen on how he'd upgraded the Council meeting from a set of squabbling bureaucrats to 'potential battle'. I hoped he was just doing it for effect.

'Now is not the time to bicker,' said the Morrigan, interrupting what was setting up to be a real humdinger, even by our standards. 'Now is the time to plan. The eye of which you speak could hold great significance, sister.

We have been taught to trust your visions, even if you do not – you are the Mother. The Seer. To ignore them would be foolhardy, even by your mortal judgement.'

I wanted to argue, but I couldn't. That would be petty. And also, she wasn't beyond taking me outside for a quick straightener, and the last time that had happened I'd ended up dragged off by my hair and left unconscious, with a very sore arm.

I nodded, studiously avoiding Gabriel's gaze. It was all his fault I was here anyway. And I was still pretty pissed off at being left with the female equivalent of a raging hard-on.

'What else is there to say?' I muttered. 'It was an eye. A huge eye, with flames in it. It obliterated the landscape, wiped out Manhattan, and blinked at me. It was all I could see, and I felt like it was coming for me. That it could see me, that it knew who I was, and that it wanted me.'

'What colour was it?' asked Carmel, resting her chin in her hands.

'I don't know! A nice shade of hazel?' I suggested facetiously. 'It was kind of . . . fire coloured, all right? Like the pupils were made of flames. It wasn't nice. And I never want to see it again. Now, do any of you wise ones have a clue what's going on, or not?'

My voice had ridden up well above the bass-line with that last sentence, and I heard another glass smash behind the bar. Jesus. This was getting tiresome. We'd be drinking out of buckets if that carried on. I reined myself in and spoke again, quietly and calmly: 'Does it have any significance to you, or is it just me being weirder than usual?'

I saw Gabriel's eyes meet the Morrigan's across the table, and their gazes hold for a few seconds. It did mean something. And they knew what it was, in typical secret squirrel style. If I was a really, really good girl, maybe they'd even tell me.

'Possibly,' said Gabriel, finally. 'The leader of the Council we will be meeting tomorrow is Hathor. Aide to the Egyptian Sun God Ra. The one-time destroyer of humanity, redeemed and celebrated. She became addicted to slaughter, and was brought back by magic. Her other name is The Eye, and her other form is a lion. She is Ra's eye on earth.'

I pondered it for a moment, then spoke: 'So, she's a serial killer deity fresh out of rehab? And she's in charge of the Council? And you think she might be blinking at me in a vision? I realise you're the experts here, but surely that's not a good thing?'

I could feel my skin goose-bumping under the sleeves of my coat. Had she been watching me? Is that why I'd been feeling twitchy?

I'd quietened my voice right down, which I knew wouldn't be a problem for Gabriel. He had ears like sonic steel traps, and he would hear me just fine.

'Why are you whispering?' asked Carmel, leaning her head across the table to look at me, frowning and now whispering herself.

'So Mr Butterfingers back there doesn't drop any more glasses!' I yelled, exasperated, and ruining the whole effect. A pause. Another smash. Of course.

I'd been pursued by countless assassins. Pushed into the River Mersey by Fintan, the leader of the rebel Faidh. I'd been attacked by the Lord of the Dead. I'd been for a pint with God, for fuck's sake. And I'd dealt with it all. Not necessarily in a stylish way, but I'd dealt with it.

And now, when I'd so been hoping for a ceasefire, Gabriel was telling me I was about to walk back into some other ancient super quarrel. My life was like an episode of *Gladiators* – someone was always trying to knock me over with a bloody pugil stick.

'Lily, calm down,' said Gabriel, reaching out to take my hand and finding himself on the receiving end of fresh air as I snatched it away. 'It may mean nothing. Hathor has shown no ill-will towards us, and we have no reason to think that has changed. We may be mistaken, about all of it.'

'Don't tell me to calm down – it just makes me feel less calm! Not long ago I knew nothing about all this stuff. Now I'm a goddess, and the all-seeing eye is out to get me? And you expect me to walk calmly in there and let this person loose on me? I thought you were supposed to protect me! Or have you changed your mind about that as well, along with the whole being my mate thing?'

He stood so abruptly he caught the edge of the table with his knees, and Guinness glasses went sliding over to the other side, where the Morrigan caught them all like she was doing a juggling trick.

I saw the familiar twitch and stretch in his shoulders, the elongation of his legs as he grew bigger. His eyes were flaming, and there was fury etched in every line of his face.

Carmel's eyes were huge, staring at me with complete girl outrage that I'd not shared this speck of information with her. Blaagh. I'd had enough. Of all of them.

'I couldn't talk to you about it,' I yelped at her, 'you weren't there. You were busy shagging lover boy over there.'

I sounded like a bitch. I was acting like a bitch. Shit. Maybe I just *was* a bitch. Everyone seemed to be making me very, very angry just then. I had never, in my entire messed up life, wanted to be alone more. To just get up, walk out, and go and live in the subway tunnels with the rats and other crazy people. And I knew I could do it now as well – Carmel couldn't stop me. The Morrigan wouldn't, if it was what I really wanted. And Gabriel? Well, we'd see who was so big and tough once I got going. Woman scorned, and all that.

Just as things were tipping over the edge into something

really nasty, the door to the pub burst open. It had been locked, and the man who'd just busted his way through looked the worse for wear for breaking it open, falling into the room on unsteady feet, rubbing at his shoulder.

He froze, dead still; a small bloke in his twenties wearing John Lennon glasses and a look of utter dread. Can't say that I blamed him, especially as Gabriel was now reaching maximum swell capacity and diverting all of his royal anger into staring down the intruder.

The man staggered towards us, specs falling forward on his nose, swiping floppy blond hair away from his face as he approached.

'We're closed,' shouted the barman, running towards him waving a beer cloth, looking even more worried than usual.

'I know. I am here to see the High King. I'm sorry to arrive like this, but I need to see him. I need to . . . seek his counsel.'

He fell to his knees in front of us, shaking and trembling as Gabriel stared him down. Carmel had immediately kicked into Champion mode, and placed herself between me and the man, knife in hand. It didn't look much – she didn't look much – but I knew she was lethal when she needed to be. The adrenalin levels in the room had notched up by a thousand degrees, and there were too many swords. Too many knives. Too much magic. Too much misplaced anger. This trembling boy could easily die by accident if things carried on like this.

I stepped up, walked towards him, ignoring Carmel's pleas and the shadow of the Morrigan as she stood behind me. I held out my hand and pulled him to his feet.

'Get him a pint, for God's sake,' I said, raising an eyebrow at the barman, who couldn't move fast enough.

'Sit,' I said, guiding him towards the table. 'Talk. We were just having a domestic, and it was going nowhere good.'

Chapter Seven

His name was Colin Murphy, and he was a twenty-five-year-old nurse at a nearby 'senior living facility', whatever the hell that was.

He was also, it was clear to see, petrified. His whole body was wracked with tremors, and the hands gripping his pint glass were about as stable as Mount Vesuvius just before Pompeii hit the big one.

His toes were tapping convulsively on the floor, and his eyes were darting from Gabriel to the Morrigan to me, over and over again. It took him several minutes, several swigs, and several stern words from the King before he was settled enough to actually talk.

'It's the place where I work,' he said, his accent pure Noo Yoik despite the fiddle-di-de name. 'There's something . . . wrong going on. And my cousin – he died, when he shouldn't have. Too many people are dying and I don't think it's right. I talked to the police, but they ain't interested. They say people die when they're old and sick; and they didn't say it out loud but I kinda got the impression they thought I was nuts.'

Hmmm. I can't imagine why – I mean, apart from the shakes, the stuttering, breaking in pub doors, and the implausible claims.

'I'm not. Nuts. In case you was wondering,' he said, looking again from me to Gabriel to the Morrigan. 'I'm scared shitless right now, but I'm not crazy. There's something wrong, and I need you to listen. My family has pledged allegiance to yours for generations, Murphys to Conaires, and this is the first time I've . . . we've . . . asked for anything, High King.'

His voice had trailed off to almost a whisper by the last few words, as he realised he'd come close to making a demand. To complaining. To cajoling. To doing things that I'm guessing aren't in the Irish Boys' Book of Royal Etiquette. His hair flopped over his eyes and the tremors intensified as Gabriel studied his face, his mouth set in a cold line and his eyes slitted. He looked every inch the big, bad monarch – aloof, distant, and derisory. I understand why he was like that: he'd been raised to rule, to fight, and he'd been doing it for hundreds of years. His life hadn't exactly been normal. But I'd been on the receiving end of that glare a few times, and it kind of made me want to punch him in the throat. Colin had obviously been raised to be more deferential than me, and looked instead like he wanted to punch himself in the throat.

The Morrigan was helping keep the warm and fuzzies up by using a penknife to gouge mud out of the ridges of her boots. Giant boots – like, maybe a size ten – which she had propped up on the table, their soles pointing in Colin's direction. Each time she scraped out a chunk of clod, it flicked – entirely possibly not by accident – in his direction. The first time it happened, he jumped, sloshing Guinness over his already damp hands.

'How did you know we were here, boy?' she eventually asked, staring up at him along one enormous leg, green eyes glinting. 'This is not an official visit by Cormac Mor. This has not been scheduled or disseminated. This is not the time for supplication to his court. The High

King has better things to do than hear the pitiful bleating of a puny mortal like yourself.'

I didn't think Colin could get any paler, but he did. Seriously, he'd make Edward Cullen look like he'd just had a course of St Tropez. I half expected him to faint, and was wondering if I should try and catch his head – the Morrigan can make the most battle-hardened of souls grovel at her feet, and Colin? Well, Colin was a nurse.

Apparently, though, that gave him the edge. That, or enormous cojones, or total stupidity. He met her gaze once, which was probably enough to turn most men to stone, then looked down at his lap. It was a only flicker of defiance, of strength, but it was definitely there – and definitely enough to swing me firmly into Camp Colin. I've always had a thing for puny mortals, I guess, especially ones who combine their bleating with a bit of bad ass. The combination of 'pathetic' and 'pissed off' was one that I somehow identified with.

'Does it matter?' I asked, as I saw Colin struggling to pull words together into a mouth that was probably dry as the bar in a Quaker Meeting House. 'I'm sure Colin has his sources. I'm sure a magical boat sailing into town didn't go unnoticed. I'm sure the logistics of this trip were complicated, and involved people who might possibly talk to each other. I'm sure that Colin knows someone who knows someone who knows someone who knows us. His family is sworn to yours and, while I'm not entirely sure what that entails, I assume it means you have a responsibility to him as much as he has to you?'

Colin looked sideways at me, nodding his gratitude.

'He's here now, asking for help, and facing up to two of the biggest bullies I've ever met,' I continued, eyeing them both up and challenging them to disagree. The Morrigan just pulled a face and carried on cleaning her boots. Gabriel was deliberately staring over my head, and I could almost hear him counting to a thousand to try and calm himself down. Everyone else was either trying to turn into the Invisible Man or, in the case of Carmel, sitting back to enjoy her own personal episode of *The Jeremy Kyle Show*.

'I'm sure he'd rather not be here. I'm sure he'd rather be doing something more fun, like electrocuting his own testicles or eating deep fried monkey brains. But he is here – so at least do him the courtesy of listening, your Royal Bollocks. And if you can't be arsed, then off you fuck – I'll stay here and have a chat to Colin instead, then maybe I'll check into a hotel, and you can go to the all-important Council meeting without me. Just tell them I'm washing my hair.'

Carmel made a 'pah' noise between her lips; Finn shook his head in despair, and the Morrigan sniggered. Colin – well, he just looked like he wanted to pee himself, really badly. I was trying to help him, but I also knew that at least part of it was fuelled by my current super-negative frame of mind towards Gabriel. Colin was taking up that tried and tested position of cowering in the cross-fire.

'If that is what you wish, Goddess,' said Gabriel, calmly, finally tearing his gaze away from the fascinating clock on the wall behind my head. His eyes were the deep, dark navy they revert to when he's back in a place of peace, when I've finished yanking his chain in my various ways – disrespect, sex, anger, contempt, falling into Mortal Danger, flirting with Luca, singing O Danny Boy very badly, the list is endless – and he's managed to wrestle back his own state of Zen.

And yes, I admit it. I felt a bit peeved about that. Screw him and screw the Zen he rode in on. I'd been needling him all day, and had no desire to stop. I was feeling so damn hormonal I could sense a full-on *Carrie* moment approaching – the scary teenager with the telekinetic killing powers, not the *Sex in the City* journalist, more's the pity. I'd rather be sipping Cosmos with my homegirls and discussing exactly how big Mr Big was, but my mood seemed to promise more in the way of exploding glass and buckets of pigs' blood.

Gabriel turned his attention to Colin, who bravely managed to stay upright throughout.

'Please. Talk. But be aware that the Morrigan speaks truly – we are here for business that doesn't involve you or your family and we may not be able to grant you succour at this time. This cannot be considered an official petition for aid or judgement but, as my lady urges, I will listen.'

'My lady.' Fah. He'd gone all old-school and formal in his language, which meant he was working hard to maintain his control. To look all noble and important and kingly. I fought down the urge to needle him some more – 'cause really, buckets of pigs' blood is never a good look for a girl – and let Colin share his story.

'Respectfully, High King,' he muttered, 'I think this is important – and it should concern you.' Major props for yet more courage, which he ruined slightly with the contrasting tremble in his fingers as he started to explain.

As stories go, it was a humdinger. It went something like this, albeit with a lot of stuttering, stammering, and spilling of beer.

Colin works in what I'd call an old folks' home. There are a lot of elderly and sick people there, all of whom could be expecting to shuffle off this mortal coil within a few years of being admitted. But Colin – eagle eyed Action Man – is also studying to be a doctor, and he reckons something is wrong. More are dying than should, and in ways that nobody had really expected. The fitter and healthier – the ones still playing shuffleboard in the rec room, the ones whose medication lists don't read like a pharmaceutical dictionary – are dying unexpectedly.

They've even been going in pairs – illustrated by a delightfully stomach churning tale about two octogenarians found dead together. Naked, apart from their bed socks and a pair of fluffy handcuffs. Death during sex, apparently, isn't that unusual for the old dears – in fact it's considered one of the most classy exit scenes around. But both together, at exactly the same time? More unusual.

Then there's the case of his cousin, Callum. Callum was sixteen and had been diagnosed with Hodgkin's lymphoma two years earlier. He'd died, in hospital, the week before. Colin's voice cracked as he told us this part of the story, and it was hard not to feel his pain and grief seeping out – but it was also hard to see why he'd thought it worthy of going to the police about. Sad but terribly true: even teenagers die of cancer.

As if sensing our cynicism, Colin went on to lay out the evidence more clearly: Callum was in remission. He'd been doing well. Hopes were high that he'd make a full recovery – and his death occurred during a routine overnight stay for tests. When he'd asked around, he found he wasn't the only one. Other kids had passed on, leaving their doctors and their families confused and battered, not understanding what had gone wrong. He'd tried making inquiries at a nearby Catholic hospice, but had had the door slammed very firmly in his face.

When he'd finished, he looked at us all, as if daring us to accuse him of being bonkers. He'd said his piece. He'd obviously been rehearsing it. And he wasn't quite done.

'Just so you know,' he said, the family Irish in his voice starting to creep in along with his agitation, 'that the facility where I work and the hospital where Callum died – they're owned by one man – Fergal Fitzgarry. My father knew him way back, growing up in Queens, and I've tried to see him. To talk to him about all this. But he's too big for the likes of me now. He's too big for everyone. Except you guys. Maybe.'

He managed to give the final word a note of challenge, and I felt kind of proud of Colin. Puny mortal or not, he'd made his case – and if it had been down to me, I'd have been out there playing Nancy Drew straight away. It certainly sounded a lot more fun than my plans for the rest of the day.

But guess what? Like most things, it wasn't down to me.

The Morrigan continued to focus on her boot restoration project, which came as no suprise. She may be my almost-big-sister, but there are a lot of differences between us. Like she doesn't really give a shit about individual lives, other than those directly around her. She gained her white-stripes hairdo through killing, not saving. And she is a Goddess of War. The deaths of a few 'puny mortals' are never going to keep her awake at night.

And Gabriel? The High King himself? Well, I knew he'd care. Or at least I thought I knew. But his sense of duty – his commitment to whatever higher cause was going on at the moment – would dictate his actions. Gabriel always had an eye on the bigger picture; he was a strategist and a planner and could on occasion make Machiavelli look like Kermit the Frog.

Colin was chewing nervously on his lips as he waited for his King's word; still twitching and jumping every time the Morrigan moved.

'I'm sorry, but I cannot help,' said Gabriel, finally. 'Not at this time. I have urgent business here that cannot be delayed and must take priority. Perhaps on my next visit—'

'Perhaps on your next visit, there'll be even more dead, Your Highness,' said Colin, bitterly.

Gabriel stared him down – centuries of arrogance

channelled into one perfectly frightening look – and stood to leave.

'You forget yourself, Colin Murphy. Be aware that I won't let it pass again.'

He strode off towards the door, followed by his gang of not-so-merry men and women. I straggled behind, pretending to be rooting round in my bag for something. Well, actually, I was rooting round in my bag for something. A tattered business card, that I eventually found wedged between a packet of chewing gum and an old ticket stub for a long-gone Kaiser Chiefs gig.

I slipped it into Colin's hand, shaking my head quickly to indicate he shouldn't speak, then followed the others out into the dazzlingly bright sunshine of a New York afternoon.

I gave him my number because, unlike the Morrigan, I did care. In fact, it was kind of in my job description to care. I'd gone to a lot of trouble to save humanity, against some pretty tough opposition, and I took it ever so slightly personally when someone started killing them off just for the heck of it.

Gabriel might have big plans for me. Big plans for us. Big plans for our future. But as ever, I had my own – and I intended to follow them. Even if I had to sneak around behind everyone's back to do it.

Chapter Eight

'Are you planning on sneaking around behind everyone's backs to help Colin?' asked Carmel, as we walked through the Bowery. We'd been graciously granted permission to call into the old punk club CBGBs, even though it was a shockingly cool boutique now. The Morrigan waited outside for us, about as inconspicuous as King Kong in drag, while we mooched around the dimly lit store.

One wall of the shop was coated with old posters from gigs past, and I ignored Carmel for a few minutes as I looked up at the flyers, and around at the preserved graffiti on the walls. Tattered rock posters and cool guitars and shady, dark corners that had seen it all. This place had been New York punk heaven: Ramones, Blondie, Talking Heads, Patti Smith. Not quite as awesome as the line-up I'd been shown by God at the Cavern – honest – but getting there.

Now, though, if I wanted to, I knew I could see it all. There was enough of the spirit of the place left: I could do my spooky time travel thing, and see Debbie Harry in all her glory. I was like a one-woman You Tube waiting to go.

Carmel poked me sharply in the ribs, dragging me back to the present and making me go 'ooof'.

'Well?' she said, raising her eyebrows at me. 'Are you? I saw you give him your card – was it one of your work ones for the paper? Do you think he's going to send you a demo?'

'Probably not,' I answered, 'but I've not exactly had time to get my new ones printed up, you know? The ones that say "Goddess for Hire – call this number for a fertile time".'

'True enough. But let me know when you do, and I'll stick some in phone boxes in Soho for you. But anyway. Back to my original question. You gave him your card. With your number on it. Are. You. Sneaking. Around?'

'If I was, then I wouldn't tell you would I?' I asked, browsing over racks of beautiful men's clothing that I could neither wear or afford. 'Because then I wouldn't be sneaking around, and where's the fun in that?'

I was keeping my tone light, but at heart I was worried. Not a full-on worry. Not a grown-up worry. More of a pre-pubescent niggle; the kind of worry so tiny it still needed to wear a training bra: could I completely trust Carmel these days? I mean, I know she's my Champion. I know she'd lay down her life for me – which is frankly nothing unusual in my social circle, they're all at it, the drama junkies. I know she would do anything to protect me and defend me. I know she's still my best friend.

But she's also . . . one of them now. The events of the past few months had changed her as much as me. She'd killed, and almost been killed. She'd fought and stabbed and battled and raged with the best of Gabriel's men – and she'd enjoyed every minute of it. Something in her had been awoken, and it was ever so slightly scary.

Now, like my High King hubbie-to-be, did she see her duty to protect me as being more important than her respect for me? What I wanted to do, the choices I made, didn't always come gift-wrapped in common sense. I worked on instinct and feeling and intuition, all of which drove Gabriel mad. I was prone to occasionally driving a knife into my own chest to distract the killing hordes, or running off into the wilds of Ireland, or hiding in wardrobes with cuddly lions while people were out to assassinate me. Yes. All true stories.

I accepted the fact that he and I would never see eye to eye on, well, pretty much anything. But what about Carmel? Best buddy, night news editor, and Champion? Now she had this official role in the Jabberwocky Jamboree, would she be less tolerant of me as a person, as Lily, and more focused on protecting me the Goddess? Especially now she was shagging one of them?

'We should have brought the company credit card,' she said, flicking through the racks of designer duds. 'This stuff would look amazing on the hunk-o-rama we hang round with, don't you think?'

'We have a company credit card?' I asked, bemused at the very thought. Maybe come January, Gabriel would start freaking out because of his tax returns, and rooting through Ye Olde Enevlope of Mystical Celtic Receipts.

'Oh yes,' she answered, grinning up at me from behind rogue black curls. 'It's usually for the boys, you know? Hardware. Weapons. Special film selections on the pay-per-view . . .'

I pulled a 'yuck' face, even though I knew she was kidding. Thought she was kidding, anyway.

'But from now on, I'm gonna use it,' she added. 'Facials. Manicures. Hair extensions. I mean, a girl's got to look good for a busy day on the front line, right?'

'I suppose so,' I replied, vowing that I would never in a million years let Carmel drag me to the hairdressers. It was long. It was straight. It was ghostly white. And I kind of liked it.

'So if, for example, we wanted to go off and get some spa treatments while we were in New York, that'd be cool with you? Especially if, you know, we didn't actually go to the spa? If we possibly just told King Shoutypants that we were off for a massage, when in fact we were doing some sneaking around behind everyone's backs to help Colin? Together?'

I felt a slow smile spread over my face.

Duh.

Of course she was still my best mate. And of course I could still trust her.

I nodded in agreement, thrilled beyond belief at the thought of squirming out from beneath Gabriel's control, even for a few hours.

'Great,' she said. 'It'll be a proper girls' day out – snooping around, poking our noses where they're not wanted, potential death, and certain mayhem. Possibly a French manicure as well. And maybe you can tell me about that other thing. That Gabriel not wanting to be your mate thing.'

She raised her eyebrows at me and I shook my head.

'Things got a bit raunchy. Then they didn't. I guess he must have had a headache.'

Carmel frowned, as though trying to puzzle something out, then nodded, once.

'I'm sure it'll all become clear with time. Now come on – we'd better head back. Luca will be up soon. Your dog needs a walk. And we have a global coalition of supernatural deities to impress.'

Chapter Nine

'Are you thinking what I'm thinking?' Carmel asked, as we stood at the corner of Central Park, looking out at Columbus Circle.

It was dark and cold, and the bare trees in the park were glistening with frost. Rows of horse-drawn carriages were lined up, waiting to give trotting tours of the park, steam snorting from the animals' nostrils to cloud up in the frigid air, hooves stamping on stone. It was only five o'clock but already pitch black, the lights from the shops and the Time Warner Center reflecting on the bonnets and windscreens of the cars whizzing around the circle, which was kind of the most glamorous roundabout in the world.

We were both wrapped up in seventeen layers of clothing, with only our mouths showing. I'd lost my gloves somewhere in the house, and my hands were bundled up in thick borrowed mittens that only had a hole for the thumb. I felt like an over-grown pre-schooler, and wondered if they should be attached to a rope.

Luca was with us, a black leather jacket casually thrown over the shoulder of his black T-shirt, muscular arms very much on show. He had a long scarf tied around his neck purely for the aesthetic, strands of silky blond hair tucked into it. People stared at him as they walked past, possibly wondering why he wasn't cold, possibly wondering if they could slip him their phone number, possibly wondering why he was with two women dressed up as the Abominable Snowman.

'Don't think of anything – clear your minds!' he said in an atrocious American accent. We both glared at him, and he shrugged his shoulders.

'What? You think I've lived as long as I have without watching *Ghostbusters* enough times to know the script?'

'That's not the point,' said Carmel, huffily. 'This is our Lame Girls' Film Club. We've put the hours in watching old movies and eating pizza, and you're not allowed to join – you're neither lame, nor a girl.'

'Thank you, I think,' he replied.

We both turned back to the view, ignoring our vampire movie buff buddy. I knew Carmel was imagining exactly the same thing as me: the Stay Puft Marshmallow Man stomping his way down the street. It still made me laugh. As well as seeming eminently more realistic, now we were standing in exactly the same place, and now we knew the world was a lot weirder than Venkman ever imagined.

We'd persuaded Gabriel we were off for a girlie spa affair, and offered to take the Morrigan – I was going on gut instinct that she'd find the thought of having her bikini line waxed about as attractive as running her tongue through a clothes mangle, and I was right. Then he'd offered Connor, or Finn, or Kevin – but we'd countered with the fact that no men were allowed.

'Fine,' he'd eventually conceded, 'in that case take Luca. He can stay outside and wait for you like a good little doggie.'

If Luca was offended at the dig, he didn't show it – he'd been asleep all day and was probably keen to get out into the big, bad city. He'd even suggested we head into town on the Subway, hanging from the rails in crammed carriages as we bounced around on the A train. I wasn't keen – being squashed up close and personal against my fellow human beings was never going to be top of my list of fun things to do – but he relished it, I could tell. All the charming smiles and gracious gestures couldn't hide the fact that he was a predator surrounded by tasty snacks. As dozens of people piled on at each stop, I'd occasionally catch a glimpse of him inhaling a pretty girl's hair, or leaning down to gaze at the exposed skin of a woman peeling her scarf off from around her neck.

I met his eyes and raised my eyebrows at him. He bared his lips to give me a quick flicker of fang, then laughed as the latest abrupt stop threw a gaggle of three students right into him. He gathered them into his arms and straightened them up, all three giggling and creating a mini-tornado with their batting eyelashes.

I'd never seen him lose control, but I knew it was there, within him. God knows Gabriel had warned me about it enough times – the dire images of blood lust and sex all wrapped together in his transparent cautionary tales, all aimed at making me realise that Luca was dangerous. In all kinds of ways.

I knew he was. And yet, I still trusted him. I'd saved his life. He'd been abandoned by the God he'd served, and by the vampires who'd been his family for centuries. If I'd let him, he'd sleep curled up at my feet with The Dog – or somewhere more intimate, given half a chance. Luca was mine, whether I wanted him or not. He also came with the added bonus – at least on this particular trip – of reciprocating all of Gabriel's contempt. When we'd explained that we weren't going to the spa at all, that we were in fact on a Top Secret Mission, he'd been thrilled. A chance to get out of the house, defy the High King, and sniff random women, all in one go.

I still half expected Gabriel to turn up, magically

appearing in a puff of smoke inside the sparkling fountains that lined Columbus Circle, looking pissed off and planning to send me straight to bed without my supper. I think it was only the fact that he was distracted by the whole killer-eye-vision-thing that bought us such an easy pass out. He'd be doing something wildly exciting with the Morrigan, like reading ancient texts or ploughing through ritual grimoires, or maybe just typing 'nasty eye Egyptian serial killer Goddess' into Google and hoping for the best.

Meanwhile, Carmel and I had a date. With Fergal Fitzgarry, the man who Colin had been trying to speak to about his whole premature death scenario. The fact that Fergal Fitzgarry didn't know it yet wasn't a problem. We'd tracked down his offices, and we'd gone so far as speaking to his press manager – claiming we were journalists over from the UK doing a series on Irish emigres made good in the States. Which was kind of half true, and we did have the press cards to prove it. We'd been told the Grand Poobah was in meetings all day, but she was sure he'd love to do it at some point in the future, and she'd 'get back to us'.

Colin had also been in touch, and I'd picked his brains about Fitzgarry's background and family connections. He reckoned he'd see us if we fronted him up, laid on a bit of charm, flirted a bit. All of which I'd have to leave to Carmel, obviously, as I had a tendency to stare at my feet and go cross-eyed whenever flirting was called for.

Still, I was feeling properly chuffed with myself, pulling the wool over Gabriel's eyes, being one half of an all-girl crime-fighting duo (not counting Luca, who was really just there for brawn and eye candy), and having a night in the pub to look forward to. We'd arranged to meet Colin afterwards, to fill him in on our progress, and to entirely possibly get a wee bit tipsy, depending on how it went. Plus, as another huge bonus point, narrowly avoiding all those spa treatments we'd lied about having. Result all round.

It took us three attempts to cross over to the other side of Columbus Circle, the traffic was so heavy – a never-ending carousel of brightly-coloured headlights, yellow taxi cabs and honking horns. We walked into the foyer of Fitzgarry's office building – one of the uglier tower blocks – and started to take off our layers. Scarves, hats, gloves, retard-girl mittens and ear muffs before we even made it to coats.

The receptionist looked on in bemusement, waiting politely until the two of us had emerged before asking us if he could help. As the receptionist was male, with the most coiffed eyebrows I'd ever seen and the high-maintenance aura of a prima ballerina, I wondered how Carmel was going to flirt her way through the first barrier. I had an instinct she wasn't his type. I'm perceptive like that.

She showed him her press card, and I followed suit, smiling inanely and waving one hand. The one still clad in a mitten the size of an oven glove. I suspected I looked like I had special needs, but hey, it was all I had right then. It's not easy getting undressed without the use of all your fingers, you know?

'Hi!' Carmel trilled, 'we're here to see Mr Fitzgarry. We spoke to his press officer, Marsha, earlier today about doing an interview with him. She said he was here in meetings all day, but he'd love to do it.'

Quite cleverly, she'd not told a word of a lie – and yet somehow managed to imply that it had all been arranged and agreed. I was rubbish at lying, and looked on enviously.

'Right, well, just let me ring straight up and confirm with his PA,' the receptionist said, taking the cards from our hands and jotting down our names on a visitors' log. This, I knew, was the moment when it could easily all go wrong – PAs never like it when people pretend to have appointments they don't actually have. They can be pesky like that.

'Perhaps you could just send us straight up?' suggested Luca, leaning right over the counter, so close he was at eye level with the receptionist. 'It'd be a shame to bother anyone, and we won't be long. What do you say . . . Devon?' he asked, reading his name badge.

Now, I've seen all kinds of movies and read all kinds of books where the vampires have clever mind control tricks. Where they can hypnotise people with one glance, read their minds, and persuade them to do the funky chicken while opening up a vein.

The vampires I've been hanging round with have never, as far as I've seen, done that. Isabella, the sumptuous singer with Luca's former band, could croon people into submission, and the rest seemed to be done on charisma alone.

So when Devon looked up at Luca, in severe risk of melting into a neat puddle of designer clothes, shiny shoes and very well-moisturised skin, I had no idea if it was down to something supernatural or just something super hormonal. I mean, Luca is – well, gorgeous. In a beyond male-model touch-of-danger kind of way. And he'd had centuries to perfect his charm, his confidence, and the way he exuded the message that if you were lucky enough, you could end up having the Best Sex Ever.

Whatever, it was working. Poor Devon was a flailing fish in a barrel, speared by Luca's bedazzling presence. It was fun to watch, and would be even more fun to do. Maybe I should get him to give me lessons.

'Well . . . I'm not sure . . . oh . . . dear . . .' he stuttered, holding his cheeks between his own hands and breathing too fast. Luca reached out and stroked his fingers, causing the receptionist to gasp. I was very, very glad I couldn't see what was going on behind the desk.

'Why don't you call his PA down to fetch us?' Luca suggested. 'And tell us where to find him. Then by the time we're finished, perhaps you'll be done for the day. We have the whole night ahead of us, after all.'

Devon sputtered a little, then passed over a small card with a bar code on it.

'You'll need this for the elevator, to access the twenty-first. I'll call Dottie. And I finish at six.'

As Dottie came down in one lift, we went up in the other, using the access card Devon had handed over. When we got out, Luca paused and pulled off both his boots which seemed, you know, a bit odd – until he used one of them to prop the door open, waiting for the other lift door to ping open and doing the same with that. So now, they couldn't go back down and rescue Dottie. Not just a centuries-old pretty face after all.

The twenty-first floor was quiet and dimly lit, and seemed inhabited only by Dottie's empty desk, sitting guard in front of what we presumed to be Fitzgarry's office. The desk was strewn with yellow post-it notes and framed photos of grandchildren with gap-toothed grins. A pencil holder in the shape of Papa Smurf with a nodding head wobbled at us in greeting. It hardly seemed like the lair of a criminal mastermind, but what did I know?

As we walked towards it, me stuffing mittens into my pocket, a far more dangerous presence made itself known – a lone man, dressed in a smart black suit that did little to hide the fact that he was some kind of tower-block office ninja. He had a headset clamped into his ear, like he was co-ordinating the dancers at a Lady

Gaga gig, and he subtly unbuttoned his jacket as he approached. I was guessing there was a weapon of some kind under there, and didn't especially want to find out more about it.

'May I help you?' he asked, his voice quiet and serious, not breaking stride as he neared us. I had no idea how we were going to talk our way through this one, as he looked like his bullshit antennae were a lot more active than Devon's.

Luca apparently decided the same, closing the distance between them in two steps so fast he almost blurred. He grabbed the guard's neck with one hand and tugged out the earpiece with the other. Within seconds, Mr Ninja was sliding to the ground, Luca draping him silently to the floor in a swish of black tailoring. He slipped his hand inside the open jacket, pulled out a small handgun of some kind, and shoved it down the back of his jeans.

Carmel walked towards them, leaning down to check his ankles, and emerging with a vicious looking knife that she stared at with relish.

I shoved the guy with the toe of my boot, hoping he wouldn't do a backflip upright and produce a taser from his arse.

'Is he dead?' I asked, keeping my voice steady. For all we knew, he had a desk with pictures of gap-toothed children on it as well. We'd come here to talk to someone, and we'd left our real names on the visitors' log, and I was pretty damn sure there'd be CCTV all over the lobby at least. It didn't seem an especially clever idea to start murdering people, never mind morally ambiguous. Luca wouldn't care about one dead guard, and I wasn't sure Carmel would be entirely heartbroken either. I was the weak link in this particular chain, burdened as I was with this pesky thing called a conscience.

'Of course not,' Luca replied, grinning at me. 'I am not an amateur. He'll be out for maybe twenty minutes, and we could get interrupted earlier. So if you want to talk to this man Fitzgarry, I suggest you do it quickly, before we have to do a *Die Hard* out of the window.'

'Stop with the film references, Luca,' I said. 'You're way too old. It's like hearing a grandad talk about twerking. I know I'm a bit retro, but you're older than the wheel.'

He feigned heartbreak, clasping a clenched fist to his chest as though I'd hit him, which was always a tempting option.

'Right. Come on. I've no idea why we're doing this, but let's get it over with,' I said, heading behind Dottie's desk towards a plate-glass door. There was no name stencilled on it, just a warm glow of light from within, but the Big Boss was presumably inside. Unless, of course, he'd heard us already, and was currently locked in a panic room calling in reinforcements.

I decided to be polite, and knocked once before opening the door.

Inside was a book-lined room, and one very small, middle-aged man. He was sitting, but couldn't be more than five-six or seven. His lean build was wrapped up in an expensive-looking suit, and his sandy brown hair was neatly parted and combed to one side. His pale blue eyes were fixed on me, and he held a phone in one hand, the other hovering over buttons.

'Mr Fitzgarry, I presume?' Carmel said, bustling past me, holding her hand out to shake. It seemed an absurdly formal gesture, considering the fact that we'd just incapacitated his security guard and left him lying in a heap outside.

Fitzgarry stood and smiled, reaching out to clasp her hand. All the time, though, he kept his eyes on me, not even taking into account the far more physically imposing presence of Luca hovering behind us. Either he had a thing for tall Goth chicks, or he sensed something about me that I probably didn't want him to.

I felt nervous and twitchy, the same way I'd been feeling since my vision but times ten, and suddenly a wee bit nauseous. His eyes were glassy and somehow reptilian, and I really, really didn't want to touch him. It was an instinct, but a powerful one – not based on my usual fears when it came to flesh-on-flesh contact, though; it was something deeper and more primeval. Something I needed to listen to.

Carmel wittered on, introducing us, spinning a web of lies about us being here to interview him, apparently oblivious to the tension building inside me.

Luca moved to stand by my side, and I could tell from his posture that he was ready to strike. Mr Fitzgarry seemed to have raised his hackles as well.

Carmel finally finished her fairytale spiel, and Fitzgarry was still standing there, smiling pleasantly, hand outstretched towards me, nodding like it all made absolutely perfect sense to him.

'I'm sorry,' I said, shaking my head and sticking my hands back in my pockets. 'I have warts. Highly contagious ones.' Lame. But the first thing that came into my slightly panicked head.

'Ah. I see,' he replied, pale blond eyebrows quirked upwards as he continued to stare at me. I swear to God, he was staring inside me. It felt like he was dismantling my brain layer by layer, despite all my attempts at guarding against him. And that was without him even touching me.

Mr Fitzgarry, I immediately knew, was not a nice man. I suddenly felt a whole lot better about the subterfuge and the unconscious man outside the room, and a whole lot worse about life in general. I could feel the energy seeping out of me, as though he was draining me of something very subtle but very important. I wavered slightly, and felt Luca's arm go protectively around my shoulder.

'You look unwell, Miss McCain. Would you like to take a seat?' said Fitzgarry, a slight smirk tugging at the corner of his thin-lipped mouth.

I would, I thought, staggering slightly and then lowering myself into a leather-backed chair. There was a desk between us, and I needed to keep it there. I needed to keep as much distance as possible between me and this apparently unimposing man. As I slumped backwards, leaning into Luca's supporting hand, it hit me: the smell.

The rancid, nostril-flaring smell of sour cider. Of rotten apples, crawling with worms. Of ripe fruit decaying into sodden flesh. The smell of the Faidh, of Fintan, of Eithne. Of people who wanted to kill me.

I glanced up at Fitzgarry, working hard to keep my eyelids open, fighting a ridiculous urge to just close them and go to sleep.

'Who are you?' I asked, my voice a barely-there whisper. 'And what are you doing to me?'

Carmel shifted forward, the knife out and in her hand. Luca stayed by my side, one hand on my shoulder to keep me steady. I could feel the tension flowing through his body, and knew without looking that his fangs would no longer be hidden.

By rights, Fitzgarry should be terrified. His guard was gone. His PA was gone. His inner sanctum had just been invaded by a knife-wielding homicidal journalist with a scar on her face and a very large vampire. Any normal human being would be peeing his pants by now.

Instead, he sat back down into his Master of the Universe chair, and grinned at me, apparently enjoying what he saw.

'I think the more relevant question here, Miss McCain, would be who you are. I feel your power. It sings out from you. And I see your interesting friends here, ready to gut me at a moment's notice. I can only assume that you are the woman I've heard so much about. The Goddess. The Mother of the Mortals. The Cauldron of Life. The one I've been keeping an eye out for. Sitting right here, in my office. Trapped, like a butterfly pinned to a board. I had heard you had arrived in my city. So very far away from home. I'd heard that your famed High King was with you, and . . . prepared for his visit. And now here you are. Without him. I can't say how happy that makes me.'

These were all names I'd heard before, all words I knew were associated with me. But right then, I didn't feel any of my power. If I was a mother, I was an ancient, exhausted, dried up crone of a hag; and if there was such a thing as a Cauldron of Life, I needed to throw myself into it. This man – this creature, this whatever the fuck he was – was taking it away. He was feeding from me.

'Get me out of here,' I muttered, my head lolling to one side and coming to rest on the skin of Luca's hand. I turned my cheek around, kissed his fingers, trying to drag myself back to my own reality, weird as it was.

'I'd prefer it if you stayed,' said Fitzgarry, reaching for the phone again. 'I think you could be a huge help to me and my work.'

Carmel physically threw herself over the desk, one lithe scurry of movement, and stabbed down at his hand with the knife she'd filched earlier.

I heard it thud into the desk, glanced up and saw that it had gone right through Fitzgarry's hand to reach that destination. The knife wobbled and vibrated, and blood pooled from the wound onto the leather topped table.

He grimaced slightly, but made no sound at all. Not even a little 'eek'. He was so not normal.

'We're leaving,' said Carmel, her voice low and menacing and a million light years from the carefree chatter she'd been spewing just moments ago. 'And if you try and stop us, I'll tear out your heart.'

'Ah,' said Fitzgarry, smiling up at her over his bleeding flesh, still not reacting to the agony he must have been feeling, 'you'd have to find it first, now, wouldn't you?'

The Irish lilt in his voice broke out as he said it, and I was reminded of Fionnula the Fair, and all the time I'd spent in her cottage outside Dublin. Of the way she'd ask if we wanted a nice cup of tea, or offer us a whiskey at bedtime, sounding for all the world like an extra from *Father Ted*.

He sounded like her, but he wasn't her. My worlds were colliding, and I was sitting in the middle, like a big fat duck with a target painted on its backside. I didn't even have the energy to waddle out of the danger zone.

At that point, Luca physically hefted me up, hooking his hands under my arms and pulling me to my feet. Once I was upright and leaning into him like a drunken hen on the town, he pulled the gun from the waistband of his jeans and passed it to Carmel.

He half walked, half dragged me towards the door, Carmel walking backwards behind us, keeping the weapon pointed at Fitzgarry. Without exchanging words, she knew to stay in the doorway, holding him still while Luca dumped me into one of the lifts.

He tore the electrics out of the other one, then hopped on one leg as he shoved his feet back into the doorstop boots.

'Now!' he shouted, holding the lift door open as Carmel sprinted towards us, leaping nimbly over the fallen body of the guard, running so fast and hard towards us that she hit the rear wall of the lift as Luca pressed the down button and the doors slid shut.

I sat in the corner, slouched in on myself, breathing hard and feeling the world spin around me. I couldn't breathe. I couldn't move. I couldn't . . . anything.

Luca crouched down by my side and held my chin in his hands, raising my face so he could look into my eyes.

'We have seconds, *bella*. Just seconds. The ground floor will be a battle zone. We will need to fight, and we will need to run. Are you with me, Lily? Are you back? What can I do to help you?'

I reached up and took his face between my hands. His flesh was cold, smooth. Beautiful. His green eyes were shining in bronzed skin, his forehead marred by the kind of frown that only I seemed able to provoke. It must really suck having your life tied to someone like me.

'Come on, now,' he said, stroking my hair back from my face. 'Be a good girl and breathe. I need you to come back to us.'

I nodded once, letting my forehead rest against his, drawing resolve from his need. That, and the fact that we were getting further and further from Fitzgarry and that puke-inducing smell, helped me claw back some energy.

'Second floor!' yelled Carmel in warning. 'We need to be ready to go! You're a fucking goddess for fuck's sake, Lily. Show some backbone and get up off your fucking arse!'

What can I say? Carmel always turns into an F-bomb when she's stressed.

Luca helped me to my feet, and I tottered unsteadily for a few moments before managing to hold myself erect. She was right. I was a fucking goddess. And I don't like lying on lift floors with the mental equivalent of the bubonic plague.

'I'm all right,' I said to Luca, patting his arm as the lift gently thudded to the ground floor. 'I'm ready. Let's get out of here.'

Chapter Eleven

As the lift doors pinged open, Carmel fired the gun upwards, straight at the ceiling, showering our greeting party with plaster, glass and bits of glitter from tasteful Christmas decorations that didn't look quite so tasteful any more.

I was fairly sure she didn't want to shoot anybody, but I never really knew these days. The very fact that she was holding a gun and seemed to know how to use it was a bit of a head-fuck.

Luca glanced at me to check on my progress, and I nodded once, feigning a steadiness that I wasn't quite feeling.

Outside, four men dressed in black were standing in formation ahead of us, weapons drawn. Luca ploughed straight into them, snarling and screeching and generally going all rabid beast on their collective arses. Carmel pulled me by the hand and we ran for the revolving door, past poor Devon, who was now cowering behind his less-than-pristine counter. His night was definitely not going the way he'd planned.

I heard gunfire, and yelling, and the hideous combination of tearing flesh and snapping bones that I knew meant Luca was doing his stuff.

As we sprinted to the door – well, as Carmel sprinted and I tried to keep up with her – another of the guards appeared from the bottom of the stairwell, taking in the scene in front of him and charging in our direction. Carmel threw herself between us and roundhouse-kicked him right in the teeth. I heard dentistry crumble and saw blood spurt from his mouth. I needed no more encouragement than that to carry on running.

I paused as I reached the still slowly-spinning door, and Carmel yelled 'Go!', presumably at me.

I jumped into one of the gaps, and fought against every instinct I had, all of which were telling me to push at the bloody glass and make it go faster. If I did that, it would stop, and I'd be trapped – back in sitting duck land, a place I wasn't keen to visit again so soon. It scored none out of ten on my Trip Advisor list.

Carmel appeared to be hugging the man she'd tackled and, even though he was a good foot taller than her, he slid to the ground, crumpling into a heap at her feet. Her hands were covered in blood, and I saw the knife sliding out of his flesh as he gripped his torn stomach.

She slipped once, then ran towards me, inserting herself in the next compartment. After what seemed an eternity, we were both spewed out into the icy night air, steam clouds rising from both our panting breath and Carmel's bloodied hands.

Luca had dealt with three of the others, who were lying in various states of dismemberment on the marble floor. He quickly looked up, saw we were safe outside, and twisted the last guard's neck abruptly to the left. The body fell to the ground, and Luca ran after us. He leaned against the glass panel, and I saw bright red imprints of his palms blossom against it, like a twisted version of a stained glass window.

The door jolted to a stop with the contact, and he

kicked his way through the glass, shattering it and climbing through, his clothes and entirely possibly his flesh tearing on the jagged shards.

More guards were flooding into the lobby of the desecrated building, and an ominous looking black van screeched to a halt in the middle of the Circle, causing an immediate traffic jam and an ear-searing onslaught of honking horns and swear words in half a dozen different languages.

Luca took it all in, and hefted me over his shoulder in an ungainly lump, taking advantage of the temporary halt in traffic to lope straight across the road, shouldering office workers and shoppers and gawking tourists out of his way as he galloped.

With each step, my upturned face bumped against his back, and I could see my white hair streaming down towards his ankles.

'Put me down!' I yelled, thumping at the back of his thighs with my balled-up fists.

'No! You can't move fast enough, so stop being a baby about it!'

'He's right!' shouted Carmel, streaming past us. 'Head for the side of the park – if we get split up I'll see you with Colin.' With that, she was gone, running ahead of us, scanning the crowds for threats as she went.

Now, if you've ever been unlucky enough to be embraced in a fireman's lift, you'll know two things: a, it's uncomfortable, and b, it's undignified. All the breath seems to be knocked out of you every time the fireman (or vampire) in question does anything especially tiresome – like, for example, jumping up onto the bonnets of yellow taxi cabs and running over them as though they were stepping stones, feet thundering against crinkling metal amid a barrage of curses.

And there really is no way to survive hanging upside down, staring at someone else's backside while they race your pathetic self away from armed pursuers, with any shred of self respect intact.

Unless, of course, you have a secret weapon. Like the fact that you're a super-powered goddess babe with the ability to flash killer beams of light from your finger-tips. Or something like that.

I twisted my head up to try and see what was happening and, sure enough, a small group of men were chasing us all the way across Columbus Circle. The Stay Puft Marshmallow Man was nowhere in sight, but that might only be a matter of time.

I tried to ignore the fact that I was upside down; that my hair was whipping in front of my eyes like a snow-storm; and that every time Luca jumped up or down all of the air was puffed out of my lungs.

Instead, I focused on my own power, my own energy, drawing it up inside me like I'd done on the ship. The last time I'd done this, it was to teach Luca and Gabriel a lesson. This time, it was in an attempt to save my own life and that of my friends, as well as ending a situation that could see any number of innocent victims dragged into our bloody mess. No pressure there then.

With another spine-wrenching twist, I curled up to look at the men again. One of them used both hands to send a young woman laden down with FAO Schwarz bags sprawling to the floor, which made my focus a lot sharper.

I drew in a breath, reminded myself I didn't really need to point my fingers, and sent a huge blast of energy in their direction; in his, in particular. I wanted to see *him* sprawled on the floor, to see all of them down for the count.

I waited for the familiar whoosh and the usual rush of power. For the tingling sensation that filled my mind, and for the resolve to control it and focus its damage on those who deserved it. For the not-very-uplifting sensation of pleasure that it gave me, that I didn't even like to admit to myself.

Instead, what I got was a big fat nothing. No power. No energy. Nothing at all.

I screeched in frustration, and pummelled Luca's thighs again as hard as I could, because that was the only target I had.

I let my face fall against the small of his back, and scrunched up my eyelids against angry tears. Either Fitzgarry had stolen something from me permanently, or I needed a goddess power top up sometime soon. Either way, it felt bad. I have no supreme physical prowess. I'm not a Champion like Carmel, or a vampire like Luca, or a member of the half immortal clan that Gabriel and the Morrigan head up. I can't leap tall buildings in a single stride, or see through walls, or snap people's necks like twigs. All I have is my power. All I *had*, that is. Now, even that seemed to have deserted me.

We'd made it completely across the Circle to the corner of Central Park, exactly where we'd started out not that long ago. Then, it had seemed like a harmless adventure – a minor rebellion against the word of the King, and a way to help out a random stranger from the pub. Now, we'd left a trail of death and destruction behind us, not to mention an angry horde of disgruntled New York motorists, and were fleeing for our lives. Well, Luca was fleeing for our joint lives. I was just bouncing up and down for mine, and not in a good way.

'Forgive me, my love, but we need a distraction,' Luca said, as he galloped towards the rows of horse-drawn carriages ahead of us. The men behind us were closing in, and even with Luca's supreme levels of fitness, I knew we couldn't carry on like this forever. I'd die of shame apart from anything else.

He made for the side of the horses, who were panting and prancing as we approached, eyes rolling in panic as

Debbie Johnson

they saw Luca heading in their direction. The vampires in attack mode are always more like a pack of wolves than anything else: they stoop and bay and howl and hunt in pack formation. The horses weren't stupid, even if they were dressed up with feathers on their heads and attached to fancy carriages and draped with velvet blankets. They knew he was a predator, and they knew they wanted to get away from him.

He reached out to one side as we ran, and I turned my head at an angle just in time to see one of the most disgusting sights I've ever witnessed: Luca shoving his fingers deep into the side of a panicked black pony, pulling the skin as he continued to run, until steaming hot blood and glistening horse flesh poured out in a foul stripe along its flank.

The horse reared, eyes huge, front legs kicking, making a terrifying, high-pitched whinnying noise that contaminated all the others with its fear and pain.

All along the road, the horses began to freak out, kicking and biting and desperately trying to escape, their confused owners trying to calm them and keep hold of their reins.

Like a row of dominos they lost control, hooves pounding onto the pavement, the screams of horses and riders and passengers and passers-by all combining in one gut-wrenching bellow. Carriages clattered into each other, and horses reared and tried to crash away from the threat. The chaos sprawled outwards onto the road, and inwards onto the pavement, blocking that entire portion of the street.

Luca paused for maybe two seconds to look over his shoulder, and I fought the urge to vomit all over the back of his legs. I was trying to hold on to my sanity, but the sense of panic was getting to me: the animals, the men, their confusion and fright all mixing in with my own over-sensitive mind to create a whirlpool of horror.

DARK TOUCH

The blood from the injured horse had slicked over the pavement, shining black in the streetlights, and a huge crowd was starting to gather. Usual rules applied: snap a security guard's neck and nobody gave a damn; injure an animal and the whole world screamed bloody murder.

As the congestion built, it formed a human wall between us and the men chasing us, effectively buying us the time to get away. As distractions went, it had worked perfectly.

I just wasn't sure I'd ever be able to look at Luca again without seeing his fingers stabbing into that poor, beautiful animal's flesh.

Chapter Twelve

I insisted on using my own two feet the rest of the way, adopting a peculiar half-walk, half-jog that amused my vampire buddy no end. Sometimes, even when the fate of the world rests on your shoulders, the most satisfying thing you can possibly imagine is punching someone in the gob. Know what I mean?

We scurried across Broadway and onto 8th Avenue, navigating New York's very helpful grid street system along to 9th until we hit the heart of Hell's Kitchen. As we passed through intersecting roads and behind the backs of car parks, the atmosphere changed.

The glitz and prosperous glamour of Columbus Circle disappeared, and the streets seemed physically darker as the lights of the tower blocks faded. There were fewer gaggles of confidently striding NY ladies in their trade-mark stylish black outfits and red lipstick; more people ignoring the red hand on the traffic lights and flicking cigarette butts at the drivers who dared to object.

The buildings were still predominantly rows of tall townhouses, but they felt more narrow, more crammed together, their iron fire escapes providing makeshift meeting places for smokers and drinkers and general malingerers. There was music coming from open windows and bars, a strange mix of Irish rock and Hispanic rap and everything in between. The smells wafting out of restaurants and cafes were just as mixed: Caribbean and Indian and Italian and Greek.

The shops changed from high-end glamour to local convenience stores; fluorescent lights flickering in the windows, boxes of fresh produce cluttering the streets outside them. Even the pavements felt less wealthy, less clean. In short, it all felt a lot more comfortable, and a lot more like home. More like a community where people would actually notice if you dropped dead in the street.

I was really hoping not to test that theory out, though, and was relieved when we made it to the pub where we'd agreed to meet Colin. Luca had been regularly checking our backs since we left the equine carnage by Central Park, and seemed satisfied we were safe – for the time being at least. I was convinced that the NYPD would swoop down on us at any minute, and freaked out internally every time I heard the sound of a siren or a helicopter swishing overhead.

Carmel emerged from the shadows of the pub doorway, looking a question at Luca.

'Clear,' he said simply, opening the wooden vaulted door and making an extravagant 'after you madam' gesture to us both.

'He's over here,' said Carmel, taking the lead, striding through the crowds at the copper-topped bar and heading towards a booth at the back. The jukebox was loud and proud, playing a souped-up cover of Don't Stop Believin' that I'd never heard before, and never wanted to hear again. A group of men in paint-stained working gear and steel-toed boots were bellowing out the chorus like an especially grimy version of the Village People, one of them giving me a leery wink as we passed them by.

I slid into the fake leather of the booth, noting with more pleasure than I can possibly describe that there was already a sweating pint of Guinness waiting for me. Well, it might not have been for me, but I was having it anyway.

Carmel took her place next to me, giving the workmen far more of an evil eye than singing a Journey song merited, and Luca nodded at Colin as he joined us.

Colin himself was looking almost as twitchy as he had the first time I'd met him. He kept swiping his floppy hair away from his forehead, and jamming his John Lennon specs back onto his nose so hard he seemed to be attempting to ram them into his frontal lobe. I suspected the short wait he'd had with Carmel hadn't exactly been relaxing. She'd have pressed him hard to find out if he'd set us up in some way. I assumed he hadn't. Or he'd probably be a bit dead by now.

'Fergal Fitzgarry,' I said, pausing to take a very long, very satisfying pull on the beer, 'is a very bad man. Did you know that?'

'Yes. No. I mean . . . you don't get where he is, from where he came from, by being nice, you know? But more than that, no, I had no idea. I'm so, so sorry, milady.'

Hmmm. Milady again. His hands were trembling on the table, and his glasses were steaming up, beads of sweat popping on his forehead. I suppose, from his perspective, he was in a truly terrifying situation: he'd been sneaking around behind the High King's back, and had placed the mighty consort of excellentness (that would be me, by the way) in significant danger. I suspected, in the La La Land of all that was Gabriel, that that could result in an anaesthetic-free bollock removal. Not a pleasant prospect for any young man.

'Well, he's more than not nice. He's evil. And I don't say that lightly. I'm sure you're right, Colin, about what he's been doing. If ever there was a man capable of draining the life out of anyone, it's Fergal Fitzgarry. He almost did it to me, and I'm not an octogenarian with emphysema. How did he know who I was?'

Colin stared hard at me, as though trying to decide if that was a trick question or not.

'Umm, well, in certain circles you're pretty well known now, milady, or at least the story of who you are and what you chose. And you look, erm, distinctive. But I didn't know Fitzgarry was anything other than a businessman. I wasn't aware he moved in this other world. I thought he was a, you know, a normal. My dad said his father was allied to the High Kings, but that ended with him. Fergal's never been part of it.'

A 'normal'? While I knew exactly what Colin was trying to say – that Fitzgarry wasn't part of our particular shade of insane – he was about as far from normal as it was possible for a human being to be. If, in fact, he was human at all.

'Well. OK,' I said. 'But he's not. Normal. He might not be part of the High King's world, but he's definitely not just part of this one either. You were right to tell us about it, don't worry. Things just went a little bit . . . tits up.'

'That's a polite way of putting it,' chipped in Carmel, who was using a small penknife to carve chunks out of the wooden table top. Nervous reflex, I guessed. 'We left a pile of bodies behind us, and you went Princess Catatonia on us, Lily.'

I nodded, wanting to apologise but not sure why I should – it's not like I had any choice in the matter.

'A pile of bodies and a very messy horse,' I replied, glancing at Luca. Seriously, even now, when we were safe – and knowing that he did what he did to get me to that safety – I still couldn't quite forgive him.

He shrugged and gave me a sad smile.

'I know,' he said. 'It will be hard to forget. You may be a goddess, but you're still an English girl who probably grew up reading *Black Beauty*. Just know that I did what I had to do to protect you, Lily. And I would do it again in a heartbeat.'

I'd heard variations on that speech many times before. Gabriel had used different versions of it to explain everything he'd ever done on my behalf – all of the mistakes he'd made, the way he'd plunged my childhood into misery, and my adult life into chronic isolation. Carmel had used it when I'd broached the issue of her turning into a bloodthirsty Valkyrie with an extensive knife collection. And the Morrigan? Well, she never even bothered – whatever she did in my name was always going to be fine with her. It was only me who ever seemed to be bothered by all the bloodletting and deception, and sometimes I wondered if I was the definition of the word 'hypocrite'.

Yes, they'd killed a gang of security guards. Yes, Luca had in all likelihood killed a very pretty pony, and injured others. All of it so they could look after me. It was thanks to them I was sitting here, drinking Guinness, and judging their morals. Maybe, if it all bothered me so much, I should just go and throw myself off a bridge.

Instead, I tried to focus on the practical.

'I think it's highly likely that we're all going to be arrested some time soon,' I said, 'and that this might be my last ever pint of Guinness. We didn't just leave a mess back there, we left evidence. Our names. Our signatures. Our DNA.'

'This isn't an episode of *CSI*, hon,' said Carmel, clearing up the wood chippings into a small pile. Neat freak as well as killer – she was a wealth of contradictions. 'And my guess is that Fitzgarry has the power, and the connections, to keep it all quiet. He clearly knew who you were. That means he knows who Gabriel is, and he didn't seem even a tiny bit scared of any of it. He won't want you in a jail cell, he'll want you back on his specimen board, sucking out your juicy marrow.'

I shivered as she said it: that's exactly how I'd felt back there on the twenty-first floor of Fucked Up Towers.

Like he was sucking out my juicy marrow. I really, really didn't want that to happen again, and realised that I felt slightly less awful about the bloody horse as it all sunk in. I'd met some pretty bad people in the last few months. Fintan had pushed me into the Mersey to die, which I'd annoyingly managed not to do, with a bit of divine intervention.

His glamorous assistant Eithne had come very close to snuffing me out in the toilets of a Liverpool club called the Coconut Shy. Donn, the Lord of the Dead, had dislocated my arm. The vampire singer Isabella had slashed my skin open to make me bleed. Numerous assassins in black had chased me through the streets of the city. And I'd also kind of stabbed myself in the chest as well.

But none of it – really, none of it – had even come close to what I'd felt in Fitzgarry's lair. He'd done that to me within minutes, without apparently even seeming to try. If I'd been there alone, instead of with my morally dubious Supernatural Hit Squad, I'd be gone now. I knew that with utter certainty. Whatever power I had, whatever life force I contained – and I was led to believe that was quite a lot, what with me being the Mother of the Mortals and all – it would all be gone, funnelled into him. Into Fitzgarry, or the Faidh, or whoever the hell it was he was working with.

That was a lot more scary than being arrested, I had to admit.

'I think she's right,' added Colin. 'Fitzgarry comes from the kind of community that would view using the police as a weakness. I think he'll use his money and his power to keep it hushed up. The guards didn't hesitate to attack you, which means they're well paid and less than innocent. He'll deal with it. I think, maybe, there is a slightly bigger problem.'

Strange as it sounded, I knew exactly what he was talking about. And he was right. There was indeed a slightly bigger problem than the whole of a metropolitan police force hunting us down. The problem in question varied between six foot two and ceiling height, usually had an angry face, and was roughly Gabriel shaped.

I knew that we should tell him everything. I knew we should come clean about the whole subterfuge, and the fact that I'd childishly delighted in lying to him to go scampering off on my own. That I'd dragged Carmel and Luca and Colin along with me. That I'd encountered a creature who seemed capable of eating me alive, metaphysically speaking. That I'd smelled the Faidh all over the place, and that Fintan could somehow be involved. That I hadn't even bothered getting my eyebrows shaped.

I knew I should, but I couldn't quite imagine how that conversation would end – other than with Gabriel swelling to eight foot tall and locking me in a body-sized safe for the rest of eternity.

Perhaps it would have been different if our snogging session had turned more serious. If the whole mate-thing had become a reality rather than a fairytale that seemed irrelevant to the reality of my life. But it hadn't – he'd rejected me, and I didn't know why. I still felt bruised about it, and still felt a bigger distance between us than I'd ever known.

If I was talking to a therapist about it, I'd probably say I just wasn't in the 'right place' to confess all. That, and I was scared shitless.

'What do you want to do about all of this, Lily?' said Luca, reaching out to hold my hand. As ever, it was a relief to let him touch me – no need to put up my guard, no need to protect us both from the visions. Just simple, comforting, non-human contact. I tried to ignore the fact that there was horse blood ingrained under his nails, and enjoy it.

'About Fitzgarry?' he continued, tightening his hold on my fingers. 'About what he's doing to the people

Colin told us about, and what he wants to do to you? And about telling the High King?'

'I just don't know,' I mumbled, feeling as pathetic as I undoubtedly looked. 'We have this fucking summit meeting tomorrow. And there's this whole evil eye thing looming over us, and the fact that someone on the Council may be out to glare me to death. And it's all just so bloody complicated. Maybe we should get one thing out of the way before we tell him? Have the meeting, sort out this Hathor thing, see if that's a real threat or just my visions playing tricks on me, first?'

I was ending every sentence as a question – a sure sign of a clear mind. Not. But I genuinely didn't know what to do. That wasn't a new feeling for me by any means, but it wasn't pleasant. It all felt big and scary and just plain wrong. I'd stumbled into a situation way beyond my control, or my ability to navigate, and I really wanted someone to just tell me what to do about it, to boss me around until I had no choice. Ironically, exactly the same thing I always complained about when Gabriel tried it.

I'd wanted freedom and now I had it. I'd have quite liked to run back to Daddy and get him to sort out the mess. Except Daddy was in the Otherworld, along with Mummy and everyone else who gave a shit, and my only options were to confess all to Gabriel and the Morrigan, or rely on the people round the ever-decreasing table (Carmel was hacking away at it again) to hold steady for another day, potentially dragging them even further into Gabriel's bad books. Luca and Carmel could handle that, they both had their own chapters in that particular tome – but Colin? I wasn't so sure.

'Your lower lip is wobbling,' said Carmel. 'You look like a tragic schoolgirl with weird hair. Pull it together, Morticia, or you'll make us all cry. And give me your hand.'

As she'd spent the last few minutes stabbing the table, I wasn't so sure I was all that keen on that idea, but she took away my choice by grabbing hold of my right paw and laying it down on the notched wood. She fiddled around in her jacket pocket, and emerged with a small bottle of what looked to my now-jaded eyes like blood.

'Chill out. It's for your nails. I have the suspicion we're not telling His Kingliness about our escapade just yet, so he'll be expecting you back ready for the runway. I brought this with me just in case. Now you're not a ginger any more, we can get away with a bit of Miss Scarlett. Just don't put those bloody mittens back on til it's dry, OK?'

I noted, with a small thrum of satisfaction, that I put my guards into place immediately, and Carmel hadn't even given it a second thought before touching my skin. Something, no matter how small, was definitely improving.

As Carmel set to work on my impromptu manicure, Colin piped up, in an incredibly small and incredibly weedy voice.

'Erm, does this mean that we're not telling the High King about all of this?' he said, his face a whiter shade of pale than my hair. All three of us nodded, and he gulped.

'Is that wise?' he asked. 'Will we not be risking more of his wrath if we don't? You could be in danger, and he should know, and—'

'Shut up, Colin,' said Carmel, without looking up at him. 'It's you who got us into this mess in the first place. Now you're just going to have to trust her Goddess-ship here to deal with Cormac Mor. She has her ways, don't worry.'

Yup, I thought, gazing on as my nails were painted a shade that would make a hooker blush, I have my ways. None of which I could rely on working.

Chapter Thirteen

I woke up the next morning with a very mild hangover, extremely pretty nails, and a king sitting at the foot of my bed.

The Dog was nestled next to him, licking his fingers as he massaged the delicate skin behind her ears. I couldn't say I blamed her. It did look pretty nice.

I did a mental check of what I was wearing, and struggled upright. I was fairly sure my bed-head resembled a work of avant garde modern art, but he didn't seem to notice. He was male. His eyes went straight to the relevant part of the little vest top I had on, where my nipples were responding to his presence by saying a nice morning hello. I was perversely glad to see I still had some power over him, even if it was only the power to make him look like a bit of a lech.

'Anything you want to tell me?' he asked, dragging his gaze away from chest and up to my face. A face which, predictably enough for me, immediately blushed as red as Miss Scarlett. Did he know? Had Carmel snuck behind my back and grassed me up? Had Colin crumbled under the pressure? Were there artists' sketches of me on the TV news as one of New York's Most Wanted, next to a photo of a dead horse?

No, I thought, buying myself a bit of time by faking a yawn and hiding my mouth with my hand as I studied him. He was his normal size. His eyes were a nice dark shade of blue. The furniture in the room wasn't shattered into tiny pieces. I wasn't in that body-sized safe. None of the usual signs of High Kingly rage were there and, believe me, I'd seen them all many times.

Instead, he seemed calm. Serene even, for him. Or at the very least controlled, which is maybe as good as it gets when you live the kind of life he does, and are saddled with the kind of mate he is. Now that I looked closer, I could see the tight lines around his lips as he tried to smile; the tension in the lines of his shoulders. The way he was using his dog-tickling as a way of distracting himself from whatever strain was pressing in on his brain. He wasn't happy, but he was trying to be. Presumably for my sake.

All of this took about ten seconds for me to compute, which kind of scared me. I'd only known Gabriel for a matter of months, but my mind was already so overly familiar with his facial expressions, his body language. The devious way he operated and manoeuvred to get what he thought was best out of a situation. I only hoped he wasn't at similar skill levels when it came to analysing my emotions, or he'd have seen GUILTY flashing above my head like a giant fluorescent beer ad. Luckily, I blushed all the time anyway, and had amazing pinging nipples to blind him with.

Even if I did seem to be getting away with it, I knew deep down that I should tell him. Fitzgarry was a threat. It was Gabriel's life's mission to protect me. Not telling him could put everyone in danger. And still . . . I couldn't. Not right then. If my first foray into independent action resulted in me running to him to cry about the scary man who'd been mean to me, I'd never escape the sometimes cloying way he tried to surround me with security. I'd accepted that my life was never going to be anything but complicated, possibly dangerous, and I wanted to at least try and cope with the first obstacle alone. Or with Carmel anyway, which was kind of the same thing.

So I ignored the warning signs my own brain was sending me, and went for 'normal'.

'Do you have coffee?' I asked, smoothing my hair down as best as I could without an industrial-sized device.

'Next to you,' he said, gesturing to the side table with his head. A steaming mug sat there, with a logo that advertised the New York Dollface escort agency. I raised an eyebrow but didn't ask. Some things are simply better off left unknown.

'What do you mean, is there anything I want to tell you?' I asked, deciding to front him up on it. Whatever he thought I'd been up to, I was pretty sure it was nowhere near as bad as what I actually *had* done.

'Well, when you got back last night, you were on Luca's back, hitting him with an imaginary whip and saying "giddy up boy". Carmel had a small bag with her that seemed to contain an entire table chopped up into small wooden pieces and all three of you stank of Guinness. I was just wondering what kind of high-end spa facility offered that kind of treatment?'

Ah. Right. It was just our normal drunken high-jinx he was referring to. Which was mildly embarrassing, but not as bad as finding out about a trail of corpses and a potentially lethal foe. Point for me. Luckily, I was already blushing, which saved me some time.

'Well, there was wine at the spa and there was a pub next to it. And . . . well, do you like my nails?' I spluttered, waving them in his face.

He took hold of my hand to inspect the rather superb job that Carmel had done, and smiled.

'Yes. Very vampish. Very . . . not you at all, really, but I could learn to live with it.'

He hadn't let go of my hand, and I felt a flutter of panic set in. I was in bed, scantily clad, with a man who could make my heart rate triple just by smiling at me. Hiding a huge, whopping secret from him. It didn't feel good at all. I had a momentary urge to confess all, and throw myself on the mercy that I knew lurked somewhere beneath all the arrogant, regal guff.

'About the other day,' he said, not looking up to make eye contact with me. 'What happened in the study.'

I pulled my fingers away and rubbed them on the duvet cover like I was trying to decontaminate them. I don't know why, but it probably didn't appear very kind, implying as it did some flaw in his scrupulous personal hygiene.

'Don't you mean what *didn't* happen in the study?' I asked, my voice emerging cracked with the bitterness I'd been trying to clamp down on in the face of far more pressing concerns.

'Yes. That. I didn't mean to upset you. I've been struggling with certain things recently. With self-control. With Luca.'

'I had noticed,' I replied quietly. Any admission of weakness was a huge deal with him, and I wasn't cynical enough not to acknowledge it. 'And nobody's perfect, Gabriel, much as you try.'

He smiled at me; a sad, sweet smile.

'Thank you. I do indeed try. Anyway, what happened between us caught me by surprise, that's all. I hadn't been expecting things to go quite that way and I wasn't prepared.'

'What do you mean not prepared? You didn't have condoms?'

I knew that was a million miles from what he meant, but I was suddenly flustered and embarrassed and remembering the humiliation that had flooded through me. He looked up, and I saw that familiar purple flare in his eyes. The one that meant I'd provoked, pushed and otherwise poked just a little bit too far. That's kind of my speciality subject with Gabriel – and, ironically, it felt far more comfortable than tender heart-to-hearts.

'You know that's not what I meant. It was about me losing control again. Doing something I didn't feel it was right to do.'

I stayed silent, but I was well aware of what my face was doing. It was saying 'I am freaked out and hurt and angry and maybe we should leave this alone'.

He made a small humphing sound, and his mouth set into a determined line.

'But if you don't want to act like a grown-up and talk about it,' he said, 'then that's fine by me. We have more important things to do today than indulge in your tendency to behave like a spoiled teenager when things don't go your way. Time to get up and get ready. I'd suggest a long shower and half an hour with a hairbrush.'

Ouch, I thought, as he slammed the door on his way out. That told me. It wasn't exactly fair, either, but there you go. What's that old saying about hurting the ones we love? If that was really true, then two people had never loved each other more.

I heard him stomping off down the stairs, and lay back down under the duvet. The Dog nuzzled close, inserting her bony head under my hand, her skinny tail thumping down onto the bed. I gave her a little scratch, and felt like joining in when she whined. I knew just how she felt: one minute he's there, stroking you behind the ear, and the next he's gone, with a face like thunder. Me and Gabriel. The gift that keeps on giving.

After a few minutes of feeling super sorry for myself, I drank the rest of the coffee and dragged myself out of bed.

The cranky nature of my cranium, combined with the fact I had to hold onto the wall as I staggered to the bathroom, told me better than Gabriel that I'd perhaps drunk a bit too much the night before. Which, considering the day I had ahead of me, was decidedly irresponsible and decidedly predictable.

My last proper memory was of taking Luca, Colin and Carmel into an alleyway behind the pub to 'test out a theory'.

From the overflowing ashtray-on-a-stick that stood outside the back door, and the overwhelming fug of smoke, it was obviously the place where nicotine lovers gathered to talk shite on a regular basis.

'Stand up against that wall,' I'd said to Luca, shoving him towards the bare brick. 'I need to try something out on you.'

'Will it hurt? And if so, will it hurt in a way I'll like?' he replied, teeth shining in the gloom.

'I have no idea if you'll like it or not – but hopefully, yep, it'll hurt.'

Obediently he stayed where he was, while I drew in my will, and focused it on dredging up my power. I needed to know if it was gone for good – stuffed away in Fitzgarry's cookie jar – or if I'd somehow magically done a Doctor Who and regenerated. The ability to use the Goddess stuff had come in handy on more than one occasion, and I'd only just started to get my head round it all. If it was now a thing of the past, I needed to know. So I would never rely on it again.

I stared at Luca, knowing that I was about to do something that could potentially floor him. I felt my resolve waver, and shored it up by thinking about horses. One horse in particular.

It did the trick, and I released what I hoped would be a supersonic wave of knock-out juice at Luca, who was standing up against the wall holding his hands up in a gesture of surrender. He was also smirking, which, given the aforementioned horse imagery, made me feel a lot better about what happened next.

The power lashed out at him, hitting him solidly in the chest. I focused hard on keeping it there, using all the control that Fionnula and the Morrigan had been teaching me, imagining it like a laser beam firing on full.

He shouted out and slumped to the ground, where he lay rolled up in a large, vampire-shaped ball.

There, I thought, dusting my hands together as though I'd just ticked off my whole lifetime to-do list. Job done. Normal service resumed, and one dead horse nicely avenged.

I turned to Colin, who was showing every sign of wanting to run straight back inside, and stared at him.

'He'll be fine. He's pretty much immortal. You can hear him groaning, can't you? That means he's alive. He'll be up and about before you know it. Now I need to test out something else. Your turn – up against the wall.'

'What? Fuck, no!' he said, grabbing the door and pulling it. Carmel reached past him to slam the door shut again, and he cowered against it, terrified.

'Don't worry,' she said, tugging him forward by his coat, 'she'll set it to stun, won't you, Lily?'

I nodded. Of course I would. Or at the very least, I'd try. I was still wearing my L plates really, but now didn't seem a particularly good time to mention that to my next, very reluctant, victim.

'You're sure?' he said, stumbling towards the wall, tripping over Luca's twitching body and rapidly apologising. 'I know things didn't turn out the way we'd expected, but I didn't mean anything by it, milady, and I'm so, so sorry, and . . . fuck!'

Poor Colin. He obviously thought this was some kind of firing squad scenario, and had turned into a gibbering wreck. I recalled how terrified the barman in the other pub had been of me, and how Colin must have heard exactly the same stories and myths built up around me. Let's face it, the stories and myths had been building up around Mabe for centuries – and I'd now stepped into her scary shoes.

Except, none of them were true, not about me. Not many of them, anyway. And I liked Colin. He seemed a nice guy, with a lot of integrity and a lot of courage. OK, so he'd got us into a mess, but that wasn't his fault. I'd never do anything to hurt him . . . until I did, of course. Until I possibly accidentally blasted him all the way to Times Square, where he might go hurtling into a neon billboard, landing splat in the 'O' of 'Chicago'.

'Of course I'm sure,' I lied, doing my very utmost, honest-to-goodness best, to 'set it on stun', as Carmel had said. Instead of imagining the beam shooting towards him like a hosepipe on full power, I imagined it on sprinkle. So if I did hurt him, it'd just be in teeny tiny droplets instead of a tidal wave. That was the theory, anyway. Physics was never my strong suit; and a lot of what I did seemed to rely on imagery, on picturing something and making it happen – so the best I could do was come up with as harmless a picture as I could.

I stared at him, drew in a deep breath, and focused, just like I had when I'd been attempting to stop Fitzgarry's men from chasing us around Columbus Circle. Then I unleashed my sprinkler from hell.

And, just like then, all I got in return was nothing. No matter how hard I tried to throw – supercharged, full power, sprinkle or rainbow striped – nothing happened. Other than Colin cringing up against the wall, holding his head in his hands, whimpering, and showing every sign of potentially needing to go to the toilet.

Nothing.

'Interesting,' I said, chewing my lip as I pondered the results of this fun experiment.

'How?' asked Carmel, frowning at me. 'How is it interesting?'

'It doesn't work on mortals,' I replied. 'That thing I do . . . the light show. The Goddess beam. Whatever you want to call it. The thing that worked on Gabriel and Luca on the ship. The thing that just worked again on Luca. I tried it earlier, when we were being chased, and it didn't work. I thought at the time it was because of Fitzgarry, but it wasn't. It was because they were human. See? Colin's fine.'

Colin muttered, 'No I'm not,' from beneath his arms, before risking a peek out at us. When nothing whacked him in the chest, he relaxed slightly, emerging from his upright foetal ball. 'Is it done? Is it over?' he asked, legs wobbling.

'Yep. All done, thanks,' I said, walking over to see how Luca was doing. I kicked him gently in the ribs, and he moaned.

'You all right down there, Horse Slayer?' I said, leaning over to check.

'Feeling wonderful, thank you,' he replied, his voice muffled by the fact that his head was still tucked into his stomach. 'Should be absolutely fine in about three years.'

I nodded, satisfied that normal business would soon be resumed, and turned back to Carmel. I stared at her, scrutinising her face. Carmel. Was she still a mortal? Or was she one of them, now she was my Champion? She'd certainly become a whole lot stronger, faster, and more lethal. I wondered . . .

'No,' she said, opening the door to allow Colin to stagger back through. 'You can fuck that for a game of soldiers. I don't know what I am either, and I'm not volunteering. Stick your ray gun up your arse, Barbarella.'

There wasn't much I could say to that, so I followed

her back inside, leaving Luca to struggle back up and wipe the ciggie butts off his jeans.

After that it was pretty much Guinness time. If there's one thing I've learned over the past few months, it's to take your pleasures where you find them – even if that involves an impromptu karaoke session with a group of workmen who mistakenly thought they were the cast of *Glee*.

At one point Luca, the Playboy of the World, had disappeared back outside with one of the waitresses, a pretty little thing with 'Kitty' emblazoned on her name badge, but she came back none the worse for wear. A little paler, a little woozy, but in fact looking pretty damn happy about life. I had no idea what had gone on out there, and thought it best not to ask. I'd probably just get some snide comment about bar snacks.

The journey home was hazy, but had obviously ended with all of the desired outcomes: i.e., getting back to the house in one piece, so I could count that as a success.

By the time I stumbled out of the shower the next morning, having carefully avoided accidental glances in the mirror, I had a welcoming committee waiting for me on the bed. The Morrigan and Carmel were sitting there together, a collection of knives laid out on the duvet. Carmel looked none the worse for wear after the night's adventures, and the Morrigan looked exactly like she usually did. Terrifying.

They both looked up as I walked in, rubbing my hair with a towel, another tied around me. Neither of them seemed even remotely concerned about the fact that I was almost naked.

'Morning,' I said, grouchily. 'Nice of you to knock.'

'Told you,' said Carmel, giving the Morrigan a look. 'She's always ten out of ten on the cow scale the morning after.'

I screwed my eyes together for a moment, hoping

they'd both disappear and leave me to bumble around on my own for, I don't know, another couple of years or so. No such luck. Life as I knew it was no longer my own, and it sucked. I'd spent most of my twenty-six years avoiding human company, and now I seemed to have it shoved in my face at every turn. I lacked the proper social skills for any of it, not that this kind of situation was likely to be covered in an etiquette book.

'What do you want?' I asked, dropping the towel and heading for the wardrobe. If it didn't bother them, it shouldn't bother me. I had no equipment they hadn't seen before, apart from that nifty scar on my chest.

'We're here to prepare you, Goddess,' said the Morrigan, 'for the meeting of the Council.'

'I am prepared,' I snapped back, taking three attempts to tug a sweater from a plastic hanger, which eventually snapped in two and clattered to the floor. It was clearly going to be one of those days. 'So you can both fuck off.'

'Your behaviour is that of a petulant child,' the Morrigan replied, throwing one of the knives at me. I froze, and it blurred past my face, thudding into the wooden door of the cupboard and wobbling there, inches from my eyes. Jesus. I needed a bacon sandwich and a Diet Coke, not near-death experiences. I was living in Crazy Town.

I would have loved to have tugged the knife out and thrown it back at her, but I didn't even try. It looked pretty embedded, and it would be embarrassing to stand there, wet and naked, trying to pull it out like some pathetic version of Arthur and the stone. Plus, even if I did manage to get it out, I frankly throw like a girl and might hit The Dog instead. She deserved better.

I ignored the interruption, and hobbled very elegantly into a pair of jogging pants and the sweater that was now lying on the ground. My hair was soggy and streaming down over my shoulders, spreading a damp patch over my back, and I knew without looking that my eyes had dark circles beneath them. Every inch the Goddess, as usual.

'Did you find anything out, last night? About the whole eye thing?' I asked, spotting with a ridiculous amount of relief that Carmel, as usual, had acted as the Diet Coke fairy and left a chilled, sweating can by the side of the bed. I sat down and popped it, taking a long, satisfying swig. I love the taste of aspartame in the morning.

'Little to concern you, Goddess. There are no signs that Hathor bears you any ill will, and the High King would not allow you to be placed in danger. He holds your safety above all else. Surely you know that.'

'Yeah. He's my own personal Health and Safety manager,' I said. 'One that I didn't even need until he came into my life in the first place.'

The Morrigan stood up, towering over me by far too many feet. Her red and white hair is swirled with marks of death, a streak for every soul she's dispatched, and it flew around her wide shoulders like a warning. There wasn't a predator alive who'd risk taking that on. No, it was only me who was stupid enough to argue with her.

Her voice was low and deep and scary as she spoke.

'I have little understanding of your mortal life, sister, but know this: your behaviour is unbecoming to any kin of mine. None of us chose our fate. To rebel against it is pointless. You have a responsibility, and you have more aid around you than many humans even dream of. You whine and complain and show less backbone than your hound. You have a mate, you have a Champion. You have me. Now stop complaining and dress in a fashion appropriate for the occasion. Do not shame us, child. You have a job to do.'

I resisted the urge to cower at her feet, and instead burst into tears. What can I say? I was very tired and very emotional. I'd had an exceptionally rough night she didn't even know about. I'd almost been drained of my life force; been asphyxiated with the smell of the Faidh; and a horse had been killed as I fled the scene. I had a hangover. My head hurt. And much as she seemed to assume it, I didn't feel any of the 'aid' she was talking about. Gabriel was my mate – but he gave every impression of being sick to death of me.

Not, I thought as I rubbed at my wet eyes, that I could blame him. I'd been acting like a bitch. He was right; the Morrigan was right. I had no idea what was going on with me; it was like a year's worth of PMS had all landed at once and floored me with wobbly hormones. All sense of perspective had gone, and I was clinging on to snarkiness as my only refuge. And totally bizarrely, I was missing my nan, who would right now be showing me even less sympathy than the Morrigan, and rasping at me to 'gerra grip girl' through a cloud of cigarette smoke.

Carmel sat beside me and held my hand.

'I'd give you a hug,' she said, 'but you look pretty snotty. Now come on. Get it together, girlfriend. You're doing that "crying but I don't know why" chick thing, and I'm not used to it from you, OK?'

The Morrigan was looking on in something akin to disgust, which was entirely justified. I felt disgusted with myself, and I must have looked unutterably pathetic from her tree-trunk perspective.

'It's OK,' I mumbled, using the sweater to wipe my face. 'I'm just . . . a mess. And she's right. About everything. I'm sorry.'

I looked up at my sister-a-dozen-times-removed and tried to find the backbone she so wanted me to discover.

'What do you need me to do?' I asked.

'You can start by preventing your eyes from leaking,' she replied, striding over to the wardrobe and tugging out the knife she'd so pleasantly lashed at my head. 'And putting on this.'

She threw a dress at me, and stood with her hands on

her hips, as though daring me to object. I looked at it, heart heavy. The last time I'd been done up for one of these ceremonial bashes was on the night of Samhain at Tara, when I'd been draped in the kind of robes you get in the sale at Virgins R Us. I'd felt like a complete tit. This time, to add to the fun, I was also acting like one.

Carmel picked up the frock and held it up for inspection. It was . . . all right. A simple shift dress, in a dark green that almost perfectly matched my eyes. Nothing horrendous at all. But still. Why did I have to dress up at all? Why was it always me who had to be shown off like a prize pig at a show? What was wrong with jogging pants and a sweater, aside from the snot and tears? Carmel always got to wear cool ninja clothes, and the Morrigan never departed from her trademark biker leather. I couldn't imagine Gabriel was standing in front of a mirror deciding if his bum looked big in his suit. It didn't seem entirely fair.

'Do not say it,' growled the Morrigan. 'Whatever petty complaint you are considering. When you have millennia of life and experience at your side, you get to choose your own garments. Now, be satisfied, and be ready.'

She left the room in a flurry of hair and fury, slamming the door behind her even louder than Gabriel had earlier. I'd really scored high in the Celtic Hit Parade today, and I'd been awake for less than an hour.

I groaned and fell back onto the bed.

'Hey,' said Carmel, poking me in the side with one finger. 'Would it help if I went and got you a bagel?'

Chapter Fourteen

The meeting was scheduled to take place in the Upper East Side, in the museum district. We'd piled into anonymous black cars and crawled through New York congestion, taking part in the honk-fest that seemed part of every journey. It was mid-afternoon, which meant that Luca was still dead to the world, and the roads were alive with traffic.

We crept up 5th Avenue for what felt like hours, passing the side of Central Park and pulling up near the Metropolitan Museum of Art. When I'd first found out we were coming to New York, I'd wanted to visit it. Wanted to stand with the other normals and gawk at the Picassos and the Van Goghs and the Monets. To browse in the gift shop and eat cake at the cafe and generally behave in the usual fashion. As I gazed up at the imposing columns and arches and steps up to the main entrance, swarming with backpackers and hazy with the smoke and smell of the fast food vans, it seemed unlikely it would ever happen. That just wasn't my world any more.

Gabriel opened the car door for me, and I got out, accompanied by The Dog. Her black fur shimmered in the crisp winter sunshine, and she leaned into my side, as though hugging me.

'Are you all right, *a ghra*?' he asked, ignoring everyone else as they assembled around us. He had also kind of dressed up for the occasion, wearing smart trousers instead of Levis, and a spotlessly white shirt that was open a couple of buttons at the neck. His dark hair curled over the collar in waves, and he smelled divine.

His eyes had shaded down to a deep violet, and he stroked the side of my face once as he looked at me. I felt my eyes swim with liquid again, and feared I'd become one of those needy women who turn to jelly at the first sign of kindness.

I leaned into him, letting my body mould into his, resting my head against the firm muscle of his shoulder and nuzzling into the smell of his neck. It felt safe and comforting and delicious there and, if only I could ignore the way we inevitably ended up driving metaphorical spikes into each other's eyes, I'd probably never move. I was sure he was confused as hell by everything I said and everything I did. I knew I was.

'No,' I replied, feeling his hands bury themselves in my hair and hold me closer. 'Not really. I don't suppose there's any way we could knock this on the head and go and look at pretty pictures instead?'

I felt him smile and shake his head.

'Sadly not, Lily. Let's get this done. I'm with you. Always.'

He pulled away, and I felt sad, and cold, and lonely. He held my hand, which helped, and led us towards a building a short distance away. I had a pashmina type affair wrapped around my shoulders, which felt all wrong, but which was offset by the fact that I'd kept my Docs on. There were some compromises I just wasn't willing to make for anyone and, knowing my track record, I'd need to be running for my life before the day was out anyway.

Except, of course, he didn't know that. He didn't know

about Fitzgarry or anything that had happened the night before. I realised, as we walked up a row of neat stone steps sided by ornate wrought-iron railings, that that was wrong. It had been a mistake not to tell Gabriel. I should have trusted him more. I should have told him every-thing. I shouldn't have dragged Carmel into the deceit, however willingly she went.

Still, I thought, too late for that now. Unless I dragged him into the loo and did a quick tell-all over the cistern. Then he'd swell to the size of a small planet, blow his top, and possibly demolish the whole house. There was nothing to be gained from it, other than me feeling a bit of selfish relief. I'd have to stick to the plan that had seemed to make a lot of sense the night before – deal with the Council, get that task out of the way, and then confess. Ideally from behind a locked door, with an armed guard, and possibly a rocket launcher as well.

We were greeted by a guy fresh from completing his PhD in How To Be A Butler. He wore a sombre black suit, a sombre expression, and even managed to take our coats in a sombre fashion. I felt like I was at a funeral, an image which wasn't exactly dispelled by the Morrigan's choice right at that moment to transform into the crow.

She perched on my shoulder, a flurry of sleek black feathers, and pecked at my ear none too gently. Still a bit peeved with me, it seemed. The Dog stayed glued to my legs, sleek and strong and solid, while Gabriel took the lead, accompanied by Connor, Finn and Kevin. In fact only Carmel was left behind me, which felt weird – they usually assumed some kind of pincer movement when they were taking their serve-and-protect duties seriously. This time, I only had Carmel watching my back. And a mighty killer bird watching my shoulders, I supposed. Caw.

The butler type dude led us up a flight of carpeted stairs that curved past a huge stained glass window, flooding the landing with sunlight and dappling The Dog's already shiny coat with shades of green and red. It looked like someone was projecting a psychedelic film track onto her skin.

I followed upwards, drawing in slow, deep breaths to calm myself. I don't like being the centre of attention at the best of times. I hide in quiet corners at gigs, usually live alone, and have a job that allows me to work in an almost-empty office. Walking into a room full of super-beings who expect me to pass some kind of test wasn't exactly going to come naturally to me. Greater dangers aside – like killer eyeballs – there was always the risk that I'd trip over my own boots and fall over. Splat, on my face – saving the Earth one trip at a time.

I'd been briefed by Gabriel on what to expect. Not, of course, that he'd ever done this before either – nobody had, for hundreds of years. They'd all been waiting for me to come along, which seemed hilarious. As ever, I found myself wondering why the Goddess hadn't found someone better to do this job. I was lousy at it.

The Council gathered on a 'regular basis', according to the High King. Which could mean once a month or could, bearing in mind their slippery grasp of time and mortality, mean once a century. He seemed to have met them all before, and he was a few hundred and counting. And the Morrigan talked about them as though they were old and familiar. Luca had attended one Council, with Donn, during World War II. For some reason the idea of that one caught my attention: I was sure there were plenty of stories to be told, once we had time. The present had a way of clouding the fact that the people I was hanging round with could tell me so much about the past. I had my very own show-and-tell history parade in my corner, with so much combined knowledge it'd make the Time Team weep.

Today, though, at that very moment, the present was

quite interesting enough. I was to be 'presented', and – although he never said it in so many words – verified, I suspected. Authenticated. Given the stamp of their collective approval.

Goodness knows what would happen if they decided I wasn't the real deal – just some random lunatic girl whom Gabriel had dragged along to be his pretend mate, like a fake date at a wedding to stop your parents thinking you're gay. Either they'd blast me into oblivion or dance with me to the Mavericks, I supposed.

The butler paused outside large double doors on the third floor, turning to look at us with a still, serious face, as though reminding us how very, very important this all was. I was suddenly glad Carmel was behind me, and nowhere within eye-catching distance. Gabriel had warned us, on the drive over, not to giggle. That might seem like a given, but we have a bad track record, especially when we're nervous. The butler opened the double doors, flinging them apart with great gusto, and bowing – yes, actually bowing – as he gestured for us to go inside. I was only glad he didn't announce us, reading our full titles from little cards as we trotted in.

The room was huge, like it had been designed to hold dances and parties and balls in more gracious times. The ceilings were high and decorated with ornate roses and intricate plasterwork. The walls were all painted white, and antique dark wood tables were laden with elaborate arrangements of fresh flowers that suffused the atmosphere with the lush scent of roses. I inhaled, deeply, testing it out for anything more . . . apple-y. Anything more scary. Nothing registered, other than a vague nostril-flaring need to sneeze. I clamped it down, pretty certain that an Earth Goddess shouldn't have hay fever.

The whole room was flooded in brilliant sunlight, cascading in from a balcony that had French windows and carved stone arches. It also had one of the most stunning views I'd seen of the city, right over the greens and browns of the vast park in its winter clothes; to the soaring points and tips of the Manhattan skyscrapers.

Right in the middle of all of this was one of the strangest groups of people (loosely speaking) that I'd ever seen, and that's coming from someone who's spent many a Saturday night out in Liverpool city centre.

I suppose I'd expected them to be around a table, like some bizarro world take on a board meeting – with Hathor at the head, and a nice electric chair set aside for me. Maybe some carafes of water, possibly a flipchart and some marker pens. Name tags perhaps. What I didn't expect was for them all to be standing there, in a circle, like they were about to join hands and start chanting Satanic verses, or doing the hokey cokey.

My first quick glance was met with a riot of colour and shine from a raging mess of costumes, hair styles and ornaments. It was like someone had chewed up the Olympics opening ceremony parade and vomited it up into a posh room in New York, without any thought as to how it would look reassembled.

There were men, women, and possibly a few that fell somewhere in between. I knew – because Gabriel had warned me – that each representative would have their own Champion, or human consort, as well as an artist. The artist bit kind of freaked me out, but he explained it was so each of them could take home a visual representation of the Goddess. The question 'haven't they heard of camera phones?' earned me nothing but the usual stern glare. We were talking millennia old beings here: I was lucky they'd moved with the times at all, or I'd be sitting there for days while someone scratched my likeness on a cave wall with a hunk of flint.

The circle parted as we entered the room, and I felt the burden of dozens of eyes landing on my face. It felt like tiny prickles crawling over my skin, and I had a very strong desire to bolt clear across the room and throw myself off the balcony. Not because of any aura of supernatural doom, or even any sense of danger – just an overwhelming blanket of curiosity folding down on me from above, smothering me in the questions I could feel buzzing around in their heads.

The first hit ran something like this, fast-forwarding through my brain in a mash-up of different accents and words and languages and tones: this-is-her-is-this-her-Goddess-taller-than-I-thought-shorter-than-I-thought-blonde-hazel-mortal-human-disappointing-impressive-scared-scary-important-weak-strong-strange-pretty-sad-joyful-skybird. There was even one long ragged scream, which I attributed to the presence of the killer crow on my shoulder rather than me, but you never know. This all came along with a few thousand other random thoughts that walloped me across the chops as I walked into the centre of the circle.

I breathed in deeply, feeling my nostrils flare with the effort, and threw up extra guards: I wasn't touching anyone, and I wasn't trying, but the power of their minds was so strong and so intense it was flooding into me anyway. There might come a time when that was helpful, but right now, collapsing in a heap with a mental nose bleed probably wouldn't do me much good. I wasn't keen on seeing visions of these guys anyway, as I was fairly sure the supernatural United Nations here had interesting pasts and interesting futures. Besides, it was all too confusing: apparently I was a buxom blonde with large breasts, a petite Asian with perfect almond eyes, a willowy African princess-type and the very embodiment of Cleopatra, if she'd had a penchant for big boots. Only one train of thought had thrown back the image of me as I actually looked, and I wasn't sure who that came from. Whoever they were, they'd seen a tall, not altogether ugly woman with long white hair, looking a wee bit petrified. The rest were seeing something entirely different, which was extremely strange indeed.

When Gabriel had said I was the Goddess to them all, I hadn't quite realised he meant I was a *different* goddess to them all. Which, if I'd paused to consider it, made perfect sense: why would a Japanese almost-deity be at all impressed with a freaky looking Liverpudlian? Why would anyone, in fact?

One woman stepped out of the rainbow-hued crowd and strode towards me. She was petite, at least physically, but the way the others deferred to her told me she was Hathor, the head of the Council. And possibly the source of my brain-wincing eye vision from Brooklyn Heights.

Her skin was a shimmering shade of gold, and her nose was prominent and hooked, not entirely unlike Carmel's, which made a certain kind of sense. She wore a floor-length gown that hid her feet and made it look like she was gliding on castors, which was entirely possible. The fabric was decorated with golden motifs, scarabs crawling over her shoulder and colliding with eagles' heads in some kind of animal face-off. Around her head, placed elegantly on her long, black hair, was a thin gold circlet. On the front of it, like she was playing that party game where you have a post-it note on your face and have to guess what you are, was an eye.

I stared at it, trying to match it up to the one in my vision. The eye stared out, and scared the shit out of me by blinking, slowly, back at me. Holy mackerel. It was made of metal, but it could blink. It was also, I realised with a sense of both relief and confusion, not the eye I'd seen in the vision at all. I know that sounds weird – I mean, how different can one scary eyeball be from another? But I knew, with complete and utter certainty, that it wasn't the same. Gabriel and the Morrigan had been wrong to suspect her – this all-seeing eye might be a nosy cow, but it wasn't out to burn my brain into oblivion. Not today at least.

On the one hand – well, good news. On the other – that meant there was still a potentially lethal mystery out there for the Scooby gang to solve. Not so good.

Hathor edged closer to me, holding out her hands. I felt the crow's feet bite into the flesh of my shoulder through my dress, and realised that was my cue. I tried to look as regal as I possibly could under the circumstances, and held out my hands to touch hers, guards well and truly up. I used to have to clear my mind with a fluffy white cloud to do that, but it was getting so much easier. Which fell into the category of 'small mercies', I supposed.

She clasped hold of my fingers and, as she closed her eyes – the ones in her shiny golden face – the one on the golden circlet closed as well.

I felt her thoughts flow into me, and automatically drew up a barricade against them. I'd known this was coming, but I instinctively didn't want it to happen. Gabriel had a habit, when we first met, of being able to randomly dip into my thoughts, back in the olden days when I didn't know how to stop him. I didn't like it and, head of the Council or not, I wasn't keen on being mind-raped by this tiny lady and her freaky third eye.

'Goddess, you must open yourself to me,' she said. In my head, and not out loud. Her lips didn't move, and nobody else responded, but her voice was there, in my mind, loud and clear. She was speaking straight at me, like a weird ventriloquist's dummy.

'I must do what I feel is right,' I threw back at her, again silently. I presumed that if she could do it, so could I, or this would be a pretty one-way conversation. I held the barricade firm, and felt a strange crawling sensation in my wrists, like dozens of tiny snakes were wrapping themselves around my bones. Fragile bones, that they could crush with one undulation. The pressure increased, and I screwed up my eyes against the pain. It felt like I was turning to powder under my own skin, and if someone slit it open, the contents would cascade to the floor in tiny calcified grains.

'The pain will increase, and you will not withstand it,' she said. 'I will crush you and send your soul shrieking for mercy. Remove your guards, and let me in. I mean you no harm, and this must be done – all of the sacrifices you and your kin have made thus far will be for nothing if you do not. Let me in, and it will all be finished. You can proceed with your life.'

Wow. Way to go with the carrot and the stick. Soul-shrieking pain or keep calm and carry on. I held her off for a moment, almost staggering with the sensation of having the tiny bones of my wrists and the base of my hands fractured and mushed together like dough in a mixer. The crow poked me again, so hard I felt her claws breach the fabric of my dress and pierce my skin. I was getting grief from all angles. I still had my eyes open, and could see Gabriel off to one side, gazing at me intently. He nodded, his eyes flashing violet, urging me to give in, to let Hathor do what she wanted to do. I assumed he couldn't hear us, and was just guessing at what was going on based on his knowledge of my naturally easygoing personality.

I didn't want to. I didn't want her in there, poking around. I didn't want her to tell me what to do. Or the Morrigan. Or Gabriel. Or anybody at all. I wanted them to just fuck off and leave me alone. But . . . I was being bloody-minded again. The inner teenager that had been emerging over the last few days was still in charge, sulking and moaning about how it all Just Wasn't Fair and how Nobody Understands Me. I'd be slamming doors and self-harming while I listened to Ed Sheeran in my bedroom if I carried on like this. 'What do you want?'

I asked, shifting from foot to foot so I wouldn't fall over. See. I'd been right. I couldn't have stayed upright with heels on.

'I want to know you,' she replied.

'What about me?' I asked, wondering why we couldn't have just had this conversation in Costa Coffee like normal people embarking on a new friendship. Hah.

'Everything,' she whispered, the single word rumbling through my body, poking at my liver and kicking me in the kidneys. Everything. Shit. I had no choice and, more to the point, I shouldn't even be fighting this – I should be embracing it, viewing it like a visit to the dentist. One painful extraction and then peace, hopefully with a bit of numbness in between. Possibly a Disney Princess sticker on the way out.

I closed my eyes, took a big girl breath, and dropped my guards. I felt Hathor sigh with pleasure, and the pain instantly disappeared. The snakes writhed away, back to whatever psychic rock they lived under, and I felt giddy and light headed with relief as they squirmed out of my flesh.

Without waiting even a single beat for me to recover, Hathor rushed into me, maybe in case I changed my mind. After the initial blast of her presence, she toned it down – but I could still feel her there, a passenger in my head. Nothing I would have noticed even months earlier, but now, with my heightened sensitivities, I felt it. It was as though my brain was a busy landscape, and she was hidden in there on the edge, camouflaged like a Where's Wally puzzle. I saw pictures of my own life flicking backwards and forwards, a kind of movie montage without the music. Almost as though I was simply lying in bed trying to get to sleep, pondering things past and things present and things future, the way you do when you're half-way conscious. Hazy memories of my child-hood, of my real parents; more defined ones of my nan

Coleen, clouded now by more affection than I'd ever felt towards her when she was alive.

School and college and work and friends. The flotsam and jetsam of a narrow life, all kaleidoscoping to and fro, skipping forward a few years then jumping back. All of it took seconds, apart from anything involving Carmel – mainly, to be fair, nights in the pub. Then she slowed down, like a car approaching a speed bump, and seemed to examine it more closely.

She was equally interested in Gabriel, and lived our first few meetings through my eyes: the night he introduced himself to me at the Coconut Shy; running from the Faidh's assassins through Sefton Park. The way I loved him and hated him and trusted him and was scared of him all at once. The way I'd seen that vision, of me having his child – which was one I was working very hard to forget.

She flittered around directing it all like an orchestra conductor, and I shared her vision of flickering scenes from my life. She watched and learned, taking in everything, right up to the present, until she found the one she was really interested in. The one that made her press the pause button.

The night at Tara, with the shrieking of the Stone of Destiny, and the crazy Otherworld horses galloping around us on a misty carousel, and Donn and his vampires closing in on me. The choice Gabriel had made to free me, and the choice I'd made to accept him. To take him as my mate, even if the only part we seemed to actually get was the bickering. She felt what I'd felt: connected to the earth, to the soil, to the roots of the trees and the burrowing insects and the heartbeat of the whole world. The scream of the Lia Fail when I'd touched it, the magical light that had flowed from my body.

I felt it boom inside me, the moment when she finally broke through the layers of Lily McCain, and all she'd experienced, to the spirit of the Goddess. Until she reached Mabe, Mother of the Mortals. The one she was looking for.

My eyes had closed during the process, and they snapped back open in time to see her smile. A big, wide grin that showed a jaw much too large for her face, and teeth much too sharp for a human. Her long black hair shimmered gold, flying around her head like a mane, and the eye on the circlet popped open. It wasn't human any more. It was a solid disk of glinting tawny gold, flecked with green. One large, dense, black pupil staring out at me. It was the eye of a lion.

Chapter Fifteen

I tugged my hands away, and she let me, smiling out at me from a face that was now entirely human. She looked smug and satisfied, and altogether pleased with the situation – which is more than could be said for me. I was trembling like a crisp bag in the wind, looking for a passing tree branch to snag on to.

Had she seen enough? Had she seen too much? Had I passed whatever crazy test it was that I was supposed to be sitting here? I glanced over at Gabriel, saw a thin, strained smile on his lips. It looked like he didn't know either.

Hathor turned slowly in a circle, facing all of the other Council members and holding her hands in the air as though she was wafting smoke around the room.

'The Goddess is here! The Earth is truly blessed once more!' she announced, her words booming out and then echoing around a room that I was pretty sure didn't usually echo. Either she was a trained stage performer, or something magical had just happened. I really hoped so – I didn't want to have to go through that again in a million years. She was one scary lion lady, even if her eyeballs weren't out to get me.

Gabriel strode from the crowd towards me, gathering me into his arms. I collapsed into his embrace as much as I could without it looking obvious. He understood how much I hated all of this crap, but I needed to maintain some kind of balance here, among these people. Assert some kind of authority, even if all I really wanted to do was curl up under a duvet with a hot water bottle and a gallon of Jack Daniel's for company. I knew I was a slightly rubbish pop writer from Anfield – but the Council didn't need to know it as well. To them I was something much more. Something important. Something that wouldn't turn into a blubbering wreck at the first sight of a mystical lion rummaging through her memories like a bargain hunter at the Primark sale.

He stroked my hair softly, and I felt a very inappropriate rush of sheer lust as his fingers brushed my scalp. Yikes, I thought, biting it back down. I'd felt that before – and last time, I'd tried to shag him in public. I wanted to enjoy it, but I wanted to control it as well, to make sure that Nympho Lily didn't escape from her cage.

I slipped my arms around his waist and clung on for a moment, my hips melding to his. He was hard, which was also inappropriate, but did make me smile a little bit. We were clearly a pair of perverts who got off on having an audience. We'd be doing a stadium tour next.

The Morrigan cawed and flew from my shoulder, leaving holes in my frock and sending the rest of the Council into a panic as she circled the room, holding their heads in their hands and looking mightily worried until she finally came to rest in the corner of the room. She transformed into her human form in a whoosh of feathers and hair, and stood tall and proud as she gazed at me, nodding once. Looked like she was pleased with me as well, which was a rare moment given my recent track record. I'd be getting a tick on my reward chart when we got home.

'What happens now?' I whispered to Gabriel, shamelessly giving his ear a little nibble as I did it, just to make him squirm.

'Umm . . . first of all, you stop that *thing* you're doing right now, Lily. This isn't the time or the place, much as I'm enjoying it. Then you will be presented to each of the Council members in turn. There will be questions asked, stories told, and possibly a rousing game of pass the parcel to finish with.'

'You're joking, right?' I asked, pulling away slightly so I could look into his eyes. Because, well, you just never know with these people. And I really dread to think what would be in the middle of one of their parcels. I was guessing it wouldn't be a packet of Haribo.

He grinned down at me. 'Maybe. About some of it.'

I didn't get the chance to find out which bit precisely, as Hathor had started to rally the troops. The grand presenting was beginning, and it was time for me to put my Goddess face firmly in place while they all, I don't know, kissed my ring or whatever.

The crowd gathered in front of me in a line, undoubtedly following some kind of ages-old etiquette I had no idea about. The Dog curled up at my feet, her diamond dappled coat sparkling even more than usual, her head buried in her tail, one eye poking out and looking up at me. I made a mental note not to move forward at all, or I'd go sprawling right over her.

Gabriel stood on one side of me, his hand placed on the small of my back, and the Morrigan walked to the other. Carmel and the boys were behind me. I felt a bit like a cheerleader in the centre of her squad, and had an absurd image of them throwing me up into the air, me doing backflips in a miniskirt while they chanted out each letter of G-O-D-D-E-S-S. Yeah. I know. It's that kind of thing that makes me glad ancient Egyptian deities aren't always roaming around in my mind. Nobody would ever take me seriously as the saviour of the human race if they could see what really went on in there.

Hathor led each group forward towards me, and I

tried very hard to look as important as I was supposed to, rather than curtsying like a kid presenting a bouquet to the Queen. There was a huge weight of power in the air, I could sense it, floating around heads and engulfing us. It made me feel giddy and slightly breathless, as though I'd accidentally fallen through the rabbit hole and ended up walking in on a G8 summit. Which was kind of exactly what had happened, I supposed – the trick was to not let them see how nervous I was. They were here to see me, not the other way round – I was the guest of honour, and I stood as tall as I could, to at least give the impression of not being intimidated.

'Mabe, Mother of the Mortals – I give to you Frigga of Asgard, and her Champion Sven the Elk Eater,' said Hathor, gesturing the first duo forwards.

I heard a sharp, feminine intake of breath behind me, and knew that it was Carmel. Trying very hard not to laugh. She was tense, she was a girl, and she'd just been introduced to someone called Frigga. Who could blame her? Gabriel had been right to warn us not to giggle, but he really should have warned us about the silly names as well, so we'd have the chance to roll around on the floor, clutching our stomachs, getting it all out of our systems in advance.

Not that Frigga looked to be a laughing matter, apart from her name. She was huge, almost as tall and wide as the Morrigan, whom she was glaring at with a hostility she didn't even try to hide. So much for me being the guest of honour. My scary, much older kind-of sibling was glaring right back, and there was clearly not a lot of love in the room. Maybe they'd fought over a boy, many centuries ago. Or a planet, or something like that.

Frigga's long blonde hair was plaited down the side of her face, looking as solid as golden chains, and in her hand she held a spear that was rusted with what I knew was blood. Every girl's ideal fashion accessory. The Elk

Eater standing next to her came as something of a surprise. He was a dwarf, rocking the Gimli beard in ginger, and looking up at me with tiny, hard eyes that were buried in folds of ruddy flesh. They must have had some especially small elks where he came from, unless he took a stepladder with him when he chowed down.

'Goddess, I am honoured by your presence,' said Frigga, holding out her spear towards me. I wasn't quite sure what I was supposed to do with it and, as I wasn't wearing CSI gloves, didn't especially want to touch it either. I was saved making a decision by the fact that the Morrigan chose that moment to kick it right out of her hand and send it clattering to the shiny parquet floor.

'The Goddess declines your invitation,' said the Morrigan, her face flickering between human and crow, which was a very shady sight.

'A pity,' replied Frigga, holding the now very angry Elk Eater back with one hand on his shoulder. 'I am sure she would have enjoyed the sight of our warriors in Valhalla, fighting to their new death.'

Umm. I wasn't so sure I would have enjoyed that at all – I'd much prefer a night in with Netflix – and was glad the Morrigan had neatly kicked that particular party off the table. Still, I had to respond in some way. I was the Goddess, and I needed to show them I could actually, you know, talk.

'I thank you, Frigga, for your kindness, and hope to accompany you sometime in the future. Elk Eater – may your sword shine bright, and may you harvest fully of Yagdrasil, the World Tree.'

The words came out of my mouth – but not entirely from me. I'd experienced this before, the spirit of the Goddess taking over the driving seat and speaking for me. Or maybe I was tapping into latent knowledge that was buried underneath all the crap, and she was just nudging me in the right direction. It had happened when I rejected

Fintan, just before he tried to murder me, and again at Tara. There were times when my own human language, and my own human experience, just didn't make the grade.

However it happened, it seemed to do the trick. Frigga nodded graciously, her blonde hair chains not budging an inch, and Sven looked entirely satisfied. Presumably I'd just blessed his mushrooms of power or something similar. They moved away, and I glanced at the line behind them. Right. One down, three to go. It was like being at the weirdest wedding in the world.

Next up was a black man with the height and slender girth of a pine tree. His face was long and looked carved, with strong lines and cheekbones you could use as a paper shredder. His colourful robes hung from him, and his hair was cropped so close to his head you could see shiny patches of scalp beneath it. His companion wasn't a dwarf, but a stunningly beautiful African woman with golden hoops hanging from her ears. She smiled, and I felt a flood of genuine warmth wrap around me. It was lovely, like the mood equivalent of a mug of Horlicks.

'Olu, of the line of the Sky Gods, and his mate, Beryl,' intoned Hathor.

Beryl? Really? She looked nothing at all like a Beryl. And much more like a goddess than I did, lucky cow.

Olu offered his hand, and I took it without a moment's hesitation, knowing that he wouldn't be able to break through my guards even if he tried. Thankfully, he didn't, so there was no need to test out that particular scrap of arrogance. Instead, he simply bowed his head, and said in a late night radio DJ voice: 'Goddess. We thank you for your bounty, and pray for a time of peace.'

My first thought was 'amen to that', but I thought that would sound a bit flippant. I was still Lily, but she needed to keep her trap shut for a while.

'I share your prayers, Olu, and welcome you and Beryl into the path of my life.'

Again, with the nifty wordplay. I was getting good at this stuff.

The two of them swished away, in a flurry of red and green, to be replaced by Sitting Bull and his pal, Hiawatha. Well, not really. But doing a pretty good imitation of it, draped in animal skins and feathers and brightly coloured beads.

The man – Nahuel – was bare-chested, some kind of tattoo of a big cat emblazoned across his skin. In his hand he held a totem pole staff, carved with birds' heads and what looked like turtles. His hair was long and sleek, hanging down his back as far as his waist, and his eyes were a blazing turquoise that didn't seem to belong in his face at all.

His Champion was a tiny woman, who looked way too short and skinny to be a threat to anyone other than naughty toddlers – but I'd seen Carmel handle herself often enough now to know that looks can be very deceptive. She was called Naira, and had eyes so large they made her look like a bushbaby. One that could rip your throat out in two seconds. She kind of scared me, she was so small and silent and serene.

'Goddess and Lifegiver,' said Nahuel, banging his totem on the floor with each word and making The Dog jump, 'we greet you, and pray that you are guided by the Great Spirit.'

For some reason, the Goddess voice in my head chose that moment to be silent. I had no ritual words to speak, and no idea what an appropriate response would be in his culture. So I nodded in what I hoped was a suitably respectful way, and simply said 'Thank you'. Naira gave me a once over with those eyes of hers, and they moved away. She was kind of cold, and worrying, evoking the opposite of the feelings that I'd had when I met Beryl. I didn't think we'd be bonding over beers and boy talk any time soon, and was more than happy with that. She probably ate her men after sex anyway, and washed down their entrails with a mug of refreshing hydrochloric acid.

Heck, maybe I'd be the same, once I started having sex – who knew?

There were only two people left in line, as well as a set of random individuals on the edges of the room who were busy with sketch pads and pencils, presumably capturing the very essence of my radiant image. Or doodling smiley faces with berets on, for all I could tell. They weren't important enough to be presented to me, though, which was all I really cared about – my patience was wearing pretty thin by that stage. There's only so much polite regality a girl can muster in one go.

The final two made their way towards me. It was the first same-sex pairing there'd been, and I wondered briefly if they were partners – in the Elton John and David Furnish kind of way – before deciding it was really none of my business.

'Honi,' said Hathor, 'descendant of the Sun Goddess Amaterasu, and his Champion Katashi.'

Honi was a Japanese man with a slight passing resemblance to Donn, which didn't exactly make me feel comfy. His jacket was spangling with dozens of tiny mirrors, about the size of the ones on the end of the tools dentists use to look at your fillings, and I saw my own face fluttering back at me over and over again from different angles. His hair was cut brutally short and was greying at the temples, and he wore a headdress depicting a bird that looked a bit like my friend the crow, only bright red.

I didn't have much time to ponder the descendant of the Sun Goddess, though, as I was slammed in the brain (not to mention other body parts) by the man standing next to him. A good foot taller, he was slender, but with broad shoulders encased in black leather. His hair was long and lustrous, flowing in a sheen over his shoulders, and his face . . . well, what can I say? It was utterly beautiful. In a deliciously tough, all-male kind of way. High, sharp cheekbones, deep brown eyes, and a nose that angled out above lips that looked way too lush for features that harsh. I actually physically wobbled, he was that handsome, and felt slightly guilty as Gabriel – remember him? – steadied me with the hand he still had placed on my back.

I was really glad my mate couldn't go nosing round my thoughts any more. Because he so wouldn't like them.

Honi was talking, and I was nodding, but frankly I didn't hear a word he said, I was so distracted by the hottie at his side. I felt a flush creep over my skin, and silently cursed. Gabriel wouldn't need to invade my thoughts now – he'd know exactly what I was thinking about.

I realised, once Gabriel nudged me a bit too hard in the ribs, that Honi was holding something out towards me. It was roughly the size of an iPad, and wrapped in red velvet cloth decorated with ornate golden cockerels.

'A gift for you, Goddess,' he said, gesturing towards it with a very Japanese bowing of the head. 'A sacred mirror, Kagami. It is said to have been blessed by Amaterasu herself, and holds the power to reflect and capture the soul. I offer it with thanks for your service.'

I smiled, and took the parcel from his hands, nodding back at him. I unwrapped the velvet, and saw a primitive looking glass shining back out at me, somewhat tarnished and framed in bronze. It didn't look any great shakes, but I could feel its power zinging through my fingers. It was ancient, and strong, and valuable way beyond the sum of its parts. I wrapped it back up, and passed it to Gabriel to hold for me. He might as well serve some purpose, other than looking pretty and silently seething at me.

'Thank you, Honi,' I said. 'It is a fine gift, and one I will treasure.'

Formalities apparently over with, Katashi grinned at me, and my tummy did a small loop-the-loop. I may have tottered a little. The grin ratcheted up a notch, as though he knew exactly what I was thinking, and he bowed slightly.

'Goddess,' he said, looking up at me from behind a waterfall of black hair, 'it is an honour. And I really like your boots.'

I suddenly knew that it was him who'd seen me as I really was. While Frigga was blonding me up and the others were all superimposing their own vision of the Goddess over my actual appearance, it was this one man who'd seen the Real Me. If that wasn't the stuff of slightly skewed rom coms, I didn't know what was. It even sounded pathetic to me, this strange version of 'he just gets me', but I couldn't help responding to it. Obviously, by blushing, and stammering, and almost having a multiple orgasm on the spot.

I'd been speaking – and hopefully saying something tremendously insightful and wise – as well as blushing, which was pretty impressive, I thought. Honi appeared to be satisfied with whatever I'd rattled out, and he backed away, sadly taking Katashi with him. The rear view was just as good, long legs and a firm behind, and I fear I may have actually licked my lips at the sight.

Woo, I thought, running my hands over my dress to smooth out invisible creases, just so I had something to do. That was unexpected. Whenever I'd imagined myself in bed with someone, it had been Gabriel. Or Luca. Or, OK, I admit it, occasionally with Han Solo, in the secret love-dungeon of the Millennium Falcon. But now I had a whole new set of fantasies to work on . . . and some very vivid images of Katashi. Wearing all that silky hair, and not a lot else. Down, girl.

While my libido was getting its party on, the formality of the gathering seemed to downgrade to something more relaxed. The presentations were done and, although I could still feel some very otherworldly eyes fixed upon me, I knew I could breathe a little more freely. The butler had wheeled in a trolley laden down with fruits and cheeses and bread, and I heard the sound of corks popping and liquid fizzing into glasses. This, I suspected, could be the prelude to that game of pass the parcel.

I risked a quick look up at Gabriel who, predictably enough, was a little stony-faced. I poked him in the ribs, hoping to let out some of his starch.

'Well?' I said. 'How did I do?'

'You did just fine, Lily,' he replied, unable to hide the tension in his voice, dropping his hand away from me. Yep, I thought. Just fine until I went all goo-goo dolls over the Japanese assassin supermodel in the corner. Jeez. Some men are just so hard to please.

'Well,' I said, keeping my voice low, not wanting anyone else to pick up on this lovely chat we were having, 'I did my best. And I couldn't help it, all right? That last thing that happened. It was nothing personal. I don't even know the guy. I'm all over the place at the moment, Gabriel, and you're not helping. I need . . .'

God. What did I need? A slap round the face? A one way ticket to Katmandu? A roll in the hay with a handsome stranger? I really didn't know, but I suddenly felt like a three-wheeled cart again, off balance and threatening to tumble over. Tears were stinging the back of my eyeballs, and my head was throbbing. I wasn't quite sure if I wanted to reassure Gabriel or set Sven the Elk Eater on him.

'Goddess, we need to talk,' said Hathor, bearing down on us with a sense of purpose that left me with an urgent need to go to the toilet. She eyed Gabriel significantly.

'Alone.'

Chapter Sixteen

Gabriel wasn't keen on letting me disappear off with Hathor alone, which came as no great surprise. He wasn't keen on me doing anything alone, which was always going to be an issue between us, as 'alone' was my default setting. He'd helped create the monster I was, and he'd have to live with it.

When he'd objected, Hathor had reached up and placed one tiny hand on the bulk of his shoulder, digging in her nails so hard I winced on his behalf. Nails. Claws. I was guessing she could switch between the two with as much ease as the Morrigan and the crow, and I definitely found the lion more threatening.

'Cormac Mor, you can trust me. I bear no grudge against the Goddess and share your joy that she is here among us,' she said. 'But now I must insist that I talk to her. There are things that she and I need to discuss, that are no concern of yours.'

Hah. I wished her luck convincing him of that – in Gabriel's view, absolutely everything about me was his concern. I could tell he wasn't happy, but he nodded once, abruptly, his face set in that I'll-go-along-but-I-don't-have-to-like-it mode I knew so well.

'Her Champion?' he asked, in an attempt to secure

me at least some protection from Her Liony Worshipfulness.

'Ah. That one,' replied Hathor, looking around the room to find Carmel. I followed suit, and saw her sitting in a love seat by one of the windows, glass of fizz in one hand and a good-looking man about the same age as her sitting by her side. Typical. Even in this kind of situation, Carmel had managed to pull. Connor was on the other side of the room, but every now and then his gaze flickered over to her. That could be a whole barrel of laughs just waiting to explode.

'She is of Menhit, and she should by rights be mine,' said Hathor, staring at Carmel with eyes that were now flecked with gold.

'No,' I responded, firmly. 'She is not of Menhit, she is of Mrs O'Grady. I don't know what the whole deal is with Carmel and her birth mother, but she is not yours, Hathor, and never will be. She is my Champion, and my friend, and she will not be heading off on a pyramid quest with you any time soon. Is that understood?'

Hathor looked taken aback by my tone, as indeed was I. I wondered if I was about to get a good snake-lashing, but instead she smiled, like I'd done well.

'I understand, Goddess. But perhaps the day will come when your Champion wants more than that – when she wants to discover who she truly is. Would you stand in her way?'

Would I? Good question. Carmel had spent vast quantities of time and cash trying to find out more about her heritage. She'd always been happy with the O'Grady clan, and who could blame her? They were loud and raucous and loving and, in my mind at least, the ideal family. She'd had a set of big brothers to teach her how to fight and look out for her, and a mother who'd kill anyone who hurt her. Even Hathor wouldn't stand a chance against Mrs O'Grady with a spatula in her chubby hand. But if Carmel wanted to know more about her 'real' parents – and she did – would I stop her?

No. Of course I wouldn't. But that was nothing at all to do with today, and with the fact that Hathor was trying to swipe my bezzie mate from under my nose.

'That will be for us to discuss another time,' I replied, suddenly feeling a lot more nervous about Carmel's new-found friend. He was, I was guessing, Hathor's own Champion – and Carmel looked fascinated with him.

I turned to Gabriel and gave him a super stern look.

'I'm going with Hathor, and we're going to chat. While I'm gone, make sure you keep an eye on Carmel. I don't trust any of them.'

'As you wish, Goddess,' he said, trying to keep the smile off his face. I'd just said an extremely rude thing, and not in a whisper, right next to the head of the Council. That was definitely more Lily than Goddess, which seemed to amuse him. I didn't even glance at Hathor, in case her face was doing something scary and I started to feel like the slow antelope at the back of the pack.

I strode off towards the balcony doors, ignoring all of the eyes that were fixed on me as I walked. Instead, I employed an old trick of Carmel's: in times of self-doubt, strut away while singing the opening chords of Jimi Hendrix's Foxy Lady in your head. It really did work. Dum-dum-duum, dum-dum-duum, ooh, foxy, lady. That was me, all right. Apart from the foxy bit, and the lady bit, obviously.

Hathor followed me outside and closed the doors behind us. I remembered as soon as I walked into the frigid New York air that it was December, that my dress didn't have sleeves, and that the almost-dead butler had stashed my pashmina. Goosebumps immediately popped on the skin of my arms, and I tried hard not to shiver.

There was a table set up surrounded by chairs, and I looked on with utter joy as Hathor also flicked a switch that made the heat lamps over our heads flare into life. My spirit may be part goddess, but my flesh was feeling decidedly human, and I sat in the chair nearest to the lamp, relishing the warm glow on my arms.

I glanced out at the amazing view, the park and the buildings and the brilliantly blue sky scudding with cotton wool clouds, and then back at Hathor, who was arranging her gown elegantly around her ankles. Which she did actually have, not castors at all. She took the golden circlet from her head and laid it on the table between us. The spooky eye blinked once at me, making me quake just a little bit, then closed. It looked sleepy and peaceful, and I half expected it to snore.

'I thought you would feel more comfortable without that, Goddess,' she said, 'as you seem to have some problem with it?' She raised one dark eyebrow at me, questioningly.

Ah. Right. Her mental rummaging had been extremely thorough. She knew about the eye vision, and about us suspecting her, and I had to assume about my adventures in the land of the evil leprechaun Fergal Fitzgarry, the night before. If we were going to be discussing this, I needed to know that Gabriel wasn't ear-wigging. I knew I needed to tell him – but him finding out by accident would be less than ideal. I stared at the doors back into the room, checking they were properly closed. Seriously, his hearing is phenomenal – and very irritating.

'Rest easy,' she said. 'This is our space and ours alone. Nobody can listen to us, and all you say will be in confidence. It leaves me to wonder, though, why you keep secrets from him. He is your mate and your protector. You were wrong to doubt my loyalties, and you are wrong to hide this threat. I felt your terror, I felt the way this man you approached drained you, and that is something of concern to us all. It is not a childish prank to be hidden away from those who care for you, and those who depend on you. You are the Goddess, and the world needs you. Why would you toy with your own safety for the sake of petty rebellion?'

Crikey. When she put it like that, there wasn't much to be said about it. It was kind of pathetic, not to mention dangerous. I didn't know quite how to respond, but settled eventually on honesty. I've heard tell that it's the best policy, though I've never been entirely convinced. The world is very often better off for a few white lies.

'I didn't expect it to happen,' I said, not meeting her eyes, but gazing out at the park instead. 'We thought it would be harmless, and had no idea of what we were walking into. I was wrong, I know that. Gabriel and I . . . well, it's complicated. I needed space to breathe. I needed time away from him. And I wanted to help Colin, the man who had come looking for aid. Gabriel didn't seem interested in helping him, and that felt wrong to me. But . . . you're right. It was childish, I know that now and I will resolve the issue.'

'Good,' she replied, nodding. 'And we will help – a threat to you is a threat to us all. Your vision showed threat from a mighty eye. That was not me, you now know – which means that it is someone else, possibly connected to this Fitzgarry. This Collector of Souls.'

I hadn't said those words out loud, or even thought them out loud, but she was right. That's what he was – he was a Collector of Souls. He'd been collecting them from the hospitals he owned, from the care homes he owned, from God only knew where else – and he desperately wanted mine to complete the set. He wouldn't give up, and I was an idiot if I thought I could make that go away on my own.

'We must work together – between us we have the power to defeat him, Goddess. But alone? Well, alone, you are nothing. We are all nothing. That is why we have our

Champions and our consorts and our allies in the mortal world. Do you understand me?'

'Yes,' I replied, feeling nothing short of embarrassment. Not for the first time this week, I was getting a proper telling off. And, not for the first time, I deserved it. There really is nothing more mortifying than a justified bollocking, and I knew there'd be much more to come once I coughed up to Gabriel.

'And you have my word, I will talk to him about it, today. There's nothing more I can do.'

Hathor smiled at me, and I wondered about her, about the days when she was young, too. When all of this was new to her. When she wasn't thousands of years old and when she didn't turn into a lion and when she made mistakes as well. It was hard to imagine, but it had probably existed. There would have been a time when life was a simple, short thing, instead of the heart-achingly long and complex path she now walked.

'You must also,' she said, meeting my eyes very solidly, as though forbidding me to look away, 'have sex with him.'

'What?!' I spluttered, feeling fire bloom on my cheeks and my fingers clench into fists. Woo. That one had come out of nowhere.

'You must have sex. With your mate. With the High King. I know that this has not happened, and it must. It should already have taken place. You are of the Earth, and you must behave accordingly. I do not understand why you and Cormac Mor have not united – he knows that this is necessary. He knows that time is not unlimited.'

Her words were calm and measured, but she was staring at me with a tinge of concern. Probably because I was bright red and looked like I could explode at any minute. Wouldn't be a good PR exercise if the newly approved Goddess went pop right on her own balcony, would it?

Still. I was shocked silly by what she'd just said.

When I'd accepted Gabriel as my mate at Tara, I'd been told it was ceremonial . . . at first. I tried to recall the exact words that Fionnula and the Morrigan had used, when we'd been having one of our fun conversations about it.

I definitely remembered the word 'ceremonial'. And I was pretty damn sure I'd been told that the 'carnal act' could be done when I was ready. That, I supposed, was the issue. When would I be ready? If I was waiting for things between me and Gabriel to calm down, that would kind of be never. And if I never committed the carnal act . . . was he still my mate? Had my choice mattered at all? If I didn't get my knickers off, would the Earth shrivel up and die, replaced by Fintan's totally creepy version of enforced Otherworld paradise? Fuck. Talk about intense. It would take more than a bit of Barry White to put me in the mood for love with that kind of pressure hanging over my head.

I processed all of this as quickly as I could, while also trying to stop myself falling off the chair, or bursting into tears. I'd been doing way too much of that lately – the crying thing. Coleen had raised me to keep my tears on the inside, as nobody cared very much anyway, and I'd possibly boo-hooed more in this last few days than I had since I was six and my parents died.

'Right. Is there a, you know, a deadline?' I asked, my voice emerging far more coolly than I thought it would. I'd anticipated Minnie Mouse after a session on the helium balloons, but I sounded OK.

'Not unless I choose to set one, as the head of the Council,' she replied. 'And I am not totally without heart, child. I have seen your soul, and I understand your misgivings. But now is the time to put them aside. I have accepted you as the Goddess, and now you must fulfil that role. If it is your inexperience bothering you, then you need not fear – ours are not the ways of the mortal

141

world. Taking Gabriel to your bed does not exclude others. The vampire I saw in your mind – one of Donn's? – he is, I know, pleasing to you. And I saw your reaction to Katashi. Belonging to Gabriel does not mean that you cannot know the touch of another.'

Humm. Yes. Nice. I'd been told that before, and hearing it again wasn't doing anything to get rid of my Code Red. And it wasn't that simple – the problem wasn't about me having sex with only one person to the exclusion of all others. The problem was me having sex at all.

I'd grown up terrified of touching anyone. I'd been cursed with visions whenever I did. That had been a deeply unpleasant experience and, as a result, I'd kept myself aloof. I had few friends, and I'd lived a solitary life. Yes, of course, I now knew how to control all of that – but it took more than a couple of months to overcome habits and fears ingrained in me throughout my whole existence. Gabriel had made the decisions he'd made, and kept me in isolation. The result wasn't quite what he'd hoped for – me, desperate for love – but something quite different. Me, desperate to be left alone.

Apart from, well, the odd occasion when I'd have quite liked to have thrown him on a desk and diddled him silly. That was all in the heat of the moment though – and this? Well, this was different. Despite the heat lamps, this moment felt very cold indeed.

'OK,' I muttered. 'I understand. I think. But . . . what happens if I don't? What happens if I can't?'

'Of course you can, you silly girl,' said Hathor, frowning and looking confused. 'Have you never heard of alcohol?'

Chapter Seventeen

We were sitting on a bench in Central Park. My pashmina was back in place, wrapped around me like a woolly second skin, and Gabriel was by my side.

He'd taken one look at my face when I'd come back in from the Balcony of Revelations, and ordered everyone else home. He did it quietly and effectively, silencing Carmel's protests with one imperious glare, giving our apologies to the Council and making it all appear perfectly normal. Just another busy day in the action-packed social diary of the Goddess about town.

Even The Dog had been banished, and I missed her warm, furry presence on my feet. It was just me. And him. And a few thousand other people, enjoying the winter sunshine in one of the biggest cities on earth.

Our bench backed up against trees and shrubs, and every now and then grey squirrels scampered across the path in front of us, their bushy tails disappearing off into the undergrowth or vertically up heavily barked trunks. Just outside, the street was lined with vans selling kebabs and gyros and giant pretzels, and the smell drifted through to us, making my tummy rumble. I'd not exactly been in the mood for nibbles at Supernatural HQ, and it had been a long time since that bagel.

At the crossroads of the three paths in front of us, a young black man wearing a hoody and jeans hanging off over his underwear was making giant bubbles with a metal hoop and a bucket of soapy water. Little kids watched, mesmerised, as he threw them into the air, running into their path and popping them, laughing with pure glee as they got their hands and faces wet. Parents looked on, tired and happy, leaning on pushchairs and rooting in their pockets for coins to throw into his collection box.

It was beautiful, and it was about to be ruined by a very heavy conversation. One I didn't want to have. I wanted to ignore it all, and run into the giant bubbles, to disappear in their oily, iridescent glow. Possibly fall through some kind of hole in the space-time-bubble continuum and never emerge again.

'So,' said Gabriel, staring at the bubble man with as much concentration as me. Maybe he wanted to run away as well. That was something I'd never really considered. He was as trapped as I was, and he'd been living it for a lot longer. Living with his sacred role and his duty and all his kingly responsibilities, knowing that his fate was sealed. Maybe it was easier if you'd never known anything different, I didn't know.

'So,' I replied, wanting to make it easier for him, but not really knowing how. There was so much to talk about, but we both seemed to have been struck dumb. I needed to tell him about Fitzgarry. I needed to ask him more about the source of the eye thing, and whether the two could be connected. I needed to make sure he didn't throw Carmel into an oubliette for hiding it all from him. And, oh yeah, I needed to shag him. Ideally not there and then, as it might scare the children, traumatise the squirrels and get us arrested for lewd behaviour.

Minutes passed. More bubbles. More kids. More silence.

'Hathor told me we need to have sex, and soon,' I finally blurted, bringing the elephant into the room and sitting on its back.

'I thought she might have done,' he replied. 'From the way you looked when you came back in. I'm sorry if the thought upsets you so much.'

I looked up at him. He was still lost in bubble kingdom, but his jaw was set and tense. I couldn't see what colour his eyes were, but his whole body was rigid, including the arm he had stretched along the bench behind me. Ouch. I'd anticipated this conversation being awkward – but not the simple fact that perhaps his feelings would be hurt. Underneath it all, he was only human. Partly, at least.

'Don't be an arse,' I said, poking him gently in the ribs. I reached out and held his face, turning it towards mine so I could see him properly. I left my fingers where they were, touching his jawline, and smiled. Because, really, it was a beautiful face – the kind that should make you smile. Yes, it was complicated – but maybe I was complicating it even more. Maybe I should just let myself make the connection that was waiting to be made.

'You know I don't find it upsetting, Gabriel. You know you're, like, the most drop dead gorgeous mate I've ever had. You know I have feelings for you, even if I don't always understand them. I chose you that night at Tara – and whatever's happened since, don't forget that. But, I didn't quite realise that my sex life was going to come under so much scrutiny. That what I did with my body was going to be a matter of public record. So – give me a break. Please?'

He leaned into my touch, and closed his eyes as I stroked the side of his face. I could feel the muscle of his thigh pressing into mine, the thick silk of his hair draping onto my fingertips, the outline of his cheekbones. He still smelled divine, as well as looking it. God. He really was drop dead gorgeous. I could feel the eyes of the yummy mummies on us, maybe wondering what we'd do next. Maybe feeling nostalgic for the time when they'd been sitting with lovers on benches, instead of pushing prams and stocking nappy bags and wondering when they'd next get a chance to wash their hair. We must have looked splendidly romantic. If only they knew.

He took hold of my hand, kissing my fingertips gently before moving it away.

'I wanted to explain,' he said, 'about what happened. The other day. I knew that Hathor might take the view she has, that we need to become mates in more than name. I wasn't certain, whether she'd even know or how seriously she'd take it, but I knew it was possible. Knowing that, I couldn't let it happen then – not without you knowing the same. Without you understanding. I didn't want it to happen, and then for you to find out what you found out today, and think that was the only reason. That I'd deceived you.'

I kept my fingers twined into his, on my lap, and turned it over in my mind. I tried to look past the embarrassment and the sting of rejection I'd felt, and see it through his eyes.

'You thought that if we'd, umm, consumated our relationship then, and later I discovered that it was somehow time critical, that I'd be upset?'

'Well, wouldn't you?' he asked. 'With our history? I know none of this has been easy for you, Lily. So much has happened in such a short space of time. Finding out about who you really are. Fintan. Losing Coleen. Being presented with me and the choice you had to make. I know you feel I've manipulated you your whole life and, well, that's true. To an extent. How would you have felt afterwards? If you found out that I'd slept with you to meet a schedule? As part of my fucking *duty*?'

He spat the last word out with complete contempt,

and I realised this was one of the few times I'd heard him swear. At least in my language.

I'd been in Gabriel's head. I'd poked around in there, much like Hathor did to me today, and I knew without doubt that he loved me. That he wanted me. That being my mate was far more than duty to him. That should have given me the confidence to brush his concerns aside, to feel strong enough to say it wouldn't have mattered.

But, if I turned the honesty beam on myself, I knew that wasn't the case. I'd felt truly shitty ever since our near miss in the study. Knowing someone loved you didn't always equate to understanding the way they behaved, or giving them the benefit of the doubt. I'd been quick to assume the worst, to take it as a personal rejection, when in fact he was now trying to tell me it was the opposite. It was an attempt to be fair, to leave my choices intact. And when he'd tried to explain it to me the next day, we'd prickled each other into submission instead.

'OK,' I said after a few moments. 'But if we had, you know, done it, then Hathor wouldn't have even raised the issue, would she? She'd have seen it my head in technicolour glory, and assumed everything in the garden of sex was rosy.'

'There was always the chance that you'd find out,' he replied. 'A passing comment, a stray thought that you accidentally picked up on. We're not exactly talking about a logical situation here. All it would have needed is for you to have taken a road trip into her thoughts, and you'd have known. And then you'd have assumed the worst – that I finessed you into sex purely because it was part of the deal. Don't deny it, you know you would.'

I would have loved to deny it, but of course he was right. There was too much murky water under the bridge that always seemed to separate us, for that. And yes, I would have felt manipulated and used and pissed off to infinity and beyond. The chances of him getting a repeat shag would have been minimal, and I may well have run off and joined a nunnery.

'That makes a certain kind of sense, I admit,' I replied, not mentioning the nunnery part. 'But you should have warned me earlier. You should have explained. Then I wouldn't have felt like the ugly girl at a party that nobody wants to snog with the lights on.'

He laughed, and squeezed my fingers tighter.

'Never that, Lily. You'll never be that. I didn't know if Hathor would find out, or how she would react. So much of this is in her hands. Then you had the vision, and that threat needed to be examined, and somehow in the middle of it all I forgot that you're female. With all those tender, sensitive feelings your type is so well known for.'

I kicked his ankles with my boots, but had to smile.

'How come, if you've had centuries worth of experience with chicks, you can still be such a dickhead?' I asked.

'Well, I suppose I've just got better at being a dickhead as I've gone along, my love. To be fair, you've only had a few decades of being an unreasonable bitch, but you're already excelling at it. So maybe we should call it even.'

The atmosphere had lightened, and I felt better than I had for a while. Still nervy, still hormonal, still on the verge of tears. But better. It was really quite tragic to realise how much his apparent rejection had affected me. Now I had a clearer idea of what had really been going on, I felt like the black cloud had at least partially scudded off to one side.

'So,' I said again, my new favourite word. 'That still leaves us with this situation to deal with. Hathor told me she's not setting any kind of deadline as yet, and she's not sharing the happy news with the rest of the gang. She's giving us a chance to . . . you know. Sort it out between us. Negotiate some kind of resolution.'

'It's not a business deal, Lily,' he said, frowning as he weighed up my words. 'At least I don't want it to be. I know you can't rest easy around me because of everything I've done in the past – but I can't change that. All I can change is the way I act now, and in the future. I wanted it to happen . . . naturally. I hoped it would.That this whole situation would be null and void by the time we got here. All those centuries of experience with "chicks", as you say, did at least teach me to recognise it when a woman finds me attractive. And you do.' Ah. A little flare-up of his usual arrogance. He must be feeling better as well.

'Well, what can I say? I'm made of steel. And if you'd tried a little harder to persuade me – using all those special ages old techniques you've undoubtedly perfected – then maybe we'd be at home, in bed, right now. Rocking the Kasbah. Instead, you've kept your distance. Been respectful and careful and guarded. That's not the way to make a woman feel wanted, you know.'

He nodded, and snaked his hand into my hair, where it started to gently explore the skin at the base of my neck with fingertips that seemed to be wrapped in velvet. Gulp. Like I said, ages old techniques.

'You're right. But I wasn't sure what was going to happen here, and I took a gamble. If I didn't have to rush it, I didn't want to. I wanted you to make the choice, as you seem to be so keen on insisting you like them. Maybe I could have seduced you, Lily – but would you have respected me in the morning?'

I let my hand drift up his thigh, feeling the ridged muscle beneath, and wondering what it would be like to touch when it was unclothed. To really give in, to be sweaty and naked and panting and desperate and not to be thinking about all this stuff. Not to be thinking at all, in fact. Surely that'd be pretty damn good.

'What makes you think I respect you now?' I said,

looking up at him, my head tilted, possibly a big sign on my forehead saying 'Kiss me now'.

He did, and it was awesome. Definitely the best kiss I'd ever had, which I realise might not be saying much. It was slow and deep and incredibly effective, if the aim had been to raise my heartbeat to near nuclear levels, make my hair really, really messy, and leave Gabriel squirming awkwardly as his body responded to mine.

When he finally pulled away, his hands holding my face steady and his eyes sparking violet, we were both earning a few looks from the parents. And the kids. And the bubble man. A few squirrels stood off to one side, shading their eyes with their paws in shock. Passing spy satellites probably noticed a global warming hot spot right there, in a quiet corner of Central Park.

'Lily,' he said, not letting me move away, even though my usual retarded embarrassment was kicking in a bit, now he didn't have his tongue in my mouth. 'I love you. You know I do. And I want you, so much. Yes, this is something we have to do – but I think it's something you want to do as well. There is so much passion in you, so much need, and if you continue to try and ignore it, hide away from it, then—'

'I might actually explode. I know,' I replied, 'I've been thinking that myself.'

It was all starting to make a bit more sense now. The way I'd been feeling – the tears and the moods and the crankiness. The frankly whorish way I'd responded to Katashi.

There were two people living inside my skin, and they weren't getting along too well. Lily McCain was an emotionally stilted human who would happily spend the rest of her life locked in a broom closet with a good book and a well-stocked iPod. She just kept getting dragged out of it by the Goddess who, it seemed, really needed a good seeing to. It was logical, in a fucked up kind of way – Mabe was of the Earth, as I kept getting told. She was a symbol of fertility, a giver of life. She recognised Gabriel as her mate, and was keen to get the party started. It was just the rest of me holding the whole process up.

It was time to stop viewing us as separate entities and get on with life. I was Lily, I was Mabe. I was both of them in one mind and one body. Maybe I'd change my name to Milly and rebrand myself – but I needed to stop tearing myself apart, clinging on to one at the expense of the other. And this man, this arrogant, contrary, domineering hunk of gorgeousness, wanted both of them. I was clinging on to my precious virginity like a Jane Austen heroine, because I was clinging on to being just Lily. To my old life, my old identity. I didn't even know why – it's not like it had been an especially good life. Just stubborn, I suppose. And possibly frightened and confused as well.

'OK,' I said. 'You're right. I do want to. I'm not keen on the whole being backed into a corner thing, but I'd be crazy to say I want to live like this forever. I want you, Gabriel. I'm just . . . scared. Scared that if I stop being Lily, some catastrophe will happen. Or that I'll turn into a sex monster. That I'll like it too much, and lose all the control I've been fighting to maintain. That I'll get some fucking awful vision in the middle of it. Or that . . . well, that I'll be rubbish at it, and you'll be disappointed, and I'll compare badly to the thousands of women I'm told you've already bonked.'

There. It was out. The super-sad confession that I'd been hiding even from myself. The rest of my concerns were real – but at heart, I was suffering from a whole lifetime of performance anxiety. I'd felt rejected by Coleen as long as I'd been in her alleged care, and I hadn't had the usual rite-of-passage heartbreak and rebuilding that would allow me to emerge stronger on the other side. I was doing a fast forward from lonely child to grown woman in a few minutes flat, and it wasn't easy.

Gabriel pulled me into his arms, and squeezed me so tight I thought my lungs might pop out of my mouth.

'I understand all of that, Lily,' he said, 'and we can deal with it. Together, we can deal with it. And I promise – no more secrets.'

Coming from him, that was quite a vow. He was like the High King of Secrets, all of which I'd had to drag out of him. I knew there were probably more, and that had been one of the reasons I'd never entirely trusted him – centuries worth of scheming and deception, all centred around me and my role in the world. And now here he was swearing them off, to try and make me feel more secure.

It should have been a lovely moment. It should have filled me with joy. It should have been heralded by a choir of angels and the sound of celestial harps. Instead, it just made me feel a bit sick. Because he wasn't the only one with secrets. He wasn't the only one who'd been lying through omission. I felt the guilt and the panic curl up in my stomach like a fist, my mouth going suddenly dry.

I had to tell him about last night, and about Fitzgarry. And telling him here and now, in a very public place, might be the best way to do it. Here, he'd at least have to fight his urges to turn into Godzilla and trample tall buildings with his feet.

'Gabriel,' I said, feeling the heat of the kiss drain from my skin, along with all other evidence of being alive. 'There's something—'

At that exact moment, both of our cell phones went off. Mine with the shrill beep of a text landing, his with the insistent thrum of a dial tone.

We both immediately fished around in our pockets to find them. Him, because he's a good and conscientious king always on the alert for the call of duty; me, because I was desperate to avoid the conversation we were about to have. Even if it was a cold call offering to reclaim my PPI, it was better than that.

I flipped open the phone, while he snapped 'Gabriel' into his.

Half listening in to what he was saying, I pressed the icon and read the open text.

I paid you a visit today, Miss McCain, it said. *But sadly you were not at home. I left a gift for you and your High King. Hope you like it.*

The number was coming up as unknown, but both the swirl of nausea in my stomach and the fact that it was signed off with the initials FF told me everything I needed to know. Fitzgarry. He'd found my number, and he'd found Ash Street. Things were about to go very, very pear-shaped.

I shoved the phone back into my pocket, just as Gabriel did the same. He stood up, abruptly, and held out one hand.

'We need to go,' he said, his voice tense. 'Now.'

Chapter Eighteen

We jumped into a cab to get back to Ash Street, the driver thankfully ignoring us as he rocked out to Chinese synth pop. I kept quiet as well – eavesdropping on the frantic conversations Gabriel was having on his phone. I couldn't make it all out, hearing only one terse end of it, but the proverbial shit had clearly been well and truly flung into the fan. The main thrust of his concerns seemed to be ensuring it was safe to go back there with me in tow. Presumably if the answer had been 'no', I'd be driven to a top secret location and stashed with the other family heirlooms.

We paid the driver and walked through the court-yard gate to the bright red front door, Gabriel keeping me behind him, shielding me with his body as we opened it.

Inside, the first thing I saw was Carmel screaming, very loudly, with tears streaking down her face. Carmel is not by nature one of life's criers, and when she looked up at me with huge, damp eyes, I knew that something very bad had happened.

The Morrigan was bellowing from the front living room, loud enough to raise the dead. Or even Luca. Finn ran into the hallway as we arrived, sword in hand, meeting Gabriel's eyes and shaking his head in a sad 'no'.

I pushed past them towards Carmel, who was now busily kicking the shit out of a coat stand, punching the jackets and yelling at the scarves that were draped from it. A random deerstalker hat fell to the floor, and she stamped on it like a cockroach, grinding the flaps into the ground.

'Stop it!' I shouted, grabbing hold of her fists and trying to keep her still. I could feel the fury and tension and the sheer need to kill something fizzing through her body, and her wide, whisky-coloured eyes glared in frustration as she realised it was me. The one person she couldn't hurt.

'What is it?' I asked, stroking the tears from her cheeks in an attempt to calm her down. 'What's happened?'

She took in a deep breath, broken with a body-wracking sob, and shook her head.

'Go in there. You'll see. And it's all our fault. We did this.'

I hugged her, once and hard, before letting her go. She sank slowly to the floor, holding her face in her hands and continuing to cry. I looked up and saw Connor staring at us. He wasn't covered in blood, or injured, or screaming – which meant he was the nearest thing to a glamorous assistant I could find.

'Look after her,' I said, before bustling away to follow Gabriel into the front room.

He was gathered with the Morrigan, Finn and Kevin, looking down at the hard wood floor. I froze in the doorway for a moment, taking it all in. The mahogany panelling on the walls. The leather Chesterfield. The desk, piled high with books and papers. The unshuttered windows ushering in pale fingers of sunlight. The deep, sonorous tick of the carriage clock on the mantel. The sounds of Carmel's anguished sobs filtering through, accompanied by the gentle 'shush' of Connor's voice as he tried to console her.

'Let me through,' I said, stepping forwards.

'No, Lily this is not—' said Gabriel, blocking my path and not managing to get a full sentence out before I interrupted him.

'This is not the time to protect me, Gabriel. Now step out of my way before I make you.'

Right. So much for the delicate detente we'd established earlier. I'd worry about our relationship's power balance later. Just then I needed to see exactly what it was that had turned my Champion into a blubbering wreck, and made the Morrigan scream. It had, after all, been left there for me.

His face was set and dark, and his body was twitching bigger, but he did at least move. Which was a relief, as I really didn't want to have to force him. His men followed suit, and the Morrigan met my eyes once, nodding her agreement.

I walked on, one quaking step at a time, the ticking of the clock accompanying the sound of my boots as I closed the distance. Gabriel placed one hand on my shoulder, and I shrugged it off, pushing past him. Whatever I was about to face, I needed to do it alone.

In front of me, lying naked on the floor, was Colin. Colin Murphy, with his floppy blond hair and his nerdy courage and his little John Lennon specs.

The glasses were still on his face, but the round lenses were shattered, a spiderweb of cracks that would have prevented him from seeing anything at all. If he'd still been alive. Or if he'd still had eyes.

Behind the smashed lenses and the twisted wire frames, all I could see was darkness. Blood had dried and crusted in rivulets down the side of his face, stiffening on a few strands of his too-long hair, like he'd used a rust-coloured spray on them.

His bare chest had been carved up, used as an etching board by something sharp enough to cut cleanly and precisely, and by a hand that didn't shake. It wasn't a random mutilation – it was a design, drawn to perfection on a human canvas. A design of a huge, malevolent eye, looking out at me in exactly the same way it had in my vision.

There would be a time – probably very soon – when that would frighten me. But right then, all I could feel was fury. Pure, raging anger. The kind that wouldn't let me cry, or scream, or panic. The kind that made me want to march into Fergal Fitzgarry's dimly lit office, and plunge my hand into his chest until I held his beating heart in my grasp.

'Cover him up,' I said, simply. 'Then I'm going to kill somebody.'

Chapter Nineteen

'Balor,' said the Morrigan from her seat around the study desk. 'It must be. Even to my memory it is so distant as to be a tale told by scolding mothers, but we have ruled out Hathor.'

Balor. Hathor. What would be next? Eeyore? If it was, I'd be knocking the stuffing out of him, and mounting his head in my living room.

While Colin lay, covered in blankets, carved up and desecrated, we were sitting around. Talking. Part of me understood the need for it, the need to plan and discuss and prepare, but part of me just wanted to get out there and wreak havoc.

This was a new feeling to me and, I have to say, it made life a lot simpler and a lot clearer. It was like me and Carmel had swapped personalities for a while. She was still upset, holding it together but occasionally screwing up her eyes as though stopping herself from leaking again. I knew I'd be there with her at some point, two girls bleating on each other's shoulders, but I wasn't there yet. I was still in Angry Town, hoping to very soon be travelling to Murder Village.

Luca was up, and had taken in the sorry sight of Colin's bloodied corpse with a sad, slow shake of his head. He'd looked, long and hard, then turned back to me, reaching out to hold my face in his hands.

'It is sad, my love. But it was not your doing. Now is not the time to blame yourself. Now is the time to be strong, and focus on what needs to follow.'

'I know that,' I'd replied, gently moving his hands away. I understood why he'd said it, why he'd made the assumption that I'd be drowning in guilt and regret and self-recrimination. I probably should be, but in truth I didn't need comforting. I didn't need anyone trying to make me feel better. I just needed to be making Fergal Fitzgarry feel a whole lot worse. Like, dead.

'What is going on? Why would this be Lily's doing?' Gabriel had demanded, immediately alert to the unapproved Luca fondling, as usual. This time, though, he had a point – we weren't flirting. We were touching on a subject that Gabriel now, more than ever, needed to know about. Keeping my little girl secrets had entirely possibly resulted in the death of an innocent man, and that was a far more sobering thought than my earlier fears about confessing. Gabriel couldn't possibly do anything worse than this to me, however angry he was.

So we'd all trooped through to the study – the War Room, as I'd thought of it days ago. Back when the most pressing thing on my mind was whether my boyfriend still fancied me or not. And I'd told him. As quickly and clearly as I could, deliberately not looking at him as I spoke, staring off into the distance instead.

I could hear the shocked sighs of his men, and the Morrigan slammed her mighty clenched fist onto the table, so hard it vibrated, but I still didn't slow down or quaver or jump off my chair and hide under the desk. Gabriel, I knew, would be quivering and expanding and sending out warning signs with his eyes. He'd be furious, and disappointed, and frustrated. And he'd be right to be all of those things.

I'd ignored his decision to refuse Colin his aid. I'd lied to him about going to the spa, and instead snuck off behind his back to go on an adventure. I'd faced a very real threat to my existence. I'd encountered the tell-tale smell of the Faidh. I'd been involved in multiple homicide, mortal and equine. I'd dragged Carmel, Luca and Colin along with me in the deception.

And for Colin in particular, that hadn't worked out too well.

When I'd finished my tale of woe, I finally turned to face Gabriel. Carmel was wrenching at her hair, staring at the table, and even Luca looked uncomfortable, as the whole story flooded out, ending with Colin, lying like a gutted fish on the living room floor.

I expected Gabriel's head to be brushing the ceiling, and for him to be quaking with rage. I'd steeled myself for it, prepared for it, knew I deserved it. But instead, he was still. Silent. Looking at me as though he didn't know me at all, as though I was a complete stranger who'd wandered in from the street. That, I have to say, was so much worse. Not so long ago I'd been snogging this man on a park bench and planning on getting naked with him. Now . . . well, now he looked empty. Closed off, rather than pissed off. I realised that I wanted him to be angry. That I wanted him to shout and scream and give me the telling off I thought I deserved. That then, I'd feel a tiny bit better about what had happened to Colin.

Maybe he knew that. Maybe he was just finding his own way to cope. Maybe he was totally, one hundred per cent sick to death of me. I didn't know – and he wasn't telling.

Instead, he nodded. Looked around the table at everyone else, took in the silence. They were all waiting to see how he'd react, waiting to see how long it would take for this particular bombshell to detonate. The Morrigan's handsome face was taut and drawn, and I thought Carmel would wither into her own misery and disappear in a puff of self-loathing. She hadn't just contributed to Colin's death – she'd let me walk into danger, and betrayed her loyalty to the King. In Champion-speak, that was tantamount to catastrophe. She was clearly wanting to fall on her own pocket knife right about then.

Gabriel might be seething inside, but somehow, he wasn't showing it. None of the tell-tale bodily changes were there. None of the swelling or shouting or physical transformation that I was used to. He simply sat, quietly, mulling it over. One finger tapping on the desk was the only sign that he was even still alive.

'Well,' he finally said, still not meeting my eyes, his glance skimming over me as though I didn't even register on his radar any more, 'thank you for sharing, Goddess. You've all been busy, obviously. And there will be a time when we discuss this further – but now, we need to plan. To find this threat, to understand it, and to neutralise it. Morrigan – the eye. What are your first thoughts? What does it bring to mind?'

That's when she started to talk about Balor. Balor, the most powerful weapon in the arsenal of a once-mighty race called the Fomorians. The Fomorians, it turned out, were old. Older than the Morrigan, older than the time she judged by, older than the Earth itself. So old they were only legendary figures to the equally legendary figures sitting around the table.

'The Fomorri were the children of Domnu,' she explained. 'They represented all that was dark and evil in the universe. Balor, their warrior and mascot, was possessed of a single eye, an eye with special powers – the ability to destroy all it looked upon.

'This all culminated in a mighty battle, where Balor fought against Lugh, who was armed with the sword that is now in the possession of the King. Lugh was victorious, making a slingshot from blood and sand and using it to knock out Balor's killing eye. His last gaze fell upon his own men, who died on the spot. The nearby river ran with blood; and more men died than there are stars in the sky, and the earth shook to the keening of the warriors as they looked on at their slain comrades.'

The others nodded solemnly as the Morrigan told the tale. It sounded horrific to me, but was probably exactly the kind of bedtime story Gabriel and his men were raised on. Not that long ago I'd have dismissed it as a particularly grim fairytale, but now? Now I knew that while it might have been embellished – as age and countless retelling tends to do – there would be truth in it. Enough, at least, to make me go very cold indeed.

The especially lovely epilogue to the tale was of Domnu, who took the form of a crow to issue a prophecy – that her rivals would be driven from the world. That the summers would be flowerless, that the cows would be without milk, and the seas without fish. That the men would be weak, the women shameless, and warriors would betray each other. That there would come a time when there would be no more virtue left in the world.

Again, I could dismiss it. But I knew at least one other person who could take the form of a crow. And I remembered from my history lessons with Fionnula the Fair that at least part of that prophecy had already come true – Domnu's rivals were driven from the world as we know it, leaving the mortal plane and instead settling in the Otherworld. Bar the occasional skipping back and forth that Gabriel and his ilk did, the two remained separate. It was a delicate balance, and one that Fintan had tried to disrupt – a disruption that would have ended in the destruction of my world. Of the world I grew up in. The world where I was a pop writer on a local paper, not a fertility goddess with the fate of humankind on my shoulders.

And all that stuff about cows having no milk? Again, it sounded weird and irrelevant to my modern ears. I mean, you run out of milk, you go to the supermarket, right? But the older part of me knew and understood what it meant. It meant the end. It meant infertility, and famine, and death. A lot of responsibility to place on a Friesian I know, but that's what it signified. I'd made my choice at Tara to avoid the destruction of the Earth and now we were facing up to the fact that it might not have worked. That there was a new bully on the school playground, intent on taking everyone's lunch boxes away. For the rest of eternity.

As her story finished, I saw a look on the Morrigan's face that I'd never seen before: fear. That alone was enough to calm down the rampaging killing machine that was gurgling around inside me. She was the scariest person I'd ever met, right at the top of a long list of pretty scary dudes. If she was anxious, the rest of us should be petrified. And I probably would have been – if not for the sight, burned into my brain forever, of Colin and his mutilated body. He'd trusted me, and I'd let him down. I'd failed him.

'I failed him,' I said out loud, the words barely more than a whisper, echoing around the still, silent room. I looked up, and Gabriel at last decided to meet my eyes. I stared at him, looking for something. I didn't know what – comfort? Forgiveness? A cheeky wink?

I didn't get any of that. All I got was hard, cold steel.

'You did, Goddess,' he replied, 'you failed him and you failed us. And the reminder of that is lying on the floor in the other room. By fighting against your destiny, you helped to end his mortal life. I am aware of your youth, your inexperience, the obstacles you have faced. But this is the result of your actions, and you should never forget how this moment feels.'

He was right. I would make sure I never forgot. His comments were harsh, but I deserved them.

Carmel, though, didn't appear to agree.

'No,' she said, forcing herself to look at Gabriel even though her hands were trembling against the surface of the desk. 'It was not her fault, High King – I should have stopped her; I should have—'

'Yes, you should have,' he interrupted, staring at her ferociously, 'but you didn't. You were both too busy pretending you were just normal human girls to stop and think of the consequences. And now, we will have to take Colin's body back to his family. They will have to deal with the loss of their son. They will have to bury him, knowing he died in terror and pain. They will carry that burden for the rest of their lives – and so will you.'

Luca looked at me across the desk, and gave me a small, lopsided smile. He didn't say anything. There was no point. We couldn't argue with Gabriel on this one. I was sure he carried a few burdens of his own, was sure he'd caused deaths that he'd always regret, that he'd made decisions that still tortured him. His life had been long and full and not in any way easy, but he never bleated about it. Now, it was my turn to grow up and face my new reality.

'You are right, Gabriel,' I said. 'About all of it. But as you say, now is not the time for this conversation. We can save that one to look forward to at some point in the future – if there is a future. Because from what the Morrigan has just told us, Colin's death is linked to this Balor character. And his death was caused by Fitzgarry. Which means that Fitzgarry is connected to Balor and possibly to Fintan. The power I felt from him was overwhelming – he was draining mine away from me, without even lifting a finger. So now I have to ask a question of you. When I first had a vision of an eye, why didn't you connect the dots? Why didn't you think of Balor then? And why does this man also hate you? He spoke of you with . . . well, contempt, when we first met. And his text today said his "gift" was for both of us. If you don't even know who he is, how can he hate you?'

I wasn't trying to shift blame, or shirk my own part in all this, but they were questions that needed to be asked. I trusted Gabriel and the Morrigan to be the know-it-alls in our group. They'd been around for a lot longer than anyone else – bar Luca, and this so wasn't his natural world – and they had the collective folk memory of a herd of elephants. I was genuinely concerned that they'd overlooked what seemed to me, now, to be glaringly obvious. Instead, they'd gone off at a tangent, pursuing a theory that the eye was instead related to Hathor – and while there was plenty about Hathor that disturbed me, her particular eyeball wasn't the source of all my current woes. It wasn't responsible for Colin's death, or the potential armageddon that we were now sitting and calmly discussing around a table in a very pretty house in Greenwich Village.

The Morrigan shook her head sadly, her red and white hair flowing over broad shoulders that looked a little less defiant than usual. Her posture was slack and defeated, and it felt like a pillar of the world had collapsed.

'Child, I do not know,' she replied. 'As I said, the story of Balor is an ancient one – one that we were told as children. One that we have discounted as legend. But you are right, it should have been in our minds. On that point, we too have failed, and I challenge Cormac Mor to disagree with me on that. As to his own role, I have no clues.'

She looked up at Gabriel, and I could see that he wanted to do exactly that – challenge her. But challenging a centuries old harbinger of death wasn't a sensible option. Especially when she was right.

'Is it possible,' said Luca, leaning back casually in his chair, draped in shadows, 'that you could have been, how do you say, messed with? That some power could have exerted its influence over your minds? Could have – please forgive me – blinded you to this possibility?'

'No! Of course not!' snapped back Gabriel, finally showing signs of the fury that I knew must be lurking beneath his icy calm demeanour. His eyes sparked, and I heard the creak of the chair as his body started to expand. The question was a solid one, but as it had come from Luca's mouth, it provoked anger rather than consideration. Good to know that some things never change.

'High King,' said the Morrigan, pointing at him from across the table, 'your arrogance is not appropriate. The creature makes a fair point. Even you are not immune to all the power of the universe, even I am not. The Goddess had a vision of an eye that threatened her. We can posture all we like, but we assumed it was Hathor without any thought of an alternative. We were blinkered, and saw only what we wanted to see – the false threat. We were fools, and we must accept that, and move on.'

Gabriel didn't look much like he wanted to move on. He looked like he wanted to move around the table and rip Luca's throat out for daring to exist. He was glaring at him with dazzling purple eyes, and I could see his clenched fists swelling and expanding, the skin on his fingers cracking. I'd seen him in full-on battle mode only twice before – when we were being attacked by Faidh assassins outside my fake nan's house in Liverpool, and during a hellfire battle on the waterfront – and it had been terrifying. He actually sprouted claws, and snapped necks, and bit off body parts with his teeth. The fact that he seemed on the verge of doing that again, now, here, in this situation, felt wrong. No matter what he thought about Luca's existence, going all Animal House was a definite over-reaction. And in close quarters like these, it could be disastrous.

'Gabriel,' I said, quietly. 'You need to calm down. To think about what's happening to you, and why. At this moment in time we need to be thinking clearly, and I can tell that you're not thinking at all. You're feeling nothing but blood lust, which won't help anyone. Stop, and breathe, and think.'

He barely looked at me, he was so intent on Luca. Just a flicker of those shining eyes in my direction, then back at Luca, who, for his part, was trying to help by staying very still and very quiet. He knew what was happening. He'd fought by Gabriel's side when this kind of transformation happened. It wasn't the kind of thing you wanted heading in your direction in an enclosed space, without full body armour and a squad of paramedics on standby.

The chair Gabriel was perched on finally gave up, popping as he expanded, the arms crunching and splintering wider to accommodate his growing body. His face was twisting and churning, like there were spiders crawling under his skin, and I could see the glimmer of claws emerging from the tips of his fingers. It didn't seem to hurt – or maybe his feelings were so extreme when the rage took hold of him that he didn't even notice.

Kevin, Connor and Finn all shoved their chairs back, a chorus of wood and metal scraping against the floor, and stood up, looking on in horror. He was their king, and they lived to serve – but right now, if this carried on, he could be the enemy.

I got up and ran to the other side of the table. I pushed myself in front of him, shoving the wrecked chair backwards to make room, and stood between his legs. His whole body was enormous – even still just about sitting, he was taller than me. His hands were now spread on the table, claws digging into the wood, as though he was trying to lodge himself there. I realised that was exactly what he was doing – part of him knew what was happening, and he was desperately trying to cling on to sanity, to keep himself seated and still, as opposed to standing, moving, and randomly slaughtering.

I leaned into his body, holding the sides of his face with my hands. I could feel the bones moving beneath his skin, and the strength in his thighs threatened to crush me as they closed around my body. His eyes gazed into mine, sparking and flashing and pleading, as I stroked his cheeks, made soft soothing noises, and pushed myself even closer to him.

'Gabriel,' I murmured gently, kissing his temples, his jaw, his lips. Part of me was wussing out, scared he'd just bite my head off – literally – but most of me knew he wouldn't. Most of me knew he loved me, and had dedicated his life to protecting me, and would do anything to keep me safe. Most of him knew that as well – it was just the tiny part that didn't that was worrying me. The tiny part that didn't seem to be totally under his control.

'Calm down, my love,' I whispered. 'Come back to us. Come back to me. It's Lily. And I need you. I need all of you.'

I threw my arms around his shoulders, and found they were too wide for me to hold him properly. I nuzzled into his face and neck, kissing him and talking to him, all the while aware of his strength and his power. Power that I'd always taken for granted would be on my side.

Around me, Carmel and the men were furiously talking to each other, but I couldn't make out a word they said. The Morrigan had transformed into the crow, and was flapping around above our heads, circling over and over in a loop, a gentle gust of air from her wings lifting strands of my hair. She could kill him, like this. She could land on his shoulder and invoke her magic and take him away from me. I batted at her with my hand, and she flew wonkily off course for a moment, before returning to her circuit.

'Gabriel,' I said, more urgently. 'I know you can hear me. I know you're still in there. You're going to hurt me if you don't stop this. You're crushing my legs right now, and if you carry on, something's going to break. You're going to break me, Gabriel. And you don't want to do that, do you?'

I was exaggerating. A bit. It was hurting, the way he was squeezing me, but I didn't really think I was about to snap. I was just trying to get his attention, to distract him, to make him feel a bit more Gabriel, and a bit less Bruce Banner.

I heard Carmel shouting at Luca to get out of the room, and Luca talking back to her in a quiet, calm voice, refusing. Explaining that if he moved, if he ran, then he'd be prey – and the hunter would chase. I knew, instinctively, that he was right, but I moved my body slightly, angled it so I blocked him from Gabriel's line of vision. All of his anger, all of his frustration, all of his rage – along with the residual powder puff of the potential mind-fucking he'd been given – was focused on Luca. Luca, who'd led me astray. Luca, who paraded around buck naked in front of me at every possible opportunity. Luca, who had spent the whole journey over here pretending to slice me up and eat me in the form of an apple. Luca, who kinda deserved a good ass-kicking, when you viewed it from Gabriel's perspective – but not the kind that would result in him potentially being ripped into teeny tiny pieces. Gabriel would regret that almost as much as Luca would.

So I hid him from view, and carried on stroking Gabriel's face, and kissing him gently, and burying my fingers in the thick waves of his hair, and ignoring the fact that my body felt like it was caught in a vice and I could hear claws scraping on wood behind me.

'Come back, Gabriel,' I murmured, 'come back. You can't go all nuts on me now. You haven't even told me off properly. And we haven't even had sex. Come back . . .'

I don't know whether it was the prospect of getting

to yell at me at some unspecified point in the future, or the reference to sex that did it, but the grip of his thighs started to ease off a little. As I kissed him, I was aware of needing to lean down a little to do it. As I twined my fingers in his hair, I noticed his head was slightly lower. Inch by very slow inch, he started to recede – to revert to his usual size.

That left his face eventually buried in my chest, with my hands on the back of his head, holding him there and stroking him, muttering soothing shushing noises and praying it was all over. After a few more moments, he wrapped his arms around me, pulling me in almost as tight as he had before. I heard a soft groan coming from him, before he eventually emerged again. Normal size. Eyes dark blue. Claws all gone. In control.

I sagged with the relief, and he kept hold of me, helping me stay upright. I stroked his hair away from his face, and scanned him all over. Yep. He looked OK. A bit embarrassed. Maybe a bit ashamed. But basically OK.

'Lily,' he muttered, his breath warm against me. 'I'm so sorry.'

I nodded, still scanning his face.

'That's all right. Nobody, as I think I've mentioned before, is perfect. But you really should apologise to Luca.'

'Luca's a big boy. He can cope,' he replied, which I knew was as close to an apology as we were going to get. I heard Luca grunt behind me, acknowledging it.

'Now,' said Gabriel, 'we really have to find out who's messing with us. And stop them from ever doing it again.'

Chapter Twenty

Within an hour, we were ready to leave. Gabriel had ordered Kevin to stay behind for the time being, to deal with Colin's body and to find out everything he could about Fergal Fitzgarry.

We'd been told to pack a bag, and pack it light, in case we needed to get the hell out of Dodge with any speed. Carmel had also been instructed very firmly to leave her shoe collection behind. She looked a tiny bit crestfallen but didn't object – a sure sign she was still suffering. As the shoe collection in question included the Jimmy Choos she'd saved up for three months for, she was clearly still suffering a lot.

Gabriel had decided that he needed to go to the Otherworld to gather intelligence and, I silently presumed, to try and clear his head of whatever influence might still be lingering there. They hadn't discussed it out loud, but I could tell from the Morrigan's wary words and cautious movements that she believed it was true – that she had somehow been 'messed with', as Luca had said. She was questioning herself, and that wasn't something that came naturally to her. There'd been nothing more said about Gabriel's near transformation, but it was still fresh in all our minds. If those two could be interfered with, we all needed to be on high alert.

That, apparently, extended to me as well.

'Fitzgarry knows where we are,' said Gabriel. 'He knew where to leave Colin. He seems to know all about me, and us, and our affairs here. That means he'll probably have people watching us, waiting for our next move. I don't want those watchers to see you leaving, Lily. I want him to think you're still here, still—'

'Crying in a heap in the corner?' I finished for him. He nodded once, grimly. The tears still hadn't come. Maybe they never would. Maybe I'd lost too much to feel any more. I was still clinging on to the belief that Fitzgarry would get what was coming to him, that despite his apparent strength, we would find a way to defeat him. If that meant hiding, pretending to cower, cloaking myself in weakness, then that was fine by me. Whatever it took.

What it actually meant was going out in disguise. But this being me, and my life being like a collection of scenes from a Stephen King film these days, it wouldn't involve a French beret and a fake moustache. It would involve, I was told, my future self.

'It is nothing, child,' said the Morrigan, taking me to one side as the others scurried around packing rucksacks and sharpening swords and stoically ignoring the fact that there was a tattered corpse lying beneath a patchwork quilt in the front room. 'It is a small piece of magic, one that will not harm you.'

I'd looked at her suspiciously – the lady was protesting far too much for my liking – but agreed to sit, still and silent, while she pulled her latest party trick out of the bag. It started with her telling me to relax – yeah, right – and clear my mind. I knew now, even with my limited experience of this crazy shit, that clearing your mind was both the most basic and the hardest to master of building blocks.

I did as she said, invoking a quiet, white space where the kaleidoscope of my thoughts usually lived, letting her take hold of my hands as she started to chant: a whirl of words, long and lyrical and almost alien; the soft cadences and guttural breath of the ancient form of Gaelic she used. I was aware of Luca, looking on as the others worked, keeping a watchful eye on the proceedings, long legs stretched out along the sofa as he stared. The Dog sat at his feet, watching just as intently, her narrow face tucked into the curl of her tail.

As the Morrigan's words intensified, as her language turned in on itself, I felt strands of my hair lifting, floating into the air, like they always did when spells were being worked. I began to understand individual words, thrown up like offerings into my consciousness: matrona, Cauldron, crone, and a bizarre phrase that my brain translated as 'river of knowledge'.

As she worked, I became aware of changes in my body. Not just the flyaway hair that needed a hefty dose of Frizz-Ease, but of more subtle changes. A nagging ache in my left hip. A gnarling of my fingers, and a cracking sound when I clenched them into a fist. A slight fuzzing of the words flowing around me, like I was hearing them through cotton wool buds stuffed into my ears. Luca and The Dog became more hazy, and I had to squint to see them properly: Luca, now alert and perched on the edge of the sofa, leaning forward to stare at me intently. The Dog with her ears pricked, sniffing the air as though searching for a familiar scent. Whatever they were seeing, it wasn't me.

The Morrigan became quiet, and stood back to survey her work. She looked me over, and nodded once in satisfaction. Even though she was close, I still couldn't see her clearly – she was just a huge outline, a blur of red hair, my mind filling in the dots of her appearance.

'It is done,' she finally said. 'You are the Crone.'

That, I realised, standing up and planning to find a mirror pretty damn sharpish, didn't sound good. I knew about the three stages of the Goddess's being – the Maiden, the Mother, and the Crone. I was guessing that my real self was still firmly rooted in the land of the Maiden, and my future self was the Crone. Luckily she'd skipped over Mother, or we might have had some very inconvenient extra complications to deal with.

As I got to my feet, the nagging ache in my hip sent a jarring pain searing down my thigh, making me stagger slightly. I looked down at my hands, and saw wrinkles and creases and liver spots that hadn't been there minutes before. My knuckles were swollen and twisted, and felt sore whenever I closed my fingers.

I didn't just look like the Crone, I bloody well felt like her – and it wasn't nice. My mind involuntarily skipped back to Coleen in the hospital in Liverpool, lying on her deathbed, hooked up to monitors and fighting for every breath: her papery skin and bird-like bones, fragile and weak and twisted. The rasping sound of lungs that didn't want to work any more. The way she'd always held the small of her back as she made a cup of tea. The reading glasses she kept by her bed, alongside a bottle of Gaviscon. The paraphernalia of an ageing body.

A stray song title sang its way across my mind: the Inspiral Carpets, and This Is How It Feels. Except I didn't feel lonely – not any more than usual anyway. I just felt . . . old. And tired. And battered by decades of life that my body hadn't even lived. It was a cheat, a fast forward, and it made everything ache, even my teeth. If I still had teeth, I thought, running my tongue around the inside of my mouth to search for dentures. No. I'd been spared that, at least. Just a couple of unexpected holes where a demon dentist had yanked a couple out.

Luca was smirking at me, and I glared at him as hard as I could. I suspected it didn't look especially threatening, not coming as it did with a short-sighted squint, and from eyes that were milky with untreated cataracts. The Dog ambled over, licking my fingers, and I stroked her head as smoothly as I could with my arthritic hand.

I walked – very slowly, aware of every painful step as the sciatica kicked in on full – to the hallway, where there was a full length mirror. My steps were hesitant, as my feet appeared to have shrunk half a size, my toes swishing slightly towards the end of my Docs.

I gazed at myself in the mirror. Even knowing what I was going to see, it was a shock. It was still me – still recognisably my face – but so much older. My skin was puckered and lined, sagging around my eyes as I squinted at my own reflection. My hair – which I'd always thought of as glossy and white and luminous – was dulled down to a yellowing shade of grey, clinging lankly to the sides of my puffy face. My body was almost the same, but with rounded shoulders and an extra bit in the middle that I wasn't at all keen on. A bit that almost met my boobs as they drooped downwards. My legs were skinnier, the material of my leggings creasing at the knees, and felt so horribly weak. I reached out, leaned against the wall for support. Uggh. If this was old age, I'd be giving some consideration to Kurt Cobain's famous 'burn out don't fade away' quote, if not his chosen method of fulfilling it.

'Please tell me this is only temporary,' I said, my voice emerging with a wheeze. The Morrigan, standing behind me and meeting my eyes in the glass, nodded. 'It's only temporary,' she agreed. 'But it is real. It is your future.'

Huh. That sucked. How come she and Gabriel got to prance around for hundreds of years still looking – and presumably feeling – so good? How come if I was a Goddess, I got lumbered with a bad back and hearing aids? I was starting to feel slightly panicky, and was grateful for the distraction when Carmel arrived, burdened down with a pile of clothes.

She skipped down the final few steps with annoying agility, and skidded to a dead stop in front of me. She froze there, and stared, mouth hanging open. For a moment I thought she'd laugh, but one look at my face choked it off in her throat. Which was a good thing, because if she'd so much as gurgled, I'd have been doing some choking of my own. Assuming that my raddled old hands would let me.

'I found this stuff in the cleaning closet,' she said, dumping the heap at my feet, blinking at me once, then turning and fleeing in the opposite direction. Traitor.

I leaned down to rummage through the pile, and stopped abruptly when my back seized up. I froze where I was, clutching at myself as the pain rushed through me, then straightened up, very slowly.

'A little help, please?' I said, drawing in deep breaths to try and calm myself. Jesus. If this carried on I wouldn't need to worry about Fergal Fitzgarry – I'd be checking myself into one of his care homes and overdosing on morphine just for kicks.

The Morrigan squatted down, and emerged a few moments later with an old-fashioned pinafore decorated with faded sunflowers. It looked old and frazzled and like it had been through the wash a couple of hundred times. Which made it absolutely perfect for the way I was feeling. She helped me tug it on over my own clothes, and tied the ribbons snugly around my pot belly. All that Guinness had finally caught up with me, I thought, making a silent vow to pay a lot more attention to my physical fitness once all this was over. Nothing like a glimpse of your decrepit future-self to get you reaching for the green tea and a gym membership.

She tugged my hair back into a loose pony, and used a headscarf to wrap it all up, a few greying strands straggling out. I struggled into a thick plaid jacket over the top, the cuffs turned over and one of the buttons missing. The only footwear on offer was a pair of battered tartan slippers, which I kicked aside. There was looking like an old cleaning lady, and there was looking like a mad old cleaning lady – and I wasn't quite ready to add 'borderline senile' to my list of attributes. I kept my Docs on instead, which had always proved to be a good option in the past.

'You look like the domestic,' said the Morrigan, surveying my hunched form and my gloriously chic outfit. 'And now you will be walking the dog. Go past the deli on the corner, and over to the play park. We'll find you there. And don't forget your poo bags.'

She handed me the lead – The Dog on the other end of it, sniffing it suspiciously – and thrust a wad of shiny black plastic bags into my hand. Wow. My transformation was now complete. I felt like I should be scooping myself up into one of those bags. I checked the pockets in the front of the pinny for my essentials – cash, passport, magic mirror, that kind of thing – before I set off.

As I approached the front door, I saw Gabriel watching me from the top of the stairs. I felt a blast of pure anguish wrenching through me like a tornado of utter patheticness, and a blush fired up over my papery cheeks. I looked hideous. And I didn't want him to see me like this. I huddled deeper into the jacket, and walked outside without a second glance or a word of farewell.

I crossed through the courtyard, and out onto the street – after a frustrating battle with the lock on the gate, which my useless sausage fingers had real problems with. The Dog walked placidly by my side, and I said a quick prayer that she wouldn't notice a sweet wrapper or a Canada goose or some other passing goody, and go belting after it – I'd break a hip if I went over, I knew. My whole creaking body was having an Osteoporosis Party, and I added calcium supplements to my list of essential supplies.

Outside, life went on as normal. Smokers sat outside cafes, clutching espressos and tapping ash into trays; groups of bright young things trooped along the pavements four abreast, parting for me – the anonymous old lady – without any kind of acknowledgement. Cars streamed past, off to destinations unknown. Music blared from corner bars, blasts of heat clouding into the frigid evening air. The sound of the subway rumbled up beneath my feet as a train shot through, rattling the pavement.

I tried not to look around suspiciously as I walked – if Fitzgarry's men were watching the house, they wouldn't have seen me stepping out. They'd have seen an old lady, frail and careworn, exercising a dog.

I realised within seconds that it was the perfect disguise. Nobody gives the elderly a second glance in our world. They are anonymous, and boring, and of no interest at all unless they get in your way, block the road, or hit you with a shopping trolley in the supermarket. I suddenly understood why the legions of grey panthers we all encountered in our busy lives seemed so grumpy – they'd been young once. Full of themselves and their own concerns. Then, in what must have felt like the blink of an eye, they were relegated to the ranks of the unimportant. It was crappy, and I even started to mutter to myself as I walked, holding myself tight and careful as small crowds headed towards me, scared that the smallest of bumps would result in a new collection of support bandages.

We made it to the park, which was quiet and deserted in the gloom, and I let The Dog off her lead. I expected her to run and swoop and leap as she normally did, but she seemed to sense my need, and stayed with me. I lowered myself cautiously down onto a bench, shivering in the cold, and she settled at my feet. I was slightly winded after ten whole minutes of walking at a Snail Olympics pace, and took a few heavy breaths, looking around me at the shadowed form of slides and round-abouts and swings swaying spookily in the breeze.

I was in a strange body, in a strange park, in a strange land. And it all felt strangely normal.

Now I just had to wait. In the cold, and the dark, in my shrivelled old body, and hope they didn't forget about me, like the rest of the world already had.

Chapter Twenty-One

Luca eventually rescued me from my solitude a short
while later. I can't say with any certainty how much later,
as I seemed to have dosed off. When he gently shook me
awake, I had drool hanging from the corner of my mouth
and a crick in my neck. I also needed to pee with an
urgency that I'd never experienced before in my entire
life.

Luca is, given his nature, never exactly hot – in the
sense of body temperature at least – but he did hug me
to him, shielding me from the sharp wind that was now
howling through the open field of the park, swirling litter
and ruffling the longer grass that was growing near the
bench.

'Time to move, *bella*,' he said, standing up and holding
out his hands to help me to my feet. My whole body
creaked and moaned in protest, and I found myself
clinging onto him as he hoisted me elegantly up onto
aching legs. I made a loud 'oof' noise as I wavered there,
one hand immediately going to my back.

'Jesus, this is awful,' I muttered, clenching my knees
together as my need for the loo became overwhelming.
I was genuinely scared I might have a small accident,
without my Tena Lady to hand.

'Ageing is a natural part of human life, Lily,' he replied, a soft smile shining from his face. Yeah. Right. I was supposed to take that kind of platitude from a centuries old supermodel, while I danced around on my achey breaky legs?

'What the fuck would you know about it?' I snapped, brushing his hands aside and heading towards a small shed-like building that I really hoped was a toilet. Seriously, I'd betray the whole world in exchange for two minutes alone with a nice clean facility.

'It's not exactly your specialist subject, is it, Luca? You've not aged a day since you were – what, thirty?'

'Twenty-nine, to be precise,' he replied, following behind me, close, presumably in case I took a tumble or tripped over a passing centipede. 'And that was not through choice. It was never a choice I would have made.'

Hmmm. I wanted to snark back at him about that one – I mean, the way I was feeling? It didn't exactly fill me with generosity of spirit towards the eternally young, fit and gorgeous. But I held it in – partly because I was too excited at the prospect of relieving my eight-hundred-year-old bladder, and partly because he sounded kind of sad. I didn't know his whole story, but I knew he'd been married. Had children. All of whom he had potentially watched wither and die. Even as pissed off as I was, that wasn't a subject to carp about.

I fumbled with the door for what felt like several hours before Luca silently reached past and pulled it aside for me. I nodded at him, then made a shooing gesture. There are some things that a lady – even a lady of advanced years – prefers to do alone.

Following possibly the most blissful few minutes of my life – which is tragic but true – Luca led me and The Dog back out to the other side of the park, where I almost cried with joy at the sight of one of our cars. It was long, it was sleek, it was black. But most of all it had heating.

I curled up in the seat next to him, holding my crinkle-cut fingers in front of the vents as he started up the engine.

'Gabriel has gone,' he said. 'To the sidhe.'

A sidhe, I knew, was their term for a sacred hill – a kind of fairy portal that offered a route into the Otherworld, for those who knew how to use it. Or, for those of us who didn't, a place to get kidnapped by scary pixies and bundled into an alternate reality. The Otherworld – the Land of the Young – was blissful. As long as you wanted to be there, and kept your eyes wide shut to the fact that, if you didn't, it was a manicured jail cell set out like a country park.

It was the home of Fintan and the Faidh – boo, hiss – and also to my parents and the sisters I'd never known – hurrah. A complicated kind of place. I'd been there – see earlier veiled reference to kidnappings – but only for a small amount of time. The thing is, time in the Otherworld doesn't work like time here on our world. Even minutes there can stretch into hours on the mortal plain. For me, that would mean ageing at a heart-wrenching pace – if I stayed there too long, I'd come back out looking like this for good. For Gabriel, though, who was part mortal and part weird, it was like stepping from one existence that welcomed him to another. Brass bands and doughnuts wherever he went.

'What about the others?' I asked, wondering where they'd all gone. Luca himself used to view the Otherworld as paradise, as it was also the home of his God, Donn. Since Donn had cast him aside – and since he'd landed in the general direction of me – I presumed that it now held little allure, apart from being a sad reminder of all that he'd lost. Of a time when he had friends and a community and knew his place in life, rather than being the butt of Gabriel's jokes and my very finely buffed lapdog.

'They all left at different times, using different doors. Kevin is still in the house, with all the lights on, finding out about Fitzgarry. And . . .'

He glanced at me from the corner of his eye as he manoeuvred past a parked fire truck. Still worried, obviously. Still unwarranted.

'And getting rid of Colin,' I finished for him. He nodded, and stayed quiet as we navigated our way through Soho, past thronging crowds and brightly lit shops and side streets packed with restaurants. Down Broadway, and over to Trinity Place, where he parked the car in a spot about two inches longer than the vehicle itself.

'We'll stay here for a while,' he said, keeping the engine running and the heating flowing. 'You know how it is. He'll be a while yet. Maybe you could . . . take a nap?'

I examined his face for evidence of smirkiness, but found none. Which was good, because I really was feeling tired again. If he'd been winding me up, I'd have argued, out of sheer, stupid bloody mindedness. Instead, I allowed him to recline the seat for me, The Dog hunkering down in the back, and let myself drift off for a few minutes. I had a momentary panic when I remembered the drool incident from earlier, and wondered if I might snore like a freight train, then decided I didn't care. One of the small joys of getting older, I supposed – just not giving a fuck any more. Nap time was nap time – and ugliness didn't come into it.

I presumably drooled and bellowed my way into the Land of Nod for an hour or so before I woke up with a bad case of heartburn. Luca was reclined next to me, one arm thrown over my body, staring intently at my face as I came to. I stayed still for a moment – mainly because I was too stiff to move – and stared back at him. I'd often, in silent, possibly drunken moments, imagined waking up next to Luca. But in none of those imaginings had I been gagging for a Rennie and wondering if magical fairy mounds came equipped with portaloos.

'Welcome back, princess,' he said, reaching out and clearing a strand of stringy hair away from my face. 'Ready to go find our comrades and kick some evil ass?'

'Uggh,' I said, swallowing down a fiery mouthful of acid-ridden saliva, 'not feeling like much of a princess right now. And unless the evil ass plants itself right by my foot, I don't hold out much hope for the kicking either. Give me a minute to make sure all my bones are working, all right?'

After I aligned my various aching body parts well enough to move, we got out of the car again. It was night time, and freezing cold, but New York didn't disappoint – lit up and sparkling as we walked down through the building sites around Ground Zero. I kept my guards up and taut as we edged past the memorials, past the missing towers and the new towers, past the river of human emotion that surrounded it all. It was tragic, and magnificent, all at the same time – the new life and the new memories being built around the old, moving on but not forgetting.

Luca stayed quiet, holding my hand as he led me, slowing his pace to match mine as we headed to the Hudson River waterfront. The Dog silently padded along beside us, her black coat almost disappearing in the night.

I had no idea where we were going, or where we'd find a sidhe in the middle of one of the biggest cities in the world. If there was a sidhe in New York, though, the good news was that it probably came complete with a Starbucks and a pretzel van.

Instead, we arrived at what looked like a dark corridor leading into a man-made hill. At least I assumed it was man-made. Surrounded by towers and bank headquarters and brightly lit hotels, the noise of traffic roaring into the nearby tunnels, we walked into the passageway – and entered an entirely different world.

Not the Otherworld – but a different one, for sure. An ancient looking ramshackle cottage was in front of us, made of ruined stone and covered in creeping plants, casting shadows over the path. There was grass and flowers and a wild wind blowing through it all, whistling up the hill to a solitary, weather-worn standing stone. Alongside the path were rocks, each inscribed with the name of an Irish county. I saw Dublin, and Clare, and Mayo, and countless others. Despite the lights and the noise and the buildings around us, it felt like a tiny piece of forgotten rural Ireland had been transplanted here, a moment in time in the midst of modern chaos.

'Is this real?' I asked Luca, as we ambled along the pathway. 'It doesn't feel real. It feels . . . peaceful.'

'It's real,' he replied. 'It's the Irish Hunger Memorial. So many died and so many came here, to their New World. This is a tribute, to them, to their old home and their new home. That's what you feel, Lily.'

I reached out, let my gnarled old fingers brush against the rough stone, the tufts of dark heather around it. He was right. It might be a modern construction, but it was ancient emotion: hope and despair and pain and anguish and optimism all wrapped up together.

I reached the peak of the hill, and the city unleashed itself again: the most amazing view of the Statue of Liberty, torch aloft in the night sky, the beacon glimmering over the rippling surface of the river; Ellis Island beyond.

I gazed out, lost for words, not to mention short of breath. Being here, trapped in this old body, made me feel everything . . . more. Made me realise how precious it all was, each and every moment of life; each and every moment of every life.

I heard footsteps coming up behind me, and knew without turning that it was him. Gabriel. He murmured something to Luca, and I heard more footsteps. Then

Gabriel, next to me, an arm around my shoulder, gently holding me as though he thought I might break.

'It's beautiful, isn't it?' he said, kissing me softly on the side of my head. 'It always was.'

There was something in his tone that I'd heard before: wistful and worried and guarded. He'd been to the Otherworld. He'd found things out. Things that he didn't immediately want to tell me. I knew he'd get there in the end – but only in his own time. I leaned into his embrace, wanting for just a moment to forget everything that had happened in the last few hours. To forget that Colin was dead; that I was old, that Gabriel was angry with me.

'You've been here before?' I asked, knowing even as I asked that he had. Of course he had. He'd been everywhere.

'Yes,' he answered, turning me around to look back down at the hill. 'It was near here that we first arrived. The Battery. 1846. Sad times.'

'We?' I said, wondering who he'd been here with. There was so much about him I still didn't know. So much experience in there, hidden in his mind, waiting to be shared. We just never seemed to sit still long enough to get around to it. Maybe, I thought, you had to make time – before you got old and broke your hip on the way to have your blood pressure checked, you had to make time. To live in moments like these, with people like this.

'Yes. We. Me and Molly. Molly O'Shaugnessy.'

'Ah,' I said, trying out a smile and finding that it didn't break my face. 'German, was she?'

He smiled back, but it didn't quite reach his eyes. He was stroking the creviced skin of my hand, and I pulled it away. Still not quite ready to be that much of a cougar.

'Don't be silly,' he said, grabbing it back again. 'Do you think the way you look changes how I feel about you? Do you think I've never seen a woman I love age before?'

'Molly again?' I asked, forcing myself to leave my hand where it was.

'Molly, yes. Others, since then. But she was the first one I loved. Or thought I loved. You can't imagine how intense life was then, Lily. The famine. The death. It chased people here, and when they arrived, they weren't always welcome. The squalor was unimaginable, the poverty, the disease. Hard to picture it now, I know. But I watched Molly get old, and I watched her die, and she was one of the lucky ones – she lived until her fifties. We lived together, in the old Five Points, in one of the tenements.'

I tried hard but, he was right, I couldn't picture it. Not because I didn't have the right frames of reference, but because I just couldn't place him – the High King – in the middle of it all.

'I was rebelling,' he said, noting my confusion. 'I ran away from home, decided to live like a mortal for a while. I didn't always take my sacred duty quite as seriously as I should, you know? I was young once. A long time ago.'

He still only looked like a man in his early thirties, in the prime of his life, but I knew that wasn't the truth. That he had centuries on me, even as the Crone.

'Well,' I answered, 'that's good to know. I'm kind of comforted by the fact that you were fucked-up once as well. Maybe you'll bear that in mind next time I am. And one day, you can take me there – show me the places, tell me the stories. Share it all with me. Even if I am a tiny bit jealous of Molly. But for now – what did you find out? What's going on?'

He nodded, face serious, the wistful yearning of moments ago suddenly gone. All-business Gabriel was back, and he had news.

'Fintan is gone. Kevin's found out some interesting things. We have protection on the way.'

Three short, sharp sentences, and a gaping hole of actual information.

'Is that all?' I asked, looking up at him, his face half illuminated by the city lights and half hidden in shadow. Because I didn't think it was. I sensed there was more, that he was trying to somehow keep me half hidden in shadow as well.

'That's all,' he said abruptly, turning and walking away, back down the path, towards the stone cottage that was forever crumbling, lost in time.

'Now come on,' he shouted. 'Let's get you fixed.'

Chapter Twenty-Two

'Edwin Booth,' said Gabriel, gesturing to the statue in front of us. It looked kind of Roman or Greek, a bloke with bare legs, draped in robes. 'He was the most famous actor of his day. Slightly overshadowed by the fact that his brother killed Abraham Lincoln.'

'Bummer,' I replied, gazing at the statue, but slightly distracted by the fact that my body was gloriously young again. I was still wearing the cleaning lady's pinny and coat, but the rest of me was back. I kept stretching out my legs in front of me, enjoying the feeling of strength and solidity, and fighting hard to resist the urge to simply get up and run around. Just because I could. It must be how The Dog felt all the time – wanting to use her magnificent body for sheer pleasure. She was using it right then, doing unspeakable things in the shrubbery.

Not that I was magnificent, of course. I was still just me. But I was me minus the sciatica, the arthritis and the puny bladder. That was good enough for the time being, and I vowed I'd never moan again about not getting any physical superpowers from the whole Goddess deal. I had questions to ask – along the lines of 'so, do I age like a normal person or do I turn into the Crone when I'm five hundred years old?' – but they could wait for now.

For now, I was thrilled to be able to get up without cringing.

We'd left the memorial and headed all the way back up Broadway, through Soho and Noho and past the Village, to Gramercy Park. It was a strange place, New York – the way you could cross over one street and be in a whole different type of neighbourhood. Like the way Little Italy became Chinatown with the few steps it took to breach Canal Street, the red-and-white check table cloths and Sopranos-style restaurants suddenly overtaken by herbalists and ducks hanging in windows on strings.

This place was different again – and it screamed money. Seriously, it practically hung its head out of the window and yelled 'everyone who lives here is loaded'. Or at least it would have, if it hadn't been so terribly classy. Wide streets, achingly dignified townhouses, and lots of wealthy looking people with fur coats and poodles. And right in the middle of it, this – a tiny key park with a statue of the 'good' Booth brother at its heart.

We were here because Fitzgarry's home was here. Kevin had found out where he lived – in one of those swanky brownstones surrounding the park. He'd also found out that Fitzgarry, who had already made his fortune several times over, had recently announced his decision to retire. It felt out of character: men who came from nothing and made millions were rarely laid back enough to decide to pack it all in so they could go rambling at the weekend. But he'd already reduced his working hours, and declared that he was intending to concentrate on 'spiritual concerns' in the near future.

An assumption had been made, given his heritage and history, that he'd become more involved in the various Catholic churches and charities he already donated to – but I had the not-so-much-sneaking-as-punching-me-in-the-face suspicion that his spiritual concerns were more to do with ancient gods, creepy one-eyed warriors, and the annihilation of Life As We Know It. Not to mention sucking me up through a sippy straw.

We'd also been told that he was out tonight, at a charity function on the Upper East Side, and Gabriel had decided he wanted to come here. To see his lair. To get a feel for the foe we were facing, the foe who was probably working alongside Fintan, and collecting all those souls for some no doubt nefarious purpose. I loved that word, nefarious. And funnily enough, I'd actually had reason to use it in the last few months of my life in ways it actually fit much better than traffic wardens and people who pushed in front of you in the chippy.

Gabriel was staring up at one of the apartment buildings around the park, and Carmel and Finn were mooching around somewhere, doing something warrior-like and scary while we sat, and stared, and thought.

Fitzgarry had the entire top floor, and his lights were on. I became convinced that he was in there, watching us, and was torn between that delicious anger I'd felt earlier and, well, plain old terror. I wanted to slit his throat – but I had to figure out a way of getting close enough to do it without him draining me like he had in his office. I was the spirit incarnate of a mega-powerful, millennia old being – allegedly – and stuffed full of power. But he'd tapped into that with so much ease. I had no idea if he'd be able to do that if I was ready for him, if there was some way I could guard against it. I could really do with one of Fionnula's slightly-drunk master-classes right then – she was an expert in setting up barriers and protecting her territory.

'What do you think he's doing?' I asked. 'And how does it involve Fintan? And what's going on with this Balor dude? And why can't we, you know, just sneak into his flat up there and kill him? Plant a bomb or something?'

Gabriel dragged his eyes away from the shining

windows and looked at me, with that slightly delayed reaction you get when someone's just yanked you out of some very intense thoughts. I felt it again: that instinct that told me he was hiding something, and shivered. Gabriel was good at hiding things, and they often involved me. My words finally registered through his mental Eurovision-results satellite lag, and he managed a smile.

'What, you want to go up there with a cannonball with a fuse sticking out of it? Really?'

I nodded. It didn't seem that crazy. Always worked in Loony Tunes, and my life wasn't so very different.

'This Balor "dude", as you call him,' he said, 'could mean the end. If the stories are right, and the prophecy holds, then we could be defeated. I'm still not sure how the rest of it fits together, and that's what we need to know – I'm going to get you as far away from him as possible, but we can't kill him until we know what he's done, who he's done it with, and how far he's got. So far we know Fitzgarry has been catching souls. There are legends, ancient spells, that tell of the dead being resurrected through the power of sacrifice. That could be why he's doing it – and why he wants you.'

Yeah. I'd managed to piece all of that together with my own lightning powers of deduction. I was like a super-sized Big Mac meal to Fitzgarry, and everyone else was half a chicken nugget. The issue was: how did we stop him? If we weren't going with the devious fizz-bomb plan?

'The issue is,' I said, as I had that handy question ready, 'how do we stop him? And what is Fintan getting out of all of this? And what is it that you're not telling me?'

Gabriel's head swivelled sharply towards me, his eyes shining in the hazily lit night sky. His hand had been lying loosely on my thigh, and I felt his fingers clench with a small, sharp tang of pain.

'Nothing,' he said. 'There's nothing I'm not telling you. Right now, you have to trust me.'

I stared back up at him, knowing he'd see all manner of doubt flitting across my face, and being absolutely fine with that. Because if I had to compile a top ten list of Gabriel's all-time favourite phrases, that would be right up there: you have to trust me. Sometimes I did, sometimes I didn't. This was falling into the latter category, but there wasn't much I could do to change that. Our relationship was so up and down it looked like one of those graphs at the end of a lie detector, and right now, it was definitely in a trough.

Before we could get embroiled in one of our lovely chats about it, I saw Gabriel look up and away to the side of the park. His body language was sharp and alert, and his head was tilted at an angle that reminded me of The Dog when she was on the scent of something interesting. Like a dead bird. A quick glance in her direction showed me that she was doing exactly the same: they were clearly hearing something that I wasn't.

'What is it?' I asked, as Gabriel got to his feet and gazed off into the near distance.

'Someone's coming,' he replied, his stance changing to something even harder. I jumped up and stood next to him, looking off in the same direction and seeing nothing but shadow. I strained my ears, and then heard it: the tiny rattle of a key in a lock, the whine of a gate swinging on its hinges. The sound of someone else letting themselves into the park. Using the traditional method rather than the flicky-finger magic that Gabriel had come up with.

I glanced up at Fitzgarry's building. Saw the lights on. Reminded myself that he was supposed to be at some charity function. Decided to ignore that and, instead, focused on throwing all of my power into erecting as strong a shield around myself as I could. If it was him, I was going to need it. If it was some late night dog walker bringing Fido for a final pee, I was going to laugh my arse off.

Gabriel stood in front of me, and The Dog ran over, winding her sinuous body around my unsteady legs like a vine, ears flat to her head. I heard movement elsewhere in the park: Carmel and Finn responding to the potential threat, I was sure.

I sucked in my breath, and tried to shut them all out. Gabriel was here. He was strong, he was a warrior with shitloads of experience at fighting off supernatural bad guys. My Champion was here. Finn was here. And Gabriel had said we had protection on the way. It wouldn't be the same as it had been in Fitzgarry's office – but I was determined I wouldn't be reliant on them alone. I had my own strength, my own power, even if I had no idea how to use it most of the time. It was a bit like having a loaded gun and not knowing how to switch the safety off: vaguely comforting but potentially useless.

There was a slight shifting in the currents of the air around me, the gentle flap of wings, and I looked up to see the Morrigan circling overhead. In her crow form, obviously – though it would be even more intimidating to see her flying around as a brick-shithouse human in leather. I thought she'd gone back to the house on Ash Street with Luca, like Gabriel had told her to – but she was never very good at doing what she was told. Especially by Gabriel, whom she still regarded as a pup who'd failed his training classes.

We all stared at the path leading from the gate to our bench, and if someone had decided to come along and randomly drop a pin, we'd have heard it.

After a few tense moments, a small figure emerged, strolling towards us. It was short. It was wearing slippers. And it was *him*.

Fitzgarry was here. With me. In the very unimpressive flesh.

I felt a surge of emotion flood through me, so sharp and so intense I thought it might shoot out of my fingertips like a flame-thrower. I felt scared, yes, especially with the smell of sour cider wafting out from him, but more than that I felt the steadfast fury I'd had earlier: he was here. This man who'd carved up Colin like he meant nothing. This man who was draining the life out of people he was supposed to be caring for. This man who'd tried to do the same to me. I'd had even less life experience than Colin had, and I'd be screwed if I was going to give up now.

I pushed forward, shoving at Gabriel's back with as much strength as I had – which unfortunately wasn't enough in the face of that immovable object. I tried kicking him in the back of his calves, but he just reached behind me with one ever-growing arm and gripped my shoulder, holding me still.

'Be calm, and remember his power,' he whispered, shoving me backwards so I fell onto the bench. I sat there, winded and angry and at the same time realising that he was right, which made me even angrier. If I wanted to avenge Colin's death, getting sucked up by a slipper-wearing tycoon wasn't the way to do it. So I stayed calm, and I stayed still, and I concentrated once more on shoring up the barrier around me. I needed to get safe before I could get even.

The Dog was on full alert, standing in front of me, long tail erect and pointing, teeth baring and glinting in the darkness. Gabriel had expanded to the size of an oil tanker on legs, and the Morrigan was swishing frantically around my head. Carmel and Finn were out there, too, I reminded myself – and they weren't to be messed with.

'My, my,' said Fitzgarry, coming to a halt before us. 'If I'd known you were coming, I'd have baked a cake! So lovely to see you again, Miss McCain. And your so impressive friend.'

He glanced at Gabriel, twice his size, and smiled, showing a small row of tiny teeth. Most people would have dissolved into a pool of jelly after seeing the High King in battle mode – but the stealer of souls was made of sterner stuff. After all, he thought he had Balor on his side, and was well into delivering a plan that he probably assumed would leave him as the Master of the Universe. I really, really wanted to stab him.

He took a step towards me, and Gabriel blocked him with a fractional shift of his body. The Dog started to snarl and growl, a blood-curdling sound that I'd never heard from her before. I reached down and patted her head, my eyes never leaving Fitzgarry.

'I thought you were busy tonight, Mr Fitzgarry,' I said. 'Saving the world one charity gala at a time.'

I sounded much calmer than I felt – I was going for dignified-under-pressure, Princess Leia in the Death Star torture room. Stupid angle really, considering how that turned out for Alderaan.

'Well, what can I say? There are only so many canapes one man can tolerate. I sent a representative instead. Was planning a quiet night in until I smelled a delicious aroma wafting up from this park. You really are quite exquisite, Miss McCain. Unmistakable. So I thought I'd pop down and pay my . . . respects.'

He glanced up at the bird flying overhead, and his face creased into a smile. That alone was terrifying. He must have known who it was – and this was a creature who could make Gabriel and his mighty chums drop to the dirt and grovel whenever she wanted. Fitzgarry didn't seem phased at all, which was worrisome.

Gabriel was strangely silent, massive and menacing, but quiet. Apparently he was using the power of telepathy to get the answers to all those questions he had. Or maybe he was just feeling shy.

'What do you want, Fitzgarry? And how did killing

Colin help you achieve that?' I said, grateful for the sensation of The Dog's lean muscle leaning into my much weaker muscle. It felt like she was sending me strength, as though I could feel it oozing up my shaking legs.

He edged forward an inch, reaching out with one leather-gloved hand, and she snapped at the air in front of him, snarling. He snatched his hand back, and looked maybe one per cent less arrogant than he had before. Go Dog. The soul stealer was obviously a cat person.

'Well, I thought I'd made that clear – I want you, Miss McCain. And you can surround yourself with as much muscle as you like, but I will eventually have you. You will be sacrificed for a greater cause.'

'You mean the greater cause of Balor?' I asked, hoping for one of those bad-guy-confesses-all-at-critical-moment scenarios. It always worked in the movies.

He raised one sandy eyebrow, and smiled.

'Ah,' he replied. 'I see you have figured out my dastardly secret. Yes. Balor. He will return, and this world will change. The balance of power will shift, life as we know it will never be the same. And I will be, well, also never the same. And as for Colin – well, that was just for fun. All work and no play makes—'

'You an evil fucker?' I finished for him, clenching my fists so hard I was stabbing my own palms with my fingernails.

'I was already an evil fucker, as you so politely put it, Miss McCain. Now, perhaps we should get down to business? You know I want you. You might as well come now – it will all end the same no matter how much you struggle. And I'm sure you don't want any more of your friends getting hurt, do you? There are only so many eyes to go round, after all.'

Kevin. He was talking about Kevin, who'd lost an eye after fighting on my behalf. Kevin didn't seem at all bothered by it, but I still cringed inside every time I looked at him. Fitzgarry was pressing my buttons – just for kicks.

Gabriel had been looking marginally distracted, still blocking him with the bulk of his body, but not engaging in the conversation. Usually, if I was under any kind of threat, we had that whole 'I-will-die-before-you-harm-her' deal going on; mucho drama and even more machismo. This time, he was quiet, cautious, while I yapped away.

In a way I was relieved. Part of me, the part that was obviously mentally challenged, wanted to test myself against him. Against this creature, evil incarnate in bedroom slippers. My barriers were strong – I could feel them encasing me like invisible armour – and I wanted to know just how strong.

Somewhere – off in another universe – a siren wailed and there was the sound of glass shattering. Gramercy Park might be posh, but it was still in New York, after all.

'You will not be touching her, Fitzgarry,' said Gabriel, finally breaking his silence. Gabriel loomed over him, the solid block of his form casting a huge shadow that completely engulfed Fitzgarry from his toes to his sandy head. His voice was more Irish than usual, and his eyes visibly sparked in the darkness of the night. 'She is the Goddess, and she will remain the Goddess. You are nothing, and you will remain nothing.'

Fitzgarry looked up, craning his neck so he could meet Gabriel's gaze.

'You seem very confident, High King. Considering that so far in this game, I have been the winner. I wonder why you are so confident?'

I was wondering the same, too, until I heard the sound of a voice reaching out from the distance.

'Because we are here,' it said.

The air in the park seemed to shift and shimmer, like electrical currents were whirling through the night sky.

A couple of the lights were fluttering on and off, so maybe I wasn't totally wrong on that front.

Hathor strode forward towards us. She'd passed up on the ceremonial robes and opted for black skinny jeans and a dark sweater, but she still had the sinister golden eye placed firmly on her head. It swivelled in its metal socket, looked at Fitzgarry, and blinked once, very slowly.

Hathor was followed by Frigga, and my old pal Sven the Elk Eater, who came up to the same size as the shrubbery but would probably be a dab hand at ankle-slashing. All around us, one by one, the others appeared, emerging from the shadows to gather together at the feet of Edwin Booth: Olu, tall and strong, his dark face hidden, with Beryl at his side. Nahuel, still bare-chested and apparently immune to the chill December air. Naira, holding a bow erect in her hands and still managing to look as though she didn't like me. Seriously. There she was, presumably to protect and serve as part of the NY Paranormal Department, and she was still glaring. Mean Girl syndrome.

Over to my right, completing the circle, was Honi. I knew he was the more important of the two, but my eyes still fled automatically to Katashi at his side. He smiled, teeth bright, and nodded slightly in my direction. Kind of against my will, I smiled back, feeling a little tightening in my tummy. Hey. I'm an Earth Goddess. Which means there's always time to lech.

I studied them, following Fitzgarry's flickering gaze from one face to another. I realised that away from the refined atmosphere of the stony townhouse on the Upper East Side, everyone looked wilder. More dangerous. Completely lethal, in fact.

Finn and Carmel edged into the group, faces serious and stances battle-ready. The Dog was still standing to attention, and Gabriel was staring at Fitzgarry with unmistakable blood lust in his shimmering eyes.

The gang was all here. And they were all on my side.

Chapter Twenty-Three

I could feel the ends of my hair floating, gently swirling in the air around my head like there was an invisible blow-dryer puffing it up. It was the magic, giving me a supernatural makeover again.

Beside Hathor was the good-looking younger bloke I'd seen Carmel getting cosy with back at the townhouse when we first met with the Council. Hathor's Champion, I knew, even though we'd never been formally introduced. He stared at me, intently, and the name Amophet floated into my mind. Amophet. He nodded once, message received, over and out. His face was carved from the same golden wood as Carmel's, his nose the same slightly hooked shape, his whisky coloured eyes illuminated by the flickering lights overhead. He could be Carmel's brother, in a different world – one where she wasn't a Super Scouse O'Grady and he wasn't the protector of a near-immortal supernatural being. Heck, for all I knew, he was her brother.

That, however, was a question for another day. The big question for this day was 'What happens next?'

Fitzgarry was turning in a slow, steady circle, his tiny slippered feet padding on damp leaves, looking at everyone individually. Like he was taking his time, assessing them, searching for strengths and weaknesses.

It kind of creeped me out – the fact that he didn't seem shocked or even a teensy bit scared. He still seemed calm and in control. He was surrounded by deadly foes and he still had a look on his face that said: yeah, right, bring it on – I still hold all the cards in this game.

'You will leave this place, unholy creature,' said Hathor, walking towards him, circlet eye blinking. 'And you will desist in all of your false claims on the Goddess.'

With every step she took, the ground seemed to tremble, sending slight ripples beneath my feet that made it feel like the earth was undulating. Like there was something under there swimming around, waiting to come out and eat us. I felt myself wobbling slightly from side to side, and held on to the bench for security.

She was now a few feet away from him, and her face was changing: a swirling, whirling blend of Hathor's own human features and those of her lion. Her hair looked huge around her head, golden fuzz flying off into the sky. I wondered if I was the only one seeing it, and glanced over at Carmel to check.

She raised her eyebrows at me, and clawed the air with imaginary claws, like the Cowardly Lion marking his territory. Good. Not just me then. Hallucinations are much more fun when you share them with a friend.

I turned back to Fitzgarry and Hathor, now slowly circling each other, both looking supremely confident. They were eyeing each other up, like they were about to break out backflips and have a dance-off.

'Or else what?' he finally said, standing still and folding his arms in front of his narrow chest. 'You'll send me home to bed without my supper? You think I fear you, any of you? You have no idea of my power. If I do not take her tonight, I will take her tomorrow – and I won't even have to try. I have something she wants, and she will find the exchange a fair one.'

I stared at him, still feeling the ground wobbling and

shaking beneath my Docs. He had something I wanted? What could that possibly mean? There was very little I wanted in life, apart from some peace and quiet. The few people I cared about were either dead or here with me and, unlike Madonna, I'd never been a Material Girl. The plus side of having lived the kind of life I had: there were very few strings he could pull on to try and control me.

Still, I frowned and tried to concentrate. Unless I was very much mistaken, this was all about to Kick Off Big Time, and any questions I had would be lost beneath the melodic sounds of screaming warriors, hacking flesh and Gabriel going big, bad wolf.

I pushed forward, past his monolithic body, and dashed towards Fitzgarry. Gabriel reached out to grab me back, holding me by the shoulders as I reached out. I knew he would, and knew I only had one brief moment to make contact. To touch him. To try and read him, see his future, find out more about what was going on. He wasn't going to tell us anything – he was too clever, and enjoying the game too much. But I had all of this power at my disposal, and wanted to at least try and use it.

As Gabriel growled and tugged me back towards him, I stretched out my arm, my hand, my fingertips – stretching, stretching, just far enough. I managed one fleeting touch, one finger pressed against the back of one hand, before I was slammed so firmly into Gabriel's heaving chest that I could barely breathe. His arms crushed around me, and I heard him cursing me under his breath in muttered Irish words that clearly meant 'Why me?'

It was only one moment – but it was enough. In that one moment, I saw it: I saw Fitzgarry, as he was going to be. His future. His face. A face with only one eye, burning and glowering beneath its vast, wrinkled lid. It was the same eye I'd seen in Brooklyn, the one that had scared me so much then – but it was also Fitzgarry. The 2 become 1, as the Spice Girls would have said.

As the image faded from my mind, I felt the familiar tingling in my scalp that told me I was heading for woo-woo land, a blurring in my vision that was usually the precursor of a ladylike swoon. I fought it off, ferociously clinging to both Gabriel and to consciousness. I didn't want to pass out now. I could wake up to find dismembered bodies lying around me. Or I could just not wake up at all, depending on how it went while I was snoozing.

'It's him,' I muttered, barely hearing my own words above the vicious buzzing in my ears, 'He's not trying to bring Balor back – he's going to *be* Balor . . . that's what he wants . . .'

Gabriel held me tight with one arm, knowing exactly what might come next if the power of the vision overcame me.

'Get her out of here!' he roared. 'Champion, do your job!'

I heard Fitzgarry laughing, miles away in the distance of the here and now, and shook my head to try and clear the red fog. I couldn't pass out now. I refused to pass out now. I would not be carted away from here like a bundle of cleaning rags, dragged away from danger while my friends faced it. If I could just stop the whirring noise and the red flashes in front of my eyes and the trembling, I'd be fine.

I opened my eyes as wide as I could, determined to keep them open, and looked up. Up into the night sky, cloudy with city fog and neon haze, stars distant and dim behind scudding purple clouds. I saw the crow, up there, circling and swooping and cawing. I heard my nan, Coleen, and the familiar words she'd rasped out on her deathbed: gerra grip, girl.

I got a grip. I breathed deep and hard, relishing the frosty gulps of air as they chilled my throat. Blinked, clearing away the lights. And finally, finally, managed to stand on my own two feet, still cloaked in Gabriel, but at the very least upright and conscious.

Hathor stared at me, and obviously judged that I was back in the land of the living. She nodded at me once, then raised her hands into the sky, screaming something foreign and incomprehensible as she did it. It must have been some kind of signal, because just then everybody seemed to move at once. There was a blur of bodies and sound, of feet pounding and swords unsheathing and bloodcurdling screams as they attacked, running towards Fitzgarry even as Carmel ran instead to me.

Gabriel passed me over to her, running into the melee, taller and bigger and louder than everyone else, clawed hands reaching for Fitzgarry, intent on ripping him limb from limb. So much for finding out more before we killed him, I thought. He never did think clearly when the battle rage was on him.

Carmel had hold of my shoulders, and was shaking me so hard I could feel my teeth rattle.

'Don't fall over, you dizzy cow!' she said, hissing the words at me. 'I don't want to carry you out of here – come on, get it together! We have to leave, now!'

I shrugged her hands from my body, and shoved her a few steps backwards.

'I'm fine – fuck off, will you? I need to help them. I need to do something. I need to—'

'You need to get the fuck out of here, and you're going to, whether you want to or not. I swear to God, Lily, if I have to knock you out I will . . .'

I glared at her, feeling a surge of . . . yep, hatred. It shocked me with how intense it was, that I could look at my best friend, my Champion, the girl who'd got me through lonely nights, awkward work situations, and ancient rituals at Tara, and feel that level of resentment. She took another step back, clearly seeing this alien force in my eyes, gulping in shock.

'I am the Goddess, and I will do as I wish,' I said, ignoring her spluttering and walking towards the whirling dervish in the centre of the park.

Fitzgarry stood at the heart of it all – somehow untouched. Gabriel was clawing at the air around him, roaring and screaming, his beautiful face contorted into something bloody and monstrous. Nahuel was hacking at the same space with a short dagger, and Olu was brandishing a spear. Frigga, her golden hair spilling and swirling around her, was pounding away with her blood-rusted staff, Sven beside her, face purple with rage and effort. Honi was swinging a rope, like a lasso, around his head.

All of them were ferocious, and terrifying, and intent on death – nightmares come alive from picture books of fairytales and myths. All of them were powerful and vast and deadly.

And all of them were failing, their screams of frustration echoing above their battle cries, as Fitzgarry remained untouched. He stood before them, surrounded by them, overrun by them – but completely serene. Completely unharmed, smiling and laughing as he remained protected by some kind of invisible force.

Honi slung the rope, and it flickered in the air, before landing on something we couldn't see. Suspended in the air, above Fitzgarry's head, hanging there harmlessly. Naira let loose with her bow and arrow, eyes intent as she honed in on her target – but the arrow hit something, and clattered harmlessly to the ground.

The pummelling and punching and slashing and stabbing was having no effect at all. It was as though Fitzgarry was somehow enclosed and protected; tucked away beneath an invisible bell jar that kept him safe from the monsters outside. And he was loving every minute of it: watching those arrows rain down, watching Gabriel's claws slide and screech across his invisible shelter, watching Sven come near to a stroke with the amount of force he was using to try and break through to him. Eyes crinkled with amusement, mouth wide in laughter – mocking them while he stood there. So safe. So sound. So very, very annoying.

They couldn't get to him. They couldn't hurt him and they were, in fact, in danger of hurting each other – a scrambling, tumbling mass of primeval rage, climbing over each other in their desperation to reach their enemy. There were too many knives. Too many weapons. Too much magic – and none of it was doing any good at all.

I strode forward, ignoring Carmel's pinching fingers and ever more desperate pleas for me to come with her. To run. To get away. To be safe.

I looked at her once over my shoulder, relieved to find that I didn't hate her any more. As fleeting feelings went, that hadn't been a good one. It was as though the Goddess in me had asserted herself, and gained control – and now she had, Carmel was just Carmel, not an obstacle standing in my way.

'I will not run,' I said. 'I will stay, and I will fight, and I will use whatever power I have.'

I saw her face crumple as she realised what I was about to do, and felt the fear and the anger flowing from her like a river of pure emotion. She was scared – not only of me getting hurt, but of what I could do. What I was capable of. Hmm. Well, that made two of us, I supposed.

I stood before the roiling mass of violence in front of me, with Fitzgarry in the middle, chuckling like a demented ventriloquist's dummy. My eyes automatically searched out Gabriel, reminding myself of who he was, no matter what he looked like. These were all my allies, and Gabriel was my mate, and I didn't want to hurt them. Most of the time.

'Stand back!' I shouted, tapping deep inside myself to

find a stage voice that Edwin Booth would have been proud of. I heard my words echo around the park, booming against trees and whirling with the wind and ricocheting from the stars in the sky. I felt my hair floating, a white cloud around my face, and sensed The Dog nearby, snapping and growling and coiled with strength.

The violence shuddered and juddered and eventually halted, as my shout continued to resonate: those two words repeating over and over, with a life all of their own, until they finally permeated into the collective brain of the battle-frenzied Council.

Slowly, they backed away. I saw Gabriel's twisted face, eyes shining out at me in a question, Finn as ever by his side. I saw Beryl and Olu taking staggering steps backwards, spears clasped in their fists. Honi was pulling back his rope, Frigga was panting and gulping, her breath clouding out in gusts. She laid a hand on Sven's bulky shoulder, and he calmed, retreating from Fitzgarry's dome of safety. Nahuel and Naira, the latter still glaring at me as she lowered her bow and arrow. I glared back – she could just fuck right off, whatever it was I'd done to annoy her didn't matter at all now. Katashi, off to one side, long black hair wild around his shoulders. The crow above us, endlessly circling.

I paused, fixing them all in my minds, drawing from their emotions: their anger and frustration and need to protect me. Their impotent rage at not being able to. I breathed in, tasting the chill night air and the distant smells of traffic and the far-off tang of the sea. I raised my arms, feeling my power flow with the movement, feeling the roots of the trees and the birds with their puffed out chests and the hopes and dreams of a city of millions. Felt the soil beneath my feet and the weather of ages shaping the ground I stood on.

I felt it all, and added it to my own stores. Added it to my memories of Colin, and of my parents in the

Otherworld, and my nan as she lay dying, and of every screwed-up unfair thing that had ever happened to me. I gathered it all in, and knew that I was about to unleash it all – every last drop of resentment and love and pain and strength I had. I sought out Gabriel, let my eyes lock with his for one brief moment.

'Lily . . . no . . .' he said, his words a twisted gnarl of sound coming from a Hammer Horror face. He moved towards me, and I knew I needed to do it now, before he could stop me and lock me away in the Batcave.

I stared at Fitzgarry, who was looking at me with interest, his head tilted to one side like a curious bird – like I'd finally done something that surprised him. He could feel the power, and the greedy look on his face told me he wanted it. I was flaunting it, showing it off, teasing him with it. Hopefully, I might be killing him with it soon.

I concentrated on his face, on his thin lips and sparse, sandy hair; on his cold eyes and his stupid, ugly slippers. And I let it go – in one giant, enormous whoosh, I let it go, controlling it and aiming it as best as I could, the same way I did when I'd practised with Luca only a few hours before.

The power shot from me in a blaze of light, a guided missile full of anguish, cutting through the darkness like a golden arrow. It fled towards Fitzgarry, brilliant and dazzling and . . . failing. The glow hit the dome that was around him, and seemed to explode against it and around it. Like a million yellow crystals, it shattered, shooting up like a firework display, shimmering in the darkness, illuminating that perfect bell jar shape of protection. It bounced off it, rebounding, and I looked on in horror as it found a new target: Gabriel, and all of those around him. The crow chased off ever higher, wings frantically beating to outrun the mystical napalm.

She disappeared off into the night sky, but the others

had nowhere to run to, and no defence against what I'd just done to them. They all fell to the floor, even Gabriel. Even the one man who'd always managed to stand against it before. They collapsed, a pile of unconscious bodies, arms and legs and weapons heaped over each other. Hathor's circlet eye blinked once, and then clamped firmly shut.

The only ones left standing were the humans. Carmel, holding her face in her hands, as though she didn't dare peek out from between her fingers at the disaster in front of her. Beryl, kneeling down and clutching onto Olu's limp hand. And Katashi, standing tall and fierce and glaring between me and Fitzgarry. All three of them seemed to have extra powers and abilities as a result of their Champion roles – but clearly, they were all still ticking the 'mainly human' box on the census forms. I was grateful I hadn't been left alone – that they were all still conscious.

As, for the time being, was Fitzgarry. Still alive. Still well. Still hiding beneath his shelter. Still laughing.

He started to applaud, slowly, rhythmically, all the time grinning.

'Miss McCain,' he said, 'bravo! I couldn't have done it better myself.'

He made as if to step out, as if to approach me, but only managed a fraction of a movement before The Dog was there, in front of him. Her head was furiously snapping at him like the Hound of Satan, sharp white teeth clashing together and an unholy snarl shaking through the whole of her body.

He stepped back, and she kept up her attack, holding him in place – but for how long, I had no idea.

The sound of Fitzgarry's voice seemed to snap us all out of our horrified trance, and I ran towards the tangle of limbs in front of me. I pushed my way past the sprawled limbs and slack-jawed faces and glassy eyes until I reached Gabriel. I kneeled down beside him, cradling his huge head in my arms.

'Oh God,' I muttered, feeling tears of regret and worry rolling down my cheeks, 'are you all right? Please, please, please tell me you're not dead! Even if you are, just lie, will you?'

I squatted, silent and scared, and listened as hard as I could. There were sounds coming from them all; muffled breaths and muted gulps, and tiny movements; the rise and fall of air being exhaled, the twitching of fingers, the clashing of teeth. They were alive, I was sure. Just . . . out of it. Yeah. Completely out of it, Dead Zoned with my awesome Goddess power. Jesus. Way to go, Lily McCain – Number One Knob.

As rescue attempts went, that one would have to be listed under Epic Fail.

I squeezed Gabriel to me, leaning in to listen for breath, for motion, to check that he wasn't somehow the only one of the Magnificent Six who'd gone to the great supernatural shindig in the sky. I poked him and prodded him and kissed him and, when he finally opened his eyes, I punched him.

Because those few moments, those few moments where I thought he might have gone – let's be frank, that I might have killed him – had paralysed me. Crippled me with the kind of grief that I knew I could never recover from. It wasn't just me who would be mourning him: it would be the Goddess as well. And together, we would cry a million rivers and drown the world in a tide of sorrow.

'Aaagh,' he muttered, as I slammed my fist into his chest again. 'I'm not dead, OK? Now get out of here! Leave! I'll find you – but go, now!'

I heard Carmel screeching at me, and felt strong hands clasping my shoulders and tugging me away. I tried to hold onto Gabriel, grabbing him as hard as I could, but he was pushing and Katashi was pulling and between them and my shattered mental state, I didn't stand a chance.

I was dragged backwards, my boots banging on the heads and bodies beneath me as they started to come back to consciousness, groaning and moaning and slowly raising themselves upright.

Beryl looked up, still sitting by Olu's side as he woke.

'Go,' she said. 'Take her, take the Goddess. I'll stay. They are wakening. The Morrigan will return. We will be safe.'

I saw Katashi searching out Honi, and noted the weak nod that he managed, head just about held up above the dark mash of poleaxed bodies. Katashi nodded in return, then took hold of my face and turned it to his. For once, I didn't go all gooey inside – I was too scared. Too angry. Too bloody guilty about what I'd done.

'Now, we must leave, Lily. You, me, Carmel. We must leave. You understand?'

I nodded. And then, I ran.

Chapter Twenty-Four

We fled through the gates of the park, out into the shadow of perfectly groomed townhouses and looming trees surrounded by evergreen flowerbeds and dog walkers who studiously ignored us.

Katashi ran ahead, winding through side streets off Park Avenue, leading us back onto Broadway and the spooky triangular point of the Flatiron Building. We never paused until we reached it, and my lungs were burning with the effort, my heart pounding a drum beat in my ears as my blood pressure soared. I leaned back against a traffic light, feeling the glow of the red hand 'stop' sign flashing over my head, flickering in the periphery of my vision as I stared up at the Flatiron, panting. God, I was rubbish – Spiderman wouldn't have been standing here short of breath after he finished leaping all over it. Maybe I should start wearing a lycra suit and a mask.

'Subway,' said Katashi, nudging his head in the direction of the steps leading into 23rd Street. 'Now.'

I pulled in one more huge mouthful of air, and held up a hand to buy myself another moment of recovery. Carmel and Katashi exchanged glances, not even slightly tired out by our mad dash. I was sure they were both disgusted by my lack of physical prowess, but stood still and waited while the weakling caught her breath.

'My dog,' I eventually said, the words coming out ragged. 'I need my dog.'

'Really?' said Carmel, her voice so shrill passing birds probably fell dead from the sky. 'We're being chased by wannabe Balor, you just used your mighty stun-gun on all our mates, and you're fretting about the fucking *dog*?'

I had a lot to say to that, but I needed to breathe for another moment first. It probably took the shine off my rebuttal, but there you go – I am but human. Kind of.

'We're not being chased. Are we?' I said, looking at Katashi. He was standing with his hands on his hips, head swivelling like some kind of radar gun. There were hundreds of people milling around, even this late, staggering out of bars and taking selfies by the Flatiron and queuing up for hot dogs. None of them, apparently, rang his alarm bells.

'No, I don't think so,' he replied. 'But we must still move swiftly. And we simply cannot risk going back for your pet, no matter how much you want to. She will be safe with the others. Our job is to get you away from here, away from that man – and we can't do that if you fight us every step of the way.'

I looked from him to Carmel, who was fizzing with F words just waiting to explode from her mouth. I knew the signs well enough by now. I raised one eyebrow at her, and she stuck her tongue out at me. What can I say, we're mature like that.

'What he said,' she muttered, bouncing on the soles of her feet. 'And don't even think about trying that Goddess shit on us, 'cause it just doesn't work. I know you, well, love the dog. And maybe – just maybe – you even give a shit about Gabriel and Finn and the others as well. But we need to get going, get out of the city. The Morrigan will be back at Ash Street, Kevin and Connor and Luca will be ready to rumble, they'll all be OK – and it's not like they're going to leave the fucking dog there, is it, or sell her for dim sum in frigging Chinatown? She seemed to be the only thing Fitzgarry was bothered by anyway, so she's kind of like our Kryptonite. They won't leave her. And if your dog could speak, she'd tell you to get a fucking move on, all right?'

Only two 'fuckings' and one 'frigging' in the whole sentence. Not bad. She must be feeling more zen than usual.

I chewed the inside of my lip, not realising how hard until I tasted blood. I didn't want to admit it, but they were right. OK, I'd managed to stop Fitzgarry from draining the living daylights out of me – but he was distracted by a supernatural hit squad at the time. And my awesome attempt at harming him had resulted in that same supernatural hit squad falling down like a bunch of pissed up Humpty Dumpties. It hadn't been a good night for team building.

And even I had to accept that it was pretty twisted to be more worried about The Dog than the rest of them. Especially given the depths of despair I'd plummeted to during those few tense moments when I thought Gabriel was hurt. As ever, though, as soon as I knew he wasn't, everything kind of went back to normal on that front – and for some reason the fate of the lurcher was the first thing that played on my mind. I am, to put it politely, something of a fucktard when it comes to interpersonal relationships.

'All right then,' I said. 'Just give me a minute and we'll . . . I don't know, find some quick way out of here. Any ideas on that front? Magic portals and the like?'

Carmel snorted in disgust, and Katashi shook his head, black hair swaying like a curtain of ink. He pulled out a packet of cigarettes from his pocket, and lit one up. As he took a long, slow drag, I gazed at him with chronic nicotine lust. God, that smelled good.

'Want one?' he asked, waving the pack towards me. The answer, of course, was yes. It would remind me of simpler times, standing outside gigs in the rain in Liverpool, when all I had to worry about was writing a review and making sure nobody touched me and then going home on my own to talk to my houseplants. Ah, happy days.

Tempting as it was, I shook my head in the negative. No more smoking for me, not even the social kind. Just a few hours ago I'd been an arthritic old lady with the lung capacity of a tubercular tortoise. I wasn't in any hurry to prematurely engage with the ageing process, thank you very much.

'There are sacred places here,' he said, gazing off into the distance as he inhaled, making his cheekbones stand out just a tiny bit more. Oops. Looked like I was back noticing again. 'Places where Honi could access magic . . . but I, Goddess, am a mere mortal. I do, though, have a very mystical device called a mobile telephone, and I am sure I can use that to gain us transport.'

Ha bloody ha. It seemed to be my fate not to save the world at all, but simply to be forever surrounded by sarcastic bastards who made me feel a bit fuzzy in the knicker department.

I pulled a face at him, and we strolled towards the subway entrance, pausing there as Katashi finished his delicious-smelling cancer stick.

There was a man near the top of the steps, wearing a uniform and a hi-vis jacket and leaning against a cart full of cleaning equipment.

'Don't even think about putting that out on the floor, pal,' he said, eyeballing Katashi.

Katashi smiled back at him, and extinguished the smoke between his bare fingertips with a little sizzle before dropping it into a bin bag already bulging with discarded drinks cups and old newspapers.

'Never,' he replied, clasping the cleaner on the shoulder. 'But you really should be more polite – next time, I might put it out on your face.'

He gave the cleaner a friendly wink, and disappeared off into the darkness of the subway, and the rumbling of distant trains.

Great. Psychotic as well as sarcastic. Things simply couldn't get any better.

Chapter Twenty-Five

'Wow,' I said, 'this looks homely. Someone's even painted a welcome message on the door for us.'

We were standing outside a boarded-up building in a backstreet of Kensington. Kensington, Liverpool, that is, not London. They really are quite different. The windows were covered in corrugated metal with the words Nutcracker Security stamped on them, and the peeling paint on the door was adorned with the words 'Fuck the world'. There were no cars parked up nearby, just the frame of an old Raleigh Chopper, locked to a lamp post with both its wheels missing.

'Sorry, Princess Perfect,' said Carmel, shoving past me so hard I staggered back down one of the front steps. 'I didn't have time to order the gold-plated jacuzzi and the shagpile carpets. I just hope nobody left a pea in the fucking bed to disturb your beauty sleep.'

Ah, the joys of a six hour flight with nothing but crates full of unlabelled pharmaceuticals for a pillow. Not even any fun pharmaceuticals, either. Carmel was clearly not in the best of moods, and seemed to be wholeheartedly agreeing with our new home's motto as she fiddled with the padlock. Eventually, she let out a mighty screech of frustration, and simply kicked it so hard the wood around it splintered and cracked.

I stood well back, joining Katashi at the bottom of the steps. He was looking on in amusement, hands shoved into the pockets of his leather jacket, hair tied back in a loose pony tail that the brisk Scouse wind was whipping around, along with a few stray crisp packets.

The journey hadn't bothered him in the slightest, which was lucky – Carmel did enough complaining for all of us. True to his word, he'd used his mystical telephonic device to have hurried conversations with unknown people in fast, staccato Japanese. There was a lot of hand gesturing and head bobbing and stuff that sounded vaguely threatening in any language, and eventually we'd been told to make our way to a private airstrip about sixty miles north of the city.

It hadn't quite been the champagne and Brad Pitt movie bonanza that Carmel had been hoping for – but it had been a flight. A flight for a group of people who couldn't be too fussy, and only had one passport between them. That would be me, by the way – I'd had it tucked away in my old lady pinny, like a geriatric girl guide. I wasn't sure if money changed hands or favours were promised or if Katashi just smiled really nicely, but within hours we were on our way home, or at least to Manchester. There, in the middle of a barren industrial estate glinting white with winter frost, he'd managed to acquire a car, probably dubiously, which Carmel had driven like an insaniac all the way back along the M62.

She stopped once for a comfort break, and to buy one of those giant trays full of Krispy Kreme doughnuts, before bringing us here. To the safe house. Not that it looked all that safe. Kensington was just on the edge of the city centre, and was part way through a shedload of regeneration – which meant that shiny new estates and playgrounds and health centres sat side-by-side with

streets like this, terraced rows with a few die-hard inhab-
itants, weeds and litter in the front yards, and the names
of the local 'grass' (police informant, to those unfamiliar
with the bucolic form) spraypainted on the nearby
fencing.

On the plus side there were some good pubs, and
absolutely no sign of Fergal Fitzgarry, Balor, Fintan, or
anyone else who was planning on killing me. Party time.

It was the best we could do, anyway. We couldn't risk
hotels, we'd be too conspicuous and it would be too
obvious. We couldn't go to the homes of anyone we knew,
for the same reason, and because we'd be putting them
at risk. This place was abandoned, empty, unwanted. The
perfect place to hide.

'Bet you could have kicked that door in much better,'
I said, nudging Katashi as we watched Carmel trying to
batter it even further open.

'Naturally,' he replied, 'but I find it best to leave angry
women to kick in their own doors. Your Champion seems
insulted by the world at the moment, and perhaps needs
to break a small bone in her foot to cheer herself up. She
is making a lot of noise, though.'

'Yeah, well,' I said, glancing round the dimly lit and
completely deserted street, tied-together trainers swaying
overhead as they dangled from the phone lines, 'it doesn't
look like the Neighbourhood Watch is out in force
tonight.'

He frowned, and I realised he didn't get the reference,
what with being from Japan and all. I shrugged, too tired
to try and explain. I was exhausted, and smelly, and I
missed my dog much more than I should have.

Gabriel had texted us to say, in as few words as
possible, that everyone was well, and telling us where to
go when we landed. Katashi had been in touch with
Honi, and been given permission to stay with us for as
long as he was needed. I can't say that displeased me.

He was amusing, and could probably do secret samurai squirrel things and, well, wasn't exactly hard on the eyes. A goddess has got to take her pleasures where she finds them, after all.

Carmel stepped back from the half-shattered door, reared up her right leg, and slammed her boot into it as hard as she could.

The wood finally gave, and the door creaked open. She turned round and gave us an evil grin, accompanied by a less evil thumbs-up, then walked through into the hallway.

Seconds later, she was lying on her arse at our feet, swearing. As soon as her foot had crossed the entrance, she'd been physically blasted away – landing back in the street in a crumpled heap. It was as if the house had simply not liked the taste of her and spat her back out.

The door was now wreathed with smoke, slinking out into the night, illuminated by a single dazzling torchlight glaring into our eyes. It was so bright I felt like I was about to be interrogated by the Gestapo, and didn't object when Katashi stepped in front of me.

I shielded my eyes against the glow, and tried to scrunch up my eyelids enough to look around his shoulders and see what was going on.

'Oh for feck's sake, it's you! Why didn't you just knock, you stupid girl?'

An exasperated, very Irish voice – matched by an exasperated, very Irish woman, appeared in the doorway. She tottered there in high heels, wearing leopard print leggings and a low cut top showing way too much middle-aged cleavage.

The smoke fluttered around her, like dry ice at a Def Leppard gig, as she stepped out into the courtyard and looked down at Carmel, who was possibly concussed and most definitely pissed off.

Fionnula the Fair – or Witchy Bitch, as Carmel always

called her, during our stay at Fionnula's cottage in Ireland.

I felt my face crease into a smile, and I moved out of Katashi's shadow and into the squidgy embrace of my former mentor. We'd spent days holed up with her in County Dublin at the start of this whole thing, learning about gods and goddesses and the Otherworld and fate and destiny and cocktails and make-up and lots of other important things. Most essentially of all, it had been Fionnula who had taught me how to control my visions – how to build and maintain the barriers that would protect me from them, and allow me at least a rudimentary chance to interact normally with the rest of humanity.

It was still unspeakably wonderful to see her. She wasn't huge and deadly like the Morrigan, and she didn't live to serve me like Luca did, and she wasn't my Champion like Carmel. She was just . . . Fionnula. Powerful in her own way, and exactly the sort of person who would booby trap her own makeshift safe house.

She was also, I could tell from her breath, already a wee bit tipsy. Some things never changed.

'Darlin', how are you doing?' she said, pulling away and studying my face for any signs of injury, or possibly for poorly applied mascara.

'Oh, I'm fine thank you!' interrupted Carmel, back on her feet and fuming. 'Thanks for asking, and no, I didn't crack my skull on the way down!'

Fionnula turned to look at her, eyes narrowed and glinting.

'I'd be more worried about your skull cracking the pavement, girl. And what did you expect? That I'd just let any old trash walk in from the street? You should have known better, *Champion*.'

She let the sarcasm drip from the last word before teetering away back up the steps and into the house.

'You'd better come in,' she said over her shoulder. 'And bring the hunk with you.'

I looked at Katashi, who had watched the entire exchange in a respectful – or possibly just horrified – silence.

'I think she means you,' I said, raising my eyebrows.

'Without a doubt,' he replied, grinning as he walked past a still-swearing Carmel and through the battered door.

Inside, there was a hallway empty of everything apart from a huge pile of rotting free sheets and a tattered collection of junk mail. Someone had also, for reasons that probably made sense to them at the time, posted a small collection of dead snails through the letterbox, all in a plastic sandwich bag. Bare wooden stairs were right in front of us, leading up into the darkness of the upper floors.

The layout was the same as my nan's old terraced house in Anfield, so I knew the kitchen would be at the end of the hall, with a small back yard behind it, and that the living room would be behind the door on my right. It was, and inside it I found Fionnula feeling up Katashi. Groping his biceps and grinning, she was pointing to a huge gap in the lounge wall.

She'd somehow blasted a massive hole in the brickwork, creating a doorway just high enough for me to walk through, as long as I didn't have a beehive and was willing to stoop a little. The edges of the wall were still charred and blackened by whatever magical boom she'd conjured up, with ragged layers of wallpaper hanging off – about eight generations worth of different styles. The first one, an explosion of huge anaglypta sunflowers, would probably be back in fashion by now.

'I've done some remodelling,' she said, pointing down into the grim beyond. I stooped down, and walked through – right into the living room of the next house. This one was also boarded up, and the only light came from candles that she'd strategically arranged on the mantelpiece and dusty window ledges. There was a huge cuddly Winnie the Pooh in one corner, the kind you won at the fair, that had obviously been left behind when Kensington's Christopher Robin moved out.

I glanced into the hallway, and through the open door across from me – seeing, as I'd suspected I would, that the next room was exactly the same. A great big hole where the wall should be.

Knowing Fionnula, she'd got tanked up on Bushmills finest, and blasted her delicate way through the entire terrace. I just hoped she'd stopped at the end, or it would be getting pretty damn cold in here tonight.

'How many?' I asked, raising my eyebrows. I mean, nobody was living there, and they were probably scheduled for demolition anyway, but still . . . it felt a tiny bit extreme. The good Catholic girl hiding inside me was feeling guilty about the property damage.

'Four,' she replied, sounding a wee bit defensive, and ending the word with a small hiccup which she tried to hide with a hand to her mouth. 'Gabriel and the others will be back tomorrow, and he doesn't think it wise to return to his home here in case Fitzgarry knows where it is. For now we have to make do here, and I didn't see the point in us being cooped up together when we didn't need to be. There are three bedrooms in each one, and, well, I've done my best. It was all short notice, you have to bear in mind – but I still managed to get to Asda and stock up a bit.'

'Yeah, right,' said Carmel, peering over my shoulder at the devastation in front of us, 'but did you stock up on anything that isn't vodka?'

'I stocked up on sleeping bags and candles and food,' Fionnula answered, swerving over towards us and wagging an angry finger, 'and just for you, a huge roll of duct tape to slap over your big fat mouth.'

I saw Carmel start to splutter a reply, and held up my hand to pre-empt it. I was so not in the mood for one of their catfights. On a good day, they could be entertaining – kind of like Supernatural WWF – but this? So far, this was not an especially good day. I for one was glad that Fionnula had vandalised an entire block of houses, once I thought about it – it meant I'd at least have a chance to spend some time on my own. Away from the murder and mayhem and magic. That stuff just got tiring after a while. And Gabriel was right – joyous as it would have been to go back to his swanky waterfront penthouse, with its Dolby surround sound and rain-forest showers and squishy leather sofas, it would also have been dangerous. Fintan was somehow in league with Fitzgarry, and he knew where it was. And where my own flat in Sefton Park was. And where my nan's house was. We couldn't risk it.

'It's fine,' I said quickly, before Carmel could launch into a slanging match. 'Thanks, Fionnula. Now, what's going on? As far as you can tell?'

She was still glaring at Carmel, her nostrils flaring, probably with the effort of not turning her into a three-legged piglet dressed in a baby's bib. She held a candle in front of her, dripping wax onto a saucer, and the fire-light was dancing off the bonnet of her bleach-blonde hair.

'Give me a moment to make us more comfortable, child – no need to act like savages, even if *some* of us clearly are,' she said, gesturing for us to follow her back through the ad hoc brick doorway and into the first house. I shoved Carmel, hard, to make her move.

Fionnula pointed to a pile of boxes in the corner, and looked over at Katashi. He had remained impassive throughout the whole exchange, showing an impressive level of self-control. If it'd been me encountering those two together for the first time in circumstances like this, I'd have laughed, cried, and tried to do a runner.

'Could you be a gentleman and help with these?' she said, walking over to the pile. 'I've been waiting for someone with big . . . lungs.'

He smiled at her, and started to tear open the boxes. He looked momentarily confused as he pulled out piles of fluorescent pink plastic, before glancing at the pictures and realising they were inflatable chairs. The kind teenagers sat in while they played the Xbox for twelve hours straight. Still, right now, they looked like the height of luxury.

'Go on then,' I urged, nodding at him. 'Get puffing.'

Within a few minutes – because Katashi did indeed have big lungs – we were at least all sitting down. Fionnula and Carmel both looked happy enough, but Katashi and I were having to stretch our longer legs out in front of us. He'd been provided with a bottle of fizzy water, and I was happily swigging a can of Strongbow. All we needed was some Grateful Dead and a few spliffs and we'd have the perfect bedsit party going on.

'Right, so, is everyone all right? Does anybody want any peanuts?' said Fionnula, once she'd stopped fussing over everyone apart from Carmel and finally settled herself on a squishy chair. She moved as if to stand up again, presumably to fetch the bloody peanuts, before I said 'No!' as loud as I could.

'Please stay there, stop wittering, and tell us what the fuck is going on. We don't want any peanuts – we want an update.'

She feigned shock and surprise and, eventually, even went for wounded. Yeah. Right. It was all fake – and I didn't have time for it. I needed to get an update, and I needed to get some sleep.

'No need to be rude, child,' she said, sitting her half-raised backside down into the chair again. 'Like I said, the others will be with us tomorrow. I've spoken to Gabriel, and they all managed to get back to the house on Ash Street. This man Fitzgarry was apparently held at bay by your hellhound until they all recovered enough to retreat. I've been doing some research, looked at some of my older texts, consulted some of—'

'Can he do it?' I interrupted, knowing that Fionnula could not only talk for Ireland, but that she was doing her best to avoid getting to what was called, in technical terms, the nitty gritty. I'd seen her evade like this before – back when I'd been trying to get to the truth of the role Gabriel had played in my miserable childhood – and needed to cut through the seventeen layers of fake-Mrs Doyle crap that she was hiding beneath. She'd talk about her books for five minutes, and about how hard it was to research for another five, then she'd ask us all if we wanted more drinks, then she'd have another herself and, eventually, we'd all be too drunk to talk and I wouldn't know anything more than I did at the start. It was like a non-stop carousel of booze and confusion.

'Fitzgarry?' I said abruptly. 'Can he become Balor, and do all this crazy end-of-the-world shit? And what does he have that he thinks *I* want so much? How does Fintan play into all of this? And how can I protect myself against Fitzgarry? Because I have to say, the usual stuff you spout about just trying really, really hard might not cut it this time. If he gets me, he gets Balor, it's like a BOGOF deal – so how do I prevent that from happening?'

She pursed her lips, frowned, and took a not so lady-like gulp of whiskey that saw half her plastic tumbler-full disappear down her gullet in one mouthful.

'Always with the questions, Lily – you're always so good at asking, never so good at listening.'

I gave her a hard look that said 'I am not going to rise to your bait, you old bat', and waited a few beats until she continued.

'Right. Well, I think the answer to the first question is maybe. Probably. There was an occasion in what you would call the seventh century, where the Norsemen used a similar technique to bring back one of their long-dead chieftains. They wanted him to lead them into battle when they raided in the new lands, despite the fact that he'd been dead for three generations. There was a sacrifice. Not just of animals, but of people. And not just their bodies – one of their seers is said to have carried out a ceremony that drained others of their souls. The ritual left some of them alive, but mindless – and this being the age it was, they were taken out to the forest and left to die. A whole fishing village was lost to the spell, so the gods would allow that one man to walk again.'

Uggh. Nice. But no worse than what Fitzgarry was doing – he just had a shedload of unwilling souls stacked up in care homes and hospitals, waiting to be collected. He didn't even need to dump them in a forest.

'Did it work?' asked Katashi, leaning forward so far his inflatable chair was in danger of unbalancing. 'Did the chieftain rise?'

Fionnula nodded, her eyes darting around the room as though looking for monsters in the shadows cast by the dozens of flickering candles. It was stranger than usual, this whole setting: the empty, desecrated shells that had once homed entire families; the tattered wallpaper, the blasted brickwork and the strange corridor into the next building, giving us a telescopic view through the walls like something from a post-apocalyptic *Charlie and the Chocolate Factory*. The boarded up windows, the candles, the musty, damp smell of a long-empty building. The too-true ghost stories from another time. It all made me shiver.

'So the stories say, yes,' said Fionnula. 'He rose again, and led them into battle, and . . . well. They were even more brutal times than these. I'm sure they saw the loss of one village as nothing compared to the riches and land they found across the sea in England and Ireland.'

Probably not. And we all know from history lessons – and possibly from TV shows featuring impossibly sexy Nordic types – that the Vikings went forth and multiplied. There were loads of Viking place names around Liverpool, and all over the rest of the country. As well as the rape and the pillage, they'd settled and farmed and married and produced children and contributed to the genetic make-up of the whole country. I suspected the Big Bad Balor thing would have a less organic ending, if Fitzgarry pulled it off.

'But if he manages it – if he raises Balor, or becomes Balor, because that's what my vision showed me – then he won't just be getting in a boat and wearing a hat with pointy horns, will he?' I asked. 'He'll be fulfilling this prophecy, the one Domnu made in the form of a crow? The one about all the milk going bad or whatever?'

'I know that is what you saw, Lily, but you must remember what I told you – your visions can be changed. They don't have to come true. We must find a way to unmake it.'

'And just how do we do that?' asked Carmel, her eyes drooping closed even as she spoke. She was so tired, her can was starting to slip out of her hand – a sure sign of chronic fatigue, potentially wasting alcohol.

'Because everything we tried in the park in New York failed,' she continued. 'Even Lily's great big monster ray gun, and the Morrigan and Gabriel and all the magic arrows and swords and other shiny crap we threw at him. Even that funny rope that Honi had—'

'The shirukume,' interjected Katashi. 'It is made of magical rice straw.'

She snorted and shook her head so her now-matted curls bobbled. 'Yeah. OK. Even the magic rice rope failed, big fucking shocker. Should've tried pasta. What else have we got? What else can we do? And how long will it take, 'cause we're due back in work in another two days? And it's my mum's birthday next week and I still haven't got her a present.'

She sounded exhausted and angry and borderline blow-in-a-paper-bag hysterical. And, of course, there was a bit of a logical shortfall in her statement. If we failed, then we wouldn't have to go back to work. I would be gone for sure – sucked dry and metaphorically dumped in a forest. There would be no world as we knew it, no Liverpool as we knew it, and definitely not a *Liverpool Gazette*. Her mum, along with the rest of the O'Gradys and every other human on the planet, would be either dead or on their way to getting dead. Maybe Balor would turn them all immediately to stone, maybe there'd be a charming intermediate survivalist phase where they all died of famine or disease or from getting whacked in the head by looters or eaten by desperate cannibals, but one way or another it would all be gone. Either instant annihilation or Road Warrior slow-fade.

She knew that, I was sure – but clinging to our own reality is one of the only ways we'd survived the last few months. In the face of gods and supervillains and vampires and magical ropes made out of food, we both needed to remember what mattered in the life we'd had before: getting drunk, meeting deadlines and, in her case, her family and the random men she encountered. In mine, it was more the latest *Kerrang!* roadshow and cosying up with a box-set of *Lost*, but there you go. Our world might not be much, but it was the only one we had.

Fionnula and Katashi were both silent in response. The only sounds were the candles hissing, the distant rumble of traffic in the busier streets nearby, and the sound of a lonely dog barking that almost brought tears to my sore eyes.

'I don't know, Champion,' replied Fionnula eventually, voice soft and, for once, gentle. 'But we will find a way – we have to find a way. And the Goddess hasn't as yet reached her full power. Perhaps when she has, when she has all her strength about her, things will be different.'

I noticed the way her gaze flicked towards Katashi as she spoke, and knew she'd have been a lot more blunt if he wasn't in the room. Carmel frowned, looked confused but was too tired to question it. I stayed silent, fighting with no effect at all the blush that was sweeping across my face. I knew what she meant. It was the same thing Hathor had meant. It was the same thing my body had been telling me for a while now. I needed to get me some man-flesh. Eeek.

Fionnula had left a lot of questions unanswered, I also noticed. Accidentally on purpose. But as I saw Carmel's grip finally give up, and the now-empty can fall from her tired fingers to the frayed, stained carpet left behind by the house's previous owners, I knew they'd have to wait until tomorrow. We were all too tired to save the Earth right now.

Chapter Twenty-Six

The next morning, Carmel and I took an executive decision that we were heading into town to do some shopping. It wasn't quite that simple, and was preceded by a set of vocal exchanges between the four of us that went something along the lines of, 'No, it's too dangerous for Lily, the fragile flower', 'I'll protect her', 'You're rubbish at protecting her', and 'I'll protect myself – now all shut up because I NEED SOME CLEAN KNICKERS!'

It was a crisp, clean, cool December day, with blue skies dotted with fluffy white clouds and the perfect mix of fresh air and car engine fumes as we walked into the city centre. Ah, the smell of home. All of Katashi and Fionnula's moaning aside, it felt good to be out – almost on my own. And being with Carmel was as close to being alone while in the company of another human being as it could get for me. We'd known each other a long time, and watched a lot of films together, and had no trouble at all with enjoying a nice, pleasant, comfortable silence.

Which is exactly what I'd been hoping for before she started winding me up about Katashi.

'So, what do you think about Sexy-San?' she said, as we made our way past the Dental Hospital on London Road. We passed the School of Tropical Medicine, and worked our way round a gaggle of backpacked student types all staring at a street map that kept folding back up in the breeze.

'Sexy-San?' I repeated, stopping as I always did to look at Galkoff's, the old kosher butcher's shop. 'Isn't that a bit racist?'

'Nah,' she replied, bouncing around impatiently while I enforced a pause. 'If anything it's demeaning him through objectification, and I like to be an equal opportunities sexist. It'd be rude not to. *Why* do you always stare at this place? It's just an old shop . . .'

She was kind of right. It was a run-down mid-Georgian terrace, still covered in dark green tiling and Hebrew symbols – but I'd always been fascinated by it, even when I was younger, and had no idea why. Now, of course, I knew that if I tried hard enough, I could mentally do a time tunnel and see it the way it was: shiny and clean and bustling and full of the chatter and comings and goings of the city's Jewish community. Another time, and maybe I would.

We carried on walking down the hill, past the Turkish fast food places and the bed shops and the antiquarian bookseller and the pawn shops that offered the very best prices for unwanted gold jewellery, until we hit the corner of Lime Street.

'So,' she prodded. 'Come on. We're talking about men.'

'No, *you* are,' I replied. 'I'd rather talk about dogs. Or duckbilled platypuses.'

'Ooh, kinky,' she said, nudging me and guffawing like Sid James. 'But anyway. Katashi. Luca. Gabriel. Seems you are currently surrounded by blokes who'd be happy to bonk you. So what's the problem? Pick one and get it on, you lucky cow.'

'You're hardly going short – Connor and you are getting plenty,' I replied, hoping to shift the focus away from my lack-of sex life to her very noisy one.

'Yeah, but that's just fun,' she replied, in that primary-school-teacher explaining tens-and-units voice she used when she thought I was being especially dim. 'Blowing off steam – among other things. It's not, like, a great love affair, or, you know, going to save the fucking world or something.'

Ah. So she'd figured it out. I felt my cheeks flare red, as per usual, and ignored her. Carmel had always thought that sex could save the world, and my situation seemed to be proving her right.

'I don't want to talk about it, OK?' I said, weaving through a throng of people at the bus stop outside the train station and heading for the traffic lights.

'You don't need to talk about it,' she replied. 'You just need to fucking do it. And stop acting like a martyr about it, all right? It's not like you're some sacrificial virgin waiting to have her throat cut on an altar. There are gorgeous men in your life, all of whom would be happy to oblige – and don't give me that "Oooh, my visions!" bullshit either – Luca doesn't even give you those, and the rest of the time now, I know you can control them. Look, see, no visions!'

With the last few words, she reached out and poked me, hard, on the forehead, with one pointed finger. I stopped still, and she carried on poking me. One jab at a time, bobbing me backwards as she jabbed me. I took a deep breath and reminded myself that really, deep down, I didn't want to kill her at all.

'Stop it!' I yelled, slapping her hand away so hard I heard the flesh connect in a sharp sting. 'Just because I *can* be touched doesn't mean I want to be, OK? I've spent my whole life at the mercy of other people, of their decisions, their version of what's best for me. Being controlled and manipulated and wondering what the hell was going on. So please forgive me if I'm not quite ready to give up everything just yet, because some stupid supernatural

woo-woo crap says I should! This is the first time I have
ever – *ever* – had control of my own body. So you, and
Gabriel, and Hathor, and Fionnula, and every other nosy
parker who thinks they can boss me around can just go
screw themselves!'

We'd attracted a bit of attention, which was impressive.
Normally you have to walk naked on stilts while
breathing fire to get noticed in Liverpool city centre. But
St George's Hall seemed to have been transformed into
some kind of Winter Wonderland grotto, and a massive
queue of mothers and kids was snaking around the
plateau outside it.

I felt a few glares from concerned mums, and toned
it down the only way I knew how – by walking away,
off down the cobbles of William Brown Street, stomping
down hard with my Docs as I tried to regain my cool.

William Brown Street is one of the most picturesque
in Liverpool. On one side there are the gorgeous museums
and galleries and the library, on the other there's land-
scaped gardens at the back of St George's Hall. It's usually
one of my favourite places, but right then I wasn't feeling
the love. I was angry with Carmel – she was my best
friend, and she usually understood me. Even Gabriel
understood me on this one, and deliberately avoided
getting too hot and heavy until I felt more in control.
More like it was all my choice instead of some bullshit
destiny thing; something I chose to do instead of being
pimped out by fate. She seemed to think I was acting
like some prima donna brat, and it made me feel raw
and misunderstood and lonely.

Carmel ran up behind me, then to my side. 'Slow
down, Usain Bolt,' she said, falling into step. 'I *do* get it.
I just think also that you need to . . . get over it. None
of us asked for what we're given in life, Lily – but you
know that thing about when you're given lemons? You
chop them up, make a big jug of gin and tonics, and get

pissed. So stop being a baby. Anyway, enough about you. I wanna call in here. Come with me if you like, or just walk moodily round the streets of Liverpool in a big fat sulk.' She flounced off towards the grand entrance to the World Museum, freshly washed curls flying around her head like a swarm of angry snakes. Carmel can be a world class bitch – but she can also be right. I followed her, but held on to my big fat sulk. A girl's got to have some pride.

She passed the giant carved totem pole in the cavernous lobby, and pinged up the steps like they weren't even there. I landed there a few minutes later, and found her in the Ancient World. To be precise, in Egypt. I'd been here with her before, gazing at the mummies and the amulets and the statues. This time, she was staring into a glass case full of miniature people. Shabti dolls. The information panel helpfully told me they were representative of servants taken into the afterlife, to help the deceased carry out work for Osiris.

'Wow,' I said, standing next to her, seeing our own faces reflected in the glass. 'That would suck – being taken into the afterlife as a servant? Doesn't seem fair somehow . . .'

'I know. I wonder what I'll get to take with me when I go into the afterlife?' she replied, clearly distracted. Her encounter with Amophet had obviously rung a few bells, and I'd not been listening to the chimes. I could now add 'selfish bitch' to my list of flaws. Carmel had been fascinated by her heritage and tracking down her birth parents, for as long as I'd known her. She'd probably been totally freaked out by Hathor and her Champion, and the fact that they knew so much more about that world than she did. 'Well, if you go before me,' I said, 'I'll be sure to pack your tomb with a shed load of booze and some Terry's chocolate orange, and, well, are you OK? Is this all a bit weird? What did Amophet say to you? And do you want to . . . I don't know, go shack up with them or something for a while?'

I tried to sound calm, but I was slightly panicked at the thought of her leaving me. She'd been my Champion for a lot longer than I'd known I was a goddess. She smiled at me, even though her eyes looked big and sad.

'Nah,' she said, shaking her head. 'Maybe I'll visit with them for a bit, once everything's calmed down. I have a lot of questions that they can probably answer. But I'll never really leave you, Lily. We're a dynamic duo, never to be parted.'

'Like Batman and Robin?' I asked.

'I was thinking more Laurel and Hardy, but whatever floats your boat. Now come on. We've both indulged ourselves in a bit of flouncing. Now we need to buy some knickers, and save the world.'

An hour or so later, we'd shopped 'til we dropped, dressed in new clothes, and temporarily parted ways.

I'd managed to convince Carmel that I would manage, against the odds, to stay alive for twenty minutes without her Champion-ly presence, and was sitting – blissfully alone – in the gardens of the Bluecoat Arts Centre. Just me, a big steaming cappuccino, and a few back copies of the *Gazette*. She'd given in gracefully because she wanted to visit one of her brothers, Joe, who worked in the Apple shop. The O'Grady clan are nothing if not protective, and if she didn't check in with one of them at some point, Mama O would be trampling over Manhattan like one of the Transformers, flattening buildings with each stomp of her mechanical feet.

The Bluecoat is the oldest building in the city centre, a grand 18th-century confection that started life as a school but now hosts galleries and events and all kinds of bohemian shenanigans. It also has this beautiful little courtyard at the back, one of those total oasis-in-the-city deals.

I needed the space, the feel of air around my body that nobody else was breathing, the sense of solitude that would let my seething brain settle down to something less than boiling point. Even Carmel was too much after a while, especially after the topsy-turvy road we'd travelled today.

I had a lot to think about. Fitzgarry. Balor. Fintan. Sex. How To Be A Goddess. Lots of very, very important stuff. So, instead, I caught up on the latest Liverpool news – which betting shops had been robbed at gunpoint, who was starring in that year's pantomime, and which celebrities made the best bowls of Scouse, our parochial term for a pan of stew. I'd done two of my pop pages in advance before going to New York, but had to start thinking about my next one. Working on the assumption that there would be a next one.

I was enjoying an especially interesting feature about childhood obesity when the automatic doors into the main building opened with a gentle hiss.

I glanced up from my paper, frowning. I really didn't want anybody to come and bother me right now, not even the cute waiter with the ginger hipster beard and the buff gym body under the tight black T-shirt. Not that I noticed stuff like that.

Instead, I saw a young couple walk through into the courtyard, both of them the very epitome of Liverpool chic. The woman was small and slim, and had huge blonde hair that was curled up in extravagant rollers, bobbing round her head like a parody of a 50s dolly girl. That might sound odd, but it was a common sight in Liverpool, especially at the weekend. The gorgeous girls came out with their curlers in, wearing them like a badge of honour that declared to the world: I Am Woman, And I Am Out On The Pull Tonight.

She was wearing skin-tight black leggings that were stretched so transparent I could see the pattern of love hearts on her underwear, and six-inch spike-heeled boots that would provoke most mothers to say something like 'you'll break your ankle in those', or 'be careful you don't have someone's eye out'.

The bloke she was with was like a negative carbon copy of anti-glamour, wearing head-to-toe black, tracksuit bottoms, and a billowing coat with the words North Face on them. His head was shaved, and he looked like he was fresh from stealing milk money from school kids. On the making-an-effort scale, she was about 100, and he was a minus 7. I quickly looked away from them, and moved my eyes back to the newspaper. Hopefully they were just cutting through – the courtyard led out past the craft shop and back into the main shopping complex. They walked towards me, the girl's heels clacking loudly on the paving as she moved. I carried on reading, hoping they weren't going to ask me if I had a light or if I knew the way to San Jose or anything, until they stopped. Right by my table, casting long shadows over me in the winter sunlight.

I looked up, ready to be polite but distant – and that's when the smell hit me. The familiar scent of rotting apples and long-dead fruit, oozing from them and clogging my nostrils like toxic perfume. I felt a small gag rise in my throat as they sat down opposite me, and immediately felt my defences go up. I was *so* getting better at that.

I stared at the man, silently, taking in his little piggy eyes and the fact that one of his front teeth was badly chipped and that he had the corner of an Everton tattoo peeping out of his coat sleeves. That she was made up to the max, with bright red lippy and matching shellac nails, now tapping away on the table surface. They were Faidh, I knew that much – that smell was only ever associated with them. The smell of all that should be good somehow perverted and corrupted.

'Hiya!' said the girl, in a sing-song voice. 'You going out tonight?'

It was exactly the same question hundreds of Liverpool girls were probably asking each other in salons and hairdressers and on street corners all over the city at that exact moment in time. For a brief second I wondered if I had it wrong, if my olfactory senses were having some kind of hallucination. Then she smiled, and I knew I was right. 'It's been a while, Lily,' said the man, gazing at me intently. 'You look well, considering. The hair's a nice touch. Very . . . ethereal. Almost otherworldly, you could say.'

He had the accent as well, but the words he chose didn't match it. Not to mention the smell, or the fact that he knew who I was. I must have looked confused, and he gave me a predatory grin.

'Want a clue?' he asked, then mimicked drinking from an imaginary cup. 'Mmm . . . Ireland's finest!'

I recognised the gesture. I recognised the words. And now, I recognised the man – even if he did look completely different. First time we met, it was in Bewley's coffee shop in Dublin, although I didn't know who it was then.

Now, despite the body-swap, I did. It was Fintan, leader of the Fintna Faidh, and the creature who had tried to kill me several times. The creature who, as far as I knew, still wanted me dead.

At first he'd tried the good, old-fashioned assassin route. When that failed – mainly due to Gabriel, Carmel, and some well-placed terracotta plant pots – he'd started talking straight into my brain. Kind of like Emily Sandé, telling me his version of events, trying to persuade me that my lacklustre view of humanity meant he was right – that it didn't deserve to survive.

Eventually, when he got tired of all that subtlety, he

stole the body of a near suicidal Irishman called Larry Hoey, and tried to kill me by breaking my fingers and pushing me into the River Mersey the same night my nan died. All to try and stop me making my choice at Tara.

Except I'd made the choice. I'd rejected him, humiliated him, thwarted him. And now, he was sitting opposite me wearing a body that could probably snap me like a twig.

The woman with him had to be Eithne, his Girl Friday and all round evil bitch. She was also a member of the I Tried To Kill Lily McCain And Failed club. All things considered, I should have been scared. Terrified. Quaking in my Docs as I faced two deadly foes, both of whom had tried to send me off to the great beyond. Except, well, they'd failed. I was still here. I was still the Goddess. And they still smelled really, really bad.

I had a lot more power now than I had then, and was fairly convinced that I didn't need my High King or my Champion to protect myself from these two. I examined myself for a racing pulse or the sting of tears, and found none. Stupid? It wouldn't be the first time. I wasn't scared of them – but I was scared of what their sudden appearance could mean.

'Ah. Fintan,' I said, eventually. 'And I'm assuming your glamorous assistant here is Eithne? You've both borrowed a couple of bodies to walk round in, is that it? How did you manage that? I thought you were limited to the Otherworld apart from at Samhain. Have they finally kicked you out for bad behaviour?'

Eithne snorted, and reached out to swipe the tiny biscotti that was sitting on the side of my saucer. I slapped her hand away, so hard she snatched it back and rubbed her fingers.

'That's my biscuit,' I snarled. 'Get your own.'

'My my, you have changed,' she replied, amusement

dancing in blue eyes that I knew weren't even hers, curlers bobbing away in hair she had no right to. I hated how they did that – stole people. It was just . . . icky.

'Who does that body really belong to?' I snapped, needing to know. To find out a name so I could check on them afterwards. I'd always meant to do that with poor Larry Hoey, but had never followed through. Scared of what I might find, I suppose.

'This old thing?' she said, looking down at her perfect, toned figure. 'This is Sophie Duffy. Nineteen years old, studying to be a massage therapist, and for some unfathomable reason in love with this oik here.'

Fihtan smiled, and added: 'And the oik in question is James Hennessy. Twenty years old, and studying to be a petty criminal. A man devoid of charm, intelligence, or integrity. Neither use, nor ornament. Honestly, I still have no idea why you'd want to keep this useless species alive.'

He looked genuinely confused about that, and always had been. In his mind, humanity was defunct. It had outlived any usefulness it ever had, and he wanted it gone.

'You never will understand that, Fintan. We just have to agree to differ. Now, how are you here? And why are you here?'

'Well, the how is down to a certain mutual friend . . . nice chap, vertically challenged. New York accent. I'm sure you know who I mean. He already has great power, with an absolute bonanza on the way! He asked us to pay you a little visit. Make you an offer you can't refuse, you know?'

He lapsed into a fake Godfather accent for the last few words, and Eithne giggled through Sophie Duffy's perfectly made-up mouth. I sighed. God, I hated these two.

It's funny how I'd once been so terrified of them, and

now found them annoying instead. Fitzgarry, however, was a different matter. Even without saying his name, the racing pulse I'd been checking for earlier kicked in. I bit my lip so hard I tasted blood, and tried to keep my face neutral. Fintan alone no longer worried me. Fintan with Fitzgarry was an entirely different prospect.

'We've been following you around for ages,' Eithne said. 'Waiting for a chance to be alone with you. I can't believe you considered getting that fluffy cashmere thing in pink, by the way – it would have been a disaster with your colouring!'

I hated to admit it, but she was right. About the sweater at least.

I stayed silent, looked at my watch and frowned, as though I was rushed for time. I might be quaking a tiny bit inside, and desperate to run in case Fitzgarry appeared with a slice of cheesecake, but I didn't need to show them that.

'Fine. Now you have me. Could you get a move on though, 'cause I have things to do today? Plus, I'm sure Sophie and James would really like to have their bodies back in time to go clubbing tonight.'

I saw a snarl twist Eithne's lips, and a subtle change in her body language: a softening of muscles, a loosening of limbs, a stretching of tiny bones. Like a snake about to strike. I'd been struck by her before, and it hadn't been nice.

Fintan placed one hand on her forearm, calming her down.

'Now now, my love, don't do anything hasty. For the time being, we need her alive, don't we? He wants her for himself, in person.'

He looked back at me, and I made a big fake deal of sipping my coffee and licking off my frothy cappuccino moustache. Fintan and Eithne I could handle – I could blast them all the way into the lingerie department in

Next if I needed to. But what if they were somehow 'more' now? What if some of Fitzgarry's power had given them the same level of protection from me that he seemed to enjoy? What if they were like Mario after powering up on a Super Mushroom?

'You seem very relaxed, Lily,' said Fintan, leaning forward across the table until his face was inches away from mine, and I could see the warmth of his breath curling out into the air. James Hennessy, I could see, had once had a very bad case of teenaged acne that left tiny pits across his skin. 'I remember not so long ago you were a frightened child, crying in a locked room with your evil nan downstairs. Sobbing for your parents, and fantasising about someone who would rescue you. Someone who would *looooove* you. Poor, abandoned little girl – weak and alone.'

'Yep, well, I'm not that little girl any more, am I, Fintan? And I'm not weak. Not so long ago you seemed a lot more scary than you do now. The all-powerful Fintan, leader of the mighty Faidh – except . . . well, last time we met face to face I seem to recall that all I had to do was touch you, and you fell to pieces. Something like this.'

I reached out, and quickly placed my hands on either side of his forehead. I zinged up just enough juice to hurt him, a tiny little bit. OK, a bit more than I'd planned on inflicting on James's borrowed body, but he probably deserved it. There was a little sizzle, and smoke started to rise from his skin. 'You weren't that impressive then,' I said, tightening my grip, 'and you're not that impressive now. And I don't need to use my visions to realise that none of this is going to end well for you, Fintan – what do you think will happen to you when Balor rules the world? Haven't you ever watched a horror film? It *never* works out for the evil henchman . . .'

Fintan's hands were clenched into tight fists on top of

the table, and I could feel his knees juddering and shaking against mine, like he was in the electric chair getting fried. I was causing it, but I also felt distant from it, like an interested observer looking on from afar. The coffee cup was rattling and shaking, spoon clanking against china, and his face was turning a really nice shade of red. It was kind of fascinating, to be honest, and I was interested to see what would happen next.

What did happen next was that Eithne bit me. She just opened her mouth, leaned over, and chomped down on my wrist so hard I squeaked and let go. I pulled my hands back in shock, and saw bright red lipstick smears on my bruised skin. There was even a patch of blood where she'd broken it. Jeez, I was going to have to bathe that in a vat of Dettol – it was worse than getting snacked on by a rabid dingo. But, well. I was kind of glad – I'd not quite got full control of this goddess stuff, and I'd have been in a mighty huff with myself if I'd accidentally blown North Face's head off.

I glared up at Eithne, fighting my instinct to retaliate. To hurt her. To tear *her* head off. Because it wasn't even her head, and I had as little right to it as she did. Silently, though, I vowed that if I ever came across her in her own form, things would be different.

'Time to stop playing games, Goddess,' said Eithne, her eyes slitted and glittering. 'Your pathetic demonstrations of what you think of as power are nothing but distractions from our real purpose. We are here to make you an offer.'

I pulled a bottle of water out of my bag and unscrewed it, splashing some of the liquid over the bite mark. I noticed my phone vibrating in there, and knew it would be Carmel. Her spidey senses had probably kicked in, and she was checking up on me.

Whatever it was these jokers had to say, they didn't have long left to say it in. Carmel would be here, going all ape-shit Champion crazy, and these poor puppet bodies would sustain a lot more damage than they had so far.

'So talk,' I said, looking up at them. 'Stop trying to mess with me, and talk. What did your boss send you here to say? What could you possibly have that I would be interested in?'

Eithne took a sideways glance at Fintan, who was still leaning so far back in his chair he was in danger of up-ending it. His eyes were grey and glazed, as though someone had turned down the dimmer switch in his brain.

She made a little noise that sounded disgusted with him, uttered a word under her breath that sounded suspiciously like 'Men!', and turned back to face me.

'We have,' she said slowly and clearly, 'your parents.'

Chapter Twenty-Seven

All of the calm that I'd been partly feeling and partly faking deserted me, and I stared at Eithne across the table.

She was smiling at me, clearly delighted at the way my face had fallen into a state of slack-jawed disrepair. Taking advantage of the fact that I was now completely poleaxed, she reached out and grabbed the biscotti from my saucer, popping it between her bright red lips and munching it up.

'Mmm . . . almonds! Yum!' she said, once she'd swallowed.

'You can't have my parents,' I eventually said, trying to drag some sense out of my brain and into my words. 'They're in the Otherworld. They're safe there.'

She had to be lying. They had to be safe. Allowing anything else to be true would be too horrific to contemplate.

From the age of six onwards, my life had been hellish – and the only happy times I could recall were spent with Francis and Sarah Delaney, their Fairy Princess, loved and cherished and adored. Secure in a way I've never known since.

They *had* to be safe.

Through everything that had happened – fighting off Fintan, seeing my nan die, making my choice to be the Goddess – I'd at least been able to take solace from the fact that while I might not be with them, my parents were safe. Untouchable.

And now, smirking and pouting away opposite me, Eithne was telling me that they weren't safe. They weren't untouchable. And that they – and Fitzgarry – had them.

I realised that that was what he'd meant that night in Gramercy Park, when he said he had something I wanted. Something that would make me come to him voluntarily. And I also realised what it was that Gabriel had been hiding from me.

He'd known – he'd found out when he entered the Otherworld through the Sidhe at the Hunger Memorial. He'd come back calm and sad and burdened with a knowledge that he didn't want to share with me. I felt a familiar sense of fury and frustration swirl in my stomach – no matter how many steps the two of us took forward together, he always found a way to leave me behind. We were supposed to be partners, but his high-handed arrogance and determination to protect me against everything from paper cuts to parental kidnapping meant that we would never be equal. At least not in his eyes.

'Nope,' said Eithne, licking the last few crumbs from her lips. 'Not safe. Not safe at all. Mr F has already amassed a huge amount of power from the souls he's sacrificed. He obviously thinks you'll be the icing on the cake, the final boost he needs to resurrect Balor and finally end all this . . .' she paused to look around her, contemptuously, '. . . nonsense. But he is even now stronger than the combined force of the Faidh, or the Gods we know, or your precious High King. Stronger than all of us. And he's used some of that power to give your parents a little holiday. A kind of mini-break!'

'Where are they? And why should I even believe you? You could be making all of this up!'

'I could be,' she replied, grinning. There was still a glint of red on her teeth where she'd bitten my arm, and it made me shudder. 'But I'm not. Would you like to see them, get some – what do they call it in the human movies? – proof of life?'

My mind was racing, and I took a deep breath, hearing the cold air rasp in my throat. I needed to stay calm. Not freak out. Not cry, or panic, or accidentally kill Eithne, leaving her to rot before she even got a chance to take those rollers out. I needed to take my hatred for her and Fintan out of the equation, and concentrate on this one thing. On the fact that these bastards had somehow dragged my parents – the only people who'd ever shown me unconditional love – out of their peaceful world and into this totally messed-up one, all in an attempt to manipulate me.

'Yes. I would like to see them,' I finally said.

'Only if you say please,' she replied, her voice rising on the final word in a parody of girlish flirtation that probably suited Sophie Duffy a whole lot more than it suited her.

'Please,' I murmured through clenched teeth, repeating to myself over and over again: must not kill Eithne, must not kill Eithne. At least, not yet.

'Oh all right then, since you asked so very nicely. You can find them in your happy home. In that lovely little house where the mighty Cormac Mor abandoned you with that old hag Coleen. We thought you'd like that, as a special treat. Circle of life and all. They're waiting there for you – but you *must* go alone. None of those meddling kids you call your friends. The slightest whiff of a Champion or the Morrigan or even that booze-drenched witch Fionnula, and all deals are off. Do you understand me, Goddess?'

'Yes,' I said, leaning closer to her. 'I understand you, Eithne. And when all of this is done – when I've looked Balor in his mighty fucking eye and destroyed him – I will find you. I will find you, and I will kill you. Do *you* understand *me*?'

She lurched back, the legs of the chair scraping against the paving stones, and for a fraction of a second I saw her fear, an ancient thing flickering over Sophie Duffy's pretty young face. She covered it up straight away, but I'd seen it – and it was delicious.

I grabbed my bag and stood up. Without a word, I left her, sitting there looking great and smelling awful, holding on to Fintan's hand as he drooled quietly away next to her. I marched through the arts centre and back out onto the street, pulling my phone out of my satchel and furiously texting as I strode past the packed shops with their Christmas decorations and saccharine window displays and piped carols.

I told Carmel I was fine, to give me another half hour, and headed off for the taxi rank. She'd be furious at being ditched, but what's a goddess to do? If she knew, she'd insist on coming – and after Eithne's warning I couldn't risk it. She immediately asked what I was doing and if I was all right. In return, I told a small text lie. Claimed to be buying fancy underwear 'just in case', to give her already healthy sense of curiosity about my love life a push in a distracting direction. She sent me a series of winky faces in return.

I didn't like fibbing, but it was better than explaining I was going to visit my already-dead parents who'd been kidnapped from their afterlife and stashed in my also-dead nan's terraced house of horrors.

I jumped in a black cab, slamming the door behind me. Time for a trip back in time.

Chapter Twenty-Eight

As the black cab shunted its way through the city centre and towards Scotland Road, weaving in and out of match-day traffic, another text landed from Carmel. Telling me, with much glee, that Luca had actually been transported back to the UK in a coffin, which she clearly found hilarious. That Gabriel was back, and so were the others.

After quickly replying and checking that The Dog was with them, I switched off the phone and took out the battery. I had no idea how sophisticated Gabriel could get, but I'd seen enough episodes of 24 to have a vague idea that he could somehow use it to find me. Plus I suspected the damn thing would be humming away with multiple calls sometime very soon, and I was too busy to deal with an irate Goddess Protection Squad.

I paid the driver, and climbed out in front of my nan's house. My house now, technically speaking. She'd left me everything in her will – which didn't amount to a great deal; no priceless jewellery or Ming Dynasty door-stops or anything likely to excite the boffins on *Antiques Roadshow*. Basically just this small, two-bedroomed terraced house – which I wasn't even sure I wanted.

The street was buzzing, with cars lined up head-to-tail along both sides of the pavement. Groups of lads were wandering down towards Anfield, all dressed in their uniform of red and white, eating from open bags of chips and laughing with each other. The rest of the time it was quiet here, but on match days, a river of life ran through it. I could hear the distant chanting in the background, and the vague clop-clopping of police horses patrolling. The squeals of excited kids, a muffled voice coming out of speakers, and the sounds of thousands of people gathered together at their chosen place of worship.

It had always driven Coleen mad, predictably enough. She was a grouchy old cow at the best of times, and the noise and the litter and the drunks cutting through from the footie pubs nearby just piled on the joy. Once I'd left home, and found my own flat several miles and a different world away in the south end of the city, I avoided coming here on match days at all. Not that that was a problem – she was never in a hurry to see me anyway.

I'd learned since that it wasn't all that simple. She wasn't only an evil, miserable bitch – although that was most definitely in there with the other, more complicated, stuff. Her life had been difficult. She'd suffered great loss, and been forced into a role she never wanted to play – my guardian. It was a blow that she'd never quite recovered from, and neither had I, thanks to Gabriel's masterful handling of the situation. I'd survived – physically at least – so I supposed he saw it as a victory. I saw it as a black flag that would forever hang between us, fluttering in the breeze of bad memories drifting by.

The taxi left, reversing all the way out of the cramped side street because there wasn't enough room to turn. He'd shown no interest at all in the circus going on around him, just pulled faces and made comments about the 'knobheads' getting in his way. He must, I deduced, be an Everton fan – and they weren't playing 'til tomorrow.

I was left there, standing alone outside the house. The door was still the same shade of cream, the windows still covered by thick floral curtains on the inside, and now several layers of grime on the outside. The step was still painted red, but the top coat was flaking, and it needed a good sweep. I really needed to do something with the place. Put it on the market or rent it out or just get Fionnula to give it one of her SOS Home Makeover demolition jobs. My memories of it would be forever sour, no matter what deathbed reconciliations I'd had with Coleen. Outside, in my brave new world, I was a goddess and could hold my own with supernatural pseudo-deities and Otherworldly bad guys.

But inside that house? Inside I would forever be the tiny, crumpled mass of snotty heartbreak that I was when I first arrived. The small, sobbing six-year-old girl that Fintan remembered. The one who wept for her mummy and daddy, and didn't understand the abusive new life she'd been abandoned into. It would always be a place of sorrow and sadness and regret. I'd not been there since the night Coleen died, and I never wanted to set foot in it again.

But, I reminded myself, I had to. Because this is where, with a cruel flair you had to admire, Fitzgarry claimed he had my parents. Even the thought of them in this awful house, with its cold rooms and unloved furniture and echoes of the miserable lives Coleen and I had endured there together, felt wrong, corrupted. The ultimate poke in the eye from a master player.

A collection of blokes ranging in age from maybe fifteen to seventy walked past, three abreast across the pavement, flowing around me as I stood and stared. They were in fine spirits and loud voices, and one of them – he looked to be somewhere in the middle of the multi-generational group – muttered a timeless classic as he walked by. 'Cheer up, love,' he said. 'It might never happen.'

Hah, I thought, grabbing the keys and my courage

and getting a tight grip of both. Maybe not in his world – but in mine? Anything was possible.

They marched off down towards the ground, and I fitted the old-fashioned Yale key into the lock. I turned it and pushed the door open, expecting a small mountain of junk mail, and to be assailed by the familiar and unwelcome smells of the house: stale cigarette smoke from Coleen's incessant puffing, and the latent tang of the chemical air-freshener plug-ins she used to try and hide it.

Instead, as I took a step inside, it smelled clean and fresh and vaguely of cut grass. I looked around me: the narrow hallway was gone. The stairs that led straight up to the bedrooms weren't there. The corridor that linked the living room and the kitchen had disappeared. It should have looked similar to our hidey-hole in Kensington, but . . . it didn't.

I'd walked through the door of a tiny terraced house in Anfield, and into something entirely different.

I was in a spacious lobby, the walls all painted cream. The door behind me, as I closed it, was wider and more solid. Decorative stained glass above it cast flickers of red and yellow, and next to it was an overflowing coat stand, draped with anoraks and fleeces and colourful scarves.

There was a small side table, and on it an old-fashioned telephone – the kind with a big handset and a dial instead of buttons. Next to it was a vase of fresh lilies, which explained the smell. There was a white envelope propped against the vase, with my name on it. I hesitated, then picked it up and opened it quietly. It was, as I expected, from him. My fingers recoiled as they touched the ink, knowing that he'd touched it before me.

Enjoy your trip down Memory Lane – FF.

I frowned, shoved it in my pocket, and shouted out: 'Hello! Anyone home?'

Nothing. I could hear sounds coming from elsewhere in

the house, small voices that rose and fell in dramatic arcs. I squinted – which for some strange reason I thought would help me hear better – and realised it was a radio play.

I looked up and all around me, at high ceilings and intricate plaster cornicing and a decorative rose circling the hanging lights. Sunshine flooded in through a large picture window, and the radio play ended with applause.

I took a few steps, over varnished bare wood floors covered with rugs that looked old and Oriental, and knew I'd been here before. It wasn't Coleen's house, that was for sure, but it was, somehow, still mine.

It felt so familiar, like a half-remembered song I'd known as a child and almost forgotten. Even the sound of the cuckoo clock ticking sounded right, like a rhythm I already knew.

I walked further into the hallway, seeing a wide staircase leading upwards. The banister was painted white, and more sunlight streamed down, picking out flecks of dust hanging in the air around me.

There was a door, a few steps on. Again, painted with white gloss, its handle a shining rustic brass. I could hear movements coming from inside and, again, the sound of voices. Of quiet chat and gentle laughter and then an easy silence.

'Hello?' I yelled again, not wanting to scare anyone. It was entirely possible that I'd suffered some kind of psychotic breakdown and wandered into a complete stranger's house in a fugue state. Fintan could have played some kind of mind magic and sent me off to explore random houses in Grassendale, for all I knew. Except . . . it still all felt so very familiar. I gripped the brass door handle and twisted, noting as I did that it felt smaller than it should. I remembered it – my body remembered it – being much bigger, so bulky I struggled to wrap my hand around it. It definitely used to be bigger – or, of course, I used to be much smaller.

I walked into a spacious room and stopped, frozen, as I looked around. Again, high ceilings, walls painted shades of neutral. A piano in one corner, and a TV in another. Old fashioned again, with a big back, and no sign of any modern essentials like a satellite box or a DVD player. Just a bulky old VCR, with some video boxes on top of it. *Working Girl*, with Melanie Griffith grinning up from the cover, and *Rosemary Conley's Hip and Thigh Diet*.

The walls were lined with crammed, over-flowing bookshelves, and two more paperbacks were lying face-down on the arms of a huge cream-coloured sofa. One of them was *Silence of the Lambs* by Thomas Harris, and it was almost finished.

I knew this room. I knew this house. I knew these bookshelves, and this sofa, and I knew the people who lived here. It gushed back into my mind like a stream suddenly un-dammed: memories I'd blocked out, for so long, because they were just too painful to deal with.

The contrast between the early days of my childhood and the ones after Coleen took me in was so sharp you could slit your throat on it. After a few months of misery with my new 'nan', praying for the return of my real family, I'd realised they were gone and not coming back – and thinking about them only made the hurting worse. So much so that I'd buried it, and tried to forget it all – my old name. My old parents. My old home.

Now, I was back here. In our house in St John's Wood. The only real home I'd ever had – somehow transported and crammed into the space occupied by Coleen's joyless mid-terrace in Liverpool.

I wandered to the windowsills, and remembered them afresh – so wide a small person could perch in them and watch the world go by. Assuming she was very naughty and moved all the photo frames first. The pictures were still there, the collection of different sizes and different colours and different faces, all standing to attention like a small memory militia. Framed photos of my parents together when they were younger, wearing some hideous late 70s clothes, her with huge hair and him with a stupid smile, standing outside an old VW camper van.

Pictures of an elderly couple I didn't recognise, but my mind logged as my mother's parents. Various scenes – on beaches, at parties, in the garden. In the middle of them all, the one I remembered the most – the two of them at their wedding. A huge bouffant frock and a Princess Di haircut. A grey morning suit. Dazzling grins in the sunshine outside a church I didn't know.

I picked the photo up, careful not to get fingerprints on the glass, and stared at it, smiling, before I put it back in its place. I looked again at the collection, and realised that something was missing from it. To be precise, someone was missing from it – me.

Filtered through a child's eyes, I could vividly recall these photos – and vividly recall me, at the heart of them. Me a gurning baby in my mother's arms, wrapped in a pink blanket. Me as a chocolate-faced toddler, grin splitting a chubby face. Me as a child, in a school uniform, with my ginger plaits sticking out at the side of my head like handles. All kids are egomaniacs at heart, and I'd accepted my dominance of the windowsill display as my given right. Of course I was in the middle of it all – why wouldn't I be? I was the Fairy Princess, after all.

Except now, I wasn't. I wasn't a Fairy Princess and this house shouldn't be here. And if it was, where were my photos? Why weren't there any toys, or little girls' coats hanging up in the hallway? Why was there no sign of me at all?

I straightened the pictures, and walked through the room, noting subtle differences from the way I now remembered it. It was so much tidier and so much more spic and span, and the smell of flowers was everywhere.

I took in a deep breath of flower-scented air, and opened the door that I now knew led into the kitchen. They were there. My parents. He was sitting at the big old pine table, a mug of tea in front of him, and a newspaper spread out, turned to the sport section. Cricket. He was reading about cricket, which felt right.

She was over by the counter, next to the sink, with a vast pile of flowers laid out there. She was holding a small paring knife, and trimming the stems, preparing to place them in a large glass vase.

'Lilies again?' he said, smiling, but not looking up from his paper.

'Of course,' she replied, smiling back as she worked. 'You know I love lilies. They just, I don't know, remind me of something, something good.'

'Me!' I shouted, approaching her. 'They remind you of me! I'm Lily!'

There was no response at all. My dad carried on reading about the cricket, occasionally tutting to himself. My mum carried on stripping leaves and placing each single stem into the waiting water, humming quietly as she did it.

I reached out, tried to touch her, but my hand went straight through her long blonde hair. They couldn't hear me, or see me, or feel me. I was the ghost in the house – the ghost of a child who, in this existence, had never been born.

I looked around at the kitchen. There were none of my crayon drawings of rainbows and smiley-faced sunshine pinned up on the corkboard. No sign of childish food, or the brightly coloured plastic bowls I remembered eating my breakfast cereal from. Nothing at all. Fitzgarry had somehow moved them from the Otherworld, to this place: this fake replica of my childhood home. One that had been happy and bustling and noisy and full.

'What shall we do today, love?' my dad said, finally folding up the paper, and leaning back in his chair.

'I don't know,' my mother replied, bringing her own mug of tea over and sitting with him. 'I keep feeling like there is something we should be doing, but I can't quite put my finger on it. Like it's on the tip of my tongue.'

'That's what you always say when you're watching *Mastermind*,' he said, nudging her gently in the ribs. 'But I know what you mean. I feel like I've forgotten something too. Oh well. Must be getting senile in our old age. I suppose I'll just potter in the garden then, if that's all right with you.'

'Course it is,' she said, tucking a stray strand of hair behind her ears. She reached out and took the newspaper, unfolding it in front of her before frowning and looking up. 'But I wish I could remember what it is that's missing . . .'

I felt the tears slowly rolling down my cheeks before I knew I'd even cried them. I wanted to talk to them, to scream at them, to shake them until they woke up. Until they remembered. Until they realised exactly what it was they were missing.

But I knew it wouldn't do any good – wherever they were, whatever Fitzgarry had conjured up around them, I wasn't part of it. They weren't dead. They weren't in the Otherworld. They were here, trapped in some kind of comfortable suburban limbo. It could have been worse – they had their cricket and their tea and their fitness videos to keep them amused. But for me, it was heart-wrenching – seeing the few happy memories I had wiped out of existence.

I dragged clenched fingers across my cheeks, wiping away the tears, and took one final look. At them. At the old pine table. At the view of the garden from the back window, with its neat borders and its bird bath and its toolshed. At the home that I'd once known, but had never known me.

And I left.

Chapter Twenty-Nine

I staggered my way back through the living room, and the hallway, crashing into the coat stand as I approached the way out.

My hands fumbled against the door as I tried to open it, and eventually I half stepped, half fell back out onto the street.

I steadied myself with a hand against solid brick, and looked around. I wasn't in St John's Wood any more, Toto. I was very much back in Anfield, and was also very much in the dark – literally.

Whatever sphere of alternate reality Fitzgarry had created in there, it had been running on Otherworld time. Which meant that even though I'd only been inside for minutes, hours had passed in the 'real' world.

The match day cars had gone, and only a few discarded McDonald's wrappers remained as evidence of the heavy footfall the street had seen earlier. I glanced at my watch, and saw that it was almost 8 p.m. Shit. I'd left Carmel in the early afternoon and told her I'd be back in an hour. They'd be going absolutely apeshit by now. Gabriel's head had probably exploded with the anguish of not being able to protect me 24/7.

I rummaged around in my bag, knowing I needed to

let them know I was still breathing, then decided I needed a drink more. I mean, that whole revisiting the past thing was a major league head-fuck. The kind that only a quick pint or six can cure.

I headed out onto the main road that led all the way into Liverpool, which was lined with bars and pubs of varying levels of style, business, music and propensity for violence. I wandered into one that looked only marginally rammed with drunken idiots, and also seemed to be hosting some kind of low-key 80s disco.

There was a small dance floor off in one corner, and a bored-looking DJ who looked about eighteen was spinning some Sade. A less than smooth operator was clumsily trying to grope all three of the middle-aged women who were trying very hard to ignore him as they danced. I bought two pints of lager, and found a table as hidden away as I could. After a few uplifting gulps, I finally reassembled my phone. It took a few attempts, my fingers were trembling so much – plus, you know, I had an idea of what was waiting for me once I switched the damn thing back on.

Sure enough, the beeping started almost immediately. I drank some more, then looked. Sixteen missed calls from Gabriel. Twelve from Carmel. About the same amount of voicemails from both. A text from Katashi. And a message from British Gas telling me my boiler was due for a service. I deleted them all apart from the one about the boiler – safety first.

I needed a bit of space and a bit of peace to think about everything. To think about Fitzgarry and my parents and the end of the world. About Gabriel and Luca and my dog. About what the fuck I was going to do next.

I hated Fitzgarry with a passion I'd never quite felt before in my life. I was fizzing with it. With sheer fury at what he'd done to poor Colin, at what he'd done to the poor souls entrusted to his care in homes and hospitals. At what he'd done to my poor parents, who deserved so much better. At the reckless way he was willing to tread over the rest of humanity simply to acquire power.

I wouldn't give in to him – I refused to. I'd rather chuck myself in front of a Northern Line train to Southport than submit to him. He wanted my power, needed it to complete his plans. I could take that option away from him right now by ending my life. But I wouldn't do that either – I'd only just started it, and he could fuck right off. I wasn't his, and I never would be.

If I had to sit here all night coming up with a master plan to the backdrop of Deacon Blue, I'd do it. I would find a way to defeat him, to rescue my parents, to do it all. I just needed some inspiration to go with my resolve, and I'd be all sorted. I knew that what I should do was go back to Kensington, talk to the masterminds I called my friends, and see what their devious schemes amounted to.

Except up until now, they'd failed. They'd completely, totally, one hundred per cent screwed up, even by allowing Fitzgarry to get this far. I needed to stand on my own two feet, and *think*. There had to be a way.

I sat like that for most of an hour, drinking my beer, glaring at any men drunk or stupid enough to come near me, and singing along to Wham! songs almost against my will. Eventually, something started to germinate. To take root, to blossom, and to do other vaguely horticultural things. I supposed the bullshit in my mind provided it with lots of fertile ground.

I bought another pint, and realised as I started it that I was marginally drunk. I must have been. I really wanted to dance to Depeche Mode. But . . . I had something. Admittedly something that probably would only work in a big-budget film, the kind that needed a John Williams soundtrack, but it was something. Something better than suicide or submission, at least.

I pulled my phone out of my bag again. Two more missed calls from Gabriel. None from the boiler man. I sighed, knowing I had to do something to put him out of his misery. We'd been apart since the showdown in Gramercy Park. The showdown where I thought I'd lost him, and fell momentarily to pieces. He'd be feeling the same now, not knowing where I was or what had happened to me. It wasn't fair to torture him, and now I had those budding ideas sprouting in my brain, I felt more in control. More able to simply breathe.

I decided on a text. Less chance of getting screamed at that way. 'I'm fine. Be back in an hour.'

I pressed send, then straight away composed another one. This time to Luca, simply telling him to go outside and call me in private. I knew he would – not just because he was my slave and all, but because he lived to sneak around behind Gabriel's back.

I gathered up my stuff and walked – a tiny bit unsteadily – towards the door. One of the women had finally given up, and was doing an ungainly slowie with the balding sex pest in a Pink Floyd T-shirt. Amazing how your standards dropped the more you drank.

As soon as I was outside, the phone rang, and I answered it straight away.

'I am outside a derelict house in Kensington,' said Luca. 'With your dog. She misses you. I miss you. We have all been worried.'

'Yeah,' I replied, huddling in the doorway to try and shelter from the rain that was slashing down through the street-lit sky. 'I can imagine. Sorry. I'll explain later. I need you to do something for me.'

There was a pause. I heard the dog bark, once and sudden, as though saying hello.

'All right. Anything. What is it?' he eventually asked.

'You're not going to like it, I warn you now,' I said.

'I suspected as much from the tone of your voice, and

the fact that you're not asking the High King for this particular favour. But I live to serve – now, what is it?'

'I need,' I said, 'to see Donn.'

Yep. Donn. The Lord of the Dead. The now one-eyed bastard who'd treated me like shit at Tara. Luca's former master, and the kind of man you'd cross the street to avoid even if the other side of the street was crawling with brain-eating zombies.

Luca, predictably enough, didn't like it one little bit. He faffed and growled and argued and complained and eventually agreed to try and reach him. And also, of course, not to mention it just yet to Gabriel. There were things I needed to do alone. Away from the High King and his soldiers. Away from Carmel. Away from Fionnula and the Morrigan and everyone else.

I ended the call by blowing a kiss to the dog – yes, indeed, totally tragic – and leaned back against the wall to bite my lip and catch my breath. I had one more call to make before I went back to my des-res in Kensington. The one I least wanted to make.

Right on cue, as I called up his number, I heard Tears for Fears kicking in on the dance floor. Everybody Wants To Rule The World. Don't they just, I thought, pressing the dial button.

Minutes later, it was arranged. I would see Fitzgarry the next night. I would allow him to use me. I would let him sip my soul, and drain me of my power. I would, as he had predicted, go to him voluntarily.

Now, I just needed to see exactly how much power that was.

It was time to go and be a goddess.

Chapter Thirty

Another rainy night, another black cab ride. This time back to Kensington.

I could hear The Dog scraping and whining at the makeshift door someone had knocked together as I approached, and felt my heart literally about to burst with affection for her. It was likely to be the only un-ambiguous welcome I received, bearing in mind the others had all been stressed out of their minds for the last few hours.

I walked into the living room of house number one, and was faced with some kind of bacchanal. The interior design had been stepped up a level, presumably with a few more trips to the shops. The whole floor was now covered in thick duvets and fleecy blankets and huge cushions, like a nest. Candles were lit and placed around the room, making the whole place look warm and cosy and cute, a boutique hotel going for the luxury bedouin tent vibe.

Someone had acquired a battery-powered CD player, and Fionnula was shaking her booty to Beyoncé's 'Crazy in Love'. Katashi was looking on in amusement, drinking from a can of Red Bull. The rest of the gang was lounging around on the floor and cushions, drinking from cans of considerably stronger stuff. Carmel and Connor were snuggled up in one corner, and Finn and Kevin were playing what appeared to be a Nintendo DS in another. So much for their stress levels. Obviously once they knew I was fine they'd slipped into default R&R setting. I'd seen it happen before – there's only so long you can be battle-ready for. Fight hard, play hard.

Luca was nowhere to be seen, and both Gabriel and the Morrigan weren't around. Possibly they were in the kitchen whizzing up a big jug of Margaritas. Not. I looked around, taking it all in as The Dog furiously licked my fingers.

'Hi honey, I'm home!' I shouted, waiting for Gabriel to emerge. Carmel raised her can at me in salute, but gave me a very evil eye at the same time. Yes. Well. There'd be a price to pay on that front, but it could wait. Fionnula, breathing heavily from all her crazy grandma dancing, landed in Katashi's lap and started to play with his hair. He tolerated it, like the very nice person he was, and smiled at me over the top of his Red Bull.

My triumphant return was considerably less triumphant than I'd expected it to be, but also considerably less fraught with interrogations as well, so I took it as a win. I did, however, need to break up the party. We had a big day ahead of us and, in my case, a pretty big night as well.

I put my bag down, and walked over to the CD player, The Dog superglued to my side. I switched it off suddenly, enough to hear Finn's raised voice finishing off a sentence he'd been shouting with the word 'arsehole'. I glanced at him and he blushed slightly. Glad I wasn't the only one suffering from slapped cheek disease.

'I need you all to leave,' I said. 'Now.'

Fionnula started to struggle upright on Katashi's lap, and I heard a 'but . . .' start to form on her overly-glossed lips.

'No buts,' I announced. 'Time for you all to fuck off to the pub or something.'

I heard footsteps on the stairs, and assumed it was Gabriel. I felt a small tremor run through my tummy at the thought of seeing him again, of facing him after all the deception, but clamped it down. I didn't have time to be a girly-pants right now.

Everyone started to get up and move around and pull on shoes and boots. Part of me was surprised that they'd listened – I'd tried to put a load of Goddess oomph into my words, but wasn't sure how successful I'd been. Carmel came towards me, still hopping on one leg as she shoved her left foot into an unlaced Converse.

'What gives?' she said, frowning at me. 'First you dump me in town and go AWOL, now you kick me out? If this is the new you, I'm not sure I like her.'

I owed her an explanation. And a hug. Possibly a cruise to the Caribbean with Gerard Butler as her sex slave. But again, I didn't have time. I stared into her eyes, and reached out to briefly touch her hand in apology.

'I'm sorry,' I said. 'But not now, OK? Tomorrow. I'll tell you everything tomorrow.'

She was gazing over my shoulder, and I knew Gabriel had arrived. She looked from me, to him, and back again, the frown growing deeper by the second as she weighed up the situation.

'You better had,' she said simply, flouncing past me as she followed Connor to the door. After a few moments and a lot of complaining, I heard the makeshift door being pushed shut, scraping on the ground as it went.

I stayed facing away from him, buying myself a few moments as I shrugged off my jacket and kicked off my boots.

'Am I supposed to be fucking off to the pub as well?' he eventually asked, after what felt like hours of him standing behind me. He walked into the room, wearing a pair of Levis and nothing else. He'd obviously braved one of the cold showers, and his slightly too long hair was dripping water over the ripped muscle of his shoulders and chest.

Good, I thought, taking in the view and feeling my breath catch. That certainly helped.

'No,' I said, closing the distance between us and reaching up to place my hands on his shoulders. His skin was cool, but his eyes flamed at the touch – a scorching violet that shone in the candle light. 'I need you here.'

I moved closer, until our hips connected, and tugged his head down to kiss him. I had no idea how to do seduction, so I thought it best to simply get started. He hesitated, tried to pull away, but I kept hold of him, standing on tiptoes so I could press my lips to his.

I let my hands roam over the smooth, firm flesh of his shoulders, his back, his sides, coming to rest on his perfectly denim-clad arse and holding him even closer. I felt his response, and shamelessly wriggled into it, a small fire starting to burn inside me.

I pulled away a few inches, breathless, flustered, and delighted to see his face lost in lust. We'd been here before, and this time it wasn't going to end with frustration and tears. I started to pop the buttons on his jeans, one by one, distracted by the sensation of his hands slipping beneath my sweater, his fingers making gentle contact with flesh, the touch of his lips nuzzling against my neck as I worked on the Levis.

'We should talk,' he said, his actions at odds with his words as I felt my bra strap pop open. His hands drifted around my waist, reaching up to stroke first one nipple, then the other, all the time kissing and sucking and softly nipping at my neck, my ears, my shoulders. I felt a tingling sensation start to run through me, a kind of white noise in my ears, a build-up of need so strong that for a moment I thought my barriers had failed and I was about to pass out with some hideous vision. I wobbled slightly, then stretched up my arms as he pulled my top off, throwing my bra to join it. I leaned into him, feeling my bare flesh connect with the ridged muscle of his torso for the first time, and my whole body singing in response.

He cupped one of my breasts in his hand, leaned down to kiss it, to lick its erect peak, and suck it gently into his mouth.

'No,' I muttered, grinding into him, rubbing my body against his groin, feeling him hard and ready and groaning with pleasure. 'We talk too much. Nothing good ever comes of it. We should fuck.'

Chapter Thirty-One

Afterwards, I allowed myself the luxury of lying in his arms for a few minutes. I felt physically exhausted, drained by the exquisite things we'd done to each other, my body still humming and singing as I rested my head on his chest. God, if I'd known it would be like this, I'd have insisted on starting earlier.

We were lying on a heap of duvets, a blanket thrown over us, candles burning down and going out one by one. He was stroking my hair, kissing my forehead, one leg thrown territorially across me.

'These are not the surroundings I'd imagined for this,' he said, one hand drifting across my body, fingers caressing still fluttering skin.

'What? An abandoned house in a Liverpool back-street?' I said, letting my own hands wander as well. He was so bloody beautiful. Every part of him was perfect, and I'd waited a very long time to get the chance to touch him. I could have stayed here and stroked him for a few more years, if it wasn't for the impending apocalypse and all. 'No electricity and sheet metal windows? Surely that's every girl's dream?'

'Probably not,' he replied, shifting slightly in response to my touch. 'But you're not exactly every girl, are you?'

I smiled. No, I wasn't. I was the Goddess and, for the first time, I felt it. All of that nagging – Hathor, Carmel, Fionnula. They'd been right. Mabe was created to bless the earth, to bring fertility and prosperity and milk and honey – and I'd been doing it all on auto pilot, until now. Now, I felt like a supreme mega-being from another planet. I felt full and strong and powerful – as though I could leap tall buildings in single strides. There had been no brass bands, or choirs of celestial angels, but I felt the change inside me – the unleashing of power that had been there all along, latent, shackled by the battle raging between Lily McCain the Untouchable, and the Goddess. Now, I felt them both meld – and it was glorious.

And I also felt . . . sad. Sad because this had to end. This perfect moment, this one oasis of tenderness in a life of conflict, had to end. I needed to drag myself away from this man, this place, and do Big Important Stuff. I had to see Donn. I had to make a deal. I had to face Fitzgarry. All I really wanted to do was stay here, under these covers, cocooned with Gabriel – but a duvet day would have to wait.

'What are you thinking?' he said, breath warm against my face.

'Isn't that what the girl's supposed to ask?' I replied, avoiding the question. I didn't want to explain to him how perfect this all felt, and how I knew it was merely one gentle moment of calm and serenity amid the turmoil. I just wanted to lie there, quietly, in his arms, and enjoy it. He gave me a look – like he knew exactly what I was doing – and said: 'I'm not like other men. And when I ask what you're thinking, it's not because I'm being needy, or I'm looking for marks out of ten. We both know I'm an eleven. It's because you're distracted, and I can feel you preparing to do or say something that I won't like. Because we *should* have talked. Because there are things we need to think about, and there are things you need to know.'

Ah. His bossy boots tone was back. The one that always made me think he was about to channel Picard, and say 'make it so'. Looked like the honeymoon period was over, after five whole minutes.

I worked my way out of the blankets, and stood up. I was shocked at how brazen I felt, how I didn't scurry for cover, or try and hide my nakedness, or worry if my bum looked big in this. Gabriel might indeed be an eleven, but I was a frigging goddess.

I started to get dressed, and he followed suit. Our delicate truce was over, replaced by a tense silence as we messed around with knickers and socks and buttons. He didn't have a T-shirt to put on, which I was kind of pleased about. It put him at a disadvantage, and gave me something to look at while I spoke.

'I know about my parents, Gabriel. I know Fitzgarry has them.'

His face twisted, and his eyes dimmed to a sombre navy blue. He reached out for me, and I pushed his hands away. He opened his mouth to speak, and I shook my head, feeling a surge of anger creeping in already. Now we were out of bed, we didn't seem to quite fit again. This was my life, not a Mills & Boon – maybe it would always be that way.

'No, don't bother, Gabriel – I know you're sorry, I know why you did it. I know that, as usual, you were trying to protect me. But now you have to understand something. I don't need protecting any more. What we just did? It was amazing. It was the best thing ever. But it wasn't just great sex, was it? It was more than that. It was about me, becoming who I'm supposed to be. About me, finally accepting this power. About me, Lily McCain. Mabe. Whatever – all of it's the same now. I'm stronger than you can imagine. I have power that you don't. The days of you protecting me are gone – now it's time for me to do what I'm meant to do.'

The final candle sputtered and hissed out of existence, and all I could see of his face was illuminated by the weak rays of street lighting that filtered through the cracks in the boarded-up windows.

He paused. Stared at me so intensely I thought I might evaporate. Then he shook his head, still-damp hair swishing against his shoulders.

'Would it be too needy,' he said, trying to smile, 'to say I feel somewhat . . . used?'

I laughed despite myself, despite the circumstances, and reached out to poke him in the chest.

'That's what you were put on this earth to do, big boy – and I didn't hear you complaining when I was using you all over the floor a few minutes ago. Now, I've got to go out. I have to do something – alone. And you have to let me. Tomorrow, we face Fitzgarry. We free my parents, save the world, and we kill him. Either we do it together, Gabriel, or I do it without you. Really, what did you expect? One shag and I'd be at home cooking your dinner for the rest of my life?'

He grabbed hold of me, slamming me into his bare chest so hard my breath was knocked out in an ungainly gust. He held me there, arms wrapped around me so tight I couldn't move, could barely inhale. He buried his face deep in my hair, and whispered: 'No. I never expected that, Lily, nor would I want it. But I have waited for you for centuries, and loved you for years, and much as you mock me for it, would give up my life for you in a heartbeat. All of that is as it has always been – and always will be. What did you expect? One shag and that would change?

'Now go, if you say you must. But remember this – you're not *the* Goddess. You're *my* Goddess.'

He let me go so suddenly I staggered with the

unexpected release, and he turned away. I took one more moment to admire the breadth of his shoulders, the way those Levis hugged his body, then grabbed my bag and left.

I kneeled down to The Dog before I departed, letting her lick my face, scratching her ears to try and reassure her. She whined as I went, which made me feel like the world's biggest shit, but it had to be done.

As soon as I was outside, in the cold damp air, winter drizzle kissing my skin, I let go of the breath that I didn't realise I'd been holding. Of course it hadn't been easy. Things with Gabriel would never be easy. But if I didn't get my act together, things with Gabriel would simply never be anything. We'd all be gone, and Fitzgarry's new world order would take care of the rest.

I found my phone, and checked for messages from Luca. I pulled my face at the destination, but felt satisfied that at least one part of my plan was coming together. There was a long way to go yet, though, so I'd save my victory dance for later.

I walked into Liverpool, having had enough of black cabs for the day. There's only so much meaningless conversation with middle-aged blokes listening to Radio Merseyside that you can handle. Besides, I needed the air. I needed to feel my body working. I needed to see the world, and all it had to lose.

Admittedly, the walk from Kensington to Liverpool on a rainy Saturday night might not have cast the world in its most flattering light, but I still needed it. I needed to walk past Galkoff's again, and remember the history of it. I needed to see that raucous gaggle of hens, dressed up in pink latex hot pants and L-plates, as they staggered out of the pub. I needed to see those drunk blokes, whistling at them. I needed to see the whirl of headlights and the sound of screeching brakes at the Queen Square bus station. I needed to hear the music blasting out of the Cavern as I passed by, and to notice the young couple snogging next to the John Lennon statue, and to smell the waft of garlic and coriander oozing out from Spice City on Stanley Street.

I needed to take strength from it all, to remind myself why I even existed. Of why it was worth fighting for, even without the added threat of my parents spending eternity trapped in a lifeless semi in a fake London suburb. I hadn't always been convinced – there was a time when all of this would have left me cold.

But now, it was mine. I felt my possession of it zinging through my veins, knew that the whole messy hotch-potch was mine to protect. People fucked up. They loved and they lost and they lived and they died. But they should always have the chance to do all of those things – Fintan and Eithne were wrong. And Fitzgarry was insane. And I was marching at the speed of light through this reality of twenty-first-century Liverpool, with ancient power and righteous anger searing through me.

It only took what felt like minutes to get there. My breathing was steady, even though I'd been Olympic-level speed walking, and my heartbeat was slow and calm. Looked like I was finally getting a few superpowers of my own to play with.

I'd been taking sneaky peeks behind me the whole time, fully expecting to see Gabriel lurking in the shadows, no top on and wielding the flaming Sword of Lugh as he charged to defend me from *Big Issue* sellers or drunks offering to share their chips. I didn't see him – but that didn't mean he wasn't there. He'd kind of been stalking me my whole life, which wasn't as creepy as it sounds – and I suspected he wasn't ready to give up yet. I knew he loved me. I'd been in his mind and seen how much. I'd felt it during every minute of our love-making. And sometimes it was pretty awesome to be protected. But other times? Like when I was sneaking around developing a dangerous masterplan that he'd totally disapprove of? Not so much.

If he was out there somewhere, I wondered what he'd make of me striding brazenly into the Tease Me Please Club off Dale Street. Tucked away near the business district, not far from the *Gazette* offices, its signage announced it was a 'high class' gentlemen's establishment. I had my suspicions that any place needing a sign to prove it was high class probably wasn't, and that the 'gentlemen' in question weren't going there to place their cloaks on muddy puddles to allow the fairer sex to keep their pretty feet dry.

I handed over my £20 cover charge to a bored-looking doorman with a shaved head, walked down the carpeted steps, and entered a world of fake glamorous sleaze. The walls were painted purple and silver, and covered in dozens of mirrors with gilt-edged frames. The bar was all dark wood with more mirrors, and the lounge area was completely bedecked in red velvet and tassels. It was Dracula-chic meets whorehouse.

None of the staff raised an eyebrow at me entering, so I was guessing more women came to these places than I'd thought. A few of the men sitting in the booths, though, cast me questioning glances and the odd hopeful smile. Yeah. Right. I was so not up for a paid-for threesome with Barry from Accounts. I reminded myself of all the positive thoughts I'd been cultivating about humanity during the walk here, and moved on, down into some kind of dimly lit stage area.

The music was ferociously loud, the kind of anonymous pumping house tunes you probably need ecstasy to appreciate, with a driving rhythm that I could feel vibrating through the soles of my Docs. I took a couple of steps down, saw a small performance area, lit up with neon spotlights and fluorescent poles. Two women were whirling around them, wearing nothing but thongs and smiles, their fake tans glowing as they writhed and wiggled with pretty damn impressive athleticism.

Around the stage, there were smaller booths, red velvet banquettes where more women gave lap dances. I started to stalk around, looking for Luca and Donn, noticing the mixed expressions of the men as I went. Some were sitting on their hands, obviously worried they might break the no-touching rule. Some looked drunk and lecherous, as you'd expect. Others looked scared and worried and a little bit embarrassed. Others had the glazed eyes and slack postures of people who'd consumed so much lager they might as well be at home in bed for all the fun they were having.

In front of them was a lot of bare, gyrating female flesh. Girls of different ages and shapes and sizes and colours, doing the bump and grind and smiling like their tips depended on it. I registered mild surprise at the sheer variety of chicks working there: there were the slender, toned young things I'd expected, but some a great deal older, with a lot more meat on their bones, who seemed to be just as popular. I don't suppose one hour of sex really made me an expert on men and their needs, did it?

One bloke shouted out at me as I passed, waving a handful of notes in the air. I gave him a look that said 'desist or die', and accidentally bumped over his pint with my hip as I edged by the table. I mean, come on – my hair was white and messy, and I was wearing seventeen layers of clothing with jeans and Doc Martens. Unless someone had a Morticia Goes To College fetish, I should have been low on the list of options in this place.

Finally, I spotted a familiar face tucked away in a red velvet booth in the far corner. A face that was difficult to forget, as it only had one eye. The Morrigan had pecked the other one out, which was only fair – he had just dislocated my arm, tried to have me raped, and then attempted to rip my head from my shoulders.

He wasn't alone, which I suppose I should have expected. A ridiculously lithe blonde was straddling him, her chest fully loaded with boobs that she appeared to have stolen from a much larger woman. I wondered how she ever managed to stay upright with those barrage balloons strapped on.

Donn didn't seem to mind. He was leaning back, a slight smile on his face, enjoying the show. I stood to one side, knowing that he'd seen me. He might only have one eye, but he was the Lord of the Dead – he had power that I was only just beginning to understand.

His long black hair was pulled into a ponytail, and he was dressed in black leather pants and a matching waistcoat. Kind of Medieval Asian cowboy.

I sat down next to him, looking on with interest as the dancer turned round and presented him with a rear view, which she proceeded to shake vigorously. I found it more fascinating than embarrassing, and noted the surprising absence of the Incredible Blush Machine that is usually my face. I realised right then why Donn had chosen this place for us to meet – he wanted to embarrass me. To humiliate me. To throw me off balance. Things had not ended well for Donn after our night at Tara, and I was undoubtedly very low on his list of favourite people.

The music came to an end, and the girl turned back round and gave us a dazzlingly white smile. She leaned in towards me, those inflatable bazookas right in my face, and said: 'Do you want a dance, hon? I'm sure your fella would like it . . .'

'He's not my fella,' I replied, leaning back slightly to avoid getting poked in the eye, 'but thanks for the offer. Maybe later.'

She seemed satisfied with my answer, or possibly the £20 note Donn passed over to her, and tottered off towards her next client.

'Ah,' he said, stretching out his arm so it was behind me in the booth, like a parody of a teenaged boy trying it on with a girl in the cinema. 'Alone at last! How have you been, Goddess?'

I was sure he had a pretty good idea of how I'd been, but decided to answer anyway.

'Oh, you know, the usual – fighting megalomaniacs, fleeing for my life, meeting with supernatural Councils. Shopping for handbags. That kind of thing.'

'I see. Busy girl. More than that, as well, I believe – you are changed. I can feel it in you . . .'

He stared at me, and I stared back. I was so not going to start chatting about my sex life with the Lord of the Dead. Too weird.

'Now, what is it you wanted of me, Goddess? I was surprised to be contacted by your dog, Luca. I thought I had made it clear that he was no longer any child of mine, but he was most insistent. And I am also curious as to why you don't have Cormac Mor with you, defending your honour as usual?'

He glanced around the room, and I detected a slightly nervous twitch in his one eye. Like me, he obviously suspected that Gabriel would be lurking around. They were allies – of sorts – but united only by their belief that humanity deserved the chance to die out all by itself, rather than being snuffed.

'He may well be here for all I know, so don't get too comfortable. And I asked Luca to contact you because I need your help,' I said. 'You know, I'm sure, of the threat we are facing. Of Fitzgarry, the mortal man who plans to resurrect Balor.'

'I had heard the tales, yes. The Morrigan was fluttering around the Otherworld just today, gathering information and scaring people. I did not believe it was true – that Balor could be returned. His body was trapped under-water in the Northern Seas, along with the rest of the

278

Fomorians. If it is even true, and not merely a story told to frighten our children. Are you telling me that it is the case?'

I took his drink – a glass of something cold and fizzy – and sipped it.

'Yes, it's true. I've met Fitzgarry. I've looked into his soul, such as it is. He is already part way there – Balor already lives within him, I think. But he needs more power to complete his transformation. Power that he intends to take from me. If I'm right in my understanding, Donn, you are the gatekeeper to the Otherworld. For the souls that dwell in it. You decide who is allowed in, who is moved on, who gets to stay.'

He nodded once, his angled eyes fastened intently on mine.

'And you may have noticed that you're missing a couple. My parents. They've somehow been taken, hidden. Fitzgarry is using that as leverage against me, to force me to submit to him. If I do – if he gets what he wants – then everything will change. Everything.'

I saw him weighing up my words, formulating a response. Donn, I knew, had never wanted to see the world end. He liked humans. He found them amusing. He had fought the Faidh with Gabriel, and loaned us the use of his vampires to turn the tide of battle. I didn't think he would be ready to give up on all of that just yet, no matter how much he despised me.

'And why do you think that would be a bad thing, Goddess? Change? Why would I care?'

'Because you are with us on this, Donn. You always will be. We might disagree about methodology, but we want the same thing. For the human race to survive. Me because it's my job, you because . . . I don't know. Maybe because you get to look at fake tits whenever you want. I'm guessing there's not much of that around in the Otherworld. If this all goes, we all lose.'

Debbie Johnson

He glanced off at the women on the poles, and smiled to himself.

'That would indeed be a loss,' he finally said. 'So, tell me about your plan. How you, a mere mortal child playing dress-up in the Goddess's clothes, plan to defeat the most mighty warrior any of our planes have ever seen.'

'I plan,' I said simply, 'to die.'

Chapter Thirty-Two

We spent the best part of an hour together. Some of it talking, some of it me looking on as Donn paid for increasingly raunchy lap dances in a failed attempt to make me squirm. For a Lord of the Dead, he certainly seemed to love life.

He, of course, thought my plan was ridiculous. Mainly because it was. But he also believed me when I told him of Fitzgarry's power – the way he'd been able to drain me so easily when we first met. The way he'd messed with the minds of the High King and the Morrigan. The way he'd been untouched by the attack of the Council. The way he'd been able to take my parents away from the safety of the Otherworld. The way he had recruited Fintan and the Faidh to his side. If Balor's body had been trapped underwater, then his spirit could have survived, and the children of the Otherworld – the Tuatha – would never have known it.

As it stood, we really didn't have many options – we'd thrown everything we had at him and failed. The Morrigan may have been on some kind of recon mission, and Gabriel would undoubtedly be planning some kind of heroic, testosterone-fuelled attack – but both of them had been scared of Fitzgarry, of Balor. Both of them had been head-fucked by him, and totally freaked out by the thought of Balor returning and making Domnu's prophecy a reality. They'd tried to hide it, but it wasn't hard to spot – not when you're dealing with super-beings so strong they don't usually feel threatened by anything at all.

I, at least, was too stupid to be that scared. I had a plan – a very rubbish one – and now I had an ally. An even more rubbish one. But it was something – it was a fraction of a chance. A long shot. It was 'help me Obi Wan Kenobi' only hope territory, and I had to go for it.

Donn agreed, eventually, that if I arrived at his gates – if I died and arrived at the Otherworld with my back stage pass – he would refuse me entry. He would wield whatever power he had to return me to the mortal plane, to send my spirit back to my human body. I didn't trust him, but had to work on the assumption that he would keep his word. Not because he was honourable – but because I had no other options.

'Tell me,' I'd said, 'what happens to my human body when my spirit leaves it? Last time I did it, I just kind of sat there . . .'

The last time – when I'd projected myself into Gabriel's gym in Dublin to have an out-of-body chat to him – I'd been fine. But that had been a very different set of circumstances.

'That time, I presume, you did it willingly? With every intention of returning?'

I nodded.

'This time may be different – if what you tell me is true, then you will be . . . evicted from your body and sent to me. Nobody has dealt with this situation before. I cannot guarantee what will happen to *this*.'

He flicked a finger at me, wagging it up and down to gesture my human form. Obviously I didn't do it for him in the same way the lap dancer did, which was a relief.

I shrugged at what he'd told me – and decided not to pass that particular concern on. There was nothing I could do but take the risk.

'What,' he then asked slyly, 'would keep me from changing my mind, Goddess? From deciding to keep you in the Otherworld?'

'You wouldn't want me around,' I'd replied, with a lot more confidence than I actually felt. 'I'd just cause trouble.'

When we'd finally thrashed out some of the details, I asked him where Luca was. I hated the way he referred to him as my dog, or my slave, or my property. I hated the way he'd discarded him like garbage, just because he'd drunk my blood to save himself. He didn't even know what he was doing at the time – the decision was really made by me and by Isabella, the singer in Luca's vampire band and his companion for centuries.

Luca had kept his life, but had lost so much. Lost any sense of community or belonging he'd ever carved out for himself, cut adrift not only from his Lord but from his family. In return, he got me. Not exactly the deal of the century. He rarely complained, but I sensed his sadness, his solitude.

'He is outside somewhere,' Donn replied abruptly. 'Not that it is any concern of mine. He seemed to find the presence of Isabella and the others upsetting, so I sent them all away to play. Your dog was upset, and took a couple of bitches to console himself with.'

Yikes. The thought of Isabella in this place really did make me squirm. She was stunningly beautiful, sable-haired and voluptuous, but totally deadly. Any man wielding an erect penis in her direction was likely to lose it. And the thought of Luca outside with his 'bitches' was almost as alarming. Luca had a good heart, a good soul. He never killed people unless he really had to, and I'd almost forgiven him for the horses in Central Park. But an unhinged, grieving vampire on the loose with a couple of willing lap dancers wasn't a recipe for anything good.

I left Donn to the attentions of the next girl in his totty parade, and walked back outside. It was cold, and I was tired and anxious, but I needed to find Luca and get him safely home with me before he did something that he – and the lap dancers – would regret in the morning.

The club was on a small side street, quiet apart from the chat of the bouncers dissecting that day's match. They nodded at me as I passed, and I stopped and took one of them by the hand. He didn't seem that shocked – you probably developed a high tolerance for weird behaviour in his line of work. I lowered my barriers, and allowed myself to try and poke around in his memory a little. I'd expected it to be tricky, controlling the direction of my prying – finding out what I needed to know without allowing myself to see his future. But in reality, it was shockingly easy, and I realised that my newly strengthened powers had come with newly strengthened control. That was good. That was something I'd need the next day.

I looked into the bouncer's tired eyes, discarding the flotsam and jetsam I didn't need. Like the fact that he was secretly gay but worked in a world way too macho to admit it, and spent hours pretending to lech over the girls with his mate on the door. That was sad in so many ways, but not what I needed. I framed it in a question, thinking it at him rather than saying it out loud – where would a man go around here if he wanted privacy with some of the girls? And have you seen one go past – tall, blond, doesn't look like he'd have to try too hard?

The image clicked with him straight away. He'd noticed Luca, not paid too much attention to the girls. They were young, looking for fun, it wasn't unusual for them to go off and party if they wanted to. He'd had one tucked under each arm, and they looked really happy to be there, for which he couldn't blame them. And they'd probably headed off to the little flat in Old Hall Street that a bunch of the girls chipped in to rent together for the nights they were working. He knew where it was – a tiny one-bedroomed place where they crashed when they needed to, or got ready for nights out, or occasionally used to party. He'd been there, pretending to stare at the girls in their spangly knickers as they got changed. Joining in the way he thought blokes were supposed to.

I wondered if I should pull some kind of Paul McKenna and implant some positive messages about being out and proud in his dormant mind, but really, what right did I have to mess with his life like that? It was up to him to decide when to join the rainbow nation, not me. I dropped his hand, thanked him, and scuttled off in the direction of Old Hall Street, hoping I wouldn't find a trail of blood on the way.

I arrived at the flat, on the third floor above an Italian restaurant, and found the door open. There were no screams, or ambulances, which I took as a good sign as I pushed it back and walked in.

I could hear giggles and sighs and music coming from a room at the end of a narrow hallway. Somebody here was a big fan of Lady Gaga, and I practised my poker face before I walked in on them. If there was some Bad Vampire Shit going down in there, I'd have to fire up the Goddess Gun and give Luca a blast of superjuice. If there was some Bad Sex Shit going down in there, I'd have to be the number one party pooper and break up the orgy.

If Gabriel was to be believed, the two were always linked in Luca-land. I wasn't convinced he was right on that one – I'd only known Luca for a few months, but I knew for a fact that he'd both fed and fucked on a regular basis during that time, and so far he'd never given the villagers cause to run at him with pitchforks and flaming torches. I had my suspicions that it was just Gabriel's not-so-subtle way of warning me off Luca, knowing as he did – me being female and Luca being Luca – that I fancied him. And he had a point – now, having finally experienced the joys of the flesh properly myself, I couldn't help wondering what it would be like with Luca. In fact, I'd always wondered, and he'd always encouraged me to, with his constant flirtation and casual touches and the way he paraded around in hardly any clothes all the time. Now, the whole concept was just a lot more vivid.

I shut down that train of thought – it was taking me on a one-way ride to Naughty Town – and pushed at the door, giving it a polite little knock first. Not that anyone could hear me apart from Luca, who would undoubtedly have sensed me coming minutes ago.

The music was so loud in there I thought my ears might bleed, and the scene on the sofa in front of me threatened to have the same effect on my eyes.

Luca was sitting down facing me, wearing nothing but a lap dancer. She was straddled naked across him, the movements of her body leaving absolutely nothing to the imagination, long auburn hair flowing over her back. She was either screwing him, or having some kind of seizure. From the low moans coming from her mouth, I had to go with the former. Luca was holding her hips, controlling the rhythm, silky dark blond hair damp with sweat around his face, stray tendrils plastered to the tan skin of his chest.

He met my eyes over the girl's shoulder, and gave me a huge, lazy grin, before leaning his head towards her bare neck. I heard her gasp as he bit her, and knew from first-hand experience that it could hurt like a mother-fucker. But I also knew from first-hand experience that after that initial shock, it could be absolutely bloody blissful. Literally. He softly suckled on her neck, and she threw her head back, eyes wild with sensation as she continued to buck against him.

I staggered back against the wall, momentarily swept away with it all. I could hear her cries, and could almost feel her mounting pleasure, the way Luca was filling her up and emptying her out at the same time. Her heart was thudding, blood rushing, every nerve ending in her body tingling with fear and ecstasy. All the while, he was staring at me, knowing exactly what effect all of this was having on me.

I closed my eyes, and concentrated on regulating my own heartbeat. I was getting a second-hand case of the down and dirties here, and it felt too damned good. I was fighting the urge to grab Ginger Barbie by the hair and throw her to the ground so I could take her place, and I couldn't afford to get distracted right now.

'Finish what you're doing, and meet me outside,' I said, gritting my teeth and dragging myself away, out into the narrow hallway, away from the girl's yells and the music and the sex-drenched atmosphere. Away from Luca, and out, into the cold, fresh night air. The chill felt like a slap on the face, which was exactly what I needed. I turned my head up to greet the rain, allowing nature to give me a cold shower while I waited.

A few minutes later he finally emerged, biker boots clomping on the stairs, shrugging on his leather jacket and smoothing his hair behind his ears. We stood and faced each other in the drizzle, cars shooting past and shattering the oil rainbows on the tarmac.

'Done?' I finally said, my face set and tense.

'Well and truly,' he replied, grinning at me.

'What about the other girl? I thought there were two of them.'

'She's resting,' he answered, raising his eyebrows in a way that suggested she really needed a little lie down after he'd finished with her. That and possibly a blood transfusion. His eyes were roaming over my face, and he looked confused, frowning at me.

287

'You're not blushing, *bella*. Usually, the slightest hint of sex and you blush.'

Hmm. Yes. Well. I knew why that was – and after a few more seconds of silence, so did he. I saw the moment when the penny dropped, when it acquired the weight of an anvil and crash-landed on his head. His eyes clouded, the frown deepened, and a small hiss escaped from his lips.

'Ah. I see,' he said. 'The High King finally managed to get a fuck, did he?'

He was hurt, and sad, and being crude to try and make me feel the same. I reached out to touch him, and he walked away, taking quick strides back towards the city centre. I ran after him, and caught up by the pub on the corner. Karaoke night inside. Someone was slaughtering Big Spender.

'Stop, Luca!' I said, grabbing hold of his arm and pulling him back towards me. He pulled away for a moment, and I felt a sigh ripple through him. He turned around, and I saw tears mixing with the raindrops on his face. I smoothed them away with my fingers, wanting so badly to comfort him, but just not knowing how.

He gathered me up into his arms, clasping my head into his chest, his mouth buried into the damp mound of my hair. I wrapped myself into him, feeling the hard lines of muscled thigh against mine, the silken touch of his mouth skimming the sensitive skin of my neck.

'I could make you want me,' he said, sliding his hands beneath my top, stroking the flesh of my lower back. I shuddered, allowed myself one moment of pure sensory joy, the touch of his face against mine, the brush of his lips against my skin. The scent of his dark blond hair and his leather jacket and his sheer physical presence.

'I know you could,' I murmured, as his hands roamed, long fingers skilfully working their way over me, his cold flesh making mine hot. 'But please – don't. Not now, not like this. I need you. I need your help.'

He pulled away, suddenly, shoving his hands into his pockets as though to stop them misbehaving. He stood back, looked me up and down. I concentrated on getting my breath back, and not imagining another time, another place, and how it all could have ended if everything in my life had been different. I struggled to pull myself together, and to meet his eyes.

'Well,' he said, smiling sadly. 'At least I've put a bit of colour back in your cheeks, Lily.'

That was true. I could feel my skin flaming – not with embarrassment, but with physical need. I was clearly going to be a slave to my vagina from now on.

'I know there will never be a happy ending for us, Goddess, or for me at least,' he said, reaching out and fastening up my coat for me. 'But a man can dream. You say you need me. So I will be there.'

'Will you come back with me?' I asked, wanting so much to hold him, to be held, but knowing exactly how selfish that would have been.

'No. Not now. It's been a busy night. Seeing Donn, Isabella, the others. Seeing you, like this. The women. No, I can't come back now, and watch you and Cormac Mor play happy families while I sleep curled up with your hound. I'm going to find a club. With a drum kit. And I'm going to beat the living daylights out of it, imagining the High King's face under my boot with every stroke. Then, I promise you, I will come. Now, run away home, little girl. Go back to your precious Gabriel and leave me alone for a while longer.'

Chapter Thirty-Three

'So,' I said, knowing full well what kind of reaction I was going to get, 'tell me, Katashi. Exactly how magic is this magic mirror?'

'Oh God,' groaned Carmel, holding her head in her hands. I thought she might have had a hangover. 'Is this going to be one of *those* conversations? Like the time you were drunk and started a whole debate about exactly how small the Small Faces' faces were?'

I pursed my lips and ignored her. It was the morning after a heck of a night before, and we were all tired. Weary. Downright scared. We'd gathered in the living room of house number one, and Finn had been sent out on a McDonald's run. The Dog was in the corner, eating, and Luca was upstairs, sleeping off his excesses until the sun went down. Fionnula was in another part of the terrace, probably drinking.

I was nestled on a big cushion, sipping take-out black coffee and trying to explain what I intended to do.

'Carmel, I'm revealing my master plan here,' I said. 'I could do without the heckling, all right? Because unless you've got a better idea, this is it.'

Gabriel was at my side, hovering protectively as ever. When I'd arrived back at the house he was already

290

asleep – or at least pretending to be. I'd lurked in the doorway of his room for a few moments, feeling weirdly uncomfortable. I mean, were we a couple now? Was I supposed to jump in and go for a cuddle? Wasn't it a bit strange that a few minutes earlier I'd been imagining having sex with Luca instead? Would any of this ever get any simpler?

He'd rolled over, and smiled. His hair looked suspiciously wet, and I had a strong instinct that he'd not just been lying here waiting for me all night. He'd been on Goddess patrol, and forgotten to take an umbrella. He patted the space next to him, and I'd crawled into it, too exhausted to carry on the internal debate. Woman tired and cold. Man warm and yummy. End of story.

There'd been some fairly frantic and fairly mind-blowing action in the middle of the night, but also a lot of sleep. A lot of comfort. A lot of closeness that I felt unfamiliar with, and didn't know quite how to manage. I'd never shared my bed with anyone for a night, but as this was just a couple of sleeping bags, maybe it wasn't that big a deal.

And now, we were all up, and as alert as we were going to get in the circumstances. The Morrigan was back from the Otherworld, and was squatting in one corner of the room, powerful haunches perfectly balanced as she consumed her Sausage McMuffin in two gulps. It felt good to have her back. She'd nodded once at me, raising her eyebrows in a way that told me she knew exactly what I'd been up to, then stayed silent as I brought everyone together.

'Katashi,' I repeated. 'The mirror.'

Katashi looked pretty much the best of them all, due largely to the fact that he seemed to be that alien species, a teetotaller. He held the mirror that Honi had given me on his lap, and was unwrapping it from its velvet coverings. There wasn't much light getting in through the boarded-up windows, but what there was seemed to be sucked towards it, glinting and shimmering and casting dancing pinpricks of reflected sunlight over his angular face.

'Honi spoke truly,' he replied, carefully avoiding looking into the mirror himself. 'This kagami has been blessed, by Amaterasu, and in every generation since by our gods of nature – the kami. It is said that it has the capacity to reflect the true spirit. To show the soul.'

'And to capture it, Honi said?' I answered, frowning at him. This bit was kind of important. If that claim had just been posturing, I needed to know.

'That is the legend, yes. But it has not been used in such a way. The magic it contains has lain dormant for centuries. It was given to you, Goddess, as a ceremonial gift – not as a practical tool of warfare.'

'Yeah, well,' I said. 'We're now at a stage where we're digging for victory, aren't we? This may sound desperate – but we are desperate. Unless the Morrigan came up with any nuggets of information for us, like the fact that we could kill Fitzgarry by sneezing on him or something?'

I looked over at her, and she frowned in confusion. *War of the Worlds*. Not her thing, obviously.

'I suspect that would be of little use, Goddess. And what I discovered confirms what you say – that we are desperate. I cannot uncover the roots of this evil, why this mortal man took this path, but the threat is real. His family was allied with our cause long ago, but that allegiance ceased with the death of his father. There has been no contact since.

'I consulted the oldest of the Tuatha that I could find – those even older than myself – but to them also, Balor is a story. A legend. It is hard for them to believe that he is returned, that Domnu's words carried truth.'

'But we know they do,' interjected Gabriel, his arm shooting out and coming to rest on my shoulder. 'We have seen his power, and Lily has felt his strength. Now, we must act – we must hide her. We must lock her away. We must—'

'We must stop talking such nonsense, Gabriel,' I interrupted, shrugging off his arm and glaring at him. 'I will not be locked away in some tower for the rest of my life, all right? I will not hide. I will face him, and I will defeat him.'

His eyes sparked violet, and his shoulders started to twitch, and I could see his anger puffing him up more and more by the second.

'You overestimate your strength, Goddess!' he snarled, glaring at me in a way that I didn't find romantic at all. I had a moment of utter sympathy for him: born to protect me, living to love me, and still not having a clue about how to deal with me.

I reached out and stroked his hair, running my hand around the side of his face and keeping it there. We locked eyes, and I leaned forward to kiss him, once, solidly on the lips. I heard Carmel breathe in, and saw Katashi shift uncomfortably. Perhaps they assumed we were about to have full-on rocking Goddess sex in front of them.

'No,' I said softly to Gabriel, who was calming at my touch, 'you underestimate it, my love. And if you think I'm going to run, and let you lose this battle on my behalf, then you still don't know me at all.'

'This is all very touching,' said Carmel, screwing up her sandwich wrapper and lobbing it into the middle of the room, 'but I for one would like to hear the rest of the master plan. To recap, we all go to Calderstones. You let Fitzgarry have his wicked way with you. You somehow get him to look in the magic mirror, and we trap his soul. Is that right? 'Cause it sounds like the kind of plan you'd come up with after drinking mushroom tea.'

She was right. It did. But something told me I could do this. That I could pull it off. Possibly just sheer stupidity kicking in to over-ride a whole lifetime of caution.

'It's not quite that basic,' I said, scanning all their faces, and seeing different shades of uncertainty and disbelief. 'From what I've learned, Balor is not of the Otherworld. He should by rights remain in the Northern Seas, wherever they are.'

'Scandinavia,' Kevin chipped in.

'Thank you,' I replied. 'And when someone from your world, or connected to your world, dies, you go to the Otherworld, right? Where Donn is waiting for you, to send you on your path to eternal joy, or whatever. So, for example, if Fionnula there was to choke on her own spit right now, she'd end up in Donn's waiting room?'

'That is a correct parody, Goddess,' said the Morrigan, nodding at me. Of everyone in the room, I knew my biggest ally in this would be the Morrigan. Carmel would support me, but her over-riding drive would be to protect me. Same with Gabriel, and his men would follow his lead. The Morrigan, though, saw things through different eyes – eyes that could strip away sentimentality and personal feelings, and assess the strengths and weaknesses of what needed to be done. She was brutal, and I needed that.

'So. Simple. I make this big-eyed freak somehow look in the magic mirror. His body dies, and his spirit goes back to the land of ice and snow, while mine goes to the Otherworld. Donn will refuse me entry, and I find a way back to my mortal body.'

'Sounds wonderful,' replied Carmel. 'Then can we all have a tea party with chocolate cake and lashings of ginger ale? Because this is all sounding more Enid Blyton by the minute.'

'Your Champion is right,' said Gabriel, standing up and taking centre stage in an already small room. 'You should listen to her. There are more holes in that plan than in a fishing net, and we cannot take those risks. And not, before you say it, just for *your* safety, Lily – though that is high on my list of priorities. But if you fail, and Fitzgarry triumphs, then this world falls. If we hide you, we at least have a chance of delaying him until we can figure something else out, build our strength. If you force this issue now, and lose – then everyone loses. Are you ready to decide the fate of billions of people, an entire race, an entire planet, based on your misplaced confidence and a *magic mirror*? Not to mention an even more misplaced trust in Donn?'

I stood up too, wishing I could pull off his swello trick and look him straight in the eyes.

'Yes,' I said firmly, 'I am. I was given the power to decide the fate of billions of people when I was only a child, and forced to make choices I didn't want to make at Tara. It's my job – you can't talk about our sacred duty one minute then expect me to behave like a good little girl the next. And if you try to stop me doing this, things could get very nasty. I've not read the High King manifesto, Gabriel, but aren't you here to serve me, not rule me?'

'I'm here,' he said, his eyes blazing, voice raised, fists clenched, 'to protect you, and to be your mate. Neither of which you make very fucking easy for me, Lily!'

He rarely used the F-word, so I knew how bad it must be inside his head. I only cared a little bit, though. It was time for me to be as brutal as the Morrigan.

The tension of the moment was broken by the sound of The Dog letting out a huge, gassy burp. Carmel burst out laughing, and the Morrigan smirked. I tore my eyes away from the electrical current of conflict flowing between me and Gabriel, glad of the distraction. We were both a pair of bloody psychos, truth be known. The fate of the world was in very crappy hands. I really needed to have a word with God about all of this next time we were out for a pint.

At that moment Fionnula bustled into the room, holding a bundle of dirty laundry.

'What did I miss? Anything interesting?' she said, sizing up the tension in the room.

'Yeah,' answered Carmel. 'We need you to check that a magic mirror is magic enough to trap the world's most deadly warrior, before we let Lily die and get re-animated into her corpse by the Lord of the Dead.'

'Oh,' said Fionnula, screwing her face up as she tried to process the words. 'Then I'll need some coffee.'

'That's the spirit,' said Carmel, passing her a cardboard cup. Then she locked eyes with the Morrigan, who nodded once, and walked over to me, stretching out her limbs as she did.

'It sounds like a load of shit to me, Lily, but what do I know?' said Carmel. 'I'm just a little ol' Champion. But if we're going to do it, we better get ready – and that starts with Fionnula the Fairly Drunk giving the mirror an MOT. She does have some uses.'

'Yeah,' I replied, risking a smile. 'We've got ninety-nine problems, but—'

'A witch ain't one,' she said, grinning and holding up her hand for a high five.

Life is never – I repeat *never* – too serious for a good pun.

Chapter Thirty-Four

We were meeting Fitzgarry at midnight, as he was obviously never one to miss a dramatic gesture. He'd asked me to come alone, but, well, he could go fuck himself. He was unlikely to care once he had me – my power was a hundredfold what it was – he'd be too busy salivating and rubbing his tiny hands in glee to object.

Gabriel had come back stern-faced – for a change – from a phone conversation with Hathor, and refused to repeat to me the words she'd used. I was guessing they weren't pretty. And perhaps it would have been sensible to wait for them – to have stalled Fitzgarry while they came to back us up.

Sensible, however, seemed to be a distant land to me right now. I was too fired up, too single minded. Too pre-occupied with the fact that my parents were still pottering around that fake house in a fake St John's Wood, living their fake lives. I'd never felt stronger, or more determined, or more convinced that I could succeed. Perhaps it would have worked out better if I'd tripped over my own arrogance on the way out, and knocked myself unconscious.

We made our way to Calderstones Park, which was relatively close to my own flat in Aigburth, in a black van that someone had acquired. It had blacked out windows and huge chrome hub caps, and I felt like a drug dealer as we cruised through the late-night streets. Loud music was blaring from the speakers – some kind of Queen's greatest hits compilation. Finn, who was driving, had wisely skipped forward past Who Wants To Live Forever, and we were currently engaged in a shouting match about being the champions. A pep talk from Freddie for my supernatural hit squad.

As well as the nine warm bodies, one cold body and a dog, the van was crammed with weaponry. Daggers, spears, shields, and Gabriel's Sword of Lugh, lying wrapped at his feet. Luckily not emitting any flames right then. Fionnula, for some reason, had dressed entirely in black, like a member of the Supernatural Air Service. The rest of us were wearing what we usually wore – variations on jeans, sweaters, and big boots.

Luca remained as apart from the rest of us as he could be, long legs stretched out in front of him, staring out at the streetlights and the rain as it hissed against the windows. He'd not exactly been chatty since he'd joined us, but he was here, in body at least. Gabriel had been equally silent, brooding away for hours on end. Jeez. Men. Lighten up, will you?

The place we were heading to was a huge public park, which I'd visited several times. There was a playground, a lake, a Japanese garden, an old manor house and a one-thousand-year-old oak tree. By day it was a haven for screaming toddlers and ice cream vans. It was also the ancient home of the Calderstones that gave it its name – six megaliths that were probably once the marker of something sacred and powerful. For as long as I could recall, they'd been in storage – victims of the weather and modern graffiti artists who wanted to add their mark to time immemorial. The power, though, must still be there – it's the only reason Fitzgarry would have chosen it. I doubted he was there for a quick play on the swings.

We pulled up outside the fence, and Kevin leapt out with something that looked like a huge gardening implement. I had no idea why he was cutting a hole when we could a) use magic, or b) walk round the perimeter until we found another hole that some enterprising youth had already made so he could sneak in there and drink cider on the roundabouts. But, you know, whatever.

His hair was flopping over his face as he worked, and I had a vivid flashback to another time. Another place. Only a few months ago, but a different world – one where Kevin was just the long-haired barman who served me chilled Peroni in the Coconut Shy. The cute guy I chatted to between gigs. The bloke who always used to keep an eye on me if the crowd turned shady. Back in the days when he hadn't faced the Faidh on my behalf and come out of it half blind.

'Kevin,' I said, standing next to him, feeling the rain drip down from a broad-leafed tree and onto my head.

'Goddess?' he replied, squinting up at me, pausing.

'Be careful tonight. You only have one eye left. If you lose that one as well, you'll have to become a blues singer – and the world doesn't need another one of those.'

He laughed, and turned back to the job at hand. He'd never seemed bothered about the eye. These guys were very weird like that – it had taken me days to come to terms with my hair changing colour, never mind losing a body part.

The others emerged from the back of the van one by one, pale skin and eyes glinting in the moonlight, the sound of scraping metal and blades being slid into scabbards. The music was still playing as Carmel jumped out. The opening bars of Flash.

Never missing a beat, she bounded over to me with

as much giddy enthusiasm as The Dog, and grabbed hold of my arms.

'Lily, I love you,' she said melodramatically. 'But we only have fourteen minutes to save the Earth!'

I couldn't help but smile back at her, before Gabriel's glower engulfed me. He was huge, nearing seven foot, buffed up and battle-ready.

'You should have waited until we were through the hole in the fence before you did that,' I said, glowering back at him and disappearing off into the park. Sometimes I loved Gabriel, I really did. But sometimes he was about as appealing as a barrel load of dead herrings.

As soon as I made it to the other side, I felt the strange energy of the place wash over me. I stood up straight, brushing damp leaves and mud off my knees, and looked around. Maybe it had always felt like this, but I hadn't been receiving those kinds of messages before. Maybe tonight was special because we were here, or Fitzgarry was here.

But whatever the reason, the park was drenched in power. From the rubber soles of my Docs to the tips of my hair, flying fuzzily around my head in rising tendrils despite the rain, I could feel it. An ancient energy that zinged through my veins, pounded in my heart, and sent tiny electrical impulses across my skin.

I turned around in time to see both the Morrigan and Gabriel vault the fence and land athletically on their booted feet behind me. Show-offs.

'Can you feel that?' I murmured, eyes wide and fingers tingling.

Gabriel nodded, gazing around him cautiously.

'I feel it,' he said. 'It's like the power of a sidhe . . . except there shouldn't be one here. This is how it feels for me when I'm in the Otherworld. As though some of it has spilled out into *this* world.'

300

The Morrigan's hair was doing exactly the same as mine, red and white stripes levitating around her face as though they were being pulled by invisible strings. She inhaled, and I saw her nostrils flare.

'This way,' she said, heading off over a wide expanse of grass before disappearing into distant trees. We all followed her, Gabriel in front, The Dog at my feet, Carmel at my side, and Luca bringing up the rear, either keeping guard or still sulking. Finn, Connor, Kevin and Katashi split up, creeping out around us, feet silent, flanking the group at the heart of it all. Fionnula was probably out there somewhere, unless she'd called in at the off licence over the road for a bottle of Baileys.

The route through the trees was sodden and damp underfoot, the rain seeping through the canopy of branches, moonlight dappling the muddy ground. I heard twigs snapping as I walked, small animals scurrying for cover, the distant tinny sound of a traffic light beeping. All of it underpinned by the incessant hum of power thrumming in my ears, dancing over my flesh.

We emerged into a clearing, and standing before us were the Calderstones. Enormous, powerful slabs of rock, casting moon shadows over wet grass. They were arranged in a strange shape, almost square, not the circle formation that I'd seen at Tara. Each side of all six stones was covered in intricate carvings of circles and spirals, darker glints in deep red.

This was the source of the power – I could almost see it shining from them. I closed my eyes, and reached out with my mind, seeing long-forgotten burials and mounds of bones and ash, flickering through the centuries. Lightning strikes and running blood and prayers of reverence and screams of terror, the stones standing watch over it all, like sentinels.

'What the fuck,' muttered Carmel as she came to a

halt beside me and gazed at the stones. 'Where did they come from? They shouldn't be there.'

She was right, of course. They shouldn't be there. They shouldn't be that big. They shouldn't be that clear. And they shouldn't be conducting that kind of sizzling energy – but they were. I took a moment to register the same surprise as Carmel, then forced myself to get over it. If I was derailed every time something crazy like this happened in my life, I'd be a train that never left the station.

In the middle of the stones, I could see a flickering shape, whirling and spinning, and from this distance, apparently made up of nothing but light. I squinted my eyes, trying to make out what it was, but it was so vivid and so fast-moving that it was nothing but a blur. I knew it would be important, but needed to get closer.

We had all come to a halt in the clearing, looking out at the incredible stones and the wavering shape of light and the power that seemed to physically hover above it all, like the smoke trail left by passing aeroplanes.

Gabriel moved to take a step forward, and I held out a hand to stop him.

'Let me go first,' I said, adding a 'please' at the end to make it less confrontational. These were my allies, and Gabriel was my mate, and I needed their support – not more turmoil.

He reached out and held both my hands in his. He was so big now he made my fingers feel tiny in his grip, and his eyes were roiling shades of violet and black. He stroked my palms, then raised one of them up for a kiss. I closed my eyes and let him, a buzz of warmth flooding through me with the contact.

'I will follow you, Lily, if that is what you want. And I will die before I let Fitzgarry hurt you.'

I smiled, and squeezed his hands as tight as I could.

When he was stripped down to the bone, that's what Gabriel was, or at least what he wanted to be: my hero. He'd been playing that part for so long in his own mind that it refused to let him skip forward to the part where I was stronger than him. I loved him for that, even if it didn't make our relationship easy.

'I know that, Gabriel. And you must know that you need to let him – and trust me to make it all right. How many times have you asked me to trust you since we met? So many. Now, it's my turn to ask – trust that I have the strength to do this.'

I didn't give him the chance to answer. Now wasn't the time or place to get into a trust debate. I turned round once, let my eyes run over the faces of the group standing behind me. Carmel, fizzing with energy as usual. Finn, Connor and Kevin, backing up their High King. The Morrigan, circling overhead in crow form. Fionnula, losing her battle for camouflage because of bright blonde hair she'd forgotten to hide. Katashi, his face set and determined, knowing he had a vital role to play. Luca, further back, shoulders slumped, hair sleeked down by the pounding rain. I gave him a small smile, still feeling the tug of his sadness, and turned away, back towards the shimmering stones and the ball of light inside them.

Perhaps I should have given them a motivational speech. Some kind of Goddess pep rally. But I didn't need to – we were linked by our pledge to fight. By millennia of history. By fate and destiny and too many nights spent drunk together. Either we'd make it or we wouldn't, and no amount of rabble rousing would change that. They were all as committed as they could possibly be.

I strode ahead, feet squishing through long wet grass, towards the stones. The closer I got, the stronger their pull was. I felt a need to touch them, to stroke them. To lie naked on them in the rain, looking up at the stars. What can I say? I'm weird like that.

As I neared, I saw men posted at each of them. All dressed in black, all armed. All looking distinctly uncomfortable. They were probably human, under Fitzgarry's command, and wondering what they were doing there. Sadly, the answer to that was probably dying. I shut off any sympathy for them – it wouldn't help, and I needed all my energy focused on one thing.

On the one small figure standing in the middle of it all. Fitzgarry.

The Dog was running by my side, and started to snarl and snap as soon as we were close enough to see him clearly. I noted with a certain level of childish satisfaction that he automatically recoiled, his face twisting into a grimace.

I called her to heel, laid a comforting hand on her smooth, sleek head. I applauded her instinct, but I didn't want one of the men in black getting trigger happy. If any of them shot my dog, I'd have to kill them, and live with guilty pangs for possibly minutes afterwards. There was a darkness that came with my new strength, and I wasn't yet sure how to totally control it.

I carried on walking until I was a few feet away from Fitzgarry. He looked the same on the surface – sandy hair, nondescript face, arrogant expression. The living embodiment of short man syndrome. His eyes widened as I approached, and I saw his hands clench into excited fists. He felt it, I was sure. He felt the fact that I was no longer just Lily McCain, with the Goddess hitchhiking a ride in my body. He felt the fact that now I was both – and offering him the chance to drink in the kind of power he'd only ever imagined.

At his side were Fintan and Eithne, in their real form – Fintan a buffed-up blond, tennis coach handsome, and Eithne tall and regal and dark. They were both sensible enough to be looking cautiously up at the large black crow that was now flying over their heads, probably preparing to run if she headed for their shoulders.

Fitzgarry pulled himself together, and nodded at me respectfully, eyes straying nervously to The Dog at my side.

'Goddess,' he said. 'You honour me with your presence. And I see you brought some friends to the party.'

His eyes locked on Gabriel, who was breathing hard behind me, restraining his natural urges to leap right in and rip Fitzgarry's head off his shoulders. The Morrigan was fluttering around overhead, cawing loudly, scaring the shit out of the armed soldiers.

'I did. If this is to be my last day on Earth, then I did not want to spend it alone. Now, I am here. I am doing as you ask. Where are my parents?'

He looked away from Gabriel, and gestured to the ball of light whirling around inside the stones. Now I was closer, it was even more vivid, dazzlingly bright. I sheltered my eyes with one hand, and looked, properly, staring hard. It was like gazing into the sun, burning shadows onto the edges of my retinas.

The sphere was made of light, but it was also hollow. A crazily spinning egg-shaped container, whirling around and around like a laser show. Inside it were my parents, standing, holding hands, looking out in horror.

I met my father's eyes through the glare, and knew that he saw me now. Knew that he remembered. Tears ran down his cheeks, and he placed his palms on the inside of their prison, gazing out at me. He shook his head, and his mouth formed a silent 'No'.

Of course it would be a no. They'd rather die than see me give myself up like this – but they'd already died for me once and, as far as I was concerned, once was enough. I wanted to run over, to place my palms against his, to speak to them and reassure them and tell them that I loved them.

Instead, I turned away. Stored up all of that anger and pain and fury and faced Fitzgarry. I wanted so badly to hurt him – but for now at least, he held all the cards. If we killed him – assuming we even could – then my parents would be lost. I wasn't willing to sacrifice them, and I wasn't convinced it was a battle we could win. He had made all of this happen – the stones, the spinning prison, my parents. His power was immense, and the only way I could hurt him was from the inside.

I took a step closer, and The Dog howled as I shooed her back. I was going somewhere she couldn't go, and she sensed the impending abandonment.

'I'm here. Let's do this,' I said.

I hadn't given much thought to the practicalities of it, and was momentarily freaked out when Fitzgarry touched me. I wobbled, but stood firm as he placed his hands either side of my forehead. I felt Gabriel move closer, heard his sharp inhalation, and waved my hand behind my back to caution him away. As my fingers waved and dangled there, The Dog started to lick them. Or at least I assumed it was The Dog.

That, bizarrely, was the last coherent thought of my own I had, and it wasn't exactly a classic.

I felt his fingers rubbing the side of my head, like some kind of perverted massage, and then my eyes closed. At that point, I had no idea at all what happened to my real body – because I flew right out of it and into his.

It didn't happen as quickly as it sounds, but even thinking about it makes me want to vomit. In reality, it felt like I was being sucked down an acid-lined drain, spiralling out of control, spinning and flying and flailing and having one final glimpse of the world around me before I fell, crashing, into an alien mindscape.

I gave my brain a shake, and had the urge to pick myself up, stretch my limbs, move around. Except the limbs that this brain was wired up to weren't mine, and instead I was blind, dumb, and immobile.

I pushed and searched and poked as much as I could, surrounded by blackness. Panic set in: had I really got it all so wrong? Was this it now, for eternity, trapped alive yet dead in nothingness? Was this really the end – an ever-stretching vista of emptiness?

If I'd had my own eyes, I'd have cried. If I'd had my own mouth, I'd have screamed – but I couldn't even give myself that satisfaction.

'Goddess,' said a voice. Fitzgarry's voice, but somehow deeper, stronger, more solid. 'We have a few moments together before we become as one, and before Balor returns. I thank you for your power . . . I've never felt anything like it before. All the others pale beside it. Your sacrifice has made me whole.'

'My parents?' I said – or thought, as I was still completely disembodied.

'Gone now. Back to the realm of the Tuatha de Danaan. Now, it is just you and me, and only seconds together before I evolve.'

I had no idea what was going on around my body, back in the real world. Probably death and mayhem and bloodshed and barking. All I could do was try and hold steady, to calm myself down enough to think, to plan, to act. To remember the confidence I'd had earlier that I could do this – that I could dominate Balor enough to destroy him.

Feeling as I did, like a small child locked in hell, the confidence was hard to find. For now, he was still Fitzgarry, but I could sense the changes taking place in him – sense the way my power had given him the final boost he needed to free Balor's spirit, to take it into his own. To *become* Balor.

307

'Why?' I thought, throwing out that one small word into the void. If I was going to die now – if the world was going to die with me – I wanted at least to know why.

The sensations around me shifted, like gravel rubbing up against raw skin, memories brushing my mind that weren't my own. I felt my consciousness shrivel back, clench, try to shut down the invasion, and forced myself to relax into it instead.

I recalled the lessons of Fionnula, the advice of the Morrigan, and trusted my own senses. All my instincts screamed against it, but I took the mental equivalent of a deep breath – and let go.

I saw Fitzgarry, as a child. Nine or ten, maybe. Small and scrawny and with the word 'victim' practically tattooed on his forehead. I saw his father's funeral, Irish pomp and splendour and a drunken wake in a bar in Queens. I saw his mother – grieving and desperate and poor, grabbing on to any chance to make life right again for her and her son.

I saw the choice she made – the wrong one. The man she married, in the misguided belief that he would be a good father to her son and a loving husband to her. All brawn and muscle and beer-breath. Angry, violent, living his whole life searching for someone else to blame for his failures.

I saw him going into Fitzgarry's tiny apartment bedroom at night. I smelled his sweat and felt his fury – and trembled along with Fitzgarry, a tiny, huddled boy – as he removed his belt. I heard the caustic words of abuse: *you worthless piece of shit*. Recoiled from the hiss of leather as the belt bit into his buttocks over and over again. Saw him there after, hiding under blankets that chafed on his wounds, crying for his father. Crying for the people his father had served. Saying his pre-adolescent version of prayers for help – prayers for the ears of all his father had held sacred, the High Kings and the line he'd served for so long.

Prayers that were never answered. Pleas that were ignored. A lifetime of failed hope and humiliation and abuse. Fitzgarry had grown up – but never recovered. He had always carried the scars, both physical and emotional – and the belief that Cormac Mor and his brethren had forsaken him. I had my 'why', at least. I knew why he was so angry with Gabriel. If I got out of this, I could explain – this was why the little people mattered. You never knew what they'd grow up into.

'Now you understand, Goddess?' he said afterwards, as I trembled with second-hand emotion and the fear I'd taken in through osmosis. I understood, perhaps better than most – the way a childhood of loneliness and loss and fear could scar you.

'I get it,' I replied, shaking the false memories away. They were not mine, and I did not want them. 'You had a bad childhood. So did I. That's no excuse, and you will find no forgiveness from me.'

He was silent for a moment, and the blackness intensified. I felt as though I was floating in a bath of obsidian, disconnected and disjointed.

'I do not seek it. Farewell, Goddess,' he said.

A strange pounding sensation started up – like the sound of your own blood rushing through your ears when you're trapped underwater – a booming drumbeat that threatened to shatter what was left of my mind. I was rolling, somersaulting, a fragment of fabric flapping in a tumble dryer, unable to stop or steady myself. It went on for what felt like hours, driving and hammering and tossing, until it abruptly stopped.

If I'd been in my body, it would have crashed to the floor – instead, I opened my eyes.

Or at least the one eye I had.

Chapter Thirty-Five

My vision was vast and wide. Like one of those panoramic vistas that takes in a whole seafront in one shot. I could see the entirety of the park spread out before me, curving in at the sides as though I was seeing it through a looking glass. I could see the tops of the houses beyond, and thousands of stars glittering in the night sky, all of it shot through with fine red lines, like tiny burst blood vessels.

I was still me, still there, looking out at the world, but feeling like a mosquito clinging to the hide of an elephant. I could be whisked off at any moment, and had no idea how long my own will would survive inside the crushing weight of Balor's mind.

Behind me, I could hear the hacking and groaning and yelling of battle, and knew that, as I'd suspected, the minute my corporeal body hit the grass all hell had broken loose. I wanted to turn and look, but as yet had no control of this body. I felt huge, lumbering, powerful but slow. A tank in humanoid form.

Balor's own thoughts were there, engulfing me, pouring over me like oil: find the enemy. Destroy the enemy. Avenge the deaths of his army and his people and himself. He felt blurry, unfocused, juddering. Perhaps

that's what being magically trapped under the North Sea
for millennia will do to you. I hoped I'd never find out.

I needed to see what was happening – but I also knew
that with one look, Balor could kill them all. The legends
told that his one mighty eye could turn a man to stone
with just one look – for all I knew, that's how the
Calderstones started life. I shuddered, and hid the
thought away – if they were people trapped inside megaliths . . . well, yuk.

I took a tentative mental poke with the equivalent of my
fingertip, knowing that I needed to rein in my meander-
ing thoughts before I had none left at all. Before I become
subsumed, swallowed whole, oozing into the shambling
creature of death and destruction that was Balor. I felt the
body shake slightly around me, twitch in confusion. He
knew something was there, but couldn't quite find it – like
a shadow in the corner of his enormous eye.

I felt a rumbling, shaking sensation, and realised he
was moving. Mammoth feet were taking steps; thick,
sturdy muscles were twisting. He was turning around,
to see what was going on behind him – and presumably
to destroy whatever he saw.

I tried to allow myself to meld partly with his thoughts,
with this alien being so large, so monolithic, that I couldn't
comprehend him. He was like a monster made of clay
– an ancient golem created by Domnu purely to destroy
the world that her sister had blessed. I was not dealing
with a superior intellect here – his power was primal,
brutal, domineering, and completely unquestioning. He
had one mission, and one need – to destroy.

With each staggering footfall, the earth tremored, as
though the roots of the trees were trying to escape from
their subterranean prisons. I stared out of that one eye,
hoping against all hope that I wouldn't be coming face
to face with Gabriel, and be forced to watch him petrify
before me.

We'd discussed this before, all of us – they knew the stories better than I did. We'd talked it through, amid sighs of disbelief and moans from Carmel and sullen stares from Luca. We'd planned for this, but as I was slowly, steadily turned around, a tiny hitchhiker perched on Godzilla's shoulder, I was terrified.

If they forgot – if the heat of the battle had overcome their common sense, if Gabriel had simply gone apeshit berserk, if Fionnula was too pissed to remember – then they would die. Then I'd turn into a big fat crying baby girl in here, and lose my mind forever.

Balor blinked, the physical effort of it aching through the whole body, as sinews stretched and that giant eyelid pulled itself back upright. I looked out, and finally allowed myself to breathe again.

The soldiers Fitzgarry had brought with him had earned their bonuses by being slaughtered. They never stood a chance, even with guns – not against vampires and ancient kings and Goddesses of War. Their bodies were slumped in dark heaps where they'd stood, silent and crumpled in the moonlight, covered with blood that shone viscous and black.

One had his throat torn out, which could have been Luca or could have been The Dog. Others had brutal sword wounds across their stomachs, dark body matter oozing out into lifeless hands that had tried to defend indefensible flesh. Another had a gaping, bloody smile across his throat, which I knew would have been Carmel with one of her tiny, lethal daggers.

I saw my body on the floor, tangled in hair, my legs twisted beneath me. I paused, felt a momentary stab of pure terror: I was lying there, on the grass, with rain seeping through my clothes. I was *dead*.

Except, I reminded myself, you're not – not yet at least.

Gabriel and the others were all lying flat on the floor, their heads buried in their arms, hiding their faces from

Balor. Thank God they'd remembered, and assumed the position – if they didn't meet his eye, they'd be safe.

Luca, bless his tortured soul, had The Dog clasped firmly within his grasp, holding her bony head to his chest so she couldn't get all doggy doolally and start running around trying to bite the giant eyeball that could kill her. I was monstrously relieved: she might only be a dog, but somehow, losing her would have had just as disastrous an effect on me as any of the others.

Balor took a shuddering step towards them, and I could feel blood lust roaring through his brain – that primal, basic instinct to destroy. To end things. To end their lives, and the lives of everyone on this plane of existence – to kill, kill and kill again.

I could see Katashi over to one side, his eyes covered by a red bandana, his hair draped over the sides of it like an Indian in an old cowboy movie. I could see his body shaking, and his frantic breath clouding out into the cold night air. I could feel his fear, almost taste his terror – and to Balor, it was delicious.

Hold steady, I thought, for fuck's sake hold steady – if Katashi fell now, it was all over. If he lost his steely Champion nerve, or if Honi's gift slipped from his trembling hands, it would be the end of days.

He wavered, but he didn't fall, despite the fact that the ground around his feet was bobbling and buckling as Balor strode towards him.

Now, I thought to myself, *now*. You have to be the Goddess. You have to find the strength to make this big, stupid, lethal behemoth do your bidding – you have to bend his will to yours, and end him.

I started to gather strength from everywhere I could, pulling it in from the grass and the trees and the silent birds roosting in damp branches and the thousands of tiny insects burrowing beneath Balor's feet.

I pulled it in from the moon and the stars and the

flowers and the fish swimming in the pond of the Japanese garden. From the grey squirrels looking on, from the hidden foxes, from the bright glimmer of warm souls that I could feel in the comfortable homes around the park.

I pulled it from myself, and my memories: from my parents, and Carmel, and Coleen, from Luca and the Morrigan and The Dog. Most of all, from Gabriel – replaying the passion and the fury and the need that we shared. The anger and despair and joy of it all, the flirting and fighting and loving, and the knowledge that I was meant to be right here, right now, with him, doing this. I was the Goddess, and he was part of that. That he was mine, and I was his, and we *would* be together again.

I felt my strength growing, felt as though the space I was occupying in Balor's twisted, one-track mind was growing. I was spreading, stretching, expanding – creeping out further and further. I could feel his limbs as my own, their thickness and power and solidity. I could feel his breath as mine, rasping and vast, pulling in huge clumps of oxygen with each heave of his mighty chest.

I felt the moment when he noticed. The moment when the mosquito finally bit the elephant, and made him mad. I felt as though I'd been slapped, hard – so hard that if I'd had physical form, I'd have fallen. He was confused, and angry, and distracted, not knowing what was happening to him, not knowing why his simple urges and his earth-crushing power were being resisted, invaded.

There was a sizzling white noise around me, and I felt myself weakening as he turned his attention away from the bodies lying around him, away from the curled-in forms of Gabriel and the others, away from his all-consuming need to finish them. He turned, instead, inwards – and set about trying to crush the mosquito.

I needed more power. I needed to be the Goddess to

Infinity and Beyond. I cast my mind around, desperate for a new source – and saw the Calder-stones, shimmering with their own magical mysteries. With the last bit of energy I had, I forced Balor to raise one enormous hand, and bring it down on the nearest stone. It tremored beneath his palm, trembling visibly as the slap connected.

Instantly, it soared into me: millennia of power and energy and sheer, raw magic. It burst through me, singing and glorious, searing into my soul and seeping through my mind.

I had to do it now. Balor was aware of the threat, was trying to crush it and swipe it away, and I would never be stronger than this.

I took all of that power – from the stones and the land and the people and myself – and threw it into one command. One instruction. One final, desperate demand. *Look*, I told it, told the body that I was now part of. *Look* . . .

Twisting and groaning and creaking, fighting all the way, he looked. He turned that one mighty eye towards Katashi, quivering with his covered eyes and flailing hair. Katashi dropped the velvet covering of the mirror, and held it aloft.

I felt Balor fighting me, bucking beneath my control, screaming against me in a low, rumbling voice that sounded as though it was emerging from the bowels of the earth he wanted to destroy. Again, I surged on – I refused to let him look away, and refused to let him close that eyelid. I held it open, and could feel the cost of it almost as though I was snapping tendons and ripping muscle and tearing hamstrings in my brain.

Look, I repeated, clinging on to the elephant's back and simply refusing to let him go. *I am the Goddess, and you will* look.

He looked.

And we both fell.

Chapter Thirty-Six

I was standing in the garden of a small, neat cottage. The borders were teeming with honeysuckle, buzzing with bees. I felt the sunlight warm on my head, and turned my face up to meet it. I sighed, enjoying a moment of harmony and peace.

I was in the Otherworld. I'd *done* it. I'd defeated Balor, and saved the world. Yay for me.

I looked down at myself, seeing my real body there, but not feeling especially connected to it. I felt wobbly, as though my limbs were made of bouncy castle, and if I took one step I'd end up doing enormous moonwalks. It was different from the time I'd left my body before: then, I'd been able to walk, to see myself, to be seen. This time, it was more as though I was a shadow – looking at a body that was no longer mine.

The door to the cottage opened, and Donn emerged. His hair was tied back, and he was wearing his trademark black leather. So this was where he lived. I'd imagined something grand and Gothic and threatening, but it was a small, pretty cottage in the middle of a meadow, a bubbling stream running through its grounds. Donn was the gatekeeper to the Otherworld, the Lord of the Dead – and he lived in the little house on the prairie. Weird.

'Goddess,' he said, squinting his one good eye at me as he approached. 'Against the odds, I see you made it.'

'Kind of,' I replied, trying to move my arms and finding them weak and soft, apparently made of cheese strings. 'What has happened to Balor? Is he here?'

'No,' Donn replied, drawing up close to me. 'He is not a creature of Tir na nOg. His soul is – I presume – trapped in Honi's toy. As for his physical remains, I have no idea.'

He paused, his head tilted to one side as though he was listening out for something. All I could hear was the music of the skylarks and the gushing of the stream pouring over rocks.

'Ah,' he finally said. 'Perhaps he will be able to tell you.'

Before I could register the word 'Who?', Gabriel tumbled onto the lush green lawn. It was some spooky Star Trek shit, with him literally falling out of the clear blue skies, and rolling himself to his feet in one smooth movement.

He stood tall – very tall – and smiled at me. It was a good smile, wide and deep and heartfelt. I'd have probably gone over and given him a big snog if I'd been capable – but I wasn't sure my ankles would sustain any movement just then. It must be some kind of hangover from being dead and all.

I grinned back at Gabriel, running my eyes over him to check for damage. A few scrapes and tears, and a dark purple bruise under his eye, but other than that he looked fine. The Sword of Lugh hung at his side, dark with blood, and he walked towards me and took me in his arms.

It felt good in so many ways – the relief of seeing him whole. The knowledge that nobody I cared about was dead. The very un-modest surge of pride I felt at being strong enough to defeat Fitzgarry, and Balor. The one way it didn't feel good was physically. Because, you know, I couldn't actually *feel* it.

'Go on,' he said, nuzzling his face into my hair and kissing my neck. 'I know you want to say it.'

'What?' I replied, faking innocence.

'I told you so?'

'Well, yeah, I did. But I assumed you weren't listening to me, as usual. I take it that everyone is all right?'

He nodded, and pulled away slightly. I felt weak without his touch, and staggered slightly. He reached out to hold me steady, then frowned, turning to look at Donn over his shoulder.

'She is not returned?' he said, one eyebrow shooting up. 'Why is she so weak?'

Donn smiled, and it wasn't such a good smile. In fact it was so un-good that it made my stomach fill with roiling worms. I was clinging on to Gabriel, sure that if I didn't, I would collapse right there in Donn's garden, and never be able to get up again.

'Donn?' I said, feeling those worms crawling all over me now. He was looking too smug, too satisfied. 'We had a deal. Turn me away. Refuse me entry to the Otherworld, and help me get back to my own body on the mortal plane. You're the Lord of the fucking Dead – you can do this!'

'Oh, I know I can, Goddess,' he said, smirking. 'But that doesn't mean I'm going to. You have insulted me at every turn, you have stabbed me with your puny knife, you have stolen one of my souls. Your tame crow even took out my eye. Now you have dealt with the threat of Balor for me, why would I want to do anything for you?'

'Because,' I hissed, feeling weaker with every word, 'you *said* you would!'

He laughed, loud and hearty, and clapped his hands together like I was a child giving an especially precocious performance in a school play.

'Your naivety is refreshing. As is your obvious weakness – you are separated from your body not by choice, but by force. It is back there, where time is passing, and you are here, so reduced, with me, in my domain,' he replied. He was still smiling. Still smug. Still begging for an ass-kicking that I knew I couldn't give him, not the way I felt. I wouldn't even have the energy to swat away one of those buzzing bees if it landed on my nose.

Gabriel lowered me gently to the warm grass, and I sat there, feeling pathetic and furious all at the same time. He stroked my hair back from my face, and kissed me slowly. I grabbed hold of his hands, trying to keep him at my side even though my fingers couldn't connect. He pulled away and walked over to Donn.

'We have been allies for many years, Lord,' he said, drawing close to him, towering over him. 'And we have never had cause to fight among ourselves. I ask you now, return the Goddess to her human form.'

Donn stared up at him, not at all daunted by his sheer size and the violent glow of his eyes. I suppose he'd seen it all before, many times.

'Cormac Mor,' he said steadily, 'we have indeed been allies. We have shared the same goals, and fought the same foes. Our aims have always been aligned – the preservation of the human world. Well, the Goddess came. The Goddess made her choice at Tara. And the Goddess, I know, fulfilled her role in the blessing of the world when she mated with you, High King. She has despatched Balor, and saved the world from the blight of Domnu's prophecy. She did it all, and she did it well. But as far as I can see . . . I have no more use for her. Her job is done, and I think I shall keep her here with me, like this. I will enjoy playing with her in her weakened state, and enjoy taking my vengeance for the humiliations I have suffered.'

The blood was roaring through my ears so loudly it felt like there was a freight train stuck in there. I could barely move at all now, not even to wipe away the tears that were rolling down my face – tears of anger and sorrow. I would rather die forever than stay here with him, like this.

I searched Gabriel's face, and saw his steadfast refusal to let the words Donn was speaking take root. I knew exactly how his thought processes would be working right now: it was his sacred duty to protect me, and it seemed that he had failed. His fingers were twitching, and I saw his hand lurch towards the hilt of his sword.

'I could kill you right now, Donn,' he said, quietly and calmly and all the more terrifying for it.

'That,' Donn replied, following the movement of his hand, seeing it come to rest on the sword's pommel, 'is debatable. You are powerful, High King, but I am a god. If you strike me down, I will return – you cannot defeat me that way.'

Even amid the turmoil and the panic and the shortness of breath, I registered a Darth Vader moment, and hoped it wouldn't end with one of them disappearing into a flurry of cloaks on the Death Star floor.

I tried to dredge up enough energy to move, to crawl, to blast Donn down where he stood, but it was useless. I was useless. I wanted to scream with frustration – I'd been through too much for it to end like this. To be trapped in the Otherworld with a sadistic god, drained of all the power I'd been so smug about just a few moments earlier. I'd allowed myself a moment of pride, and now I was wallowing in the inevitable fall. The spirit of the Goddess was still mine – but without a human body to house it, it was only that. Spirit. Maybe there was a way I could kill Donn with spirit alone – but I didn't know how yet.

'Gabriel!' I shouted, with as much force as I could muster. My cry broke the tense impasse between the two, and he turned to look at me, irritation momentarily fluttering over his features. Good to see that even now, here, like this, I could still annoy him.

'Yes?' he asked, replying to me but not walking back to me. I punched the ground in frustration, and yelled: 'Whatever it is you're thinking of doing – don't! Go back to the others, make sure everything is done properly. We still have a very nasty soul trapped in a mirror to dispose of. We still have things to do. Now is not the time for you to start scrapping – leave me here for now. I'll find a way back, you know I will.'

'He knows no such thing, Goddess,' said Donn, before Gabriel could answer. 'He knows that you will be released only when I choose to release you – and that might be long after your mortal body has rotted and seeped into the earth, food for the worms.'

Yikes. Lovely image. I gritted my teeth and refused to cry any more. If Donn wanted to keep me here, I'd make him regret it, I swore. I'd do everything I could to drive him nuts. I'd argue when he wanted silence and I'd go dumb when he wanted me to talk and I'd sing at the top of my voice when he wanted to sleep and I'd spit in his face whenever he got close enough. I would get stronger, and meaner, and eventually, I would break him. Because just as Gabriel couldn't really kill Donn, Donn couldn't really kill me. I was a goddess, and he couldn't end my existence. If he wanted to share it with me, I would make it my very long life's mission to bring him pain.

Something of what I was thinking must have seeped out into my face, and I saw uncertainty crease his forehead.

'Yeah, you better worry!' I shouted. 'You better bloody worry you miserable cheating bastard!'

Gabriel turned away from me, and back to Donn, but not before he gave me a sad, small smile. Yeah, I was still a screaming harpy.

'Will you make a trade, Donn?' he asked. 'Will you

bargain for the Goddess's life? Because like her, my job is done. The job I spent centuries waiting to do is finished. The burden is lifted from me.'

I so didn't like the way that sounded, and slowly began to drag myself, inch by tortuous inch, across the grass towards them.

'Burden?' I squeaked. 'I'm not a burden, I'm the love of your fucking life, and we're not finished with each other yet!'

Donn stared at me, crawling across his lawn like an insect he'd pulled the wings off, still spitting fury and yelling abuse at the High King like the good Scouse fishwife I was capable of being. His frown deepened, and he took a step back, even though I must have looked as threatening as a sleepy panda.

'What do you offer, Cormac macConaire?' he said, never taking his eye off me. My fingers were gouging holes in his lawn as I approached, adopting a demented technique of digging my fingers into the rich earth and pulling until my body followed. He'd need a whole lot of Patch Magic to sort this lot out.

'I offer myself,' said Gabriel simply. Donn flicked his head back around to Gabriel, who had immediately gained his attention.

'Why would I be interested in that?' replied Donn, though his tone implied that he was interested – very interested indeed.

'Our alliance is clearly over, Donn. You seek revenge. And in seeking that revenge, you have caused harm and threat to the Goddess. That is a line which you should not have crossed. If I leave here and she stays, I will hound you for the rest of my days. When I am dead, my men will hound you. Her Champion will find you and slice off your balls. Her vampire will use your secrets against you. The Morrigan will find you, and remove that other eye, before she shoves it down your throat.

Hathor will unleash her lion and tear you limb from limb. You will never rest easy again – never. I swear that on my own life and those of my ancestors.'

I was close enough to see the way that Gabriel's words affected Donn. His good eye narrowed, and I saw his skin pale beneath its olive cast. He tried not to gulp, and choked on it.

'Do not,' I screamed, close enough now to grab his ankle, 'even consider accepting this trade, Donn! It is not his to make!'

He kicked off my hand and moved away, and I started my desperate crawl to chase him, in extremely slow motion, around his own garden. It would have been completely amusing if not for the whole life or death scenario playing out around me.

Donn looked scared, and angry, and confused. Gabriel was a rock. I was an extremely hard place. And he was trapped between us.

His eyes flashed from me to Gabriel, and eventually, after minutes of silent deliberation, he said: 'High King, I accept your offer. You will remain in the Otherworld. The Goddess will return to the mortal plane. And all debts between us will be considered settled.'

'No they fucking won't!' I shouted, still inching towards him.

Gabriel nodded once, and swiftly pulled the Sword of Lugh from its sheath. He uttered a quiet word beneath his breath, and it flamed into life. Birds swooped from the apple trees and flew away, and the bees seemed to still in the sunlight. All that could be heard was the gentle hiss of the blazing fire licking around the edges of the sword.

'Gabriel!' I screamed. 'No!' I frantically tried to reach him, feeling fingernails snap and blood flow as I did.

He turned to me, and held the fiery sword to one side so I could see his face.

'It's all right, Lily,' he said. 'I've lived for hundreds of years. I lived long enough and well enough and lucky enough to see you grow into what you've become. Your life will go on. Mine will too – I'll just be here, in the Otherworld, instead of following you around Liverpool in the rain.'

'That is *not* all right,' I said, scurrying closer. 'I want you following me round Liverpool in the rain – that's your bloody job! I'll get into all kinds of trouble without you. I'll . . . I'll die without you!'

The last few words came out as a wail, and I finally stopped scrambling across the grass. Something had to give right then, and I suspected it was my sanity.

'No, *a ghra*,' he said quietly, 'you won't.'

And with that, he raised his arms high, and plunged the Sword of Lugh – flames and all – into his own stomach.

Chapter Thirty-Seven

I'm not brilliant on geography, but the Red Sea really is quite a long way from Liverpool.

We were standing together on a beach somewhere near a town called Marsa Alam. We'd been in Egypt for a couple of days already, and when I left that night, I'd be leaving without Carmel.

It was January, but still hot. I could imagine that these beaches would be crammed with sizzling European flesh in tourist season, but right then it was relatively quiet. Possibly because it was 6 a.m.

The Dog was there, and the Morrigan, her hair fluttering wild in the coastal breeze.

I gazed out at the sparkling water, the sun flickering over the waves, and unwrapped the mirror. Time to get rid of at least one problem.

'So, I just lob it in, then?' I asked.

'Indeed,' replied the Morrigan. 'Just lob it in, as you say, child. The tides will carry it out, and Fionnula has bespelled it to sink deeply. Balor will never rise again.'

I nodded. Yeah. That was a good thing. With his body mouldering away somewhere beneath the earth, and his soul trapped in the Middle East, I was betting that was one threat we'd never see again. Fitzgarry's little plan hadn't quite worked out the way he'd wanted it to. I tried to feel some sympathy for him – for the pain of his childhood, the twisted events that blackened his heart – but I couldn't really manage it.

I wasn't really managing much at all in the way of feelings, truth be told. I'd come to in my own body at the foot of the Calderstones, realising as soon as I blinked open my eyes that several hours had passed. The sun was rising, pale golden fingers crawling over the stones around me.

I'd sat up, and was immediately treated to a warm tongue bath from The Dog. Carmel had been sitting beside me, her eyes rubbed red raw from fatigue and tears. The others all swarmed as soon as they saw me move, gathering around me in a protective circle. Luca was hiding beneath the broad branches of a huge oak tree, sheltering from the encroaching sun, but I saw his face dissolve into relief when he realised I was back.

'Where's Balor?' I said, stretching out my legs and finding them solid.

'The earth swallowed him,' said Carmel. She noted my expression of disbelief, and continued: 'No, honest, it fucking swallowed him! The stones did something weird, almost like they dug holes, it was like they had roots. And he tumbled straight in, and the soil poured on top of him, and he was gone. And you were gone, you just looked dead, or like you were in a coma. And Fintan and Eithne were gone. Then Gabriel was gone. And we all sat around like nonces, for hours and bloody hours, waiting for you to come back!'

I gave her a sad smile. She always got angry when she was upset – she didn't like feeling vulnerable.

'Well, look see, I'm back,' I said, standing up and brushing the worst of the mud off my jeans.

She stood up next to me, frowning deeply. She grabbed hold of my arms, and shook me hard.

'You're back,' she said. 'But where's Gabriel?'

I shook my head, and closed my eyes. I should probably be in hysterics. I should probably be screaming and tearing at my hair and getting fitted for a straightjacket. Instead, I just felt a cold, calm anger.

'Gabriel's not coming back,' I said, simply.

Much wailing and gnashing of teeth ensued, and the last month had been an orgy of grief and anguish and recriminations and, in the case of the Morrigan, a declaration of war against Donn. Some of them had visited Gabriel in the Otherworld – I had not.

I was still too angry with him. And too busy – if Fitzgarry had found a way to bring back Balor, and to remove my parents from Tir na nOg, then I would find a way to bring Gabriel back to us. It might take months. It might take years. But I *would* find a way.

There was a gentle splash as the mirror landed in the water. I saw it float on the surface for a few moments as it was taken out by the tide, and looked on as the Morrigan transformed into the crow and flew out to check on its journey.

'Good Guys two, Bad Guys nil,' said Carmel, smiling up at me. 'We are so fucking awesome.'

She was right. We were. And in Carmel's case, probably about to get even more so – she was spending a month here with Hathor, and who knew what she'd come back like? Changed in some way, undoubtedly. I wasn't sure I was happy about that – I liked her just fine how she was – but change is life, as they say.

And she's not the only one to change, is she? I've gone from lonely pop girl to goddess in a few months. I went from Maiden to Crone and back again in New York. And now, my body was telling me, the middle stage wasn't as distant or as impossible as it once seemed.

The Matron. The Mother. I let my hand gently flutter across my stomach, and turned to walk back to the car.

Acknowledgements

I might not have been on quite as much of an adventure as Lily and her pals, but it's been quite a ride. A lot of people have helped me along the way, and I'd like to thank my agent, Laura Longrigg of MBA, for her constant belief in me. The team at Del Rey – Michael and Emily – and my fellow fabulous Del Rey authors have also been awesome. The Royal Society of Literature helped me see New York first hand, and the wonderful Fabrice from www.realnewyorktours.com brought it all to life.

On the home front, I couldn't have done any of this without the love and understanding of my family – Dom, Keir, Dan, Louisa, and the Newton Gang. Love you all. I include my wonderful friends in the category of 'family' – so thanks for the chats, the quiz nights, the beers, the childcare, and listening to me witter on: Sandra Shennan, Pamela Hoey, Jane Murdoch, Jane Costello, Ann Potterton, Louise Douglas, Vikki Everett, Ade Blackburn, Helen Shaw, Rachael Tinniswood, Danielle Sharpe and Paula Woosey. Thanks to all of my various work colleagues, especially those at the *Liverpool Echo*.

As ever, an apology to any serious scholars of Celtic mythology or the Irish language. I'm afraid I used both to suit my fictional needs – some of the names are

Debbie Johnson

intentionally wrong, and I've lifted legends and messed with them just so they sounded the way I wanted them to. Same goes for the wonderful cities of Liverpool and New York – I've played fast and loose with geography, but hopefully retained their spirit. The Irish Hunger Memorial in New York is real, very poignant, and well worth a visit – I can't promise you a portal to the Otherworld though.

Thanks also to everyone who reviewed, recommended, bought or otherwise suported *Dark Vision* – both Lily and I appreciate it!